In Times Like These

In Times Like These

Nathan Van Coops

Skylighter
Press

St. Petersburg, Florida

ISBN-13: 978-0989475501

ISBN-10: 0989475506

Cover design by Damonza.com
"Books Made Awesome"

Author photo by Jennie Thunell Photography

Skylighter Press, St. Petersburg 33704
Printed in The United States of America
First Edition 2013

For series updates visit
www.chronothon.com
and
www.nathanvancoops.com

ACKNOWLEDGEMENTS

I am deeply thankful:

For the true life friendships that helped inspire these characters and relationships. Morgan McGuire, Jakzeel Nuñez, Kelly DeWitt, RJ Schamp, Kristen Keller, Stephanie Haines and Bobby Angel.

For the beta readers who read my early drafts and kept me encouraged, Marilyn Bourdeau, Stephen Cook, Kristina Van Coops and Patricia McGuire.

For Emily Young, who shared in this book-writing journey as both friend and editor, and provided me with a wealth of encouragement and constructive criticism.

For all the amazing friends who have loved and supported me through this entire adventure.

This book is dedicated to all of you.

Chapter 1

"Don't assume that because you know something in the future won't happen, that you can do nothing. Sometimes the reason it doesn't happen is you."
-Excerpt from the journal of Dr. Harold Quickly, 1997

I have far too much of my life in my arms to even think of reaching for my phone when it starts ringing in my pocket. I concentrate on getting the key in the lock. That and not dropping the shoes, water bottles and mail I've hauled to the door of my apartment. I get the door open with my free fingers and just make it inside when one of the water bottles escapes, and the next moment, all but my useless junk mail is on the living room floor. I leave it there and open my phone the moment before it gives up on me.

"Hey Carson, what's up?"

"Dude. You coming to batting practice?"

"Yeah, I'll be there. Just got home from work."

"All right, can you check the weather while you're there?"

"No problem. Be there in a few."

I toss my phone and the junk mail onto the couch and locate the remote in the cushions. The station is still on commercials, so I head for the kitchen. Depositing the remote on the counter, I turn to the refrigerator out of habit. It's still just as sparse as the last time I checked. I settle for my one remaining bottle of water and head for the bedroom to change. I can hear the news broadcast come on from around the corner.

"Welcome back to News Channel 8. In a few moments we'll get your Drive Time Traffic and weather, but first, a look at today's top stories.

"Today was the conclusion of the eight month trial of Elton Stenger, the man accused of murdering fourteen people in a series of vicious car bombings and shootings throughout the state of Florida and around the country. Judge Alan Waters ruled today that Stenger be convicted, and serve fourteen consecutive life sentences, a record number for the state of Florida. Stenger is being transported today into Federal custody and will be tried in the state of New York for three additional murders."

I pull my paycheck from my shorts pocket and lay it on the dresser. It'll be gone in a week. Emptying the meager contents of my wallet out next to the check, I extract enough cash for a couple of post-game beers. *Minimal celebrating is still better than no celebrating.*

"Today is a monumental day for St. Petersburg and the entire scientific community, as the St. Petersburg Temporal Studies Society gets set to test their latest particle accelerator, what they claim may be the world's first time machine. They will attempt to launch a number of particles through time and space in their laboratory here in St. Petersburg today.

"We have correspondent David Powers on the scene. David, what's going on down there?"

I get into my athletic shorts and snag some socks. *Where the hell did I put my uniform shirt?* I cruise back through the living room to head for my laundry closet.

" . . . and while the potential applications of the experiment are yet to be determined, one thing is for certain, these researchers won't be wasting any time. Back to you, Barbara."

I glimpse the blonde woman grinning on screen with her co-anchor. "Next thing we know they'll be rolling out a Delorean. Certainly a day to remember. Now we go to Carl Sims with our weather update."

I know what it's going to say. Hot. Chance of thunderstorms. This is Florida. I locate my wrinkled *Hit Storm* shirt in the laundry basket, and slide it over my head as I walk back around the corner to the TV. Just as expected, the little cloud and lightning symbol dominates the entire week.

When I arrive at the field, most of the team is already there. I spot Carson's orange hair as he's out on the mound throwing batting practice. As I step out of my car, the moist, sweet smell of clay and grass clippings makes my shoulders instantly relax. Each step I take toward the field helps the tension of my workday ebb away. Robbie is donning his cleats in the dugout as I walk up.

"Hey, man."

"What's up, Ben? How's it going?"

"Hoping we're going to get to play this one," I reply.

"Yeah me too, I'm going to forget how to swing a bat if we keep getting rained out." Robbie stands and stretches his arms toward the roof of the dugout. My arms would reach it. At 5'8" Robbie's come up short. What he lacks in height he makes up for in fitness. Despite his on again, off again

2

cigarette habit, he can still out-sprint anyone on the team. His lean and muscular physique is contrasted by his relaxed demeanor. His constant state of ease makes me feel like I'm rushing through life by comparison.

"Have we got enough people tonight? I know Nick said he was going to be out of town in Georgia or something like that." I kick off one of my flip-flops and start pulling on a sock.

"Yeah, I think Blake's going to second and Mike's filling in at catcher. We should be good. There's Blake now." Robbie gestures with his head while he leans forward and stretches his arms behind his back.

Blake's Jeep pulls into the space next to my truck. I'm happy I'm not the only one who has missed most of practice. Blake and I have a lot in common, including our propensity for arriving fashionably late. Blake's my height, and while his hair borders on black compared to my brown, we occasionally get mistaken for brothers.

"You wanna throw?" Robbie asks, as I finish lacing up.

"Yeah." I grab my glove and the two of us toss the ball along the sideline until Blake joins us.

"Is Mallory making it out to the game tonight?" I ask Blake as he lines up next to me.

He stretches his right arm across his chest and then switches to the other one. "I doubt it. She has to watch her niece and I don't think she wants to bring her out."

We never get many fans at our games. Blake's girlfriend is the most frequent but even her appearances have gotten rare. I keep inviting people, but apparently Wednesday nights are more highly valued elsewhere. *Can't remember the last time a girlfriend of mine made it out to a game. Three seasons ago? Four? I suppose managing to keep one longer than a few months might help.*

Carson pitches us each a bucket of softballs, and I knock the majority of mine toward an increasingly dark right field. We ignore the clouds as much as possible and concentrate on practice. Once everyone has hit, we mill around the dugout, stretching, while Carson gives me his appraisal of our chances.

"These guys should be cake for us. I watched them play last week. I think we're going to crush them."

I consider the big athletic guys filling the opposing dugout and realize that Carson might be overly optimistic, but I don't argue. "We're definitely due for a win."

Carson starts jotting down the lineup. He's full of energy today. I admire that about him. At twenty-six, he's a couple years younger than me, but about a year older than Blake. He has no trouble organizing things like this. Sports are his arena. He's naturally talented at all of them. I could outrun him. Blake could outswim us both, but Carson has everybody beat on all-around athleticism. He makes a great shortstop in any case. The other teams have learned to fear both his fielding abilities and his trash talking skills. Blake and I flank him on the field at second and third base respectively.

We walk out to our positions and are waiting for Robbie to throw the first pitch, when a thunderclap rumbles through the clouds. The umpire casts a quick glance skyward, but then yells, "Batter Up!"

I'm digging my cleats into the dirt at third when I notice my friend Francesca walking up from the parking lot. She catches my eye and sticks her tongue out at me before sitting down next to Paul, our designated hitter. I scowl at her and she laughs, and then turns to greet Paul. *What do you know? We did manage a fan tonight.*

The crack of the bat jerks my attention back to the game as the ground ball takes a bad hop a few feet in front of me and impacts me in the chest. It drops to the ground and I scramble to bare hand it, making the throw to first just a step ahead of the runner. I rub my chest as I walk back to my position. *That'll be a bruise tomorrow.*

Robbie walks the next batter as I start to feel the first few drops of rain. The third batter grounds to Blake at second. He underhand tosses the ball to Carson who tags the base and hurls it to first for a double play, just as a bolt of lightning flashes beyond right field. Carson's yell of success over the play is drowned out by the boom of thunder. I head for the dugout, hoping we'll get a chance to hit, but as the outfielders come trotting in, they're followed by a dense wall of rain. I step into the dugout before the heavy drops can soak me.

"Hey Fresca, What's shakin'?" I plop down next to Francesca on the bench.

"I finally make it to one of your games and this is how you treat me?" She gestures to the sheets of rain now sweeping the field.

"I ordered you sunshine and double rainbows, but they must not have gotten the memo."

"I was worried I was going to get arrested getting here, too. Did you see all those cop cars downtown?"

I think about it for a second, then remember the newscast. "It's probably for all that trial stuff going on."

"Oh, right." She turns to Blake as he sits down next to me and props his feet on the bucket of balls. "Hey, Blake."

4

"Hey, Francesca. Thanks for coming."

"Looks like I'll be witnessing your drinking skills instead. Are you all heading to Ferg's now?"

"I think we're going to wait and see if this passes first." I watch the puddles building on the field.

Carson dashes back into the dugout from his conference with the umpires and drips all over the equipment as he explains the situation. "We're on delay for now. They're going to see how wet the field gets."

I play along with Carson's optimism. Most of our team has already gone to their cars to wait, but I'm not in any hurry to leave the company of my friends. I can tell that this storm isn't likely to be over fast. Anyone with a few years of Florida weather experience gets to know the difference between a quick passing shower and a prolonged storm, and this one appears to be settling in for the evening. I'm bummed to not be playing for another week, but even rainout beers are better than being at work.

"I guess those guys don't think it's going to let up," Robbie says, noting the opposing dugout clearing out.

Carson picks up his clipboard. "If it stops and they don't have enough players to re-take the field, we win by forfeit."

"I came here to play. I hate winning by forfeit," Robbie grumbles.

"What's new with you, Blake?" Francesca steers the conversation away from our glum prospects.

"Did Ben not tell you the news yet?"

"No, he's obviously slacking in the gossip department. What's your news?"

Blake looks at me. "Should I show it to her?"

"You have it with you?"

"Yeah, it's in my Jeep."

"What is it?" Francesca's curiosity is now piqued.

"Be right back." Blake gets up, walks past Carson, who is in deep concentration over the stats sheet, and dashes into the rain toward the parking lot.

"What's he got?" Francesca looks back to me, brushing a strand of dark hair out of her eyes.

"It's pretty impressive." I grab my flip-flops out of the overhead cubbies and start changing out of my cleats. Robbie follows my example.

"It's not looking good," he says. I nod in response and a minute later, Blake dashes back into the dugout holding a plastic bag. He sits next to Francesca and unwraps the package. He holds out a small jewelry box.

"Oh for Mallory?" Francesca exclaims. Blake pries open the lid and displays the diamond ring inside. "Ooh, you did good Blake!" Francesca takes the box and looks adoringly at the ring.

"Well it's time," he replies.

"How long have you two been dating now? Four years?" Carson asks, his interest waning in the statistics sheet.

"Yeah, I wanted to wait till she finished grad school, but now that she's almost done, we're taking the leap."

"That's awesome, man." Robbie pats Blake on the shoulder.

We pass the ring box around, admiring it as the rain beats down on the dugout. Under the bright lights of the baseball diamond, the ring sparkles even more than the last time I saw it. *Mallory's going to love that. I need to find a ring like that. I need to find a girl like that.* I close the ring box and pass it on to Robbie. As I do, an exceptionally bright lightning bolt sears across the sky and hits what can only be a few blocks away. The thunderclap is deafening and immediate. The bench is a symphony of expletives for a moment and Francesca clenches my arm and pulls herself against me.

"Holy shit that was close!" Robbie says.

A high-pitched whine like a jet engine begins to emanate from the direction of the strike. It grows louder and is followed by an explosion of bright blue light that domes up through the rain and illuminates the cloudy sky.

"What the hell—" is all that escapes my mouth, before a deafening bang from a transformer blowing behind us drowns me out. I'm still too startled from the shock to move when the severed end of a power line whips into the end of the dugout and lands on the far end of our bench. The last thing I sense before blacking out is the sight of my friends glowing with a pale blue light, and the sound of Francesca screaming.

Chapter 2

"If you meet an experienced time traveler, you can usually trust that they are intelligent. The nature of this business rapidly weeds out the morons."
-Excerpt from the journal of Dr. Harold Quickly, 2110.

I open my eyes to bleary but bright sunlight. I'm lying on my back staring at a clear blue sky. The bright light worsens the ache in my head, so I close my eyes again. I can feel the heat of the sun on my face and the dry itchy feeling of grass on my arms and neck and the backs of my ears. There's definitely something crawling on my arm, but I'm too unmotivated to care. I monitor the slow progression of little insect feet, trying to gauge the threat. *Lady bug maybe? Spider?* I consider the most likely candidates. *Shit, if it's a fire ant, there's probably a zillion more around.* I open my eyes again and angle my head slowly upward, trying to locate the intruder in the crook of my elbow. My eyes adjust to the light and I make out the ant. Not a fire ant. I lay my head back and stare at the midday sky. *Why is it daytime?*

A low moan comes from my right. Francesca is lying next to me, her dark hair spread out around her and her fingers clenched in the grass. My eyes travel down her back to the wisp of smoke rising from the backside of her jeans. This moves me to action. "Francesca you're on fiaargh." My body objects to movement, and I collapse back onto the ground. *Son of a bitch that hurt.*

I try again more slowly this time. I roll up to my elbow and reach a hand out to Francesca's shoulder. "Hey. Fresca. You okay?" She doesn't respond. Beyond Francesca, Blake and Carson are likewise lying in the grass. Blake's legs are still extended over the bench of the dugout, only there is no more dugout. I twist and look back toward my feet. The bench is there but the roof of the dugout and the cubbyholes where I had stashed my glove and water bottle have disappeared. The opposing dugout is gone too. In its place is only the cement slab and the bench. I twist farther and see Robbie sitting up behind me. "You okay?"

He rubs a hand across his face. "Yeah, I think so. What happened?"

"I don't know."

"Are the others all right?" He tries to get to his feet, but staggers a little and sits down on the bench instead. "Agh. There's something wrong with my feet!"

I shake Francesca again and she rolls onto her back, but doesn't open her eyes. Blake sits up on the other side of her and looks at his hand. There's a red scorch mark across his palm. He rubs it with his other hand as Robbie slides down the bench and nudges Carson. As Blake turns his right foot toward him, I see a hole through the center of his cleat with melted edges.

"Hey, you okay?"

He looks at me. "Yeah. Looks like we got a little crispy though."

I feel around my backside and find a singed hole in my athletic shorts. "Ah, man . . ."

"What?"

"Nothing. I just apparently got shocked through my butt cheek." Francesca's eyes are open now. I lean toward her. "Hey. You all right?"

She tilts her head toward me. "I feel awful."

"Yeah. Join the club."

"What happened?"

"We got electrocuted," Blake says.

"But what happened to the field?" Robbie inquires from the bench. Carson is sitting up now also, staring blankly past me.

"I don't know. That's throwing me off too." I stare at the open sky where the roof of the dugout ought to be. I blink twice, half expecting to see the illusion disappear and the dugout rematerialize. The vacant space refuses to yield. I climb to my knees and gingerly take a seat on the bench.

"You've got to be kidding me." Francesca has her hand around the backside of her jeans and has discovered the burn hole. "I just bought these." She mutters a little more and extends a hand for me to pull her up. She twists to inspect her butt again and then sits down next to me.

"What time is it?" Carson climbs to his feet and brushes some grass clippings off the shoulder of his shirt.

"Looks like the middle of the day," I say, looking at the sun.

"Were we out here all night?" Francesca asks.

"I don't see how. When I woke up, your jeans were still smoking."

"What?" Francesca pivots to check her backside again.

"Yeah, something weird is going on." Blake is fingering the chain link fence between us and the field. "None of this looks right."

"Dude, where are our cars?" Carson springs off the bench and begins hobbling toward the parking lot. I follow him. Blake limps along with us. The only car in the parking lot is a dark red Ford Tempo. Carson looks fruitlessly for his pickup truck. Mine is gone too. "This is so not cool." Carson holds his hands to his orange hair.

Good thing my truck is a piece of junk. Who the hell would want to steal it though? I walk over to the Tempo. The paint job is shiny and clean. The interior looks pristine as well. I lean down and note the original stereo system. *Somebody has really gone to some pains to restore this thing. Who would restore a Tempo?*

"We need to call the cops," Blake says. He shouts back to Robbie and Francesca, "Do either of you have your phones?" I turn away from the car and follow him back toward the bench. His fingers go to his pockets as he's walking, and he shouts again. "Hey! Anybody see the ring?"

I stop and inspect the ground as Blake hobbles toward the bench. "I think I had it last," Robbie says. He stands up and looks around, evidently no longer in possession of it.

I'm working my way closer when I hear Francesca exclaim, "Is that it?"

Blake vaults over the bench to the place she's indicating and snatches the ring box out of a clump of grass. The muscles of his face relax as he opens it and finds the diamond still inside. He slips the box into his pocket.

"That would have sucked," Carson says. Francesca removes her phone from her pocket and opens it. "Did it get fried?" Carson asks.

"No, it's still on, but I'm not getting any signal." She hands the phone to Robbie. "Here. You mess with it. I'm cold. Is anyone else cold?"

"It is kind of cool out," Carson responds.

"So what are we doing? Are we trying to call the cops?" I look around the empty field and see no sign of our other teammates or the opposing players.

"Yeah, if we can get any kind of signal." Robbie holds the phone up and walks around.

"So wait, I don't get what's going on," Francesca says. "What happened to the field? Are we at the same place? What happened to the dugouts?"

"I don't know what the hell is going on." Robbie shuts the phone.

Blake is looking at the scorch on his palm again. "We should probably get ourselves checked out at a hospital. Some of these burns might need attention."

A door opens in a house across the street and a woman walks to the sidewalk to check her mail. As she collects it, she takes a side-long glance in our direction before going back inside.

"Did you see that woman's hair?" Francesca asks. "It was huge."

"Pretty out of control," Carson agrees.

"Nice mom jeans too." Francesca scoots over for me to sit down next to her.

"Are we getting pranked right now or something?" Robbie asks. "Why is the field different looking?"

"If somebody thought pranking us after we just got electrocuted was funny, I would probably kill them," Carson says.

"Who would be capable of doing something like this?" I ask. "This would be really elaborate. Besides, the only people who ever prank me are sitting right here."

"Maybe the electrocution messed with our heads," Francesca suggests. "Maybe we're just remembering it wrong?"

"All of our batting gloves and mitts and stuff were in those cubbies. We had bats and balls and water in the dugout. It's all gone. How could we remember that wrong?" Carson asks.

"My batting gloves are actually still here." I pull them up from between where Francesca and I are sitting on the bench. "I guess if we moved, these managed to come with us." I stroke the leather of the gloves between my fingers. *What happened to the rest of my stuff?* I have a nagging at the back of my mind like I'm missing something. I stare at the baseball diamond, trying to make sense of the changes. I feel like it's there, right in front of me, but I just can't see it. "Did you guys see the power line hit the end of the bench?" I look up at the poles near the street, the power line hanging benignly between them.

Francesca shakes her head. "I just remember the noise."

"And the results." Blake holds up his scorched hand.

Carson shields his eyes from the sun while looking up at the lines. "I saw it. But it's back up there now."

"Maybe Francesca's right," Blake says. "Maybe our brains are fried, because none of this is making any sense."

"You guys want to try to walk to find a place where this phone will work, or maybe find a payphone?" Robbie scratches the back of his head. "There might be one over on Ninth Street."

"Walking? Really?" Francesca says. "We just got electrocuted."

"Well, we can sit here I guess, but without a phone, I don't really know that we're going to get much help," Robbie says. "You can try to ask mom-jeans across the street I suppose."

"And tell her what?" Blake asks. "That we got shocked by a phantom, self-repairing power line? I think we're better off not trying to convince people of that one, till we know what's going on."

Francesca stands up. "Fine, but I'm walking in back so none of you guys look at my butt."

"You can't see anything. You're fine," Carson replies from behind her.

"Hey, stop looking!" Francesca shoos Carson in front of her.

Blake smiles and looks over at me. "You okay, man? You look dazed."

"Yeah, I'm okay. I'm just trying to figure out what on earth happened to us."

We walk to the street and turn east.

"I'm so pissed about my car!" Carson spouts. "I had my iPod in there, and all my stuff for work. My wallet's in there, my phone . . ."

"Who would steal all of our cars? And how would no one notice five people lying on the ground all night, or notice and not say anything?" Blake asks.

A couple cars pass us and we get out of the way. *Something about the cars. What am I missing?*

"These people are all staring at us funny. I know I'm looking smoking hot, rocking these grass clippings in my hair, but seriously, what's their deal?" Francesca says.

"Smoking hot in the literal sense today," Carson adds.

"Ha ha. Shut up, Carson."

"Well it's true. And you smell like a charcoal briquette. You should really market that scent."

Francesca scowls back. "At least smelling odd is a change of pace for me, electrocution had to improve your B.O."

"That's just real man smell." Carson smiles. "You never used to mind it before."

"Before. Oh, before that night you left me sitting at home on our date night so you could go drink with the girls' swim team?" Francesca says. "That before?"

"You always bring that up. We weren't even serious," Carson says. "And I told you, it was a fundraiser. They needed help."

Francesca turns and faces him, stopping them in the road. "It was our two month anniversary. And no legitimate fundraiser involves belly-button Jello shots." Blake looks at me and raises his eyebrows. I smile and we keep walking ahead. "But you're right, Carson, it wasn't serious, because you never take anything seriously," Francesca continues.

"Hey. Don't take out your frustration about this out on me," Carson says. "I didn't ask you to come to the game."

"I'm still going to blame you, Carson," Francesca fumes. "We probably only got struck by lightning because God is smiting you for being a jerk!" She turns and grabs Robbie's arm and keeps walking.

"You got electrocuted too," Carson says. "So what does that make you?"

Francesca ignores him. I decide to interject. "Hey, guys. When do you think the Ford Tempo came out?"

"The car?" Robbie asks. "I don't know. Late eighties maybe? Early nineties?"

"I'd say mid-eighties," Carson contributes, trotting to catch up and escape Francesca's fury.

"Do they still make them?"

"I don't think so," Robbie says. "Why?"

"That car back in the parking lot was a Tempo, but it was in pristine shape, like it was brand new. I was just thinking how long it's been since I've seen a car like that new. All the cars that have been driving by us and the ones we've been walking past have been older models too."

We look around at the cars parked in driveways and on the street. A line of three cars is ahead of us on the right. As we approach, Robbie speaks up. "Yeah, these are all older cars. That last one is a Datsun 280Z. Those are definitely older. My brother used to have a '78, till he wrecked it."

As I walk around the first car, a Dodge Aries, my mind is wrestling with what I'm beginning to suspect. I look in the windows and notice the radio. "This thing has an original stereo. Not even a tape deck."

"Dude, this one's registration is a little out of date, wouldn't you say?" Carson comments from the back of the next car, a slightly battered Plymouth Duster. "It says June of '86."

"This one is December '85," Blake adds from the rear of the Datsun.

I look at the silver Datsun with its black vent fins and my mind flashes back to the blonde on the newscast. *"Next thing you know, they'll be rolling out a Delorean."*

Delorean. Tempo. Mom-jeans.

"Shiiiit," I blurt out, drawing out the syllable as I look at the license plate of the Aries.

"What is it?" Francesca inquires.

"Francesca, go look at the license plate of the car in that driveway." I gesture across the street to a Volkswagen Beetle under a carport.

"What am I looking for?" Francesca asks, as she walks over to the car.

"The registration sticker on the license plate. What does the date say?"

12

"July '86," she calls out when she reaches it.

It can't be. But what else would make any sense of this. "Guys, I hate to tell you this, but I think we might be in the eighties."

"What?" Francesca exclaims. "What?"

It sounds even crazier out loud.

"Ha. That's funny," Carson says. He looks at my face. "Wait, are you being serious?"

Everyone stops moving.

"There have to be plenty of other explanations," Robbie says.

"What are the odds that four cars on the same street would have registration stickers from 1986?" I contend.

"Yeah that's weird, I'll give you that, but that doesn't mean we're in the eighties," Robbie says.

"Look. Today, before I got to the game, I caught a little bit of this thing on the news. They said there was an experiment going on in town. I wasn't paying that close of attention but they were talking about something they were trying to make travel through time. I didn't think anything of it till we saw all these cars. But now that I'm looking at it,"—I gesture to our surroundings—"Does any of this look like it belongs in 2009?"

No one speaks for a moment as we look around.

"Are you saying we're part of an experiment?" Francesca asks.

"I don't know, I'm just saying what I heard. They were doing something weird. They called it the something society. Time Society or something like that."

"This is crazy," Blake says. "There's no way we're in 1986! Let's get off this street and figure out where we are. Four cars on a street having old stickers doesn't mean we're in the eighties, or being experimented on. Something is wrong here and we just need to find out what it is." He turns and reads the street sign on the corner. "Look. We're on Thirteenth Avenue. Mallory's house is only a couple blocks over. We'll go there and we can sort out what happened to us. She can give us a ride to the hospital too if we need it. We're obviously just having some sort of group hallucination or something."

I look at him and consider what he must be thinking, and then decide to stop arguing. Blake walks away with determined strides. I linger behind for a few moments, then follow reluctantly. I catch up to Robbie and say quietly, "I hope I'm wrong about this, but if I'm right, this could be a really bad idea." Robbie gives me a quizzical look but doesn't respond.

We walk in silence for the next three blocks, only casting occasional glances at the cars and houses we pass. I notice that Blake is not even

13

looking at any more of the cars, but directing his attention straight ahead, as if hoping to avoid any additional oddities in this day. I keep watching for things that would only exist in 2009. I scan yard decorations and patio furniture, check bumper stickers and even glance in backyards for signs of a Powerwheels car, or anything I know was not invented yet in the eighties. I spot a few more eighties registration stickers. Everything about the neighborhood seems either authentically dated or impressively retro. The whole experience is surreal. My conclusion of being in the eighties seems like a ridiculous guess and I don't actually want to believe it myself. I feel that at any moment a more plausible explanation will prove me wrong and I'll be able to laugh along with how outrageous my suggestion was.

The only sound is the clacking of Carson and Blake's softball cleats on the sidewalk and the steady slapping of the flip-flops worn by the rest of us. When we reach Mallory's house, Blake pauses briefly to consider a car that I don't recognize parked in the driveway. He then proceeds to the front door and rings the doorbell. I join him on the porch.

The awnings on the windows have changed color to a brilliant blue, and a number of children's toys are strewn in the yard, along with a Big Wheel tricycle. The gutters of the house still have Christmas lights strung along them. Not getting any response from the bell, Blake pounds on the front door. A few moments later, Mrs. Watson opens it, looking younger than I've ever seen her. She smiles pleasantly and takes a brief look at Blake and me on her porch, then glances at the others standing on her front lawn.

"Hello, Mrs. Watson . . ." Blake begins, obviously shaken by her youthfulness and lack of recognition of any of us. "I'm looking . . . is Mallory here?"

"Mallory?" Mrs. Watson responds with a confused expression. "She's sleeping. I just put her down for a nap. I'm sorry, who are you?"

Blake stares at her as if willing her to recognize him. "I'm Bla—"

"Pardon me," I interject. "I think we have the wrong house. I'm sorry to bother you Ma'am." The words feel strange coming out. *I think she's younger than me.* I grab Blake by the arm to pull him off the porch. Blake looks awkwardly at Mrs. Watson, at a loss for words. She gives us a half-smile and watches me turn Blake around before she closes the door.

Francesca walks to Blake and holds his other arm. Carson and Robbie follow us back onto the sidewalk, where we stand in silence for a moment. Blake is staring, shell-shocked, into space. A middle-aged man with a Labrador walks around us and begins to walk away, when Robbie calls out to him, "Excuse me, sir?" The man turns. "I'm sorry, but do you happen to know the date today?"

14

"It's the twenty-ninth," the man replies.

"Of . . . June?"

"December." The man looks at Robbie curiously now. He turns and continues walking a few more steps before Carson calls out to him this time.

"Sir, I'm sorry, but could you tell us the year?"

The man looks as if he's going to say something sarcastic, but seeing the seriousness of all of our faces, he simply replies, "1985." And continues walking.

It's true.

No one says anything for a minute as we look at our surroundings with a new sense of wonder. Francesca finally breaks the silence. "It's no wonder I'm cold. It's freaking December." Robbie rubs Francesca's bare arms, which indeed have goose bumps on them, though the temperature can't be much lower than seventy.

"This is the weirdest day of my life." Carson holds his hands to his head.

"I call bullshit," Robbie says. "That guy was in on it."

"You saw Mrs. Watson," I say.

"I never really met her before." Robbie crosses his arms. "Maybe she got a facelift."

"We're in the eighties." Francesca points her finger toward two kids walking down the sidewalk on the other side of the street. "No little kids are brave enough to dress like that in 2009."

The two boys are wearing T-shirts and high cut running shorts with stripes down the sides. One has a pair of blue striped tube socks stretched almost to his knees. The other has the same socks in red. Both have backpacks and one is carrying a basketball under his right arm.

"Hey, kid!" Francesca yells. She walks across the street toward them. The two stop short on the sidewalk, unsure of what to make of this young Latina woman headed their direction. I follow her out of curiosity. The boys look to be elementary school age.

"How old are you kid?" Francesca addresses the taller one in the blue socks. The boys exchange unsure glances. "You're not in trouble or anything. I just have a couple questions for you."

"I'm ten," the boy replies.

"I'm ten and a half," the shorter boy chimes in.

"What's your favorite band?" Francesca says, still addressing the tall boy.

"I don't know."

"Doesn't even have to be a favorite. Just name a band you like."

It's the shorter boy who responds. "John's mom doesn't let him listen to much, but I like Springsteen."

"I can listen to stuff!" The tall boy shoves his friend's shoulder. "Remember, it was me who got that one album from my brother when I slept over at your house."

"That was Wham. That doesn't count."

Francesca turns to me. "See? They know about Springsteen and Wham. No ten year-old in 2009 knows Wham." She nods to the shorter kid and heads back to the others.

"Was that it?" the tall boy asks me.

"Yeah," I say. "Thanks, guys."

As the boys walk past me, the shorter one switches the basketball to his left hand, and with his right hand, holds his fingers to his ear like a phone. He mouths, "Call me" to Francesca. She smiles, but her eyes are still serious.

When I get back to the other side of the street, I notice Robbie has both of his arms extended toward the sky. "Hey, man. What're you doing?"

"We're dreaming," Robbie says. "That's the only logical explanation. And if I'm dreaming, I should be able to fly."

Carson smiles. "How's that going for you, dude?"

Robbie looks back at us and slowly lowers his arms. "Shit. What are we going to do now?"

As I cross my arms, I take the opportunity to pinch myself. *Damn. I'm not dreaming either.*

Robbie speaks up again. "If we're really in the eighties, and Mallory is a little kid, then we would be too."

"So we can't go home?" Francesca continues the thought.

"I don't know who was living in my apartment in 1985, but they probably don't want company," I say.

"Our parents are going to freak out if we show up saying we're their kids from twenty years from now," Robbie says.

"My parents aren't even around here. Neither am I. My family was in Oregon in 1985," I reply.

"My parents would be in Miami," Francesca says.

"My parents would be here," Carson says. "But, if we're really in 1985, I think we would totally screw stuff up by interacting with ourselves when we were young right? Wouldn't we change our own lives like *Back to the Future*?"

"This is really messed up," Robbie says.

16

"We have to find a way back." Blake hasn't said a word till this response but he becomes alert now. Confronting Mrs. Watson was obviously enough to convince him that my theory is true. "We're going back."

"But how did this happen?" Francesca asks.

The blinds on the house move and I catch a glimpse of Mrs. Watson watching us. She has a phone to her ear. "Come on. Let's get out of here," I suggest.

Blake gives a longing look at Mallory's house, as if willing her to come walking out the door, but finally turns back to us. We go a couple of blocks without really having a destination.

The realization that we're actually somewhere other than home quells the conversation. I retreat into my own thoughts, feeling almost guilty that my guess has come true. I cast occasional glances at the faces of my friends to see how they are faring with the news. Blake's face is the most severe, his gaze unseeing, his mind disconnected from the world around us and likely tarrying with thoughts of the Watson house and Mallory. Francesca has linked arms with Robbie as if anchoring herself to something familiar. I watch the back of Carson's head as we walk, wondering what might be going on in his mind. When we reach Ninth Street, he turns to face us. "I'm starving. Was Dairy Inn here in 1985?"

"Yeah, it's been there for a long time." Robbie perks up. "I went there as a kid all the time."

"Let's walk down that way," Carson says. "If we see a bunch of kids blabbing on their cell phones, we'll know we're just having a bad trip from the lightning or something."

"Does anybody have any money?" Robbie asks. "I left my wallet in my car.

"I have my wallet," Francesca replies, pulling a small fabric bag from her pocket. "Did they have debit cards in 1985? I don't have that much cash."

"A card wouldn't work even if they did," I reply. "We wouldn't have any bank accounts yet. I think I have a few dollars in my pocket." I pull out the inner pocket of my athletic shorts and look inside.

We walk south along Ninth Street, relieved to have a destination, if only briefly. The telephone poles are decorated with holiday banners and the storefronts have occasional Christmas trees in their windows. Carson and Robbie lead the way while Francesca and I hang back to walk with Blake, who is merely trudging along behind. He has the ring box in his hand and is running his thumb across the top of it.

Francesca suddenly stops. "Guys . . . what if we're dead?" We stop to listen to her. "The last thing I remember before this was that power line. What if that power line killed us?" Her face has gone pale.

"And for an afterlife we got sent to the eighties?" Carson smiles. "Does that make this heaven or hell? Ha!" He turns and keeps walking. "Good one, Francesca."

Francesca narrows her eyes. "Yeah, you're right, Carson. I forgot. This couldn't be heaven, because you're here."

I smile. *I have no idea what's happened to us, but at least the company is entertaining.*

We make it to the outdoor ice cream stand in a few minutes and it looks essentially the same as it always has, but I notice there are no kids with cell phones. Francesca pulls out her money and counts it. "I've got thirty dollars. What are we getting?"

I hand her the wad of ones from my pocket as well.

"Some burgers?" Carson suggests, as he looks at the menu.

"Wow, check out the prices!" I run my eyes down the menu board. "At least we get more for our money in the eighties."

The price for burgers for all five of us comes to nine dollars, and Francesca hands the teenage cashier a ten-dollar bill. The girl takes it and stands there awkwardly for a moment. "Um, is this real?" she inquires.

"What?" Francesca asks, caught off guard.

"I haven't seen money like this before," the cashier replies. "I think I have to ask my manager about this."

Francesca looks at the bill with its peachy coloring and sees the oversized picture of Alexander Hamilton. "Ah, yeah, those are the new ones," she stammers back. "You know what, I need change anyway. Why don't you take it out of this one instead." She hands her twenty to the girl and retrieves the ten-dollar bill. The girl slides the older style twenty into the cash register and hands Francesca her change. Francesca smiles reassuringly, looks at me with wide eyes and turns back to the other guys who are congregated around a picnic table on the side of the stand.

"Well that almost didn't work," she says, as she walks up to them. She flashes the new style ten-dollar bill. "How are we going to spend this one?"

"I forgot about that," Carson responds. "How old was your other money?"

"I think it was like 2003 or something," Francesca replies. "But luckily she didn't look at the date."

"Yeah, last thing we need is to get arrested for counterfeiting while we're here," Robbie says.

The burgers come out and we sit at the picnic table eating them and sharing a couple of root beers. Francesca checks her phone, which is still searching for a signal. "I guess we don't have to call the cops about our cars. We wouldn't really have much to tell them. 'Hello officer, we left our cars parked in 2009. Can you help us?'"

I laugh. It feels good to laugh, despite our obvious predicament. I notice Blake doesn't smile.

"What're we going to do for a place to stay tonight?" Francesca asks. "I think it's getting colder." She shivers a little in the cool breeze that's wafting through the parking lot. The sun has dropped in the sky and the temperature has started to come down with it.

"How much money do we have?" Carson asks.

"Twenty-five dollars, but with the new ten it's more like fifteen," Francesca says. "Unless we find a way to spend that."

"I think a hotel is out," Carson says. "I'm a little scared to think what a fifteen-dollar hotel room would be like, even in the eighties."

"We need to find somebody who can help us," Blake says.

"Who do we know that would help us, that would be living here in 1985 and is close by?" I ask.

"What about a teacher or something?" Carson suggests. "Or maybe a family friend? Maybe we can say we're distant relatives visiting or . . ." He trails off.

An older gentleman and a little girl are at the window of the stand buying ice cream cones, and Robbie is watching them when he suddenly blurts out, "Wait, what did that guy say the date was?"

"December twenty-ninth, 1985," I respond.

"I would have been . . . four," Robbie says. "My grandparents died when I was four, but they might still be alive right now." He talks excitedly. "I could have a chance to talk to my grandparents again before they die!" He looks at me. "I don't know if that would screw things up as much as seeing our parents, but their house isn't very far away."

I consider this possibility.

"How are we going to explain who we are?" Francesca asks.

"What if we just tell the truth?" Robbie suggests. "I know it will sound weird, but it's true. I'm still their grandson."

"Are we going to totally screw up your life this way?" I ask.

"I don't see how," Robbie replies. "I never really knew them that well to start with."

"I'm okay with it," Francesca says. "Old people always have sweaters." She rubs her arms and leans into Robbie next to her.

"We need help from someone," Carson says.

"All right, then we should get going if we're going to do this." I arc my burger wrapper into a trashcan a few feet away. "We probably already screwed up the space time continuum or whatever just by being here, so we may as well be warm."

We follow Robbie north and then east into another residential neighborhood. It's about fifteen minutes later when we finally turn onto our destination street. An alley provides access for the home's garages.

We walk past a set of trashcans that have a Christmas tree lying next to them with only a few strands of tinsel left on it. Robbie sees it and suddenly stops.

"What is it?" Blake asks.

"I just remembered something," Robbie replies. "My grandma died before Christmas. I remember it. I remember being happy on Christmas that I still got a present from her, even though she'd died, and I remember feeling guilty later for thinking that. It's past Christmas, so she would have died a few weeks ago."

"How do you think your grandfather is going to be?" Carson asks.

"I don't know. Probably none-too-good. He didn't live much longer than my grandma. Mom always said she thought he died of a broken heart. It happened while we were on vacation. I remember coming home early because we heard the news."

We remain quiet, not wanting to intrude on this moment of Robbie's.

"Do you want to try a different plan?" Francesca finally asks. "We don't have to go there."

Robbie is pensive. "No. We're already here. Plus, I really would like to see him. I always had so much I wished I could have talked to him about, and this is a second chance. It's not like these opportunities come along every day."

He starts walking again and a few garages later, turns into the backyard of an old, Spanish-style home. The garage and house are tan and roofed with terracotta tiles. The lawn is green and healthy but looks like it hasn't been cut for a month. We follow a flagstone path that connects the garage to a screened-in back porch, topped by a veranda with an iron railing.

"I haven't been here in such a long time," Robbie says. He walks ahead of us and enters the screened porch, stopping at the back door of the house. We file in behind him. Francesca tries unsuccessfully to pull the back of her shirt down to cover the singe on her backside. Carson notes his reflection in the back window and makes a quick attempt to straighten his mussed hair.

IN TIMES LIKE THESE

The porch is cluttered with lawn care tools and patio furniture. A collection of colorful gnomes stare at me from a shelf like tiny sentinels.

Robbie takes a deep breath and knocks on the door. Inside the house, a dog barks. The barks are distant at first, but grow rapidly louder as the dog makes its way through the house.

"How big is that dog? Francesca asks cautiously.

"I remember him being really big," Robbie says. "But then again, I was four."

Francesca takes a precautionary step away from the door and accidentally bumps a small table, toppling a pot of potting soil off the edge. The pot shatters on the tile floor and sends ceramic pieces scattering.

"Oh crap," she mutters, and scrambles to gather the pieces together. Blake and I are closest, and squat down to help her.

The back door of the house opens and a grey-haired man in khaki pants and a light-blue Alligator polo, surveys us from the doorway. He's barefoot and supporting his right side with a cane. His green eyes travel from my potting soil stained hands to Carson's red hair and then finally settle on the face of Robbie, who is standing directly in front of him.

"And who might you be?" he inquires, looking into Robbie's eyes.

A brown-and-white, Border collie mix dog wriggles through the man's legs and proceeds directly to the three of us gathered around the remains of the flowerpot. He does a cursory sniff of the pile of dirt and then licks Francesca in the face.

"Come here, Spartacus!" the man orders. The dog returns to its master's legs, looking around happily. "Please pardon my vicious watchdog. He's been lacking in social outlets recently."

Francesca wipes her face but smiles back at his kindly gaze.

The man looks expectantly at Robbie now and says nothing else. Robbie has stage fright, faced with the awkwardness of explaining our situation. "Um, Grand ... ah ... Mr. Cameron," he stammers. "We're here because we ... we are from ... um, we need some help," he finally manages. "I'm Robbie, and these are some of my friends." He gestures to the rest of us. Francesca, Blake and I are now standing, trying to brush the dirt from our hands inconspicuously.

"I know this might sound unusual ..." Robbie pauses for a moment while taking a breath, "but I'm your grandson."

Mr. Cameron raises his eyebrows almost imperceptibly, but continues to listen as Robbie speaks.

"And we're here from ... the future."

Robbie looks to us and we try our best to appear supportive. Blake goes so far as to give a quick thumbs-up before shoving his hand into his pocket and averting his eyes. Carson has been watching Mr. Cameron's face, but when Mr. Cameron looks at him, he shifts his gaze quickly to the dog, that is panting and still looking at us with barely contained exuberance. Francesca continues to smile in their direction, holding the smile slightly longer than is natural.

"I know it might be hard to believe," Robbie continues. "but I remember you from when I was a kid." Mr. Cameron looks at him more seriously now, but remains quiet. "I know that right now I should only be about four years old, but we got sent back from the year 2009, and now we're stuck here. We could really use your help."

Robbie stops talking, holding his breath to see how his grandfather will respond. I've almost stopped hoping for an answer in the moments of silence that follow, but when Mr. Cameron speaks, it's with an undisturbed calm, like someone pulling the drain plug to empty the pool of our anxiety.

"I don't know about all this future business, but it's obvious that you're Rick's boy. You look just like him. As for you all," he continues, "I don't believe I've had the pleasure."

"I'm Carson," Carson begins, since he's closest to Robbie. He extends a hand.

Mr. Cameron switches his cane to his left side and accepts Carson's handshake. He turns next to Francesca. "And you, young lady?"

"I'm Francesca." She smiles, stepping forward and extending her hand as well. He shakes it gently, then looks over her head at Blake and me. We state our names. Blake includes a wave. Mr. Cameron smiles back politely.

"Why don't you all come inside?" Without another word, he turns and disappears into the house. Spartacus pads inside as well, but stops just inside the door and sits down, looking at us invitingly.

Francesca, Blake and I aren't sure what to do with the mess we've made, so we just leave the little pile on the floor, and follow Carson and Robbie, filing into the house one by one. As I shut the door behind me, Spartacus gives a happy bark. I lean over and scratch him under his chin.

"It's nice to meet you, too."

22

Chapter 3

"They say timing is everything. I would argue that spacing is a close second. It's no use showing up right on time, if you fuse your leg through the coffee table."
-Excerpt from the journal of Dr. Harold Quickly, 1989

The inside of Robert Cameron's house is an anomaly. The house is tastefully decorated but looks like it has been rifled through by hungry burglars, who raided the refrigerator and left dishes all over the house. As we file inside, we enter a general-purpose room off the kitchen, that leads to a large dining room to the right. The house isn't dirty, but it's disheveled, with cupboard doors left open in the kitchen and newspapers and jackets lain haphazardly on furniture. A pair of dog food cans on the kitchen counter haven't made it to the trash. Raucous cheering from a television game show emanates from a room nearby. The dining room is the only area that looks like it hasn't been tampered with.

Mr. Cameron picks up items from a roll top desk with his free left hand, but upon seeing that the waste paper basket next to the desk is already full, simply sets them back down. He looks at us, and then gestures to follow him. "Why don't we go in here." He leads the way into an adjacent room. "Less of a disaster."

We follow him into a spacious living area lined with floor to ceiling wooden bookshelves. Around the room, various comfortable looking armchairs and two love seats sit at right angles to one another. The seating surrounds a wooden table with a map of the world painted on it. I like the room immediately. It feels warm and comfortable. In the corner of the room is a birdcage, housing a pair of green parrots. The birds are chirping to one another and pay us little attention.

Robbie walks around the room in a state of nostalgia, looking at things he hasn't laid eyes on in years. I find myself just as interested. Odd knickknacks are interspersed on the shelves among the books and all of the objects look as though they have a story to tell. An ornate saber hangs on a hook with a copper hunting horn. There is a Mason jar of wooden dice and bucket of used wine corks. A wooden longbow leans on a collection of the works of Rudyard Kipling.

Looks like he's had some adventures.

Mr. Cameron works his way to a high-backed leather armchair that has been turned to face the windows. He drags it toward the circle of other chairs and sits. He gestures to us to take seats, and we do, keeping our eyes on him as best we can, despite all there is to look at in the room.

"I'm sorry the place is not more ready to entertain," Mr. Cameron begins. "I'm afraid I haven't been keeping it up to the usual standards. My wife passed away recently and I've not had the interest in maintaining the place as I once did. Call it a deficit of motivation if you will." He smiles wanly and then continues. "So tell me more about how I may be of service. You're a long way from home it seems."

"Well, yes and no," I answer. "We all live in St. Pete, but we can't really go home . . . we're about twenty-three years early, so some of us wouldn't be here yet, and some of us are from here, but are already here I imagine, so are sort of in a weird situation."

"We're all in a weird situation," Francesca laughs nervously.

"Do you mind if I ask how you all found yourself in this predicament?" Mr. Cameron asks. "Your explanation of your circumstances was a bit beyond me."

"We're still trying to figure that out ourselves," Robbie says.

"There was a lightning storm and we got electrocuted," Francesca says. "It burned a hole in my pants."

"Oh dear!" Mr. Cameron replies. "Are you in need of medical attention?"

"We'd thought of going to the hospital to get checked out but we hadn't made it that far yet. That was before we figured out where we were. The time travel thing sort of trumped all of our other problems," Robbie says. "But I think we're okay. I know we got burned a little here and there but I don't think we're in real trouble. At least I'm not. I don't know about you guys."

The rest of us express the same feelings, so Mr. Cameron continues. "So your main concern is that you find yourselves displaced, and are, I'm sure, looking for some kind of solution to the problem."

I nod slowly.

"While I've seen my fair share of Star Trek episodes, I'm afraid I'm not very knowledgeable about time travel. I do know a thing or two about being in need of a place to stay however, and I feel I would be a poor excuse for a human being if I did not at least offer you my hospitality in that area. You can see that I have more house here than I really need, and with my wife gone, all the space in here is downright dreadful."

"We'd really appreciate that," Francesca says.

"It's my pleasure," Mr. Cameron replies. "Besides, it appears I suddenly have an adult grandchild in my house, which is a rare and unexpected treat." He looks at Robbie as he says this.

They have the same eyes.

"With all the people who have come knocking on my door of late to check up on me, I've been used to visitors, but you all are certainly the last thing I would have expected. I probably ought to have my head examined for even letting you in the door with a story like yours, but it's pretty hard to argue with the truth staring you in the face." He considers Robbie some more. "I remember your dad at your age. I don't know if you've seen any photographs of your dad then Robbie, but he was quite athletic too. Middle age got the better of him around the time you were born, but that happens to the best of us I suppose. How is our lovely family doing in the future?"

"Good," Robbie replies slowly. "Really good. Everybody is pretty happy." He suddenly looks uncomfortable talking about the subject with his grandfather.

"You said when you came in that you 'remembered me from when you were a child.' I take it I'm not featuring in our family's doings much in 2009."

Robbie shifts in his seat and starts to speak, but stops himself.

"That's all right," Mr. Cameron continues, "Unless the police finally catch up to me for all those banks I robbed and put me away,"—He winks at Francesca as he says this—"I shall assume I'm simply among the departed in 2009. It's okay," he continues, looking at Robbie now. "We old people don't mind talking about death as much as you young people think we do. It's a rather unavoidable topic at our age."

He doesn't seem all that old to me. Mid-sixties maybe? I wonder what his wife died from?

Robbie relaxes a little but still seems unsure of where to take the conversation next. Mr. Cameron diverts into another topic however and it turns out he doesn't have to worry about it further. "Why don't you all tell me a little about yourselves? I've never met any time travelers before and I feel you must be tremendously interesting people." He smiles and folds his hands in his lap, awaiting our responses. We look around at each other briefly. I give Francesca a nod.

"Um, I'm Francesca," she starts. "I'm twenty-six and I work at a bank and . . . my family is from Cuba. Um, I don't really know what else. I have a cat named Toby. I'm feeling very awkward about having a hole burned in my pants."

"Wonderful!" Mr. Cameron exclaims, smiling at her candor. "And how about you gentlemen?"

"I'm Benjamin," I begin. "My family is all from Oregon. I work on boats at a marina and sometimes do boat sales. I'm pretty terrible at selling things, so it's not that great of a job, but it gets me on the water. These guys are pretty much my best friends." I look around at the others as I say this, realizing that there could be far worse people to be stuck in this situation with. "This is also my first time time traveling. It's been pretty cool so far though." I smile and stop talking.

"And all of you are friends with my Robbie here?" Mr. Cameron asks.

"Yeah, I actually grew up playing soccer with Robbie," Carson says.

"We three went to high school together," Francesca adds.

"Now we all play softball together," Robbie says. "At least that was what we were trying to do when we ended up here."

"You got here from playing softball?" Mr. Cameron raises his eyebrows.

"There was a storm and a power line hit our dugout. That must have had something to do with it. We don't really know what happened. We just know that we were playing softball last night and we woke up here this afternoon."

"It's very fortunate you are okay," Mr. Cameron says. "I was shocked once pretty badly in my younger days and I know it can be very scary. Nothing to the scale of a power line however." He looks around at all of our faces. "I'm sorry that you are dealing with all of this, but I've learned over the years that while life is not always predictable or necessarily enjoyable, it certainly holds no lack of surprises."

Mr. Cameron stands up slowly from his chair and smiles. "I feel I'm in for a treat having you fine young people as guests. I don't feel at all that you are here to rob me. Why don't I give you the nickel tour?"

We follow him out a side door different than the one we came in. We walk through a hallway that leads off of the front door and contains a collection of framed art. Most of them are impressionistic landscapes but I spot one Norman Rockwell *Saturday Evening Post* cover mixed in. The hall doesn't receive any comment from Mr. Cameron and we proceed through it into another room, slightly smaller than the one we've just left.

"This was my wife Abby's sewing room," Mr. Cameron explains. There is a wooden spinning wheel with a stool and pictures of family members hanging on the walls. A quilt is draped over the back of a couch and there are a couple of armchairs facing a TV.

"Hey, is this you, Robbie?" Carson is looking at a group photo of Robbie's family.

"Oh, look at your mom!" Francesca exclaims. "Aw, check out how young everybody looks. Your mom's hair is great."

"Wow, you were goofy looking back then too, eh Robbie?" I smile at the photo of the brown haired four-year-old.

"That was your family Christmas photo this year," Mr. Cameron says. He looks at Robbie and back to the picture. "Fascinating. I can't say as I understand a bit of this situation but it's certainly remarkable. I don't know how anyone will ever believe me. Probably say I've gone off my rocker." He pokes Robbie in the shoulder with his index finger as if checking to see if he's a hallucination. "But there you are."

He seems really intrigued with Robbie. I guess I would be too if someone showed up at my door claiming to be my grandson.

Robbie smiles and then continues to follow his grandfather, who walks to the far side of the room. Mr. Cameron leads us up a wooden staircase into an upstairs hall. "This door leads to the roof." He raps his knuckles on the left hand door closest to him. He then shows us each of the three bedrooms along the right. "You can put yourselves up in here if you like." He points out the various beds in the rooms. "These two rooms share a bathroom you can use. I'm sure you can find some towels and such if you need them. There are twin beds in the middle bedroom, but I guess one of you may have to camp on the couch downstairs, as I think we're going to be one bed short."

"That won't be a problem," I say. "We're happy to have anything really."

"Yes, this is incredibly nice of you," Francesca adds.

"It really is my pleasure." Mr. Cameron leads us down the hall to the glass door at the end. He points to the wooden door to the left before opening the glass door. "That's me."

The veranda overlooks the backyard and the path we walked to the house. A number of wooden chairs surround a circular table with a pot of geraniums on it. We spread out along the railing, taking in the yard and its lush landscaping.

"You have a really beautiful home," Francesca says.

"Thank you," Mr. Cameron replies. "Abby and I always took a lot of pride in it." He looks out over the yard and his eyes grow slowly moist. I try to think of a way to change the subject politely but I can't think of anything about the house that wouldn't relate to the late Mrs. Cameron. Mr.

Cameron straightens up and exhales a deep breath, brushing his hand under his eye to wipe away the beginnings of a tear. "Are you all hungry? I was going to fix myself something in a bit."

"We actually ate recently," I reply. "But we'll definitely join you if you like."

"Wonderful," Mr. Cameron says, still looking at the yard as if trying to avoid our eyes. "If you'll make yourselves at home, I'm going to get started on that." He smiles at us quickly, and then turns back into the hall. "Come down when you're ready. Come along, Spartacus."

Spartacus follows his master with his tail wagging. Mr. Cameron holds the door open long enough for the dog to follow him through, and closes it behind him.

The five of us make a semi-circle along the railing.

"Your grandfather is really sweet, Robbie," Francesca says.

"I wish he wasn't so sad," Robbie responds. "I feel like I'm interrupting him somehow, like I'm invading his grief."

"He seems happy to see you," Francesca says.

"Yeah, he seems very interested in you," Carson slouches against the railing. "It's great that he's up for letting us stay here. I think he took the whole time travel thing really well."

"Yeah, I was worried he'd never let us in after I finally got that out. How long do you think we'll have to stay?" Robbie asks.

"Yeah, what exactly is our plan here?" Blake inquires. "How is this helping our situation? We're in 1985. We don't have any money. No one is going to know who we are. We don't have any I.D. or even know how we got here. We're seriously screwed."

I realize that the four of them are looking to me for a response. I don't feel especially qualified to be making any decisions. The walk here has mostly just been putting one foot in front of the other and trying not to flip out.

I step away from the railing and straighten up. "I think we should spend the night and see how things look in the morning. Maybe we can look for someone to help us. They have that Time Society group here supposedly, according to that newscast. Maybe they can help us somehow. Someone has to know something about this stuff. We'll find them and maybe there's a way we can sort this mess out."

"We should have another look around the softball field too," Carson suggests. "Maybe whatever happened, is going to happen again, and we can see how it works."

"Could be possible I guess," I say.

"I need to buy a toothbrush," Robbie says.

"I need to buy some pants," Francesca adds.

"I need to get something other than cleats to walk around in," Carson looks down at the dirty softball cleats on his feet.

"Yeah, me too." Blake swats at a bug that's attempting to land in his scruffy facial hair.

"We're going to be out of money in a hurry," I say. "We'll have to figure that out soon. For now, lets go down and hang out with Mr. Cameron and see how that goes. Then maybe after, we can walk down to a drug store and pick some things up."

The other four agree and Carson leads the way through the door, trying to walk gingerly so as not to scratch the hardwood floor with his plastic cleats.

"Maybe you should just take them off," Francesca suggests. Blake and Carson both stop and begin removing their cleats.

Robbie gets a whiff of a slightly singed foot smell and backs up. "Maybe you should just leave them on."

"Oh shut up," Carson retorts. "It's not that bad."

Dinner with Mr. Cameron is rather subdued. It turns out he made extra helpings of chicken and rice for us, so we help ourselves in spite of our recent meal. We sit around the table and tell him about our lives and doings in 2009. Mr. Cameron listens politely to our conversation and asks questions, but after a few of Carson's anecdotes about Carson and Robbie getting into trouble together in college, he lapses into silence.

We likewise concentrate on our chicken for a bit and cast periodic glances at one another. I accidentally drown my asparagus in gravy from the tureen and almost make a joke about it, but stop myself, unsure of how best to break the silence. We help clear the dishes after the meal and Mr. Cameron tells us the location of the nearest drug store. Blake and Carson opt to stay behind rather than don their softball cleats again for the walk. Robbie also decides to stay at the house. Francesca and I promise to do our best to retrieve the items they need for them, and once the dishes are all put away, make our way to the back door. Spartacus follows us.

"Is it all right if we take Spartacus with us?" Francesca inquires.

"Oh, of course. You'll be his new best friend," Mr. Cameron replies. "His leash is hanging on a hook on the back steps."

"Do you happen to have a jacket or a sweater I could borrow?" Francesca asks.

"Oh yes, I could find something of Abby's in her closet perhaps, or if you want to use my windbreaker, it's on the back porch too," Mr. Cameron replies.

"That would be fine." Francesca is elated to find that the jacket is long enough to cover the burn hole in her pants. Spartacus bounds to her with his tail wagging and positions himself at the screen door of the porch. Francesca fastens the leash and Spartacus bolts through the opening in the door as soon as he can fit. He's in a state of bliss, sniffing the flowerbed and a garden hose before Francesca and I even make it out the door.

The walk to the drugstore would've only taken a few minutes, but the journey is punctuated by detours through hedges and around a particularly odoriferous set of trashcans. Upon reaching the store, I hold on to Spartacus while Francesca goes inside to grab the items we need. A movie poster for Beverly Hills Cop is hanging in the window, and I'm reading through the cast, when my attention is diverted by three police cruisers racing past with their sirens on.

As I lean down to calm Spartacus, who is barking at the sirens, a fourth police cruiser pulls into the parking lot. Driving slowly, the officer eyes me briefly before pulling into a position near the entrance. He remains in the squad car and transmits on the radio.

The police car makes me nervous, though I can't think of a valid reason why. I casually play with Spartacus, who has decided to chew on his leash to pass the time. In a few minutes Francesca comes out of the store with a bag.

"I found some cheap flip-flops in a bargain bin for Carson and Blake, and I got us all toothbrushes, but they didn't have any shorts or anything. I'm going to have to find a clothing store . . ." She catches me eying the police car again. "What's going on?" She looks over and sees the middle-aged officer watching us from the car.

"I don't know," I reply. "I think we should get back to the house. Come on, fuzzball." I give Spartacus' leash a tug.

"Is something up with officer mustache over there?" Francesca asks as we take to the sidewalk.

"Could be. A bunch of police cars went blazing by and he came into the lot really slow, like he was looking for someone. I think it might be some kind of search."

"Well they can't be looking for us," Francesca replies. I look back briefly after we have gone a half a block or so and see that the police car has idled up to the street. I'm worried for a moment that it's going to follow us, but when it pulls into the street, it turns the opposite direction. I pull Spartacus out of a yard where he's made use of the pause to chew on a Cabbage Patch Doll that was left on the lawn.

"Hey, you little terror, they don't want your teeth marks in their baby. I think those things were expensive." Spartacus drops the doll and trots happily back to the sidewalk to continue on with us.

"Seriously," Francesca comments. "Some kid is getting an earful when the parents see that in the morning." I take one more look at the diminishing taillights and then follow the dog.

When we reenter the house, we find our friends in the sewing room. Carson is sitting on the stool of the spinning wheel and has an acoustic guitar on his lap. He's strumming and singing *Champagne Supernova* quietly to himself, occasionally stopping to make notes on a piece of paper. Blake and Robbie are lounging in the pair of armchairs and watching a television in the corner of the room.

"You guys are just in time," Robbie says as we walk in. "*MacGyver* comes on in five minutes."

"Unless he's going to show us how to build a time machine from a fork and a pencil sharpener, I don't think it's really going to help us." Blake scowls from the other chair.

"Here." Francesca tosses a pair of flip-flops to Blake. She drops the other pair on the floor at Carson's feet. He stops singing and reaches down to examine them.

"I didn't remember to ask for your sizes, so I guessed. I figured they were flip-flops, so you could probably work it out."

Blake slips his feet into his and wiggles his toes around.

"Is this the only color they had?" Carson asks, looking at the blue straps on the flip-flops.

"Actually, they had pink, but I decided to be nice. I got us some burn cream too." She pulls a couple tubes of ointment out of the bag. "Let me know if you need them."

"I'll take one," Robbie replies, and Francesca tosses the tube to him.

"Where's Mr. Cameron?" I ask.

"I think he went to bed," Blake responds. "He went upstairs a little bit ago and we haven't heard from him since."

"Blake and I are taking the twin bedroom," Carson says. "You and Robbie get to fight over the other one."

"I can take the couch," Robbie suggests. "I don't really care."

"Take the bed." I slump onto the couch. "The couch doesn't bother me. That bed looked a little short for me anyway."

Carson goes back to strumming the guitar while Francesca joins me on the couch. I pull my feet up and wedge one of them in between the couch cushions trying to get comfortable. Francesca fiddles with the cap on the burn cream but doesn't open it. I lay my head back on the cushions and examine a burn on my palm. It's still red and warm to the touch, but not especially painful. Carson is partway through singing the chorus to Eagle Eye Cherry's, *Save Tonight,* when Blake suddenly snaps at him.

"Am I the only one who's freaking out here? We're in 1985! I don't see how no one else is concerned about this." His eyes have a look of thinly veiled panic. "Seriously. We're so screwed right now!"

Robbie turns down the television.

"We're all freaking out," Francesca says.

"Yeah, it's crazy for all of us," I add. "But it isn't going to do us any good to lose our heads."

"I'm not losing my head, I just think we ought to be worrying about more than *MacGyver* right now. We may have just destroyed our entire lives. What happens if we never get back? My girlfriend is two years old! By the time she's old enough to talk to me, I'm going to look like some creepy old pervert."

I keep quiet at this, considering my own losses. If I don't show up for work tomorrow, I imagine my boss will notice, but I don't think he'd exactly miss me. He'd just have to trailer his own boats. We're missing Mallory, but otherwise, most of the people I spend my time with are right here in this room.

"You said there is the Time something or other Society here right?" Carson asks.

I nod.

"Do you know where it is?"

"I think we can find it. I'm sure we can figure out where it is tomorrow and see if someone there has any way to help us."

"What if they arrest us or something?" Francesca asks. "Who's going to believe us?"

"They're a group devoted to studying this stuff, so if anyone is going to believe us, they should," Robbie says.

"I think it's our best shot," I add.

"What about Mr. Cameron?" Francesca asks. "I feel like we should do something for him since he's putting us up. Maybe we can clean his house for him or something?"

"That's a good idea," Robbie replies. "I know that lawn sure needs mowing."

"How about we see what we can do around here in the morning, and in the afternoon we can go see about finding the Time Society place," I suggest.

The other four agree to this and go back to their own thoughts. I feel like they look more at ease now that there is a plan of action. Robbie turns the volume back up on *MacGyver* and we watch to the end of the episode, before ambling to our respective rooms for the night. Robbie is the last to leave the sewing room. As I'm getting myself comfortable on the couch, he stops at the foot of the stairs.

"You know . . . I don't think it's going to be that bad. I know we're in a totally screwed up mess and all, but I can't help but feel like there's a purpose to all of it, and that somehow things are going to work out okay."

"I'm sure they will." I try to match Robbie's optimism.

"At least we aren't alone," Robbie adds.

"Yeah, definitely," I say. "I can't imagine how messed up I'd be, if I was in this by myself.

Chapter 4

"Not all time travelers you meet are out to do great things. Sure, some are reminiscent of bygone eras, some are seeking adventure, but some are just looking for a way to escape the IRS."
-Excerpt from the journal of Dr. Harold Quickly, 2052

I wake to a slobbery tongue in my ear. "Argh Spartacus!" I fend off the dog's affection and roll over on the couch. There's a clatter of dishes from the kitchen. Spartacus continues to nuzzle me in the back until I finally give up trying to ignore him. "Okay fine. You happy now?" I sit up and scratch the dog on both sides of its head.

It really wasn't a dream. I look at the sewing room around me. A pendulum clock ticks back and forth on the wall behind the TV.

I'm in 1985.

I guess it beats going to work.

I get up and walk through the library into the kitchen. Mr. Cameron is standing at the sink, scrubbing coffee mugs and laying them on a towel on the counter.

"Good morning."

"Good morning, Benjamin," Mr. Cameron replies. "I'm just trying to make the place a little more presentable. It seems I was trying to start a mug collection in my bedroom. Can I get you anything? I have some coffee brewing."

"No thank you. We were talking last night and we'd really like to help out a little in return for letting us stay here. Would you mind letting us mow the lawn or something like that? We can do dishes, whatever you need."

"That's very thoughtful of you. The lawn is in disgraceful shape, I'll admit. But I really don't mind putting you up. It's already helped get my mind off things. But I certainly won't turn down help that is offered." He dunks another cup in the soapsuds. "Plus I imagine you are all in a tight spot financially with your lives and homes nowhere to be found. I can probably find you some jobs around here worth paying you for, if you like."

I grab a dishtowel and start drying the dishes on the counter. "We're happy to just work for our keep. It's so nice of you to put us up like this. We are rather broke, but you don't need to pay us. I'm sure we'll find a way to work things out eventually."

"Okay, we'll see what we can do. I may have some clothes that might fit some of you in the meantime. I don't mind taking you shopping for some basic necessities. I know young people seem to like having holes in their getups these days, but having a change of clothes won't hurt you."

"That's nice of you. Thank you."

As I stack dishes in the rack, I spot a battered copy of H.G. Wells' *The Time Machine* sitting on the stove. "Doing some research?" I ask.

"It was the only thing on the bookshelf that seemed relevant. Not sure it's going to be much help, unless you have an upcoming battle with some Morlocks you failed to mention."

"Would've been nice if the book came with some blueprints for building your own time machine," I say. "That we could use."

When we finish the dishes, Mr. Cameron calls for Spartacus. The dog bounds to his side. "I'm going to take Spartacus for his walk this morning. I have a couple of errands to attend to. Tell the others to help themselves to the fridge. There isn't a lot in there, but maybe I can take you all to the store a little later and you can pick out a few things you like. If you want, I can show you where the lawn things are on my way out."

I follow him out to the garden shed we'd passed on our way in yesterday. The inside of the shed smells like grass clippings. There's a workbench along one wall and a board with tools hanging on it. In the center of the board is a dusty wooden plaque that was carved with the name Robert "Lucky" Cameron. Mr. Cameron shows me the mower and gas cans and the electric edger. I point to the sign and voice my curiosity.

"Do you mind if I ask why they call you 'Lucky'?"

Mr. Cameron looks up at the sign and his eyes brighten. "That's a plaque I got as sort of a gag gift from my friends. It's a long story. Remind me and I'll tell you about it when we've got more time."

My curiosity is even stronger now, but I can appreciate the need to tell a good story right, so I try to be patient.

After pointing out everything we would need, Mr. Cameron lets Spartacus off his leash and then follows him slowly out the back of the yard using his cane only occasionally for support. I go back inside and climb the stairs to the rooms of my sleeping friends. Blake is already up and coming out of the bathroom when I make it to the top of the stairs.

"Hey, man."

"Hey."

"Will you help me wake the others? I talked to Mr. Cameron about doing some chores around here and he's cool with it."

"All right." Blake rubs some gunk out of his eyes and yawns, then walks into the room where Robbie is sleeping. I knock lightly on the door to Francesca's room, then look inside. Francesca is buried under a pile of covers and I can just make out the top of her head and her right eyelid showing past the comforter.

"Rise and shine!" I call in the most chipper voice I can manage.

"Hmph. Go away," is the response I get from under the covers.

"There's coffee," I bargain.

Francesca's eye opens slightly at this, and stares at me.

"Hmm. Give me five minutes."

Twenty-five minutes later, we're out in the backyard handing tools out of the shed, when Francesca finally appears at the back door with a coffee mug, and squints at us across the yard.

"What are we doing?" she calls out.

"Yard work!" Robbie yells.

"I think I hate you!" Francesca yells back, but she descends the steps. She shuffles across the yard and Blake hands her a pair of pruning shears. Francesca takes another swig of her coffee and walks to the hedge on the side of the yard and stares at it for a bit. Eventually she sets her coffee mug down in the dried out birdbath and sets to trimming the bushes with slow but deliberate care.

Despite the lethargic start, the five of us are able to put the yard in order in good time. By the time Mr. Cameron returns, the lawn is mowed and edged and the grass is neatly bagged next to the trash cans. Francesca has trimmed the shrubbery and even refilled the birdbath. Spartacus inspects our work with avid curiosity while Mr. Cameron takes it all in and smiles.

"We've certainly made ourselves some useful friends, haven't we, buddy?"

"We made it through the yard but we didn't make it to the garden yet," Carson says.

"Ah, well, Rome wasn't built in a day. You all look like you could use a break."

We follow him indoors and gather in the kitchen. Mr. Cameron fishes some glasses out of the cupboard and a pitcher of water from the fridge. We happily accept them. Next, he unloads a couple of items from a bag he has brought into the kitchen, one of which is a packet of dog treats. Spartacus bounces up and down at the sight of it. Mr. Cameron selects a treat and tosses it through the doorway to the library, sending Spartacus flying after it. He then pulls a newspaper out of the bag and turns to us.

"I was sitting on a bench resting outside the post office this morning, when I found an interesting bit of news that I thought you might want to look at." He unfolds the paper and hands it to Carson who is standing closest. "Tell me if you have any insights on that cover story."

We crowd around Carson to read over his shoulder. The bottom section of the front page features a photo of a van crashed into a utility pole, with police officers working around it. The headline reads, "Two Dead in Mystery Crash."

"Seems a van crashed yesterday afternoon and they found two men in it who had been murdered. They appeared to be police officers or guards, but they didn't die from the crash. One was shot and one was strangled. That isn't even the interesting part. There is an odd bit in there about the van."

Carson reads aloud from the paper, "Police are checking to see if the vehicle was stolen, due to errors noted with the vehicle registration, and a model name and VIN number that the manufacturer states does not match any vehicle currently in production."

"Any specifics on the van?" Robbie asks.

"No. It starts talking about the numbers of stolen vehicles used in crimes being on the rise," Carson says.

"Can you see the model name in the picture?" I ask.

"Maybe." Carson holds the picture close to his face. "It says GMC on the back. I can't really see the model name. It's too small."

"I may have a magnifying glass in that roll top," Mr. Cameron suggests. Blake looks over the desk and finds a large magnifying glass sticking out of a cup of pens. He hands it to Carson.

"It definitely starts with an S. Maybe Sierra? What does GMC make?" Carson asks.

"Can I see?" Blake takes the paper and the magnifying glass. "I think it might say Savannah. Does that sound right?"

"I think that's a real van though, right?" I say.

"Why are we trying to find this out?" Francesca asks. "I'm a little lost. Why does it matter what it says?"

"It could be nothing," Mr. Cameron explains. "I just found it odd that it stated that bit about the van not being a model currently in production. In light of our conversation last night, and all of you present here today, it made me wonder if you all were the only ones who were affected during that power line incident. I could be jumping at shadows now that I've had a taste of the bizarre, but I thought it was interesting."

"That is interesting," I agree. "If someone else came back too, they may have some idea about what happened."

"They might know how to get back," Blake adds.

"They also could be a freaking murderer! Did you guys miss that part?" Francesca exclaims.

"Yeah. That part doesn't make a lot of sense," I say. "I don't know how we go about finding out more about it, but it might be worth the effort. Maybe we can ask around a bit and see what else they've figured out."

"Does anyone know where the impound lot is?" Robbie asks.

"We know where the police station is. I suppose we could find out there," Blake suggests.

"At least we have something to check out," I say.

"Maybe we can split up," Carson offers. "A couple of us can check out the station and ask around about the van thing, and the others can see if we can find the time place."

"I'm not going anywhere near the murder van," Francesca says.

"Okay. How about you and Blake and I can go look for the Time Studies Society," I say. "Carson and Robbie can check out the police station and see what's up. Carson can probably charm some girl cops out of some information."

Carson smiles. "I'm not the handcuffs type, but I'll see what I can do."

"Can we shower first? I feel disgusting right now," Francesca asks.

"I'll get you all some towels and see if I can find you some clothes that might fit," Mr. Cameron says. "I know my son has left more than a few things here in the past, or if not, there is my closet. And I can probably find something of Abby's for you, Francesca."

"That would be awesome," I reply.

Francesca looks skeptical but hides it quickly with a smile as Mr. Cameron passes her and heads up the stairs. "I'm going to need a job at a clothing store, like right now," she says after he's out of earshot. "Sorry Robbie. No offense, but it's going to be a little weird wearing your deceased grandmother's clothes."

"I know what you mean," Robbie replies. "At least we'll be in the same boat. We get my grandpa's clothes to wear."

Upstairs we find Mr. Cameron laying out an armful of clothes in the room with the twin beds. The guys take turns showering in the hall bathroom and we are finished at the same time that Francesca emerges from the bathroom in Mr. Cameron's room. She is wearing a floral skirt and a white blouse that she's rolled the sleeves up on, and she's carrying a knit sweater over her arm.

"Your Grandma had long arms Robbie," she comments. "And there are some benefits to elastic waist bands. She was pretty classy though. I actually really liked some of her outfits."

The guys have varied success with Mr. Cameron's clothes. Robbie and Carson find some corduroy pants to wear with some polo shirts. Blake and I are too tall for any of the pants and opt to stay in our athletic shorts, but help ourselves to some of Mr. Cameron's long sleeved T-shirts.

We regroup downstairs near the kitchen and Mr. Cameron provides us with a phone book to search for the St. Petersburg Temporal Studies Society. Blake finds the number and dials it into Mr. Cameron's phone.

"Hello. Yes, good afternoon. I was wondering what your address is?" He scribbles hastily on a pad next to the phone. "Okay, wonderful, and do you have any tours, or interviews for students interested in your work? . . . Uh-huh, would that be available today? . . . Okay, great, thank you very much." He turns back to us. "Good news. They have a designated intern for giving information on the organization and he's available till four-thirty. I got the address. That should at least get us in the door."

"Awesome. How far is it?" I ask.

"It's actually really close to the softball field. It's over on Twelfth Ave."

"Good. Robbie and Carson can hit up the Police Station on Central and see if they can find out anything about the van thing."

"I can give you two a ride down there if you like," Mr. Cameron suggests. "Central is a bit far to walk. I can't fit everyone in my car, otherwise I would take you all."

"Thanks, that would be great," Robbie replies.

"What's the phone number here?" I ask. "We can call back here if we get in trouble."

"I'll write it down for you," Mr. Cameron replies. He scribbles the number on two slips of paper and hands them to Robbie and me. "If we make it back prior to you three, give a call and perhaps I can pick you up."

"Do you have your phone on you, Francesca?" I ask.

"It doesn't work here, remember?" she replies.

"Yeah, but bring it anyway. It may be of interest at the Temporal Studies Society if we need to tell someone our story. You should bring your I.D. too."

We split up, and Spartacus is left to tend the house. It's a familiar walk back toward the softball field. Blake and I walk quickly, only slowing when Francesca is in danger of lagging behind.

The St. Petersburg Temporal Studies Society is located in a fenced in warehouse on a corner of an otherwise residential block. A small parking lot along the building is full, and a number of people in lab coats and I.D. badges are loitering around a back door, smoking. We enter through the main door and are greeted by a red-haired receptionist at the desk.

"Hello, we called about getting some information on your program," Blake says as we walk up to the desk.

"Are you students?"

"Er, yes," he replies. "We're doing a research paper on theories of time travel for our physics class."

"Okay, our intern, Elliot, will be able to answer your questions. I'll need you to sign in and I'll get you some visitor's badges."

We sign the form and pin on the badges. A few moments later a tall, lanky blonde man about our age, walks through a set of double doors and greets us.

"Hello, I'm Elliot. I understand that you're interested in getting the tour."

"Yes." Francesca smiles. "We want to learn about time travel."

"Well, we study a lot of things here at the Temporal Studies Society, everything from quantum theory, to the affects of aging. It's true that some of the scientists here have been studying theories of time travel, but that's not all we do."

"Which scientists have been working on it?" Blake asks.

"Dr. Simons is head of the department on temporal physics but a lot of the work is being done by Dr. Quickly, who came out with a published theory on the subject a few years ago, and has been considered a leader in the area. Let me show you around. There are some areas that I won't be able to show you due to safety concerns, but I can show you a few of our projects."

Elliot leads us down a hallway to an expansive open laboratory. There are bulky machines that I can't begin to identify, as well as volumes of manuals and charts laid out on tables around them. A few men in coveralls are working on one of the machines in the center of the room.

"Our creation department is devoted entirely to the construction of the equipment we need for various tests. In our field, many of the tools we need don't exist anywhere else, so we're required to custom build them to our purposes. That's one of the costs and challenges of being on the cutting edge of scientific technology."

"So what are the current chances of someone time traveling?" I ask.

"Ha, for a person, zero," Elliot responds. "Unless you live in Hollywood. We've been getting that question a lot, ever since this summer, when *Back to the Future* came out. We don't have a Delorean in any of these labs, if that's what you're wondering."

"But the theory is there, right?" Blake asks.

"Yes and no. There are still a lot of things we don't know about space and time and how they interact. We've been studying a lot of possible scenarios."

Eliott leads us through another set of doors into a smaller room that has a few large computers and a number of chalkboards and drafting tables. A dark-skinned man of about thirty is working on a drawing on one of them. "This is Malcolm. He's one of our draftsmen and also does some of the tours. He was an intern here before me and they liked him so much they gave him a permanent position." Malcolm nods from behind the table and gives a small wave before he goes back to his drawing.

"So how does Dr. Quickly propose to develop the theory of time travel further?" I ask, hoping to get the conversation back to items that can help us. "What are his methods?"

"There's been a lot of talk over the years about speed being a key to time travel," Elliot says. "Some of Einstein's theories suggest that traveling at speeds close to that of light could make one capable of time travel. The fact that you cannot make matter go that fast without first converting it to energy, obviously makes it a challenge to discuss ever sending a person through time. There have been experiments done trying to send individual particles that fast. So far there has been limited success. Most recently the science has moved into the study of wormholes, or passages through the fabric of space and time. That has of course presented the problem of finding the energy to keep such a wormhole open."

"Like electricity?" I suggest. "I thought I read something about this sort of blue electricity . . ."

Malcolm's head lifts up at this and I catch his eye momentarily before he drops his gaze again.

"I don't know that I've heard of color ever having anything to do with it, but there have been some theories in the works there also. I believe Dr. Quickly has been developing some recently. I'm not the one to talk to on that subject however. You would probably have to get that information from the source."

"Can we do that?" Francesca asks. "Can we talk to Dr. Quickly?"

"He has a pretty busy schedule. He doesn't take appointments very frequently."

We move into the next room. It has a number of steel tables in it. Some of them hold flowerpots under glass domes. The flowers are in various states of growth, from budding leaves, to pathetic withered twigs. There's also a row of cages with lab rats in them.

"Hey, it's *Pinky and the Brain*." Francesca nudges Blake with her elbow. I notice that Malcolm has followed us into the room and is fiddling with a pencil sharpener on the wall.

"This room has a number of our aging tests. I'm sorry about the heat. We keep it at a pretty warm temperature for the plants. They've been doing various longevity tests here for years. Not all that exciting if you ask me."

Francesca starts taking off her sweater. "Isn't it a little hot for these rats? I'm burning up."

As Elliot explains the nature of the tests on the rats to Francesca, she folds her sweater over her arm. Her cell phone falls out of the pocket and it bounces off of her foot and skids across the floor. Francesca mutters to herself then notices Malcolm frozen in place staring at the phone with a pencil in his hand. He looks from the phone to the three of us with wide eyes for a moment, then quickly composes himself, and walks out of the room through the doors we entered by.

Francesca grabs the phone and sticks it back under her sweater before Elliot pays any attention. She catches my eye and jerks her head toward the door that Malcolm has departed through. I noticed the reaction too and nod to her.

We continue to follow Elliot through a couple more rooms of the lab but are unable to gain any more information about Dr. Quickly or his current experiments. About fifteen minutes later Elliot leads us back to the lobby at the end of the tour.

"If you need more information on The Society, The *Saint Petersburg Times* has written some nice articles recently. They have them on file at the library. I wish you the best of luck with your research." He shakes all of our hands and disappears back into the lab.

We begin to walk out the front door when the receptionist calls us back, pointing to our I.D. badges. Francesca and I hand our badges to Blake and he walks them back to the desk.

The receptionist smiles and then leans past him and calls to Francesca. "Miss! I have a message here for you."

"For me?" Francesca raises her eyebrows and walks over to the desk. The receptionist hands her a white envelope.

"Have a great day!"

Francesca smiles and takes the envelope, and the three of us exit back onto the sidewalk.

"What on earth is that all about?" Blake asks.

IN TIMES LIKE THESE

Francesca tears open the envelope, and removes a small slip of paper. It contains only two lines.

"We need to talk. Meet me at the pier tonight, 8pm."

Chapter 5

"It doesn't pay to insult another time traveler. In fact you should make it a rule of thumb to never anger anyone today, who can go back and stab you yesterday."
-Excerpt from the journal of Dr. Harold Quickly, 2008

I'm staring out the back window of the house as Mr. Cameron pulls into the driveway. Spartacus meets everyone at the door as Mr. Cameron, Carson, and Robbie hustle through, anxious to share their news. "Dude, we ought to be detectives!" Carson declares as they enter the kitchen. "They need to make a show about us."

"I take it you got some good info," I say.

"Carson is an excellent sleuth," Mr. Cameron agrees.

"What did you find out?" Francesca asks.

"The van is a GMC Savannah like Blake thought. It's a prisoner transfer van. Only thing is, they have no idea who killed the guys in it. They're looking into the possibility that it was the prisoner who escaped. That's the assumption."

"Was there more than one prisoner in the van?" Blake asks.

"They don't know because they don't have any info on where it came from. But guess what?"

"What?"

"The police wouldn't give us any actual information on the case, because it's an ongoing investigation or whatever, but I talked to this teenage kid who was on a ride-along at the station, and he told us where the van was. It turns out he had been with one of the cops who had responded to the scene yesterday. Apparently the cop had told this kid all about the experience and even drove him by the place where they were keeping the van. He was super chatty, so we got as much as he knew out of him as he was leaving the station."

"Then Grandpa took us by the site where they were keeping it," Robbie continues the story. "The van was locked up behind a fence but it was outside. We were able to see over the fence and could see the license plate. It had government plates registered till 2010."

"Wow. So we aren't the only ones," I respond. "At least one other person is running around from the future."

"An escaped killer," Francesca adds.

"It looks that way," Mr. Cameron says.

"What if it's Stenger, the psycho bomber serial killer guy?" Francesca asks. "That guy just finally got convicted. Now he could go right back to killing people."

"We don't know it's him. There could be any number of people. There are plenty of prisoners in the world," I say, but I'd been wondering the same thing.

"Yeah, but not many driving around in St. Pete the day we left," Carson argues. "His was a special case. It wasn't even supposed to be tried here, remember? His lawyer argued something about him not getting a fair trial in Tallahassee, so they moved it to another city. They chose St. Pete, but I don't think there are many big cases like that here usually."

"That's true," Robbie agrees. "Should we warn the police here?"

"Do we want to tell them who we are?" Blake asks. "What if they take us in to question us? Who knows where we'd end up? We know the future. I don't plan to spend my time being interrogated. We need to get back."

"Speaking of that topic, what did you all ascertain on your adventure?" Mr. Cameron asks.

We describe our tour of the Temporal Studies Society and show the others the cryptic note we received.

"We're thinking it's from that Malcolm character who was acting so suspicious, but we can't know for sure," Francesca explains. "But whoever it is wants to meet us."

"Are we all going down there?" Robbie asks.

"That's actually a good question," I reply. "We don't really know how much we can trust this person. Since they only saw three of us, maybe it's a good idea for you two to keep a low profile till we know more. That way we aren't showing all our cards at once. I'd like to know more about what we're into before we go telling just anyone our story."

Spartacus trots into the room and drops a toy at Robbie's feet. Robbie picks it up and tosses it for him. "Blake brings up a good point," I say, watching the dog dash after it. "We do know the future when it comes to a lot of things. That information would probably be valuable to a lot of people. We ought to be sure of who we can trust."

"I want to be around in any case," Carson says. "Robbie and I can hang out and watch from a distance. They won't know what we look like. We can observe, and if anything goes wrong, we can jump in."

"You can use my car if you like," Mr. Cameron says. "And you can call here if you get separated from one another. It's good to have a point of contact."

The temperature has dropped significantly by the time eight o'clock rolls around. Blake and I have borrowed some sweatshirts from Mr. Cameron that are slightly too small, but are better than nothing. Francesca is hugging herself in her sweater as we walk down the long expanse of the St. Petersburg Pier. The city is lit up and I marvel at the difference in the skyline without the high rise condos that I know are going to bloom up over the next two decades.

The pier itself looks less colorful than we knew it, but the pelicans still swoop along the road and fishermen are still lining the edges. The inverted pyramid building at the end of the pier has people coming and going, and I realize how hard it will be to pick anyone out in the dim light. We look for anyone who resembles Malcolm, but don't see him. We linger outside the entrance so we can be easily found. Carson has followed us up the pier at a distance and is keeping to the north edge, pretending to be interested in one of the fishermen's catches. Robbie is at the parking lot near the car.

Fifteen minutes go by as we lean against the wall, waiting for our contact. I'm starting to worry that we're going to be stood up, when at last a trolley pulls up to the entrance, and after a couple of families descend, Malcolm steps down and walks immediately toward us. He's wearing a black coat and jeans and doesn't look at anything else as he walks up and addresses us quietly. "Follow me please."

He leads the way to an edge of the pier, then pivots and faces us. Malcolm is about Robbie's height but not as athletically built. Olive skin and dark eyes make his slightly curved nose and sharp features seem exotic.

"He wants to know what you want," he says.

"I'm sorry. Who wants to know what?" I ask.

Malcolm glares at me, but seeing that I was asking sincerely, starts over again. "Why did you come to the Temporal Studies Society today? It wasn't for a research paper."

He has a slight accent. *Somewhere in Eastern Europe or the Middle East maybe?*

"We were looking for Dr. Quickly," Blake replies. "We need to talk to him."

Malcolm looks at each of us intently. He looks lastly at Francesca and sees her hand fidgeting in her pocket. "When are you from?"

"2009," I say.

Malcolm doesn't blink. "How did you get here?"

"That's what we need help figuring out," Blake replies. "We're trying to get back."

"You didn't come here on purpose?" Malcolm asks, surprised.

"No!" Blake exclaims.

This seems to change Malcolm's disposition toward us. He looks us over again, apparently deciding what to do next. "Where are you staying?"

"We'd rather not say," I respond, before any of the others can reply. "We don't know you and we'd rather not take any unnecessary chances."

Malcolm nods. "Very well. I'll discuss your situation with Dr. Quickly and see what he says. I'm sure he'll want to meet you."

"How should we get in touch with you?" Blake asks.

"Dr. Quickly isn't here at the moment. I can't say exactly when he'll be back. Meet me here again next week. Same time."

"Next week?" Blake replies angrily. "What're we supposed to do until then?"

"Try not to screw anything up," Malcolm snaps. He begins to walk away.

"But you can help us?" Blake continues, his tone more conciliatory now.

Malcolm turns around and considers us. "If you're being honest, and all you want is to get back, we can probably help you. If we find you have ulterior motives, things will not go well. Don't come by the Temporal Studies Society anymore. It isn't wise. It's especially important that you do not disturb the Dr. Quickly there." He turns and walks back to the front of the building and boards a trolley that is loading passengers, leaving the three of us to dwell on what he said.

As the trolley departs down the pier, Francesca turns to Blake and me. "What did he mean by, 'The Dr. Quickly there?'"

"I was wondering the same thing," I reply.

Carson detaches himself from the conversation he's in with the fisherman and joins us. "What did you find out?"

"More questions," Blake replies.

"But he said he would help us," Francesca says. "We have to meet him here again in a week."

"Let's go back and find Robbie," I suggest. "We have a lot to figure out."

47

"You think Dr. Quickly has a brother?" Robbie asks. We're sitting at a couple of tables in the local Taco Bell, discussing what we've found out.

"Could be. Or it could be his father or something," Blake answers. "In any case, there's more than one Dr. Quickly."

"We only want the one who can help us with time travel stuff, so wouldn't that have to be the guy at the Temporal Studies Society?" Francesca asks, as she tries to keep the contents of her hard taco from falling out onto the table.

Carson returns to the table after a trip to the restroom and interrupts our conversation as he sits back down. "So I've been thinking. We should totally be taking advantage of the fact that we're here. We're sitting on some golden opportunities right now. We should see if we can get some money and invest it all in things we know are going to do well in the next few years. Apple, cell phone companies, we could make a fortune!"

"I think we have more important things to worry about right now." Blake scowls.

"Well yeah, but we're here. There's no harm in going back wealthy, is there? We set up some investment accounts, fast forward back to 2009, and bam! Millionaires."

"Sounds like a great idea, except for the fact that we've got no money." Robbie tries to skewer a stray bean with his fork.

"Details man," Carson replies. "There are plenty of ways to make some money. We have at least a week till we get to talk to this Dr. Quickly guy. We ought to make the best of it and see if we can't set ourselves up somehow."

"We'll nominate you for that job," I say.

"All right. I'm gonna do it. I know all kinds of stuff about the eighties," Carson says. "Think about it. We know most of the hit movies and songs that are going to come out for the next twenty years. We know at least a few of the winners of major sporting events. We could win some bets."

"Like *Back to the Future II*?" I ask.

"Exactly, and *Back to the Future II* hasn't even come out yet. No one will even be suspicious."

"No one will be suspicious because they think time travel is impossible," Blake says. "Even the Temporal Studies Society scientists think it's impossible."

"Hey man, don't worry," I say, seeing the despair creeping back into his eyes. "We got here, so there has to be a way back. We'll get you back to Mallory. We all want back too."

Francesca is staring out the window at a group of teenagers hanging around their cars in the parking lot. "You think I would look good with pink streaks in my hair?" She gestures toward a girl leaning on a Camaro in a black leather jacket and neon socks. Her hair is teased out with hot pink streaks in it. "If we stick around here much longer, I may have to regress into eighties fashion. I did always want some leg warmers."

"Come on, let's get out of here," Blake suggests, grabbing his tray and heading for the trashcan.

I get up also. "I guess we should tell Mr. Cameron what happened before he starts worrying about us."

The darkness in the sewing room is nearly complete when I open my eyes. I can make out an intermittent gleam from a streetlamp on the pendulum of Mr. Cameron's wall clock as it swings back and forth next to the TV. I close my eyes again and try to get comfortable. Then I hear it again. A low growl is emanating from the hallway. I reopen my eyes and stare at the doorway. There is a clacking of claws on the hardwood floor and a shadow slides into the room. It moves across the floor and up to the couch. The growling grows louder. *Is he going to attack me?*

I stay still and Spartacus climbs over me to stare out the window. His back feet step on me slightly and his front paws are on the back of the couch as he snarls out at the side yard of the house. "What's the matter, buddy?" Spartacus turns his head to look at me for a moment but immediately returns his attention to the yard. "All right. I'll check it out."

I move Spartacus off me and look through the blinds. A dark figure is in the grass, moving slowly and sweeping its hand back and forth. "Who the hell is that, Spartacus?"

I walk to the back door and out onto the porch. I flip on the porch light and open the screen door. Spartacus shoots past my legs into the darkness. I hear barking and then a shriek. When I get around the side of the house, Spartacus has the figure cornered against the fence.

"Get that thing away from me!" the man yells.

I know that voice.

"Malcolm?" I grab Spartacus by the collar and pull him back a few feet. The dog stops barking but maintains a low growl. "What are you doing in our yard?"

"I didn't know it was yours," Malcolm replies, stepping forward. I can make out his face now in the light from the back porch. He's dressed in the same black pants and jacket from earlier, but now has a canvas messenger bag slung across his chest.

"Congratulations, I guess," I say. "You found us." The device in Malcolm's hand is blinking an amber light and beeping. "What're you doing here in the middle of the night?"

"I was investigating," he replies.

"Well, mystery solved. We're staying here, if it's that important to you. You can go home to bed now."

"That's not what I was investigating."

"No? What's your little beepy thing you got there?"

He scowls. "It's a temporal spectrometer, not a beepy thing."

"My apologies. What're you doing with your spectral beepy thing?"

"None of your business," he says.

"You're prowling in our yard in the middle of the night. Want me to let the dog go again?"

Spartacus has stopped growling now and I can see him eyeing a stick on the ground. I know he's no longer a threat to Malcolm, but Malcolm still flinches.

"Fine. I'm researching temporal anomalies in the area for Dr. Quickly," he says. "One of the temporal anomalies was here. It turned out to be you."

"What's a temporal anomaly?"

"It's a frequency shift," he replies. "The change is evidence of matter that is out of sync with the timestream it's in. Usually the frequency changes are related to time travelers. This locates the anomalies." He holds up the device in his hand. It's a small, black box about six inches wide, with a handle. A screen on the top is glowing, and a couple of lights are illuminated.

"How big is the range on that thing?" I say.

"Depending on how it is tuned, it will pick up anomalies within a few miles. Some we already know about. This house was one we hadn't cataloged yet. Now I know why."

"You have more anomalies around town?" I ask.

"This past week we've had a rash of them. I've been working around the clock, trying to get them all logged, before the traces fade or the objects move too much. Now that I've found you, I can get you to help me answer some questions. Perhaps you will come with me and see if you can shed some light on a few things."

"A little late for investigating, don't you think?"

"If you really want Dr. Quickly's help, it would make a good show of faith if you assist me."

Spartacus has rolled upside down in the grass and is gnawing on the stick he found, so I know that threats will get no more answers from Malcolm. "Fine. I'll wake my friends."

"I only have transport for one," Malcolm says. "You will come alone."

I consider the man before me. I still don't know if I can trust him. *I think I could definitely take him in a fight if things got violent somehow.*

"Okay. Let me put the dog inside, and grab some shoes."

I coerce Spartacus back indoors, and briefly consider waking Blake or Carson, but settle for leaving a note on the roll top desk. I join Malcolm back in the yard and he leads me out to the street. I walk to the passenger side of a small, silver Plymouth that's parked a door down from the house.

"No, not that one." Malcolm points ahead of the car to a sun-faded scooter parked on the sidewalk.

"This is your 'transport?'" I say.

"Yes."

"Is it pink?"

"It's red," Malcolm says with indignation.

"Looks kinda pink."

Malcolm dons a white half helmet and gestures for me to climb on behind him.

"You do realize I am 6'3" and almost two hundred pounds, right?" I ask. "Is this thing going to hold me?"

"I've had bigger people ride it," Malcolm says.

I climb on behind him and hold on to the side of the seat. It reminds me of a weed whacker as it fires up, but once we get rolling, it moves pretty fast. I squint my eyes in the wind as Malcolm navigates us through the mostly deserted city streets. *I should have grabbed a jacket.*

Our stop turns out to be along a mostly industrial street. Malcolm guides the scooter onto a dirt drive that leads to a fenced lot. The scooter stops and I slip off the back and wait for Malcolm to park it under a tree. He gestures to me to follow him and walks to a portion of the fence that has a gap in it. He pulls back the corrugated sheet metal far enough to squeeze through, and I follow behind, careful not to gouge myself on the metal's rough edges. *I know where we are now.*

Malcolm leads the way past piles of stacked cars into a cleared area where a white van is parked among a row of sedans. "Do you know what this is?" he asks.

I look at the brand markings on the van and note the paperwork taped to the driver side window that has the St. Petersburg police logo on it. "My guess is that it's a GMC Savannah prisoner transfer van from about 2009, Malcolm."

Malcolm is taken aback. He reaches his hand into his bag as if to pull something out. *Does he have a gun?*

"How do you know that?" he asks.

"We've been doing some research too."

Malcolm considers me a moment, and then instead of pulling a gun, pulls the spectrometer back out. He points the box at the van and it blinks and beeps. He then points the box at me and the unit gives the same response. "You have the same temporal frequency as this van," Malcolm says. "What do you have to say about that?"

"I don't know. Wait, are you suggesting that my friends and I arrived in this van? You think we're escaped convicts?"

"Do you have any proof that you're not?" Malcolm says.

"This is my first time ever seeing this van in person. I heard about the murders in the newspapers, but that doesn't mean we were involved. We're not murderers."

"The guards in this van traveled through time," Malcolm says. "They arrived around the same time as you, but they're dead and you aren't. It would be a large coincidence if these events were unconnected."

"We didn't murder anybody. We arrived at a softball field," I say.

"We haven't noted any temporal anomalies at any softball fields." He consults a list from his bag.

"Add it to your to-do list then," I say. "You also might want to be on the lookout for a guy named Elton Stenger. He was in our city the day we left and might be a candidate for your murderer. He was a serial arsonist and murderer in our time. If he's here, he could be a handful for the police."

Malcolm is still eyeing me suspiciously but takes the time to jot a few notes in his notepad.

He doesn't take the same route leaving the impound lot, but rather steers us downtown. The ride back is even colder. By the time we stop at the first stoplight I have goose bumps on my arms. We are sitting waiting for the green light when a fire truck passes us, slowing slightly for the red light but then blaring his horn and passing through. I plug my ears as I see additional emergency vehicles behind it. When the light turns green, we only make it a couple of blocks before we crest a small hill and come upon a sea of lights and emergency vehicles blocking our path. A uniformed officer is directing traffic around the debris scattered in the road.

Fire crews are spraying a small office building to our left. We are directed to turn before we can get a good view of the building, but as we make a right, my attention is caught by a wooden sign imbedded in a car window across the street from the smoking building. The sign is still smoking as well. In the light of a police car's headlights I can read, "The Law Offices of Waters and Kramer." Malcolm zips up to the next street before I can see any more.

"Stay around where I can find you the next few days," Malcolm says, as I climb off the scooter onto the sidewalk at the house. "I may need you to assist in more investigations."

"I don't know if you're going to get a second date, Malcolm," I say. "You didn't even buy me dinner."

Malcolm glares at me and cinches his helmet a little tighter. "Just don't do anything stupid, and tell your friends to keep a low profile. I'll tell Dr. Quickly what you said about the field. If it checks out, maybe he will still want to help you." He revs the scooter to a high-pitched whine and lurches off in what I assume to be a reassertion of his masculinity. I smile and head back into the house.

Chapter 6

"One nice thing about being a time traveler is that no matter how long your movie date takes getting ready, you can still make it to the theater on time. And if one of the previews looks better than the movie you've come to see, you just skip ahead a few months and watch that one."
-Excerpt from the journal of Dr. Harold Quickly, 1988

My alarm clock comes in the form of Spartacus's wet nose in my ear for the fourth time in as many days. I blearily stumble into the kitchen and find Robbie already there. "What time is it? I mumble.

"I don't know. Nine-ish I think," Robbie replies.

"What day is it today?"

"Thursday." Robbie holds up the morning newspaper. The front page reads Thursday, Jan. 2, 1986.

"Thursday? I thought it was Wednesday at least a couple days ago."

"No. It was Wednesday when we left 2009 but we got here on a Sunday. We've been here four days, so that makes today Thursday. Yesterday was New Year's remember?

"This is messing with my brain." I head for the refrigerator. "Is anybody else up?"

"Yeah, Blake was gone before I got up this morning. He told Grandpa something about going for a walk. Carson and Francesca are still asleep, but Grandpa is out in the tool shed doing something."

"How's it going, getting to know him again?" I pull a carton of orange juice out of the fridge and root through the cupboards for a cup.

"It's really cool actually. We got to talk a good bit this morning and it seems like he really likes having me here. I think it's helping him get his mind off things. It's nice to see him. I'm realizing how much I missed out, not having him around. He's a pretty cool guy."

"Yeah, it seems like it."

"I know he's sad about my grandma, but I imagine he needs the company. There was an odd thing though. A couple of days ago, I overheard him talking on the phone and I think it was my Dad. He was telling him that he didn't want him to come over. I'm not sure what that was all about."

"Do you think it has to do with us?" I ask.

"I thought that at first, but from what he said to my dad, I think it was just because he feels bad having to be reminded all the time that she's gone, and being around my family just makes it harder," Robbie explains.

"Wow, yeah, that is tough. Maybe he's all right around us because we don't really know what she was like."

"Could be. I don't really know." Robbie shakes his head. "I'm glad we're here in any case. I don't want him to be alone through this."

I pick up part of the paper and flip through it.

"There's a good story about the explosion from the other night. Turns out that's what all those cops and firefighters you saw were about." Robbie tries to hand the front section of the paper to me, but I'm already engrossed in an article. "What do you see there?" he asks.

"More explosions actually." I trade pages with Robbie.

"Where were you reading?" Robbie inquires, looking over the page and not seeing the article.

"The bottom one."

"What, *Education Meets the Next Frontier*?" Robbie asks, confused.

"Yeah. See the name of the teacher? That's about Christa McAuliffe, the one who is going to be on board the Challenger shuttle."

"Oh holy crap. Really? When does that happen?" Robbie asks.

"This month," I say. "I don't remember the exact day it was, but it happens during the next launch." Robbie stares at the photo of Christa McAuliffe smiling with her mission helmet alongside her back-up crew member and an American Flag. When he looks up, I meet his eyes. "We could save them."

"We're close enough." Robbie nods. "But should we be trying to change history? I'm sure we've already changed a few things, meeting my grandpa and all, but that's small time compared to this. Everybody knows about the Challenger. It's a huge deal."

"I remember it," I say. "I remember my first grade teacher was having us watch it because it was first thing in the morning out west. I don't think I really understood what was going on. I just remember her crying. The thing is, what kind of people are we if we know something bad is going to happen and we do nothing to stop it?"

"Are we allowed to alter the future?" Robbie asks. "Are we going to destroy the earth or something?"

"Well, like you said, we've changed things already just by being here. Shouldn't we at least change something for the better?"

"Makes sense to me." Robbie looks at the photo again.

"We'll do some thinking about it." I say. "Do me a favor and don't tell the others just yet. I don't want to freak them out."

"All right."

A car door slams and I walk to the kitchen window that looks out over the backyard. A woman with short, dark hair, wearing a knee-length gray skirt and a white blouse, has just entered the backyard, followed closely by a young boy of about four. "Hey, who do you think this is?" I ask Robbie.

Robbie joins me at the window. "Oh my God, that's my mom!" he blurts out. "Shit!" What do we do?"

"Dude, is that you?" I ask in amazement as I watch the little boy hopping up the sidewalk on one foot.

"Ahh. Yes it is. Damn it, we're going to blow up the universe, and it's going to be all my fault!" Robbie exclaims.

"Lets get upstairs," I say. "We should warn the others and figure out what to do."

The two of us run to the stairs and are bounding upward when I turn the corner and almost collide with Carson on his way down. Carson's hair is disheveled and he has clearly just woken up. "Dude, go back up," I say. "We have an incoming problem."

"Is Francesca up?" Robbie asks.

"I haven't seen her," Carson replies.

We go to Francesca's room and I rap quickly on the door. "You up Fresca?" Hearing no response, I crack the door slightly and peek my head in. Francesca is asleep but stirs as the three of us enter.

"Hey. What's up?" she inquires, as she rubs her eyes.

"Robbie's mom is here," I say.

"Oh wow, really?" Carson exclaims.

"Where's Blake?" Francesca asks.

"We don't know," Robbie says. "But the younger me is here in the backyard." A door slams shut somewhere in the house and Robbie quickly adds, "Or in the house."

I can hear the sound of a woman's voice downstairs and can make out the mellow tone of Mr. Cameron responding.

"Do you think she's going to figure out we're here?" Francesca asks. "What does this mean for us?"

"I'm not really sure," I whisper. "Maybe she's just popping in for a minute and she won't even realize we're here."

"Orrr not," Francesca draws out the word with resignation and I follow her eyes to the door, where the little boy is standing in the doorway, staring with an open mouth.

"Hey there, buddy." Carson is the quickest to respond. The boy stands silently and takes us all in. He closes his mouth and stares at Carson, who has stepped from behind Robbie and is making his way closer. "What's going on, little dude?" Carson continues.

The boy looks from Carson to Robbie, who is standing shell-shocked by the sight of the younger him, and finally his eyes fall on Francesca, still half buried in blankets. "Who are you?"

He seems to be addressing Francesca specifically, so she sits up and is quick to answer. "We're friends of your grandpa's. Are you Robbie? We've heard about you."

"Why are you in my grandpa's house?"

"We're visiting him for a few days and he's letting us stay here," I say. "What are you up to?"

"We're going on a cruise," the young Robbie boasts, apparently done interrogating us.

"Oh wow, that sounds great," Francesca says.

"Robert James! What are you doing?" A woman's voice calls from downstairs. The young Robbie turns around and dashes out of the room.

We stay quiet but have no trouble making out Robbie's voice as he reaches his mother. "There are people upstairs in the cat room!"

I look around the room and notice for the first time that there are a number of cat paintings, as well as a stone cat statue near the closet door. "Huh, I guess there are a lot of cats in here."

We can't make out the responses from Mr. Cameron or Robbie's mother, but a few moments later, we hear a heavier footstep on the stairs and Mr. Cameron appears in the doorway. He smiles. "I guess the jig is up! Why don't you all come downstairs and meet Mollie."

"How are we going to explain this to her?" Robbie asks anxiously.

"Oh, I'll think of something," Mr. Cameron replies. He turns and leads the way out of the room.

"I'll be right there," Francesca closes the door behind us so she can get dressed.

"Yeah, I should probably put a shirt on," Carson comments, and disappears into the other guest room.

A few minutes later, the four of us and Mr. Cameron are assembled in the dining room, with Mollie Cameron appraising us from the other side of the room. Mollie's eyes keep coming back to Robbie as she tries to contain her puzzlement.

"You remember my older brother Martin, Mollie?" Mr. Cameron begins. "I know he wasn't around much, but you'll remember the funeral of course."

Mollie nods.

"It seems that Martin was not as much of a bachelor as we had believed. You remember that he spent a great deal of time overseas and in South America. It turns out he had a wife for a short time in Argentina. She was an American who was doing some long term volunteer work there. I had heard rumor of her somewhat but never met her in person, and Martin was never much for sharing details of his personal life with me. Well, long story short, it seems he had a son. This is Robbie." Mr. Cameron gestures to Robbie and he steps forward and shakes Mollie's hand. "Robbie and his mother have been living out west and he's decided to look us up."

"It's a pleasure to meet you," Mollie says politely. Her face is unsure but she smiles at him. "And these are your friends?"

"Yes. They're traveling with me," Robbie replies.

Francesca, Carson and I introduce ourselves.

"Our friend Blake is with us also but he's out at the moment," I add.

"My name is Robbie too!" The younger Robbie exclaims, apparently forgetting our earlier introductions.

"How long are you in town for?" Mollie inquires.

"We're not really sure," our Robbie answers. "Just sort of playing it by ear."

The younger Robbie walks to Francesca and takes her hand. "Want to see the parrots?"

"Sure, thank you," Francesca replies, smiling and allowing herself to be led into the next room to the birdcage.

"We're going to be going in just a couple minutes okay?" Mollie calls after him as they leave the room. "Well, I'm glad you'll have some company for a little of the time we'll be gone," Mollie continues to Mr. Cameron.

"I'll be fine. I'm sure you all need the time away," Mr. Cameron replies. "You need a chance to have some fun and take your minds off of things. A cruise should be good for you and Rick."

"I'll have Rick stop by before we leave on Saturday," Mollie says. "I'm sure he'll want to see you before we go. He'll probably want to meet Robbie too."

"That would be great. But if he can't make it over, it's not a problem. I know there is a lot to do before then, and it's not like I won't be here in a week when you get back."

I catch Robbie's eye and see the expression of fear in his eyes. He doesn't say anything however. Mollie visits long enough for a cup of coffee before she and the four-year-old Robbie depart.

A half hour later, we're up in Robbie and Carson's room when Blake makes it back from what I suspect was another walk past Mallory's house. We fill him in on the morning's excitement. He sits on the floor with his back to the dresser.

"It was really weird," Carson says. "Mini-Robbie was totally on to us."

I sink myself into the cushioned armchair in the corner of the room and Francesca and Robbie perch on his bed. Carson has just finished commenting on how smoothly Mr. Cameron had come up with a story for all of us, when Robbie blurts out suddenly, "I just can't let him die!"

We are all quiet for a moment before I respond. "You're sure it was this vacation when it happened?"

"Yeah. We came home early from the cruise. I don't remember all the details. I don't even remember what day it was. I wish I did. This is going to be horrible. I don't know that I want to be here when it happens."

"Isn't it better to be here, than to be gone for it?" Francesca asks. "Maybe we can help him."

"Then we're going to be changing the future, aren't we?" Carson asks.

"Unless it always happened this way," I say.

"What do you mean?" Francesca asks.

I'm still trying to work out the possibilities in my mind, and am not sure I want to build Robbie's hopes up, but I try to explain my thoughts. "Tell me this, Robbie. Do you have any memory of meeting all of us as a kid? Do you have a memory of what just happened this morning?"

"I don't think so," Robbie replies. He runs his hands over his head and then back down his face. "I'm not really sure. It was a long time ago and I was really little. I don't remember much from then."

"What would that mean if he did remember it?" Francesca asks, sitting up straighter on the bed.

"I think there are a couple of possibilities. If he did remember it, it could mean that we haven't actually changed anything. It could be that we were always here, and that this always happened in the past. Did any of you ever read that book *The Time Traveler's Wife?*"

The three guys shake their heads. "I saw the movie," Francesca says.

59

"I was in a book club with a girlfriend one time where we read it. The guy in that story has that problem. In that scenario, time is linear, and no matter what you do, you can't change the past. It just always happened. They did it in *Lost* that way too, I think."

"What's the other scenario?" Blake asks.

"Well there's the *Back to the Future II* scenario where you change something and now you've created a whole alternate time line."

"The evil Biff takes over the world timeline," Carson says.

"Exactly."

"So if Robbie remembers this morning happening, it could mean that it always happened this way, and we haven't actually changed anything?" Francesca says.

"Theoretically," I reply.

"What if he remembers it now because it happened this morning, but it never happened that way the first time?" Carson asks. "What was that movie where the guy keeps changing things and then ends up with like forty years of memories in his brain even though he's like twenty-five?"

"Are you talking about *The Butterfly Effect*?" I ask.

"Yeah. That movie had all kinds of craziness going on."

"Didn't that guy get a brain aneurism or something?" Francesca says. "I don't want that happening to me."

"I don't know. Do any of you feel like you've acquired any new memories that you can't explain since we've been here?" I ask.

"No. Not really," Carson says. The others also shake their heads.

"Would we notice?" Robbie asks.

"I don't know. Let's work on the assumption that if we're changing things, we're probably not going to automatically get all the memories. That idea always seemed a little far-fetched to me anyway." I pull my legs in below me and hold my knees.

"How do we figure out if we are actually changing things, or if nothing we do matters?" Carson asks.

"Well . . ." I look at Robbie, wondering if he has figured out where I'm going with this, since he knows what I want to suggest. He isn't looking at me however, and the next thing out of his mouth reminds me that he has more on his mind than my plans to try to save the Space Shuttle.

"We see if Grandpa dies this week."

I forget about mentioning my plan for the moment. "Do you know where he died?" I ask. "Was it in the house?"

"Yeah, what if we take a trip with him?" Francesca suggests. "We can change our location and see if that changes the way things turn out."

"I don't mean to be insensitive here, but why are we talking about deliberately changing the future now?" Blake asks. "Isn't that exactly what that Malcolm guy said we shouldn't be doing?"

"It's easy for you to say," Robbie retorts. "You just don't want to screw up our chances of getting back to Mallory. But what about me? I have family I love right here."

"You all have lives back there too," Blake says. "Our lives are in 2009, not here."

"He has a point," Carson says. "I mean, I like your grandpa a lot too Robbie, but he was never around when we were all growing up. What happens if he is now? How much of all of our lives are we going to change? I like my life the way it's going. What happens if we get back and everything about us is different?"

"Yeah, but we don't know if we can even get back yet," Francesca interjects. "Are we supposed to just let him die? He's letting us live in his house. We're eating his food every morning for breakfast. How can you guys be so cold as to just say you're not going to help him if he's dying?"

"We didn't say we wouldn't help him if he's dying," Carson counters.

"It sure sounded like you did," Francesca says.

"Hey, guys, I think we're getting out of our depth," I say. "I didn't mean to start an argument. I was just trying to figure out if we could learn something useful from this whole experience of Robbie's this morning."

"Have we?" Robbie asks.

"I don't know," I say.

We sit with our thoughts for a few moments, then I decide to take the conversation in a new direction. "I say we form a new plan. I think we should contact Malcolm at the Temporal Studies Society and see if we can get a meeting with Dr. Quickly sooner. Monday seems like a long way away right now, especially since Robbie's family leaves Saturday. We don't know what day we need to worry about in particular with Mr. Cameron, so every day counts. The sooner we figure out if we're screwing up the universe, the better."

"Do you think he's going to be upset about us contacting him there when he told us not to?" Blake asks.

"We have extenuating circumstances. He should've had time to check out the softball field and our story by now. If he's mad, I guess he'll just have to deal."

The others all seem agreeable and Francesca volunteers to be the one to call him. We file downstairs to the roll top desk and crowd around the phone as Francesca dials. "Hello. May I speak to Malcolm please?

. . . Okay." She covers the mouthpiece and turns to us. "She's going to get him."

I grab a pen and pad of paper from the desk to be prepared. Francesca straightens up as someone picks up on the other end. *That was fast.*

"Hello, it's Francesca, from the Pier. Oh . . . Hello." She looks confused for a moment. "Yes. I know. But we have a situation. We would like to meet sooner . . . yes. It is very important . . . okay."

She grabs the pad of paper and pen from me and starts scribbling. "Okay. We'll be there. Thank you." She puts down the phone and tells us the news. "He'll meet us tomorrow."

"Malcolm?" Carson asks.

"Quickly," Francesca replies. "I was just talking to Harold Quickly."

Chapter 7

"Cheating on a woman is always a bad idea. If your girl happens to be a time traveler, that's worse. And if her father is a time traveler too . . . well, now you've really messed up."
-Excerpt from the journal of Dr. Harold Quickly, 2010

The St. Pete Shuffleboard club is as busy as I've ever seen it. The 1986 crowd seems a good bit older than the young demographic I'm used to in 2009, but the enthusiasm is the same. A squat, middle-aged woman named Annie greets us in the main building as we walk in, and asks if we've been here before. It occurs to me that technically we have been here after, and not before, but I simply nod and say yes. She points us to the tangs and I root through a couple, trying to find one with solid tips.

"Are we actually going to play?" Carson asks.

"We are a little early," Francesca responds. "We can probably fit a game in."

We all grab tangs and head toward the courts. I notice a framed movie poster has been hung on the wall advertising *Cocoon*. Annie spies me looking at it and is at my elbow in an instant.

"Did you know they filmed a scene right here? I got to meet Ron Howard myself. He's such a sweetheart."

"You know, I saw that movie years ago but I never realized it was filmed here," I say.

"You must be thinking of something else, dear. This just came out this past summer. You mean you didn't go out and see it?"

"Oh, right. No. I wasn't in town this past summer," I reply.

"It was such a wonderful film. Ron Howard is so handsome now that he is grown up. And to think that we used to see him so little on *The Andy Griffith Show* and now he's shooting big time movies in our city."

Another person comes up to Annie for help and I gratefully make an exit out the door. I find my friends outside and we cruise around until we find an open lane. Blake grabs a rack of shuffleboard biscuits from a pile outside and turns back to Francesca. "How are we supposed to know when Quickly is here? Did you tell him what we look like?"

"He said he would find us here," Francesca replies. "He never asked what we looked like. He just said be here around eight and that he would find us."

"Do we know what he looks like?" Carson asks.

"I guess we keep an eye out for somebody who looks like he's looking for us," I say.

We can't all play simultaneously, so Robbie and I decide to trade off shots. He, Francesca and I walk to the bleacher side of the lane and face off across from Blake and Carson. Robbie and I play against Francesca, while Blake contends with Carson. The match is going fairly smoothly until I accidentally knock two of my biscuits into the negative-ten-zone simultaneously while trying to move Francesca's.

"Son of a—" I edit myself as I see an older woman eyeing me disapprovingly from the neighboring lane.

"There goes our lead." Robbie laughs.

"Here, you take it for the remainder. See if you can pick me up," I say, and hand Robbie my tang.

I jump up a couple of steps and have a seat in the bleachers to watch the others play. The clock on the wall in the main building shows ten past eight. *No sign of our mysterious rendezvous.* I prop my feet on the railing and adjust my pants. Mr. Cameron took us to the Salvation Army so we could raid the sale racks for clothing. I ended up with a pair of jeans and a couple of T-shirts. The one I'm wearing now features Gizmo from *Gremlins*. Carson claims to have found the best vintage treasure because he snagged an original *Thriller* T-shirt, but I'm happy with mine.

I look around at the other people in the bleachers and take in the conversations. A group of older ladies are clumped together to my right, discussing their disapproval of someone's taste in second husbands. I can hear occasional loud laughter from two men who are probably in their sixties, sitting a few rows up in the bleachers directly behind me. To my left a group of middle-aged couples is commenting on one of the games being played by their friends.

As I'm watching Blake and Carson repetitively clear each other's biscuits off the lane in quick succession, one of the older men from behind me steps past me, still talking over his shoulder. "Gotta get back to glassing the lanes. It was good seeing you. Tell Mym I said hi."

"I'll tell her," the other man replies. "She still talks about your wife's cooking on a regular basis. Probably an allusion to what she has to put up with from me."

"You two come over next time she's in town. We'll be happy to feed you both."

"See you, Walt," the man behind me says.

Walt walks in front of the bleachers, picks up the glass bead material and heads for the set of lanes around the corner. After a few moments, the second man proceeds down the steps as well, but instead of passing by, sits down next to me. He's wearing a cheese cutter hat and a tweed jacket with patches on the elbows.

I nod to him. "How ya doin'?"

I look back to my friends' game. Out of the corner of my eye, I can see him appraising me. He stretches a leg out and puts a foot onto the lower rail in front of us. "Are you a betting man?"

I turn and look at him. His eyes are friendly. He skin has the healthy sunned look that a lot of Florida seniors acquire. "Not too much. My friend Robbie likes to bet the dogs. I've never been a big gambler."

"I find a good game of shuffleboard is made that much more interesting with a few side bets. Whom would you bet on in your friends' game there, for example?"

I look at the scoreboard at the far end of the lane and see that Carson and Francesca are up by fifteen points. "Francesca and Carson look like they're pulling ahead a little bit, but I know Blake and Robbie are pretty consistent shooters. They've been known to pull off some comebacks."

"Who's your pick then?" he presses me.

"Hard to say. They're all strong."

He reaches into his coat pocket and rummages around. "Let's see what I've got for a wager."

"I really don't have much money," I reply, wishing he would just drop the subject.

"Okay, what do you have?" he asks.

I reach into my pocket hopelessly and pull out the few items inside. I have a gum wrapper, a pencil I borrowed from Mr. Cameron's desk earlier, and seventy-two cents in change. "I've got seventy-two cents for you." I hold out the change in my right hand.

He ignores it and looks toward my other hand. "What kind of pencil is that? Berol? Faber?"

I read the label. "Dixon Ticonderoga."

"Ah, not bad. A classic. Okay, tell you what, I have a ball point pen here that I'll wager against your Dixon Ticonderoga, that your lovely female friend will win it by five."

"Really?" I ask. "You want to be that specific? That looks like a nice pen."

"Confidence is key. And I've always been more of a pencil man. You never know when you might need to rewrite what you've already written."

He stares at me until I acquiesce. "Fine. I'll take Blake for the winning shot, by three."

"Now we're talking!" He smiles jubilantly, and turns his attention to the game.

In the time it has taken for us to settle on a wager, Blake and Robbie have scored twelve points to Carson and Francesca's three, making it a six-point game. Francesca notices the man sitting next to me and gives me a curious look. I shrug my shoulders and she goes back to shooting. She and Robbie both score sevens on their turns. Blake and Carson knock each other around for a couple of shots before Blake puts up two eights by replacing both of Carson's to put him within two points of the win. Francesca's third shot lands on the centerline for no points and Robbie slides one into the ten spot just shy of the line for ten points. Francesca lines up and shoots down the middle and knocks Robbie's away, neatly replacing it. She jumps up and down for joy as she's showing eighteen points in position, but Robbie eyes his last shot.

"I am going to hate you forever if you knock out my ten Robbie!" Francesca exclaims.

Robbie shows no mercy and trains his shot straight at it. The shot doesn't have the force he wants however, and when it makes contact, it's just a glancing blow, barely moving Francesca's biscuit back into the eight spot and ricocheting off to make contact with his previous biscuit and knocking it off the lane. His shot winds up on the seven/eight line for no points.

"Yes!" Francesca yells, and I see Carson's celebratory fist pump. Francesca and Carson meet in the middle of the walkway and high-five. Mentally I do the math. Seventy-eight to seventy-three.

I look at my companion. He's not looking at me, but he's smiling. "I don't know how you did it, but you nailed it." I hand the pencil over. He takes it and examines the eraser approvingly, then slides the pencil into the inner pocket of his jacket.

"I'll tell you the secret to my success."

"Psychic?"

"Cheater," he replies. "The worst."

I get a good look at his smiling green eyes and I know why I've been had. "You're Harold Quickly, aren't you?"

"At your service." He smiles and offers his hand. I shake it. My friends make their way over.

"Excellent match!" Quickly congratulates them.

"What have you two been discussing over here?" Francesca asks.

"I was simply giving a lesson in crooked wagering to your friend here," Quickly replies.

"Yeah, lesson one: Don't bet against time travelers."

"Oh! You're Dr. Quickly?" Francesca asks.

"Indeed. It's a pleasure to meet you."

Blake and Robbie introduce themselves to Dr. Quickly and take seats on the bleachers behind us. Carson and Francesca remain standing below. "I'm sorry we didn't recognize you earlier," Francesca says.

"No, that was my own doing," Quickly replies. "I wanted to enjoy the game and get to know Benjamin here. Plus I had a lot riding on your performance."

"Oh yeah?" Carson asks.

"He swindled me out of a pencil," I say.

"Oh, high stakes." Robbie laughs.

"You never can tell when you might need a good writing instrument," Quickly says. "The possibilities are endless."

"We have about a million questions for you," Blake says.

"I imagine you do. Why don't we go somewhere where we can discuss the issues at hand with a little more ease? Do you all mind riding with me, or do you have your own transportation?"

"We actually walked here, so a ride would be good," I reply.

"Very well. Follow me then."

We file out into the parking lot behind Dr. Quickly, and he leads us to his car, a sky blue convertible with tail fins and a lot of chrome.

"Wow. Sweet car," Carson says.

"This is my favorite," Quickly responds.

"What is it?" Francesca asks.

"It's a Ford Galaxie."

The six of us fit easily in its wide interior. Francesca rides in between Dr. Quickly and me on the front bench seat while the other guys share the back. We turn out around the banyan trees and cruise past the library on our way south. We take a right on First Avenue North and head west. The skyline seems vacant without the baseball stadium, and I have an unexpected pang of homesickness.

Dr. Quickly steers the Galaxie into a residential neighborhood I don't recognize. There's nothing that catches my eye about the houses on the street we turn on. They all blend together in their nondescript uniformity. We pull into the driveway of a one-story ranch house that seems, if anything, more bland than the others around it. I realize that I've been expecting Dr. Quickly to have something more elegant or dramatic in store for us, but there is nothing apologetic about his mannerisms as he cheerily welcomes us inside.

If I was confused about the exterior of the house, I'm even more at a loss when I get inside. The living room to the left of the doorway is trimmed in aged, slightly sun-faded furniture, over a dingy, green shag carpet. The kitchen we pass has Formica counter-tops that are yellowed and stained and have begun to match the tan refrigerator, whose humming is the only noteworthy sound in the house. The place looks orderly and simple, but dated and cheaply decorated. I'm overwhelmed by the sheer ordinariness of it all. Even Francesca, who is usually brimming with polite comments, seems to be at a loss for anything to say.

We don't have long to contemplate this problem, because we've sailed directly through the house and out the screened-in laundry room into the moonlit backyard. A wooden fence obstructs any view from the neighboring yards but has provided an exemplary backdrop for the mob of diverse plants that have taken over the yard. Ivy drapes the fence and leafy palms and flowering shrubs seem to fill every available inch on the perimeter of the yard.

We're led along the brief flagstone path that leads to the modest garage, entering through a corner door and coming to a stop in the mostly vacant interior. Pegboards line the side walls, and the wall that divides us from the yard we just came from has a wide workbench supported by wooden 4x4 legs that has been butted up against the wall. Miscellaneous tools are scattered on the workbench, along with a dusty, broken, picture frame. A few nails lie beside the frame as if someone had begun a repair but given up in the act and wandered off to some more interesting pursuit. I would hardly blame them. The garage is even plainer than the house, and I would have a hard time staying entertained in it for more than a few minutes. Fortunately we don't have to wait that long.

Dr. Quickly directs us all toward the middle of the concrete floor. "If you will all be so kind as to stay here for just a minute, I'll be right back."

We stand awkwardly together, not sure what direction to look, as there is nothing in particular to look at. Dr. Quickly steps back through the door we just came from but just before he shuts it, he stops and pokes his head back in to say, "Oh. Don't be alarmed." Then he is gone.

Francesca looks at me and immediately her eyes are wide. "What am I not supposed to not be alarmed about?"

"Haha. I don't know," I reply.

"You're clearly failing at following instructions," Carson says.

"Hey. If you don't want someone to freak out, you should probably give them a little more information than just, 'Hey, don't freak out,'" Francesca retorts.

"Actually he said, 'Don't be alarmed,'" Blake says. "You can freak out all you want as long as you're not alarmed about it."

"Great. We're gonna get axe murdered in a garage in the eighties and you guys aren't even concerned."

"He's a senior citizen," Carson says.

"He looks pretty spry to me," Francesca counters.

"True enough," I reply.

"I call the hammer," Francesca adds, pointing to the workbench. Before anyone can reply, there is a loud clunk. The wall she's pointing to, and the bench itself, both give a slight shudder. "What the hell was that?" Francesca exclaims.

I stare in amazement as the entire wall and workbench, including the door, begin sliding toward us. Even a section of the floor that I thought was simply a rubber mat is sliding evenly along the concrete. "Oh, sweet Jesus!" Francesca blurts out.

"Okay, is this thing gonna crush us?" Blake asks, now sounding concerned.

Carson walks to the door on the wall that is slowly advancing toward us, and tries the doorknob. It doesn't move. Blake goes to the electric garage door and tries to lift it but it doesn't budge. I'm growing concerned now too, so I join him in pulling on it.

The wall has slowly inched its way across approximately a quarter of the floor when it abruptly stops. I can hear Francesca's sigh of relief. A moment later, the door opens and Dr. Quickly reappears. He takes a look at our still-panicked faces but doesn't appear to notice our concern.

"Right this way."

I'm confused as to why we're headed back out the door we just entered, but once I step over the threshold, I can see we're not back outside at all. We've entered a space between two halves of the wall. The wall we originally walked through has been neatly bisected, including the door. I can see the other half of the door still blocking the way to the backyard. The innards of the doorknob now protrude out into space directly across from their counterparts on the other half of the door. Just to our right, the wall and workbench being moved away has revealed a set of stone stairs descending down into the ground.

"This is amazing," I say.

"I didn't know anyone could even build basements in Florida," Carson says.

"There were challenges to be sure," Dr. Quickly says, and motions for us to descend the stairs. "After you."

We file toward the stairs and as Francesca steps in front of me, she catches my eye with a stern stare and mouths two words. "Axe Murderer."

My curiosity has far exceeded my concern at this point, so I follow her down the stairs, intrigued at what we'll find.

We descend the stairs about twelve feet and turn left into a long tunnel. The hallway is brightly lit with overhead fluorescent lights, and while the floor is plain concrete, the walls have been drywalled and painted an eggshell white. We pass occasional metal doors that have numbers painted on them and I can see through the small windows in each door that there are steel ladders behind each one that extend upward toward whatever lies above us. We follow the hallway for what must be a hundred yards before we make an angled turn to the right and continue for another length that is easily as long as the first. There is a periodic humming from beneath the floor.

"What's that noise?" I ask.

"Bilge pumps," Quickly responds. "The tunnel is fairly well waterproofed, but it still manages to find its way in. The pumps keep me from having to wear my galoshes."

We are about fifty yards from the end of the hallway when Quickly abruptly stops. There are no doors visible, so I'm not sure why we're stopping. It becomes evident a moment later when Dr. Quickly pulls a remote control keypad from his pocket. He aims the remote at the ceiling, punches in a series of numbers and steps back. I watch with rapt attention as the section of ceiling ahead of us slowly tilts toward the floor. The other side of the ceiling contains a set of stairs not unlike an attic access I once had in my family house in Oregon. This stairway is easily twice as wide however, enough that a couple people can walk up side by side.

"You really like the secret doorways, huh?" Carson comments.

"If you are going to go through the trouble to build an underground tunnel, you may as well keep up the mystery," Quickly replies.

Francesca considers the stairs angling into the void above us. "No secret elevator?"

"Stairs keep me young." Quickly smiles.

We follow him into the darkness above. The stairs begin to curve once we're past the level of the ceiling. I guess that to be ground level but I can't be certain anymore. A push from another button on Quickly's remote illuminates the stairwell from light blue bulbs, evenly spaced along the curving walls. The section of the stairs from the tunnel closes behind us and I feel entombed. The feeling doesn't last long, because once we've climbed what I imagine to be the equivalent of a couple of stories, we emerge into the middle of a tall open room that is filled with moonlight. Glass windows make up one enormous wall that overlooks a busy street.

Our floor appears to be the second story of a very tall building. The ceiling of the room is at least fifty feet above us. To our left, facing the huge wall of windows, are tiers of beautiful wooden railed balconies that extend out to varying distances from the back wall, like a theatre. The room is relatively narrow. I could stride across it in a couple dozen steps. Its impressive height is accented by the fact that every inch of the balcony walls is filled, not with theatre chairs, but with wooden cubby-holed shelves holding more unique objects than I can fathom. Quickly spreads his arms wide to encompass the breathtaking space. "Welcome to the best place in the world to travel through time."

Chapter 8

"With a name like Harry Quickly, grade school wasn't easy. Losing hope of social acceptance early had its perks however. By the time I became president of the science club in high school, no one even paid attention. Then I mastered space and time and vanished completely. That one people noticed."
-Excerpt from the journal of Harold Quickly, 1999

Dr. Quickly is illuminating lights around the room while I take in the various spaces. Hanging from the ceiling high above us is a chandelier, formed into the shape of the sun. It illuminates a mosaic of dark blue tiles with constellations and planets laid out in silver across the ceiling. Smaller lamps on the balconies are now shedding a warm glow on the items around them. The largest of the balconies has a collection of leather armchairs grouped loosely near a wooden table positioned by the railing.

The dark wood railings and countless shelves along the walls give the place a feeling of age, though I can get no concept of the building we're in. It gives me the impression of a library far more than a laboratory. I've never known of anything like it in St. Pete.

Quickly invites us to join him in the center of the floor, where we find a circular table with cabinets built into the base. There are stools positioned around it and we take seats on these while Quickly himself remains standing.

"I know you all have many questions, and I'll do my best to answer them, but we should get through the important stuff first. The night is finite and we have a lot to cover to make sure we keep you all safe."

"Are we in danger?" Francesca asks.

"Well, you are in a unique situation that has natural hazards associated with it. You don't need to be alarmed, but there are some things we need to discuss to make sure that you stay with us in the here and now."

"We're actually hoping to not stay here and now," Blake says.

"Understood, but there are far worse places you could be at the present moment, and in order to get you back where you want to be, we need to make sure you don't end up someplace else. You see, the five of you are currently being affected by the results of something I ultimately bear the responsibility for."

"It's your fault we time traveled?" Robbie asks.

"Not directly, but yes. The event that sent you back in time was an indirect result of the research I started in the 1970's. I worked nearly twenty years on it, and in 1996 I made a huge breakthrough. I also made a huge mistake. I sent myself through time quite involuntarily, but by the grace of God was not killed in the process. The event was obviously traumatic and exciting at the same time. I'd made quite possibly the biggest scientific achievement in human history, and then promptly found myself out of reach of all my research materials and colleagues."

"This was when you disappeared and everyone was searching for you." I lean forward.

"Yes. I understand it made quite a stir about town for a while, and presented a major setback for the colleagues I left behind. I will confess I was quite guarded with my research, and not all together trusting as a young man."

Dr. Quickly places his palms on the table. "I had a sense of what the potential dangers were to the work I was doing and felt extremely possessive of the responsibility to keep things under control. I had not shared all of my insights with my colleagues, and when they began to piece together my work after my departure, there were a few details that most likely escaped them."

"You didn't trust them?" I ask.

"No. It wasn't really that. I think I was a bit selfish then. I should have trusted them with more, but I justified keeping it to myself by saying I was protecting them. That was half true. Their research did come together in a workable form, but the errors they made, combined with the unpredictability of Florida weather, conspired to prove catastrophic to the results." Quickly gestures to clouds in the night sky beyond the wall of windows. "The electrical disturbance at The Temporal Studies Society yielded unexpected results, that being you five coming here. The lightning caused an overload of their machinery and allowed the escape of unique particles, called gravitites, into the environment around the lab, by way of the electrical power lines. When that power line broke free of the pole and hit your bench, it transferred not just the electricity, but the gravitites as well. My colleagues had far too many of the particles in use during their experiment, and the result was a very large area being affected. The error was theirs, but the ultimate responsibility lies with me."

"Did you realize we were coming?" I ask.

"Yes. As a matter of fact, tonight is not the first time I have met you, even though it is the first time you have met me."

"You just lost me," Robbie says.

This is getting crazy.

"It's a long story," Quickly says, walking around the table and looking out the window. "I promise I'll explain it another time." He turns back to us. "For now, let me tell you a few of the things it is imperative that you learn."

Dr. Quickly walks to the wall and rolls a green chalkboard in a frame over to our table. He picks up a piece of chalk and draws a pair of parallel, squiggly lines across the board. He makes an X in between the lines at one end.

"Imagine this as a river. This is all of you in 2009." He points to the X. "You are flowing along in time along with everything else around you. The Temporal Studies Society suffered an explosion that released the gravitites into the environment around you by way of electricity. That is crucial to the events, because electricity acted in this case as not only the medium in which you were exposed to these particles, but also the catalyst for the reaction that ensued."

"You're not going to say something with 'one point twenty-one jigawatts' in it now are you?" Carson says, "Because that would kind of make me laugh if that turned out to be true."

"Hmm. No. As much as I enjoyed the *Back to the Future* films myself, I'm afraid I can't just put you in a car and zap you with lightning to get you home. The electricity played a key part to be sure, but it's a little more complex than that. These particles act as disruptors to the way individual cells stay anchored in time. The cells of your body and in all the things around you, have a gravity of sorts that keeps you in sync with the flow of time, stuck in the river with everything else that's floating with you. All of it is flowing at the same speed." He draws some movement lines in the river.

"Like going tubing down a river with your friends," Francesca says.

"Exactly. Relative to each other, it's not as noticeable that we're moving, because we're all traveling in the same direction and at the same rate. Cells that have been exposed to these gravitites are essentially released from the 'gravity' of time. You and most of the biological or organic matter around you would've been affected. It's like you took your tube to shore and hiked back along the edge of the river while the rest of your life floated on.

"The electrical current that flowed through you can react various ways with those particles. In your case, the event that ensued was an enormous leap through time." He looks at his drawing on the board. "You would have to hike for a long time in this analogy." He draws an arc back to a spot between the lines and writes 1986 above it. "It's one of the longest jumps I've heard of actually. Much more would have required an exposure that would most certainly have killed you. That was the first instance where you all were extremely lucky."

"What would have killed us?" Francesca asks.

"Oh, any of a long list of very unpleasant things," Dr. Quickly replies. "Electrocution for one, but the most likely would have been that you would have been left floating in outer space. You see, one thing that many people fail to realize when talking about time travel theory, is that one cannot effectively travel through time without also traveling through space. If we were to travel backward in time, one day, to this exact location in the universe, we would find ourselves out in the cold dark of space, waiting for the earth to get to us as it orbits around the sun." He scribbles a quick depiction of the sun and a planet and a line to show an orbit around it. I straighten up on my stool.

I feel like I should be taking notes.

"Even if we were to jump 365 days ahead so that the earth might be in the same relative position in its rotation around the sun, we would still miss, because the sun is moving too." He draws an arrow coming out of the sun.

"The whole galaxy is in fact hurtling through space at speeds that make trying to calculate for it laughable. The universe itself could be moving for all we know. We highly suspect it is. Trying to hit a mark like that would be like hitting a bullseye on a dartboard attached to a speeding train, while throwing from an airplane ... with your eyes closed. It's a useless endeavor."

"How did we end up alive then?" I ask.

"You were fortunate enough to be in contact with something that was not traveling through time, that happened to exist in more or less the same condition in the time you jumped to. In your case, it was the bench in the dugout on the softball field. It exists in relatively the same condition here in 1986 as in 2009. It was still anchored to the same slab of concrete, so when you were shocked in contact with it, you stayed fixed to it during your jump. The bench itself underwent a sort of matter fusion event, but that isn't really relevant to you at the moment. Essentially you five just went along for the ride."

"How do you know all this about us?" Carson asks. "How did you know we were at the softball field?"

"You told me. Later. Well, it's later for you. It's in the past for me."

"We tell you in the future?" Francesca asks.

"Yes. Possibly. You did tell me in the future. Whether you will again remains to be determined."

"Oh. Right. This is really confusing," Francesca says.

"Welcome to my life. If there is one thing I can promise you about time travel theory, it is that it is a complex science and there are plenty of things that I don't understand either. A lot can go wrong, but I'm going to do my best to give you the basics of what I know, and hopefully keep you safe. To that end, I have some things I want to give you."

"It's possible though, right?" Blake asks. "You can get us back?"

Dr. Quickly looks him in the eye as he replies. "You are going to get yourselves back. But I'm going to help you."

Dr. Quickly reaches down and pulls a cardboard box from under the table. From it he extracts five smaller wooden boxes that are hinged with lids. He slides one to each of us across the table. I lift the lid on mine and peer inside at the objects it contains.

This looks exciting.

Dr. Quickly pulls out a sixth box and sets it in front of himself. "These are some basic safety items. One of the main dangers you face is that since you've been exposed to the gravitites, you are susceptible to any amount of electricity triggering another jump. Even certain amounts of static electricity could possibly result in you traveling, and if you're not planning for it, it can yield some very nasty results. You don't want to end up inside a wall somewhere, or melted into the center of the earth or anything like that."

"You're really freaking me out," Robbie says.

"It's better that you know what you're dealing with. These dangers will lessen over time, the longer you stay in one place. For the first week or so after a jump of the magnitude you experienced, your cells are still very unstable temporally speaking. You'll find in your boxes an item that's going to help diffuse any unwanted electrical impulses, and keep you from jumping.

"This is a chronometer." He holds up an item that looks like a complex wristwatch. I remove mine from my box also. "These chronometers have had the time jumping portion disabled, but they have a component inside that acts as a sort of capacitor that can either diffuse or store electricity from your body. They act as regulators for jumping as well, but we haven't gotten to that yet."

I look at the chronometer in my hand. It has the basic shape of a large watch, only in place of a face with hands, it has a series of concentric rings that appear to be capable of movement. There are dials on the sides. Each is marked with different symbols and some numbers. It's beautiful, even though I have no understanding of how it works.

"Put them on your wrists," he says, and we all comply, making minor adjustments as needed. "On the full versions such as mine,"—At this he pushes up his sleeve and shows us an ornate looking chronometer that's around his wrist—"there is a pin on the side that can be pushed as a key to activate other options for you, but for the moment, yours are set to maintain the present flow of time."

"Are we going to be able to use these to get home?" Blake asks.

"In time." Quickly smiles. "Pun intended. There is much to learn before we can accomplish that feat however. I'm going to need to have all of your free time as much as possible for the next few weeks. Getting all of you to 2009 is likely to take a number of smaller jumps, as I'm doubtful about the safety of sending you back as violently as you arrived here. The odds of you surviving that again are slim. We'll need to take precautions, and there's a lot of theory and some precise calculating that needs to happen for it to work. Even so, I'm optimistic that if we all work at it, we can get you traveling home. It may take a few weeks, it could take a few months, but it should be possible."

"Well we're here to learn," I reply, happy that we're making progress. Blake has cheered up considerably and there is an air of general excitement among the others as well.

"What's this?" Francesca reaches into her box and pulls out a long wire with a plug at the end.

"Wall charger." Quickly smiles. "No fun running out of power halfway to your destination."

Dr. Quickly invites us to tour the laboratory. Behind the walls of shelves are other rooms with a few things I recognize like generators and gyroscopes, and even more things I can't recognize at all. I see a kitchen and a couple of different stairwells but the purposes of most of the rooms he's showing us go over my head. He leads us through various hallways full of lab spaces and classrooms but I rapidly lose comprehension of where we are.

"You sure have a lot of space in here," Robbie comments.

"And this is just the first level." Dr. Quickly winks.

"What's down below you?" Francesca says. "I noticed we're not actually at ground level. Was there something between this level and the tunnel?"

"Coffee shop," Quickly replies. "The ground floor has a number of retail spaces. I find it helps mask the fact that my lab is up here."

"Hmm. Coffee. Good to know." Francesca smiles.

After showing us around, Quickly tells us that we will reconvene again tomorrow as it's getting late. We agree to meet him in the morning, and he shows us out. Instead of taking the tunnel back to the house the way we came, he leads us out another exit and we descend a set of stairs and emerge from a nondescript door in a side alley of the building.

As we walk across the street, I get my first real look at the outside of the lab. It's a large, glass-paned, rectangular office building with mirrored glass. The width of the building is such that I have no concept of which windows belong to the lab. I begin to understand how Quickly has been able to hide it in plain sight between the other occupants. I doubt that the other tenants of the building have any idea what neighbors them. We walk a block to another large American car parked along the street. This one is a battered Chevy Impala. Like the Galaxie, it has a front bench seat and we can all manage to pile in. We're dropped off in front of Mr. Cameron's house.

"Thank you so much for helping us," Francesca says.

Dr. Quickly smiles. "Don't mention it. I know a thing or two about what it's like to be displaced and need help. I'm happy I get to return the favor to someone." And with a cheery wave, our new acquaintance is gone.

We file into the house and find Mr. Cameron still awake. Tybalt and Mercutio, the two parrots, are still up as well and walking around on the back of his chair as we tell him our story. Mr. Cameron listens intently and looks at our chronometers.

"How soon does he say you may be able to return home?" He asks.

"He says we have a lot to learn. Probably a couple of weeks at least."

Mr. Cameron looks a little relieved when I say this.

I don't think he is very ready to see us go.

Everyone has gone to bed as I settle onto the couch. Spartacus comes to nuzzle me briefly and attempts to lick my face in greeting, but then wanders up the stairs, leaving me to my thoughts. My mind is racing with all that has happened. I look at the chronometer on my wrist and the weight of it on my arm makes the situation seem more real. Until now I've not let my thoughts go to what we are trying accomplish, beyond getting Blake back to Mallory and the rest of us home to our normal lives. The whole experience has felt more like an odd vacation. The reality of Dr. Quickly and his accomplishments has changed that. What before seemed a massive traumatic problem now begins to look like an opportunity. We're now friends with a scientist who has successfully traveled through time and who is going to teach us how to do it.

The little boy in me that has always dreamed of super human abilities has awakened again. I think about the possibilities of what time travel might enable. I could visit moments in history I've always wanted to see. I could go to a Beatles concert, see the first person walk on the moon on the day it happened, figure out who shot Kennedy. I could go farther back, see the Wright brothers make the first flight at Kittyhawk. *What if I could witness the Gettysburg Address?*

I roll onto my back and stare at the ceiling. *How far back could I go? Could I talk to Alexander the Great? Aristotle? Jesus? What if I went back and captured some animals that are now extinct and saved them? What if I could shed light on blunders the human race has made before they ever happened? Would I ruin time in the process? What about the future? Space travel? New technologies? What if we make alien contact in the future? I could meet one.* My mind reels and I fall asleep with thoughts of medieval jousts and futuristic space ships swimming through my head.

When morning arrives, I'm awakened by an already dressed Blake, who is eager to get started. We arrive early at the outdoor post office where we've agreed to meet Quickly, and take in the passersby. I've begun to get accustomed to being in the eighties but some of the people walking by sport fashion choices that still surprise me. Francesca spends the majority of the wait alternating between snickering and admiration of the colorful outfits.

Dr. Quickly picks us up exactly on time and takes us back on the long walk through the house to the lab. When we reach it, he takes us to a side room off of the main study and sits us in some armchairs and couches he has arranged. He stands behind a desk and pulls out a stack of notebooks. He tosses one to each of us, and is about to start lobbing pens at us as well, but I get out of my chair and offer to disperse them by hand.

The next object he extracts is a globe. "We're going to get you all started on learning your time zones. Who knows how many time zones we have?"

"Twenty-four?" I suggest.

"Nope. Reasonable guess, but we actually have around thirty-nine, depending on the year. Some like Newfoundland or Iran are only half hour increments from their neighboring time zones. We're hoping to keep you in Florida and not have you venturing to Iran, but I'm going to give you a good grounding in the essentials."

Over the next few days, we spend our hours learning about time zones, places that do and don't use daylight saving time, the dates when certain times came into effect and odd concepts like "leap seconds." We all learn to use Zulu time and Dr. Quickly begins to explain how to pinpoint exact moments in time on our chronometers. The concentric rings align in various ways so that you can locate exact moments in a given year, month, day, hour, minute, second or half second. They move by activating various dials around the side of the face. Some of our chronometers are different from each other but they all operate on the same principle. We have the ability to select the time zone we're in and make calculations for whether we're using daylight saving time or not. There's also a quick set option that allows you to set a specified amount of time to jump, such as an hour or a minute.

I feel a bit overwhelmed by everything, but the excitement of what we're undertaking keeps me motivated. I find myself getting up off the couch in the mornings before Spartacus has time to lick me awake. My growing enthusiasm pales compared to Blake's. Each morning I find him in the kitchen waiting for us or coming in from walks. He's still been walking past Mallory's place in the mornings, but now instead of desperation, I see only determination in his manner. He's taken avid notes and devoured every bit of information that Quickly has given us. I begin to think that it was a wise move for Quickly to disable the time jumping portions of our chronometers. I can see the danger of Blake taking the leap as soon as he felt a grasp of the concept.

I'm a little envious that Blake has someone in his life that he can't stand to be without. While I have my share of acquaintances and associations I've left behind, I've been enjoying my time in 1986. I don't miss work or my coworkers much, and while I feel the distance from my family, it's not hard to imagine that we're just on a vacation of sorts. It's easy to think that they're just going on with their lives. I have this vision of the world we left behind, frozen in time, waiting for our return. I've not let myself think too much about how they will be affected if I don't come back. With our rapid progress toward getting home, that thought doesn't worry me. We have Quickly and his chronometers. I'm optimistic that we will be home soon. But not too soon.

Chapter 9

"There are thousands of ways to get yourself killed time traveling. Being in a hurry is the fastest way to find a new one."
-Excerpt from the journal of Dr. Harold Quickly, 1912

On the third day of lessons, we experience our first real taste of what we are getting ourselves into. We're sitting at a couple of tables in a lab classroom, where Quickly is showing us the proper method of measuring spaces for jumping into and out of tight locations, when in mid-lesson he kneels down to retie one of his shoes. Looking up for a moment, he gives me a wink and disappears. I stare at the space he has vacated for a good five seconds before I can turn to my friends. Carson has a massive grin on his face.

"That was so cool!" he exclaims.

Robbie is leaned back in his chair with his mouth hanging open slightly. He composes himself and sits up. "That's crazy."

"Where did he go?" Francesca asks. "Or is it when did he go?"

The next moment her question is answered as Dr. Quickly reappears a few feet from where he was before.

"Ta-da!" He grins. "I feel like these lessons might be getting a bit too dry, so I like to spice them up a bit."

"You certainly know how to keep our attention now," I say.

We are a mass of questions, but Quickly quiets us down to get back to the lesson.

"The key thing in jumping is to know exactly where you're going to wind up. The way we do this is by jumping to something that is not moving through time, as I explained before. In this case, I was actually using an object on the floor." He bends down and picks up a thin metallic disc about five inches in diameter. "Small objects are great for when you want to be discreet."

"Where did you go? You didn't come back for a bit," Francesca asks.

"That's true in this case," Quickly replies. "But just because the time jump involved another element. What else did you notice?"

"You didn't come back to the same spot," Robbie answers.

"Exactly. You get two lessons here, time and space. I used the first disc to jump away and returned using a second one. I could have returned to the same place, had I jumped back with the same disc, but I opted to jump back to a different location."

He walks over and picks up an almost identical disc from where he reappeared. "You have to remember that you will travel to wherever your object is going to be at the time you arrive. You can't get caught up thinking that you're merely going to jump times, and end up in the same place. You have to be sure that you know the precise location you'll end up. Had one of you happened to get up and kick this disc into the corner in my absence, I would likely have reappeared partially imbedded in the wall, and the whole lesson would have been quite de-motivating. I deliberately came back relatively soon to avoid that particular scenario, but long enough to make an impression, trusting that it would take you a few minutes before you would leave your seats and start wandering around. What else did you notice about how I disappeared?"

"You knelt down first," Carson says.

"Exactly. Anybody figure out why?" Quickly waits a moment to see if we know, then carries on. "What's missing?" He holds up his arms.

"You don't have a chronometer on!" Francesca says.

"I don't have a chronometer on . . . my wrist." He reaches down and pulls up one of his pant legs. He has fastened a chronometer to his ankle. I lean forward on the table to get a better look.

"Chronometers are designed to operate by grounding through the nearest non-gravitite-infused object your body is in contact with. Since I was using an object on the floor, I wanted to ensure that I had a good temporal ground connection to the disk. I could have left it on my wrist, but there was a chance it would have grounded through my other foot to the floor. I would still have jumped but I would've ended up back at the same spot. That would have been less entertaining."

"Where did you go in between? Were you here earlier? Or later?" Francesca asks.

"I actually was in my kitchen having a snack around two o'clock this morning. Before I went to bed last night I set up these discs in my kitchen. I needed somewhere I could monitor and it never hurts to be near your own refrigerator. I don't like working on an empty stomach. I also noticed when

I woke up that the last piece of pumpkin pie was gone, so I've been looking forward to that all morning."

"So when you woke up this morning, you knew that you had been there already, even though it hadn't happened for you yet?" I ask.

This is getting mind boggling again.

"Yes."

"What if you didn't eat the pie when you went back, even though you knew it got eaten this morning? Would you change something?" Carson asks.

"Ah. That is an excellent question Carson," Quickly responds. "It would indeed have created a bit of a paradox. That happens from time to time. Sometimes, as in this case, the paradox would be rather small. The knowledge in my mind and the location of that particular piece of pie would be the deciding changes. The universe seems to be able to handle a few things like that without much harm. In fact, little paradoxical moments happen quite frequently without us knowing it."

"So that doesn't screw up the world somehow?" Carson asks.

"The world rarely gets negatively impacted by pie," Quickly replies. "Little paradoxes rarely cause more than the occasional feeling of déjà vu for those involved. Sometimes there is no effect at all. There are things that cause major changes however. You all making a jump back here from 2009 en masse, and then living here for a bit, will no doubt affect quite a lot. You are essentially adding five new people to a time when you didn't exist before." He pauses a moment. "Well, you may potentially have always been here, it's hard to say without checking all possible permutations . . . but in any case, my presence here is equally irrational for the prior stream of time, so there is a rational basis to suspect that by being here, we have essentially caused a new timestream. One in which we exist."

"What happens to the old timestream?" Blake asks.

"It still exists. We are ranging far afield of our original topic however. Simultaneous timestreams are going to have to wait for another day. You will learn about it, but I need to get you grounded in basic jump safety first."

Quickly has us get up and follow him into the main study and up the stairs to one of the balconies. He stops in front one of the walls of cubbyholes and turns to face us.

"Francesca, tell me what variables I'm dealing with when jumping, that we've learned so far."

"Aaaah, okay. We have the date, time-zone, time of day, and location of the object. The object needs to exist in the time we're going to, and we need to know how far it is from the ground or the objects around it."

"Excellent!" Quickly responds. "Those are all key factors. One other major factor is the electrical conductivity of the object. Since we are using electricity in our jumps we like to make sure that the object we are using will be able to withstand some level of electric current. It would be really inconvenient if we destroy or alter the object we are trying to use while jumping. The results of using a piece of paper for example might be catastrophic. You could accidentally light it on fire in the process of using it and destroy your link for the jump. This might be survivable if you were traveling to a prior point in the paper's existence, but if you were trying to go forward you might be in for a rough trip."

"Have you had that happen before?" Robbie asks.

"Not me personally, but I will admit that there may be a few lab rats that I have misplaced in the course of my trials."

"Misplaced?" Francesca's eyes widen.

"A few of them turned back up, but it was not always pleasant. Let's just say, I strongly advise against that method. It can have interesting repercussions. What I've found very reliable, however, is using more durable objects."

He reaches into one of the cubbies and pulls out a round piece of solid glass about the size of a ping-pong ball. It's uniquely colored with half of the ball left clear so you can see into its interior. The interior is a swirl of various colors with what appears to be some symbols infused in the glass.

"I have a friend who is a glass blower. She makes these for me."

We pass the glass ball around. "What are the little symbols inside?" Francesca asks.

"Those denote the origins of that particular anchor, as I call them. It was created at a specific time and date that was noted, and in a particular stream of time. All of them are handmade so they are unique. This can be used to travel to anywhere this particular anchor has been in its life along that particular timestream. You will notice I have a packet in each of these cubbies that goes along with the anchor."

He extracts a small envelope from the cubby and pulls a stack of photos from it. "I have a series of photos of this particular anchor in specific locations and times. The photos are time stamped by my camera. I also make additional notes on them pertaining to their particular location in the photo. My camera is direction sensitive so it stamps a magnetic heading on each shot. That helps orient me to the direction the shot was taken. It can also give elevation in mean sea level accurate to the half inch. Very useful technology. I can use this information to safely arrive at this particular time and place, or a very near moment. We're going to be practicing making anchor shots for your own use."

I look around at the wall of cubbies, each one holding an anchor and a packet of photos, and realize how much time and research Dr. Quickly has put into making this particular collection. I imagine that even with help it has taken decades.

Busy guy.

During the afternoon's lesson, we are each given cameras and spend time learning to precisely photograph anchors on stands and denote the specifics of the anchor's location. Quickly makes us take measurements using a tape measure, compass and a watch before he eventually lets us try out his camera, which he calls the Anchor Shot Pro or ASP. We scribble notations in individual logbooks of our various measurements and locations, making frequent corrections as Quickly critiques our work.

"Is this right?" Robbie slides his chair over to mine to show me his logbook.

"I think you have your height mislabeled as feet," I whisper. "Pretty sure that's supposed to be eighty-seven inches." Robbie nods and slides back.

"Now these have all been practice notations," Quickly explains. "In the next few days we'll begin logging actual usable anchor shots. It's essential that you grasp the basics well, or all the more complicated knowledge I teach you will be useless. It's no use bestowing the theory of transverse timestream navigation on someone who is going to teleport themselves in front of a steam-roller on their first jump."

I look at the pages of scrap paper I have accrued with the dozens of crossed out entries on them.

We're all going to die.

When we make it back to the house, we're excited to fill Mr. Cameron in on our new education over dinner. He has barbequed, and we enjoy a delicious dinner of ribs and chicken while Spartacus weaves between our legs under the table, snatching up the scraps we sneak to him. We're finishing up the last of the ribs, when the phone rings and Mr. Cameron goes into the other room to answer it. I hear him chatting for about ten minutes before he makes it back to the table.

"That was Mollie. Seems you caught a crab today in the Tortugas, Robbie," Mr. Cameron says. "It apparently didn't go well for your fingers."

"I remember that," Robbie replies. "I think I hated crabs for a while." He smiles at the memory and listens to Mr. Cameron continue on about his family's vacation experiences, but I can see him grow more somber as the conversation continues. I'm not surprised when after we've finished the dishes and are up in Blake and Carson's room, Robbie tells us he's not going to attend Quickly's lessons tomorrow.

"I just need to be here for my own peace of mind."

"Do you want me to stay with you?" Francesca asks.

"No. It'll be fine. Go ahead. I'm just going to spend some time with Grandpa. I'll let you know if anything happens."

Mr. Cameron's voice carries up from the stairwell as we're talking.

"Benjamin? There is someone at the door for you!"

I get up and tromp down the stairs. Carson and Francesca follow. When I get to the door, I see the dark figure of Malcolm in the doorway. Mr. Cameron stands aside so I can talk to him.

"Hey, man. What's up?"

"I require your assistance again," Malcolm says.

"More beeps on the beepy box?"

"Just more . . . questions," Malcolm replies.

"Do you need me again, or do you want more of us to go along this time?"

"I only have transport—"

"For one," I finish for him. "Yeah, I know. One of you guys want to take this one?" I ask Carson and Francesca.

"No. It's all you, dude," Carson says.

"Yeah, it's freezing out there," Francesca says.

"Okay. Let me grab a jacket."

Malcolm's scooter is parked on the curb in front of the porch. He hands me a pair of goggles to wear this time. We don't have far to go to reach our destination. Malcolm pulls us into a rental storage facility and revs his scooter over the track after the gate opens. The rows of doors in the metal buildings are painted orange.

Malcolm steers us to the far back of the facility to a building marked Q. We dismount the scooter and he walks up to the door of unit 112. He pulls a flashlight from his bag and dangles it from his mouth by its lanyard as he fiddles with the lock. He's not using a key, but rather a set of lock-picking tools.

"Whose unit is this?" I ask.

"Someone who isn't going to be very happy," Malcolm mumbles through his teeth as he bites the lanyard. He pops off the lock and tosses it on the ground. The beam of light from the flashlight bounces around as Malcolm pulls up on the door. I step forward to help him lift it. A powerful stench assaults my nose as the door rolls up. I take a few steps backward.

"Oh God. What is that?" I say.

Malcolm pulls a handkerchief out of his bag and holds it over his nose and mouth as he shines the light into the unit. I pull the front of my T-shirt up to my face as I walk closer. Malcolm's flashlight illuminates a crowded space full of furniture and boxes. A wooden china cabinet is inserted into the center, along with a mattress set and some portable fans. Battered cardboard boxes bear labels like "Kitchen utensils" and "Dining room." A deer head with a large rack of antlers stares at the ceiling from atop the china cabinet

"There."

I step next to him and follow the beam of light to where he's pointing. "I don't see ... oh. Oh man, what is that?" A flesh-colored protrusion juts from the mattress set and joins the back of the cabinet. "Is that an ... elbow?"

Malcolm shines the light to the left of the mattress and I follow it to see a human hand jutting out the top, with a few of its fingers imbedded in the cardboard box next to it. The box is labeled "Kitchen appliances."

I back away. "That is disgusting."

Malcolm is watching my face. After a few moments, he shuffles some more of the objects around and slides himself in front of the china cabinet. I walk to the right a few steps to see what he's doing. Moving a painting of a sad clown, he reveals a human torso in a peach bathrobe. There are used facial tissues protruding from one of the pockets.

He pries open the set of cabinet doors closest to us and shines the light inside. The head of a woman is staring blankly out at me. One of the glass shelves of the china cabinet is passing through the side of her head. There is no blood. Her face looks almost serene.

"You ever see her before?" Malcolm says.

The smell gets to me and I turn around and vomit into the runoff drain between the buildings.

Damn it. Those were really good ribs.

Malcolm clicks off his flashlight. I hear him kicking a few of the boxes back inside the unit so he can shut the door. I keep leaning over, holding my knees and spitting the taste of puke and barbeque sauce out of my mouth.

"What the hell was that, Malcolm?"

"A fusion event." He pulls the temporal spectrometer out of his bag and takes a reading. He shows me the screen. The lines and squiggles on the graph mean nothing to me. "She has the same temporal frequency as you do. Just like the van."

"You can't possibly think I caused that," I say, pointing to the closed door. "I don't even know what that was in there."

"No. That was caused by temporal matter fusion, two objects trying to occupy the same space at the same time. Looks like she was using some kind of kitchen appliance when she got zapped. I just thought you might know her. She's from your time."

"I've never seen her before."

Malcolm puts the spectrometer back in his bag and pulls out his note pad. "This is the sixth fusion event I've recorded this week. All of them have your same time signature. They're likely all victims of the same incident. So far, you and your friends are the only ones I've found alive."

"This is some job Quickly has you doing," I spit again into the drain. "Time travel crime scene investigator. Do you put that on your resume? You could make yourself quite a reputation. Time travel around, solve homicides." I straighten up.

Malcolm pauses a moment before he responds. He looks away to his scooter as he speaks. "Dr. Quickly requires that I stay here. I do not time travel."

"Why's that?" I ask. "You don't get a chronometer to go with your temporal beepometer?"

Malcolm eyes the chronometer on my wrist. "Dr. Quickly requires that I stay 'constant.' He says that there are already too many variables. He needs someone he can rely on to stay steady for his calculations."

"Is that what my friends and I are to you?" I say. "Variables?"

"Yes. You come and go. Time travelers are always variables."

I check my jacket to make sure I didn't get any vomit on it, then zip it up the rest of the way. "Okay. Where to next, Constant Malcolm? I could use a drink, or at least something to wash my mouth out. Unless you want me breathing vomit breath at you the whole ride home."

Malcolm stays quiet but nods. We climb onto the scooter and get back on the road. A mile or two down the street I spot a dive bar with an open sign. We park the scooter near a group of Harleys and I smile at the bikers standing by them as we walk in. One of them consents to giving me a nod. Malcolm keeps his eyes ahead as we go inside.

We grab a booth, and a petite, dark-haired server glides over to take our order. One of her giant hoop earrings is slightly tangled in her permed, black hair. Malcolm gets momentarily distracted by her low cut T-shirt and mumbles something about needing a moment. I order a beer and a dozen wings.

"You owe me my dinner back," I say. Malcolm gives me a cool stare but then nods. He orders an iced tea.

"So what kind of other investigations have you been doing? Tell me about what else you've found," I say.

Malcolm lays his messenger bag on the table, pulls a manila envelope out, and slides it toward me. "Mostly they've been fusion events. One was more interesting though. Last night a coed at the law college got murdered in her dorm. She wasn't a time traveler, but I found evidence of a temporal anomaly around her building. I couldn't get in the dorm because they had it cordoned off by police, but eventually I'll get in. I'll see what kind of signature I can pick up."

I pull some photos and a couple of reports out of the envelope. "Are these police reports?"

"Yes. I have many contacts in the police department."

"Did you tell them about Stenger?"

"No. I haven't had any evidence of this person yet."

"You have a van with murdered people in it, and no one knows where it came from. That's pretty substantial don't you think?"

"Not conclusive enough to point to a specific suspect," he says. "If I go to my police contacts, I want to have something conclusive to offer them. I want them to take me seriously."

I enjoy the beer when it arrives. Malcolm eats most of my wings when they show up, but I don't mind. Looks like he needs them more than me anyway. Plus he's buying.

When Malcolm drops me back off in front of the house I hand him his goggles. "Let me know if you find anything else conclusive about that law student murder. I still think you might be looking for my guy. I don't know why he would be murdering college girls, but the guy is crazy, who knows what he's up to. You should be careful."

"I'll see if I can find him," he says.

"I'd bring a big-ass gun," I say.

Malcolm nods and rides away.

Or a grenade launcher.

Dr. Quickly seems unaffected by Robbie's absence in the morning and plunges us into lessons as soon as we arrive. I'm given the same tape measure I used for the previous day's lesson but today we're each given new chronometers.

"These are fully functional chronometers with timing pins installed," Quickly explains. "I want you to get used to dealing with the real thing. Exercise extreme caution with them. You know what they are capable of."

Quickly also gives us each a box with four anchors in them. Each one is unique in its coloring and design, though the internal symbols are identical.

"I had these anchors made specially for each of you. None of them have ever been used. It will be your responsibility to take care of them and take detailed notice of their existences. You'll be using these anchors to make real jumps through time. Their security is vital to your safety."

Quickly leads us into a part of the lab on the second level that we've never been to before. It's a long hallway with doors on each side. The rooms appear to be empty with the exception of an occasional table or anchor stand. I notice that each room has more than one door. On each of the rooms we pass the doors are green. We enter one of the rooms and I notice that the interior side of the door we pass through is painted blue and there is again a green door on the far wall. I'm curious about the reasoning, but assume it will be explained.

"I would like you all to note the time we entered the room," Quickly says. We do as he instructs, hastily scribbling the time into the "Location in" column in our logbooks.

Quickly has us stand along one wall of the room and he himself goes over to the anchor stand in the center. The stand itself is unremarkable. It's a steel pole mounted in the concrete floor that rises up about four feet and terminates with three short metal prongs. Quickly takes one of his own glass anchors from his pocket and sets it on the metal prongs of the stand.

"Today we're going to work on what I consider the easiest and safest manner of jump that we can attempt. In front of you we have a stationary stand. The height of your anchor from the ground will remain fixed and should not change, as we are only going to be jumping small increments in a future direction with friends here to keep your jump destination clear."

We all perk up at this news.

"Before we can get you hurtling through time and space however, we have deal with the matter of your clothes."

"Our clothes?" Francesca asks.

"Unless you would like to spend the next few hours in your birthday suit, we're going to need some clothing for you that will be able to go along for the ride. Are any of you wearing any of the clothes you had on during your original jump from 2009?"

I do a mental inventory of what I have on. I pull back the waistband of my pants and check my boxer shorts. I discover that even those are new acquisitions from the last few days. It turns out that with the exception of Francesca's underwear, none of us are wearing clothes from 2009.

"We're going to have to work on treating your new clothes with the gravitites over the next few days, but for the time being, you'll have to use some of my lab jumpsuits. There is a selection in the lockers in the hall. Use the bathrooms down the hall to change and meet me back here."

We pile into the hall and find the lockers Quickly is talking about. There are at least a dozen brown and white jumpsuits of different sizes. There are also a couple of stacks of white T-shirts and undershorts. We scrounge until we find some that match up with our sizes. When we've changed, we're back in the anchor stand room, barefoot and holding our little piles of clothes. Francesca is swimming in her oversized jumpsuit and mine is too short in the sleeves, but they are comfortable.

"Just throw your things in the corner for now. Pay attention to what you've learned so far. You will set your chronometers for a thirty-second jump. You will place your chronometer hand firmly on top of your anchor like this, being sure to have firm contact, but not touching anything else, then using your free hand, you will activate your chronometer."

Quickly demonstrates the motions at the stand for us and I pay rapt attention.

"The chronometer will automatically record the time of your jump if you are setting a specific date and time to arrive, allowing you the opportunity to log the precise moment for your records. If you are using an amount of time to jump, such as a half hour, or thirty seconds, you'll need to keep track of the time you arrive yourself. It helps to have a watch or clock handy for that." He gestures to the wall clock over the exit door. "Once you've logged it, you'll be ready for another jump."

The factual manner that Quickly is using to describe the process does not prevent my heart from pounding in my chest. It has time to calm a little as we all take turns practicing how to stand and simulating the jump. When Quickly asks us who would like to make the first jump, it's Carson who volunteers. The rest of us line up against the wall as Quickly checks Carson's positioning and double checks his chronometer settings.

"Looks like a go. Anytime you are ready," Quickly says, and steps back. Carson keeps his hand on his anchor and double checks that he's not touching the stand. He breathes out heavily a couple of times and then looks at us. I give him a thumbs up. He smiles and reaches for his chronometer. For a fraction of a second I see his red hair raise up and then he's gone. I realize I've been holding my breath and breathe out. Dr. Quickly is observing a pocket watch. I exchange looks with Blake and Francesca.

"Oh that is scary," Francesca blurts out, hopping up and down involuntarily. Blake and I say nothing. We wait in silence for the seconds to tick by. I begin starting to count in my head just to calm my mind. I watch the stand in the room and Carson's anchor sitting there undisturbed. I feel like minutes have ticked by, but know it's just my apprehension. The next moment Carson is back exactly as we last saw him.

"Did it work?" he asks.

My tension dissipates. Blake laughs out loud. Carson smiles with elation at having succeeded.

"That was the longest thirty seconds of my life!" Francesca exclaims and gives Carson a hug.

"What did it feel like?" Blake asks.

"Not bad really," Carson responds. "It felt like a shock you get in the winter from static, a little tingly but not painful."

Francesca smiles at him, and Blake and I pat him on the back.

"What do you need to do next, Carson?" Dr. Quickly asks from the side of the room.

"Ahh . . . Oh, I need to log in my time!" Carson takes to writing down his arrival time in his log. Quickly takes Carson's anchor from the stand and puts it back in Carson's box for him.

"Who is next?"

I raise my hand. "I'll do it."

Carson smiles and makes his way to the wall. He's chatting with Francesca but I tune them out. I select one of my anchors that has a dark blue swirl through it, and place it on the stand. My heart is pounding in my chest but I ignore it and concentrate on my chronometer. Set to time skip. Interval set to thirty seconds. Jump pin unlocked. Hand on top of the anchor, pressing firmly. Free hand to press the pin.

Quickly checks my settings and then gives me a nod. My friends along the wall are watching me eagerly. I look up to the clock, watching its second hand ticking past the forty second mark. I take a deep breath and push the jump pin.

I feel a tingling all through my skin. It feels like I blinked but I can't be sure. Nothing happens. Quickly's face is impassive. I look over to my friends. Carson is grinning.

"That was so cool!" he exclaims.

"It worked?"

"Yeah, dude. That was awesome."

"It's still just as crazy the second time," Francesca says.

Incredulous, I look up at the clock. Sure enough, the second hand is ticking its way past the twenty mark. "That was way less dramatic than I expected."

"I want to go." Blake grabs one of the anchors out of his box.

I pick up my anchor and pull my logbook out of my pocket. "So these books can just make the jump right along with us?"

"You can bring anything that has been previously impregnated with the gravitites. I had previously treated the books. That brings up an interesting safety concern that you should be mindful of. If you're going to be jumping to and from the same location, you have to be careful that all of your possessions are treated, because if they aren't, they'll fall to the ground where you left them, and could present a hazard to your return. If no one clears that area for you, you could end up with a pen or a necklace imbedded in your foot when you jump back. Food for thought."

Throughout the rest of the lesson, Quickly continues to casually toss out these little tidbits. "Mind that you don't sever your fingers off by picking a time when your anchor is in the box." Or, "Remember to keep firm contact so you don't end up a floater in orbit." Initially I'm shocked into wide-eyed attention, but after a while, I find I'm tuning out the fear. Quickly seems confident that we are going to be okay, so I try to be trusting.

Over the course of the remainder of the day, we all get a chance to make more jumps. We work up to jumping a five minute period at once. We've logged about seven jumps apiece by the time we call it a day.

"Celebration time!" Carson exclaims as we exit the lab onto the street. "I think this day deserves some beers."

"Where do you want to go?" Francesca asks. "Ooh, I saw a flyer for this place called the Forty-ninth Street Mining Company that had some cheap drink specials, and I think they even had karaoke."

"Let's just wander out and see what happens," Blake suggests.

Robbie pulls up in Mr. Cameron's car to pick us up, and we pile in. I roll down the window of the back seat and watch the St. Pete of 1986 stream by out the window. We pull up to a stoplight and a couple of girls in a dented BMW smile at me. I smile back and wonder if they can tell there is something different about us. I imagine myself buying them drinks at the bar.

"And what do you do?"

"Time Traveler."

Chapter 10

"Don't time travel immediately after eating. You'll waste a good meal, and leave everyone a nasty mess."
-Excerpt from the journal of Dr. Harold Quickly, 2017

"Look around you. What do you see?"

We're in Quickly's neighborhood, a few blocks away from his house, just after noon, standing in the street in our jumpsuits. Quickly is interrogating us, uninterested in the fact that we look like utility workers. At least today we aren't shoeless. We've acquired our flip-flops back after he stole them before our morning lesson and treated them for jumping. I feel very conspicuous, but the streets are quiet, and no one has taken much notice of us.

"It looks like an average neighborhood," Blake suggests.

"Indeed," Quickly responds. "Just the sort of neighborhood you would expect to find in just about any town in the country in the last or next half century. We are out here because if you're going to learn the skills you need to survive as time travelers, you are most commonly going to be using them here: quiet, average places. So how do we time travel in suburban twentieth century America? What is my first requirement?"

"We need objects fixed in time," I say, proud to use my new knowledge from our hours of lessons.

"We need clear space to work," Blake adds.

"We should avoid inclement weather so we don't get fused with falling ice or rain when we arrive," Francesca says.

"Good," Quickly responds. "What do we have here that meets those requirements?"

I consider our surroundings, trying to pick out something that looks like an anchor.

"Mailbox," Francesca suggests.

"Not bad," Quickly answers. "How would you do it?"

"Um. I guess I would stand in the yard so I don't get hit by a car when I arrive."

"Good thought. What about the grass? Do you see the danger there?"

"What, like kids playing in the yard?" Carson suggests.

"Potentially, but what I'm referring to here is that when you leave, you are pushing the blades of grass down with your feet. When you arrive back in that location, are they still going to be pushed down for you? You have to watch for that or you'll end up with a bunch of grass growing through your feet."

"That sounds really painful," I say.

"It is. I had a long stem of grass fused through my calf for the better part of a week once. It was very painful."

"What did you do to get rid of it?" Francesca asks.

"I fretted over it a few days and even saw a doctor, before I did what I should've done the instant I discovered it. I made another jump."

"That removed the grass?" I ask.

"Yes. Since the grass hadn't been infused with the gravitites, and my body had, when I made the jump, I was able to leave it behind. It still took some time for my body to heal from the unwanted intrusion, but overall I could have fared much worse. It was a valuable learning experience."

"So what would you do in the case of the mailbox?" Blake asks.

"It's not a bad choice overall, but I would use it cautiously. This post is immediately next to a driveway, so you can stand on something solid without being in the street and in danger from passing cars. You would still have to consider the possibilities of encountering a car coming in the drive, or of course the person retrieving the mail, or the mail persons themselves doing the delivery. You might have kids to factor in, or the occasional errant skateboard, but overall your probability of safety is pretty high. I would help my odds by planning to arrive at night, when you aren't likely to encounter many of these hazards. You always want to increase the odds in your favor as much as you possibly can. What else have we got to work with?"

I scan our surroundings and look for more unseen hazards, trying to picture the activity on the street. In my mind I see owners with lawn mowers, kids on bikes, sprinkler systems and rolling trashcans. I try to imagine where I would find the least activity. My eyes finally settle on a TV antenna. "What about a roof?"

"Excellent!" Quickly exclaims. "The roof of a suburban home is one of the least hazardous and least occupied spaces you can find in any town. They are often adorned with metal antennas or satellite dishes that are good conductors for jumping, and the footing, while usually sloped, is typically smooth enough to protect your feet if you are wearing adequate shoes. Most importantly, hardly anyone ever looks up there, let alone goes up there."

"What about falling off the roof?" Francesca asks

"There is that I suppose," Quickly says. "And getting up and down can be a bit tricky. These are minor details when you think about it. You have to think big picture. I will grant you that I'm climbing fewer roofs these days than I once was. Still, you are young people, prime of life. The roof is a very good choice. You can make fairly long jumps through time there with relative safety.

"I want you to work as teams. You will work in tandem to keep your partner safe. Find a location on this street to use as a jump anchor and make a jump. See if you can do thirty-minute intervals to start. Blake and Benjamin, Francesca and Carson, let's see what you've got."

I look at Blake and feel the sudden onset of stress. Quickly is certainly not shy about throwing us into these sink or swim situations. I have to believe he knows what he's doing. Blake is someone I can count on for anything, so I have no worries that he won't have my back. The stress comes from how new all of this is to me. Each day I'm learning to defy everything I've known about reality. Quickly walks down the street to give us some space, and he makes some notes in a notebook while Blake and I confer.

"What do you want to go for?" Blake asks.

"I'm not an especially big fan of heights, but I guess it would be good to go the safe route and try for a roof if we can get up on one."

We look at the houses around us. I can see a couple of them are definitely occupied. There are two or three that look like no one is home. I point to a green stucco rancher that has a wooden fence attached to the garage.

"What about just using that one?" It's the same house I spotted the TV antenna on earlier.

It's just a one-story. I should be able to handle that.

Blake nods and we head across the street into the yard, trying not to look suspicious. A van drives by and we linger awkwardly in the driveway until it's past before heading for the fence. We find the gate unlocked. We slip into the side yard, and after a tense moment of expectation that we're going to be mauled by a vicious dog, we find only trashcans and an empty, blue plastic kiddie pool. I'm happy that the garage is between the main house and us, so that even if we were mistaken about someone being home, no one is likely to hear us. We close the gate and I peek over the fence to see that no one is watching. Blake checks around the corner to the backyard to see if there is anything we need to be concerned about, but comes back immediately.

"Just a swing set."

I put a foot on the bottom brace of the fence, and grabbing the top, boost myself onto the corner. I sway precariously for a moment, then get my balance and sit. I put a foot on the top support of the fence perpendicular to the garage, and with one hand on top, lean forward and grab the roof.

Don't look down, Ben.

I realize that other than the gutter, there's not much to grab onto. I use my height to my advantage and jump, flopping the top half of me, and my right knee onto the roof. I stay low to keep from sliding back off. From this position I'm able to lean my weight forward and get my other leg onto the roof.

Hallelujah.

Blake has scaled the fence now and is positioning himself to lean over and grab the roof. I sit up and position myself as securely as I can, bracing my feet on the gritty shingles.

He stands and grabs the roof. I reach out an arm and clasp his, helping to pull him onto the roof as he flings himself up. For a moment, my flip-flops slip on the shingles and I slide forward, sending bits of sand and rock dancing into the aluminum gutter, but we're able to keep our weight low and hang on as Blake rolls onto the roof. Satisfied with our success, we crawl cautiously up to the ridgeline.

Once on the ridge, I take a pause and look into the street. Francesca and Carson are nowhere in sight, but I can just make out Dr. Quickly through a gap in some trees. He appears to be collecting dandelions from someone's front yard.

"So he's not watching us at all?" Blake asks.

"I guess not."

"He's kind of a weird guy."

"I agree. Seems awfully trusting we can do this though."

"I guess we'd better get it right."

We continue down the ridgeline, walking as lightly as we can until we reach the antenna mounted on the far end of the house. Another car passes, but the driver doesn't look up. Blake and I position ourselves around the antenna.

"Okay. Half an hour from now," Blake says, setting his chronometer.

I rotate the dials on mine also. "Okay, are we able to go at the same time using the same anchor or do we need to go separately?"

"Um. I don't know actually," Blake responds. "I don't think he covered that in class."

"I guess we'd better do separate. You want to go first and I'll follow?"

"Sure. Do you want me to get out of the way first or just stay in position till you arrive?"

"Good question. I guess as long as we're in different positions here, we'll be fine then too," I say.

"Okay. I just won't move till you show up, then we can climb back down together."

I get in position with my arm below Blake's, but not grabbing the antenna yet. He grabs the pole near the top with his left hand and uses his right to reach for the chronometer on his wrist. He breathes out deeply and looks at me. "Here we go."

His fingers squeeze the pin on the chronometer, and the next moment he's gone. I can feel my heartbeat pounding. The climb onto the roof had gotten it started, but the sight of Blake vanishing amplifies that by at least double. I take a couple deep breaths to calm myself and then get into position, careful not to put any part of myself where Blake has just been. I release the safety on the chronometer and take a look back to the street. I can no longer see Quickly. I wonder where Francesca and Carson are, then turn my attention back to my task. I squeeze the pin.

The world goes black. I feel the antenna shake in my hand and something strikes me in the face. I close my eyes and fall back from a noisy chaos around my head, grabbing frantically for a hold on the roof. I sit down forcefully and painfully on the ridgeline. I roll over and grab at both sides of it, opening my eyes and trying to balance myself. I get stabilized and catch the last glimpses of a flock of birds disappearing into the darkened sky.

My body shakes as the adrenaline pounds through me. I stay straddling the ridgeline and put my head down on my hands to calm my nerves.

What happened? How am I here at night?

I try to look at the chronometer settings on my wrist, but in the dim light I can't make out how the concentric rings are aligned. *Did I get my settings wrong? Is something wrong with it? How on earth do I get back?* I realize that I don't even know when I've arrived. *How badly did I screw this up? I could be a year off for all I know.*

A car drives by and pulls into a driveway down the street. A couple of lights are on in a few houses, so I know there are some people still awake. I wish I could tell the time from the night sky. I shimmy down the roof toward the garage where Blake and I came up. I can see a dim light shining into the backyard from inside the house. Someone has apparently come home since I climbed up.

I peer over the edge to see the fence I stepped up from. It looks much farther away in the darkness. I pivot myself and dangle a foot over the edge trying to catch the top of the fence with my foot. It won't reach. I slide a bit farther, balancing on my stomach and bracing my upper body on my forearms. I touch the top of the fence with my foot but it glances off and my flip-flop slips from my foot, disappearing into the darkness below.

Damn it.

I shift my body a little more and land my bare foot on top of the fence. It's jagged and sharp on my skin and I don't want to put any weight on it. I decide to shimmy sideways to get to the lower edge of the roof and just drop off from there. I make it to the edge and try to find a good grip with my hands. Just as I'm about to swing down, I hear a sound from the backyard. It's a thwap thwap of something swinging open and shut. My mind places the sound just as I hear a snuffling noise from the yard. *Dog door.* I grip the edge of the roof, hang momentarily and drop. I crumple and roll backward, but get right back up. The snuffling noise has stopped, and a moment later, I see a pair of eyes shine around the corner.

The dog doesn't look that large, but I don't wait to get a closer look. It barks loudly, and as I turn and leap for the fence, I hear it advancing. I ignore the jagged wooden tops of the fence boards this time and roll over top of the fence as fast as I can. The dog catches the pant leg on my jump suit as I clamber over, but my momentum pulls me free and I manage to land on my feet on the other side. I'm short a shoe, but I have no intention of going back for it.

I make a beeline for the sidewalk and turn left, trying to get as far down the street as I can before the dog's owners come out to investigate. My forearms are scratched and stinging. I don't know if the scratches are from the roof or the fence but I suspect a combination of both. A couple of them are bleeding slightly, but I simply pull the sleeves on my jumpsuit down to cover them. A half a dozen houses down I make a left onto another street, and once I'm out of view, I stop and remove my one remaining flip-flop. I briefly consider putting it in one of the jumpsuit pockets but then realize that I'll never have a use for it again without its mate. I deposit it in a trashcan in the next alley then walk to the closest streetlight to get a better look at my chronometer.

The last quarter of an hour has been a rush of stress, so I try to relax and concentrate. I count off the rings on the chronometer. The outside bezel is set to time jump and not a specific date jump. *That's correct.* Scan to the center to the time interval. I was jumping half an hour, the minute ring should be advanced to thirty. The minute ring is still at zero. *Why is that not set right? How did I even go anywhere?* I look at the next ring up and realize my mistake. I had involuntarily moved the twenty-four hour ring by half instead of the minute ring. *I just jumped twelve hours.*

Looking at my chronometer in disbelief at my carelessness, I see something else amiss. The little slider on the side of the chronometer that has been in the same position since our training began, has changed from the upper right to the lower right. I stare at it, trying to remember what it was for. I take the chronometer off my wrist and examine the side. I hold it up to the light and see inscribed in very small writing, the letters *FWD*. The word above the slider now reads, *Back*.

I haven't jumped forward twelve hours. I jumped backward. I must have bumped the chronometer climbing the roof, or at some other point, and not noticed that I changed the slider's position. *Great job, Ben. Twenty-three years wasn't far enough. You had to go back farther.*

I look around and take in my situation. This changes things. If I've arrived at last night, I can't just go home to Mr. Cameron's house. I could wake myself up and change my whole morning. That didn't happen. I'm not really sure what would happen if I did that now. I'm not eager to find out. I could try to jump forward again using another anchor, but given my recent double error I'm not feeling confident of getting it right. *I'm lucky I didn't kill myself as it is.*

I'm not far from Dr. Quickly's house. If there's anyone whose help I can use right now, it would be him. I don't know if meeting him twelve hours in the past will screw anything up for us, but he seems like he would be knowledgeable enough to figure out a way out of this mess. I decide to find his house and give it a try. The streets are quiet and I make next to no noise walking barefoot along the sidewalk. It's a little cold on my feet, but other than the occasional acorn I step on, it's an easy walk. Within fifteen minutes I'm standing in Quickly's driveway. The house is dark. I pull back the screen door and knock a couple of times. Nothing stirs. I knock again but I get the sense the house is empty. *Quickly could be anywhere.* I try the doorknob, but it's locked.

I'm getting cold and wouldn't mind getting indoors. The one plus to arriving after midnight from noon is that I'm not the least bit tired for that hour of the night. I walk back out to the street to keep moving, and start walking east to get to a main road that might have some open businesses or gas stations. I don't have any money, but I might be able to use a payphone to call Quickly and leave a message. I rummage in the pockets of my jumpsuit and pull out the logbook and pen, the only two items I possess at the moment. I know I wrote Dr. Quickly's and Mr. Cameron's phone numbers in the back.

I forgot to log my jump.

I stop and open to my log page. I look at the time of arrival column and realize I'm just guessing at what time I arrived. *Sloppy work, Benjamin. Quickly would be appalled.* I fill in the columns as best I can with what I know about where I am. I check that the phone numbers are in the back of the book and then stuff it back into my pocket. *Where do I even find a payphone?* I make it out to a main road and see the lights of a gas station shining through some trees to the north.

When I get to the parking lot there are two other patrons gassing up. A blonde woman in a Toyota is leaning back into her car window for something, and a middle-aged man at the pump diagonal to her is watching her backside. He inadvertently overflows a can of gas he's filling on the ground and he swears as it gets all over the can. I stick to the sidewalk and walk past the station because I spot a pair of payphones on the far side near the street.

I enter the phone booth on the street side, careful to keep my feet clear of the garbage that people have littered on the floor. As I pick up the receiver, the headlights of the Toyota sweep over me as the blonde pulls out of the station. The man with the gas cans is still following her with his eyes. I get my first good look at his face and something about him seems familiar. *Something about those glasses maybe?*

The car turns right. The man's eyes follow, and as it passes me, our eyes meet. He holds my gaze for a moment, then turns back to the gas. I pull my logbook out of my pocket and flip to the back to the phone numbers. I glance back to the man with the gas cans. He caps the last one and straightens up to pull a pack of cigarettes out of his pocket. He taps the packet against the side of his pickup truck and then pulls out a cigarette and lights it.

I turn my attention to the payphone. I have the phone number in my hand, but no change for the phone. *Was 1-800-Collect around in the eighties?* I start to try the number to find out, but get distracted by the proprietor of the shop poking his head out of the door of the station and yelling at the man at the pump. I can see him gesturing at the cigarette.

"No smoking at the pumps!"

The man with the cans has finished setting the last one up in the truck bed and turns to look at the proprietor. He rests his left arm on the side of the truck, and staring blankly at the man, draws another long drag on the cigarette. He holds the smoke in, then blows it casually in the proprietor's direction.

The proprietor is out of the doorway now, standing on the cement step with an indignant look on his face. He continues to gesture at the cigarette and I hear a couple more admonishments from him, but the customer ignores them. He closes the tailgate on the pickup and walks to the cab. Opening the door, he begins to climb in. The proprietor is off the step now and yelling.

"Hey! You haven't paid for that! Where do you think you're going?"

I lose sight of him as he crosses on the other side of the pumps. I can't quite make out the details of what either is saying for a few moments but then I see the man with the cigarette walk briskly to the back of the truck and grab one of the gas cans.

"Is this what you want?" he yells. "You want it back?" He unscrews the top of the can and sloshes some of the gas toward the proprietor, the cigarette still dangling from his lips. The proprietor backs into view from behind the pumps again. He has his hands out in front of him, and the anger on his face has now turned to concern. The man with the gas cans advances past the pumps. "Go on and take it back!"

The proprietor is authentically frightened now. "Are you crazy or something? I'm going to call the police!"

"That's not smart, to threaten your customers," the man responds. He advances quicker now, still sloshing gas toward the proprietor, who's trying unsuccessfully to get out of the way. His pant legs are soaked. The proprietor is taller and a good thirty pounds heavier than the medium-sized customer, but the man with the gas cans keeps advancing.

The proprietor turns and dashes for the door of the store. He opens it and tries to close it behind him, but the man with gas can grabs the handle and yanks the door out of his grip. The proprietor is frantic now. He searches the street, and for a moment, his eyes fall on me. I can see him yell something to me but I don't hear it. The next moment he disappears into the store.

The man with the gas can turns and follows the man's last glance and our eyes meet again. This time he smiles at me. It's that crooked, leering smile that triggers his name in my brain. *Stenger. We were right. He is here.*

I slam my thumb down on the receiver. I dial 911 as fast as I can and it feels like an eternity waiting for it to ring. I get a dial tone again. *Damn it. Don't they have 911 invented here yet?* I push zero and wait for the operator. I can see nothing of either of the men inside the store now.

"Hello, Operator? I need the police."

"What city?"

"Saint Petersburg, Florida."

"One moment."

I hear a banging noise coming from the store. The phone rings four times before someone picks up. "Saint Petersburg Police. What is your emergency?"

"You need to get someone to the Minute Mart gas station on Sixteenth Street right away. There's a crazy guy throwing gas on the guy working here. He's really dangerous." I see the lights in the store flicker once and then go out. "Get here fast!"

"Okay sir, what is the—"

I drop the phone, leaving it hanging from its cord and run toward the darkened store. *Please don't be dead dude. Please don't be dead.*

I get to the doors and stop. I can see next to nothing inside, except a few dimly lit display cases on the far wall that are reflecting the streetlights outside.

I didn't see any weapons on Stenger other than the gas can, but that doesn't mean he doesn't have any. I look back at his truck and the driver's door is still ajar.

Where did you go, you psycho bastard?

I pull the right side glass door open slowly and peer inside. There's a puddle on the floor just inside the door and I can smell the fumes. I poke my head inside and look to the left. The main counter is to that side, and in the light from the window I see the corner of a hallway leading to the back of the store. I slide into the doorway quietly, trying to keep my feet on the raised rubber doormat to stay out of the gas. My eyes adjust to the darkness and I can see signs of a scuffle behind the counter. A display of chewing tobacco has been knocked over and cans of Skoal and packets of Red Man litter the floor. The quiet is unnerving.

"Hey! Are you okay?" I yell into the void of the back hallway. My voice triggers some activity and I hear someone knock something over. I brace myself with one hand on the door to make a quick exit. I hear the sound of a door opening and slamming in the back.

"Get away from me, asshole!" comes a disembodied and somewhat muffled voice from the back.

Thank God he's still alive.

I move cautiously toward the hallway. The floor is slick with gasoline under my bare feet. As I lean around the corner, I can see the exit sign glowing dimly over a back door past a pair of mop buckets and a horizontal freezer. There are two other interior doors along the right side wall.

"Hey, man, it's the guy from outside!" I yell. "What happened to the guy with the gas can?"

There's a pause and then I hear the voice of the proprietor coming from the second doorway.

"He was right out there!"

I pick up a wooden mop and grip it with both hands as I eye the other door closest to me with suspicion. The roped end of the mop drips dirty water all over my right leg as I slowly reach for the doorknob.

"Where's this other door go to?" I yell.

"That's the storage closet." The proprietor sounds more optimistic now that I'm here talking to him. I yank the door open and swing the mop handle quickly around it but only make contact with some bottles of cleaner that go tumbling off a shelf. It's a small storage space and I can see that it hasn't been disturbed until my awkward mop attack. I shut the door again swiftly and move to the back door. It's unlocked. I kick it with my foot but it doesn't open.

My head is starting to swim a little from the gas fumes. I step up to the door and push with my shoulder. It moves a fraction of an inch but then stops. Something is wedged against the other side. I push my face up to the door and breathe from the crack for a moment.

"Hey, I think you can come out now," I say, addressing the co-ed bathroom sign on the door. "I called the police. They should be on their way. I think that guy must have gone out the back."

The bathroom is quiet for a moment, then I hear the proprietor come to the door and turn the lock. I step back from the door as he cracks it open. His black hair is a sweaty mess on his forehead and his dark eyes are wide in the dim light.

"You sure he's gone?"

"Not absolutely sure. Where are the circuit breakers?"

"Behind you."

I turn around and feel for the breaker panel on the wall behind me. I flip open the door and strain my eyes to try to see what has been tripped. I locate the main breaker with my fingers and press it back into position. As I shut the panel door and turn around, the fluorescent lights flicker on at the front of the store. My heart jolts in my chest as I see the figure of Stenger leering in at the glass doors. He stares at me and scowls. He lifts his gas can and dumps the remaining contents all over the front door.

Through the haze of liquid I see him grab an auto sales magazine from a rack outside and pull a lighter from his pocket. He casually lights the magazine and then watches the flame slowly grow, while with his other hand he pulls a cigarette from behind his ear. He draws off of the flame and then looks back to me, smoke streaming from his nostrils like a dragon.

Stenger disappears behind a wall of flame as he lights the door. The fire spreads to the ground immediately. Through the flames and smoke I watch Stenger walk to his truck. Most of the gasoline spilled on the ground outside earlier has evaporated, and the flames don't follow him. The proprietor runs past me to the wall behind the counter and grabs a fire extinguisher. He moves to the door.

"Keep that door shut," I advise.

The flames on the other side die down. The auto sales magazine is still curling itself into oblivion in the flames on the doormat but the fire has not spread inside the door. Sirens sound in the distance. I look back to the parking lot with a glimmer of hope, but Stenger's truck is gone. They won't catch him now.

The proprietor is aiming the extinguisher at the crack in the door to avert disaster at the first sign of flames leaking through. I can't remember ever being in a more vulnerable position than trapped in a convenience store full of fumes with my legs and feet wet with gasoline, but watching the auto magazine flames turn into smoldering ash on the step, my fear dissipates with it. It's not going to get inside.

My anxiety starts to return when I see the first patrol car pull into the parking lot. *I don't want to be questioned. How long will it be till they start asking what I was doing barefoot in the parking lot with no ID or money, in the middle of the night? What is my explanation going to be?*

"Hey I'm going to go wash this gas off my feet," I declare to my companion as I slowly back away from the door. He's not paying attention to me. He looks like he's in shock from the attack and is still staring transfixed at the door. *He might be high from all the fumes.* More squad cars and a fire engine have pulled into the lot. I turn and head for the bathroom. Before entering, I give the back door at the end of the hallway another quick shove. Nothing. Stenger must have jammed something against it when he went out. I slip into the bathroom and lock the door behind me. *How do I get out of this?*

I turn on the faucet, stick my right foot into the sink, and begin scrubbing frantically. I pump some soap onto it, rinse it off and repeat with the left, careful to try to keep my balance on the slick floor. Dirt from my walk here swirls down the drain in a dingy whirl. I don't know why the state of my feet matters to me when I'm going to get them dirty again walking around anyway, but once they're free of gasoline, I do feel a little better about my situation. I throw a handful of paper towels on the floor and step on them to dry my feet. I can hear the sound of voices out front. *Now what do I do?*

The bathroom is small, with a single toilet and sink and a fake palm tree in the corner. I look at the ceiling, hoping there might be some sort of way out, but there's nothing. I'm trapped. My eyes fall onto the shiny stainless steel rail that's been mounted along the wall next to the toilet as an aid for the handicapped. *Stationary metal object. Good conductor.*

I look at my chronometer. *I can get out of here. I need a time to arrive. The future is no good. Who knows what's going to happen in this bathroom once the cops start searching this place. Might be closed for a while. Plus I locked the door from the inside. They'll have to find a way in, maybe break the door down. So when do I go? Quickly said arriving at night is frequently safer since there are less people around, but does that apply to gas stations? What's the proprietor going to do if I just show up in the middle of the night and startle him? I feel bad for the guy. He's already had one bad scare.*

I decide on arriving in the daytime. I'll just need to find a way to do it where I won't end up colliding with someone using the bathroom if someone happens to be in here when I show up. I look at the toilet and try to visualize the least occupied space around the rail. I grab more paper towels and wipe the seat of the toilet. I toss the towels toward the bin but only a few make it. I don't have time to care.

I set one foot on the toilet seat and grab the rail with my left hand and then step up onto the back of the toilet. Using the corner of the walls, I turn myself around till I'm squatting above the toilet with one foot on the tank and one on the rail. I try to reach down with my left hand to grab the rail but it's too awkward of a position to maintain my balance. I need my chronometer to be closer to my grounding point. I unfasten it and transfer it to my right wrist.

I check my settings. *Six hours ought to do it.* I'm guessing at the time, but I figure six hours ought to put me somewhere around 7 pm, a fairly normal hour of day to escape a gas station. *Directional slider to Back. Got that right this time.* I reposition with both feet on the tank and just my right hand grabbing the rail. I reach over with my left hand for the chronometer.

Someone knocks on the door and tries the door handle.

"Hey, are you in there?"

Nope. Not anymore.

IN TIMES LIKE THESE

I push the pin.

Chapter 11

"If you find a timestream you can live with, don't be afraid to stay a while. The grass isn't always greener. Sometimes they don't even have grass."
-Excerpt from the journal of Dr. Harold Quickly, 2208

There is a little girl sitting on the toilet, humming to herself. Her feet don't touch the floor. The light swinging of her feet as she hums is making the fake flower on her headband bop around. I get the impression that she's in no particular hurry.

That is not working very well for me, awkwardly perched above her on the toilet tank. My right hand on the railing is barely outside of her peripheral vision. Any moment now she's going to hear my breathing or I'm going to slip off the top of the toilet and scare her to death.

The girl starts to sing softly to herself. I can only make out occasional words, something about a pony. *Did "My Little Pony" have a theme song?* This girl's mom or dad is going to wonder how she's doing in here soon. Then this is really going to look bad.

I decide I'm just going to have to make something happen now. I have so much height working for me that the shortest way off of the tank is actually going to be over top of her, provided I don't crash into the ceiling. I reposition one of my feet quickly and then leap. I clear her easily and land on my feet and one hand in the center of the bathroom floor. I know I should probably just bolt for the door, but I can't resist turning around to see the girl's reaction. Her wide eyes and open-mouthed expression are pretty funny. I smile at her and she doesn't look scared, only incredulous. That doesn't seem to stop her from doing the one thing I was hoping to avoid. She screams. It's one of the ultra high-pitched ear-pain inducing screams that little girls seem uniquely capable of.

That's my exit cue.

I throw open the door, praying that I won't immediately run into a parent. The hallway is clear. I catch a glimpse of the proprietor behind a rack of roadmaps. I duck instinctively. I have no idea what happens if he ends up recognizing me later on tonight. I don't want to find out. I turn and kick the back door open with my foot. This time it opens easily to a back parking lot and a dark blue sky still catching the last rays of twilight.

I'm out the door in a matter of moments and sprinting for a low chain fence that borders an adjoining residential yard. I'm over the fence and into the backyard as fast as my legs can take me. The fence at the side yard turns from chain link to wood as it wraps around the back of the house. I stop once I'm behind the wooden fence and deposit myself between two leafy ferns at a crack between the boards. I watch the back of the station and see the proprietor poke his head out and scan the parking lot. There are voices behind him but no one else emerges. He strides into the lot and looks around the corner to the pumps, then looks the other direction toward the dumpster before heading back in and shutting the door.

Close call that time.

The backyard has a gate to the alley. I slip out without a second look at the house. I know there could be some little old lady leering out her blinds as I cut through her yard but I'm not worried about it. I don't plan on sticking around. I stop and gingerly pull a pair of sand spurs out of the arch of my foot and then head away from the station. The gravel and dirt alley makes for slow going with my bare feet and the dim light. *I never did get my phone call. I'm not going back to that payphone again.*

I figure I now have about sixteen hours till I disappear off of that roof. *You're going the wrong direction, Ben.* Blake will be waiting for me to reappear next to him. *Maybe I can still get there.*

Successfully escaping the bathroom has given me more confidence in my abilities. Perhaps I could find a way to make it back without having to call Quickly or have any more run-ins with serial arsonists. I reorient myself to where I am and begin walking back into Quickly's neighborhood. I need another safe anchor. The roof had been good when I had shoes on, but barefoot I'm less confident of jumping from shingles. The smooth porcelain of the toilet top hadn't been a concern but outdoors I'm going to need to be more selective. I scan people's yards as I pass them, looking at their yard ornaments and fixtures. One porch has a wooden cuckoo clock hanging over their Adirondack chairs that catches my eye.

Shit. I forgot to log my jump again.

I pull the logbook from my pocket and flip to the page for the newest entry. Time of departure. *Not really sure. After midnight. 12:30?* I scribble it in. Location of departure: *Gas station on Sixteenth Street. What was the cross street?* Location of arrival: *Same.* Time of arrival: *That I don't know.*

I walk up to the porch and try to get a good look at the cuckoo clock. I think I arrived sometime around 6:30 pm. Should be close to seven by now. The clock reads three o'clock. I don't hear any ticking. *Well you're no help.* Time zone: *Eastern Standard Time. At least I know that one.* I look over the empty columns of information I don't know.

I'm a terrible time traveler.

I stuff the logbook and my pen back in my pocket and continue down the sidewalk. The old pavers are uneven and the littering of acorns makes me move slowly. I keep my eye out for possible safe anchors. The neighborhood is quiet overall, with only occasional cars passing. Some of the streets are brick and the houses are from a variety of eras, mashed together in time. I reach a small lake tucked away in a park in the heart of the neighborhood. A lone streetlight is shining on a playground in the adjacent park.

Jungle gym. That's not a bad anchor.

I walk to the play area and am happy to find no sign of kids. Ending up in a locked bathroom with a little girl was awkward enough. I don't really need to add lurking around children in parks to my image. The redwood bark mulch around the playground equipment is uncomfortable to walk on, but I work my way over to a set of monkey bars. There's also a swing set, a long metal slide and the type of merry-go-round that you race around and jump on to get dizzy. *I loved those as a kid. Wish they hadn't gotten rid of them. Safety really took the fun out of playgrounds.*

I climb up the two side steps of the monkey bars and then clamber to the top where I can dangle my feet over the edge. I'm happy to be off the bark. A large Banyan tree obscures the streetlight, so I doubt that I'm very visible from the street. I hear the flapping of some kind of waterfowl next to the lake, but otherwise the area is quiet.

Positioning myself as comfortably as I can with my legs hanging over the edge of the front rail and my lower back resting against the back rail, I set to work arranging my chronometer settings, tilting it to catch some light as best I can. *Next time I really need to bring a flashlight.* I decide to try to jump forward to the wee morning hours first. *Shouldn't be anyone using monkey bars at three in the morning.* I realize I'm still guessing at what time I'm leaving from again. Jumping in the lab with a clock on the wall was a lot easier to manage. I set the chronometer for a seven-hour jump. It should put me somewhere around 3 am. *Do I have it set to FWD this time? Yes. Learned from that mistake.*

I switch my chronometer back to my left hand where it feels more natural, and clamp down on the monkey bars. *Here we go again.* I close my eyes and push the pin. Opening them feels like nothing has happened. *It does seem a little darker out, doesn't it? Yeah. Definitely darker.* I'm trying to convince myself because nothing else seems to have changed. I double-check my chronometer settings. Everything looks right. *Damn. Did it work?*

I'm going to need some way of checking this. Quickly never mentioned this problem, but it probably just slipped his mind. I look around for things that might have changed in the last seven hours. Looking up, I can see a lot of stars but no constellations I recognize. They should have moved anyway. I study the star patterns above me, then take the pen out of my pocket and draw one of the shapes on my hand. *Okay. Diamond-shaped cluster above the Banyan. You should be moved in an hour.* As I'm staring at it, I see a dark spot drift across it. Another cluster disappears next to it and then it reemerges. *Don't get cloudy on me now when I need you!*

The little diamond cluster is back to shining at me so I decide to take my chances. I set my chronometer for an hour and jump again. This time I keep my eyes open and stay staring at the cluster of stars. I push the pin on the chronometer and they disappear. All the stars are gone. In their place is nothing but a charcoal blackness. As my eyes probe the darkness, I can just make out the reflection of the city lights in the layer of cloud. *Figures. At least I know it worked.*

Another idea occurs to me and I climb down the monkey bars to the last rung of the ladder and bend down to grab a piece of the redwood bark mulch. I carry it back up the monkey bars to my perch on top and set it on my lap. *When I jump it should fall back to the ground.* I nestle back into my space between bars and recalibrate my chronometer settings. *Okay, it ought to be sometime around 4 am now. Playground still should be safe for a couple of more hours.* I set my chronometer for a two-hour jump and grab the bar next to me.

The moment I push the pin, I see the sky light up. The blackness is now a predawn blue. The clouds are gone again. One bright point of light is still shining in the sky and I imagine it must be a planet. The neighborhood is now clearly visible around me. I can hear cars on the street a block over. Off to my right, beyond some trees, a car door slams. Saint Petersburg is awake. I twist around to look behind me and am surprised to see a young blonde woman on the walkway, jogging toward me around the lake less than fifty yards away. She seems concentrated on the sidewalk ahead of her feet. Had she been looking up when I arrived, she would have had a clear view of the whole event.

She looks up and sees me. Our eyes meet and she looks surprised. After a moment, she turns her attention back to the path and it curves away behind me following the contour of the lake. I pivot around to watch her but she doesn't look back. I watch her colorful figure disappear behind the next curve of foliage before turning back to my chronometer. *She was cute. Probably doesn't go for grown men hanging out on top of jungle gyms . . .*

I look down at my lap and see that the piece of bark is gone. I lean to my left and look at the ground, but can't identify my piece among all of its contemporaries. *Clearly I'm going to need a better method.* With the early morning light I can see well enough to fill in my logbook for my last few jumps. I climb down and carefully walk across the bark to a picnic table sitting under the Banyan. I sit down and flip to my log page. One of the columns I've been leaving blank catches my eye. It's labeled "Duration of stay." *What was that column for?* Quickly's lessons obviously did not stick as well I would like. *Is it for how long I stayed in a particular time, or a particular location?* I decide to just write in both and try to list my stints on top of the monkey bars throughout the night as best I can.

Six more hours and I'll be about caught up with when I left. It's an odd feeling to be thinking of a specific time as being home, but I'm realizing more and more how much it matters to me to be in the same flow of time as my friends. We're all displaced, but being displaced together is much less stressful than being stuck away on my own. I know I can walk over to Mr. Cameron's house right now and find them all sleeping. In the next hour they'll all be getting up and getting ready to head for Quickly's place. It would be so easy to just go join them, the only problem being that I'm already there. I'm going to be getting up and making myself some toast and jelly before too long. Banana. Bowl of cereal. Breakfast feels like a long time ago. It's odd to realize it hasn't happened yet. My stomach is feeling pretty empty. I'd been looking forward to lunch when we got done with Quickly's lesson in the neighborhood. That's a long way off now.

There are a couple of grade school boys walking down the street with backpacks. They get to the corner of the block and stop. They're joking around with one another. One boy pushes the other off the edge of the curb. The slightly thinner boy immediately jumps back onto the sidewalk even though there are no cars coming. They linger around the stop sign. It appears to be a familiar routine.

Having my monkey bars so near a bus stop puts a damper on my traveling for the immediate future. The random activity on the street is now becoming a factor too. The odds of someone seeing me depart or arrive have gone up significantly. I stand up and slide my logbook back into my pocket. I walk back out of the park and check the intersection street signs. I realize I'm almost an equal distance from Mr. Cameron's house as I am from the street where we were practicing with Quickly. An idea occurs to me and I start heading for Mr. Cameron's house.

It takes me about half an hour to navigate the neighborhood barefoot and arrive at Mr. Cameron's street. I don't head for the house immediately. There's a bicycle shop at the end of the street that is not open yet, but I can see the clock on the back wall through the plate glass window in the front. The clock reads ten past seven. I still have a little waiting to do.

Dark clouds are moving across the sky as I walk down the sidewalk a half-dozen houses away from Mr. Cameron's house, then cut through someone's side yard to the alley. We were picked up in the front of the house this morning but we went out the back door and walked around because Spartacus had wanted to get out into the yard. *If I can get a good view of the back of the house, I can see all of us leave.*

I sneak into the garden shed and look out the dusty window. A few minutes go by and I hear the back door. Spartacus dashes out into the yard and begins sniffing the flowerbox near the screened porch. I duck instinctively when Mr. Cameron appears. I peer over the ledge of the window. Francesca files out after Mr. Cameron, followed by Carson, and then there I am. A shiver runs down my neck. *This is so weird.* The other me is followed by Blake, then Robbie comes to the doorway and lingers, leaning on the doorframe. Mr. Cameron stoops and hooks a leash to Spartacus's collar. I see us saying pleasant goodbyes and watch as I lead the way around the side of the house and disappear. I know it will be only a couple of minutes until we are picked up.

Mr. Cameron is patiently taking Spartacus on a tour of the yard. Robbie has stepped back inside. I slide over to the door of the tool shed and peer out of the slight opening. Mr. Cameron and Spartacus draw slowly closer. *What if he comes in here?* I hadn't thought of that eventuality. *I might startle him to death. What if I end up being the reason Mr. Cameron dies?* My mind races with awful possibilities. My worries quickly ebb as I see Mr. Cameron pull on the leash and steer Spartacus toward the house.

I have so many questions to ask Dr. Quickly when I see him. My detour has raised all sorts of variables and problems with time travel that had not previously occurred to me. I'm eager to get back in sync with my life here so I can be less stressed about my actions.

I watch Mr. Cameron go back inside and then wait another ten minutes before leaving the shed. *We have to have left by now.* I work my way up the walk to the back door. I'm struck with the compulsion to knock, even though I basically live here now. I compromise and give a quick couple of raps on the door with my knuckles before turning the knob and poking my head inside.

"Hello?" I call.

Robbie appears around the corner of the sitting room doorway. "Hey. You forget someth—" He stops talking as he gets a look at me.

I look down and realize that in my dirty jumpsuit, cut up arms and no shoes, I do differ greatly in appearance from the version of me that just left.

"Hey, man."

"Hey. What happened to you?"

"Is Mr. Cameron handy? I may as well fill you both in on this at the same time."

Robbie goes and gets Mr. Cameron and we sit down around the kitchen table. It takes longer than I suspected to tell my story, largely since Robbie frequently interrupts with questions. I tell them my whole experience and how I encountered Stenger. That fact does not affect them as much as I had imagined but they are still largely surprised that I'm from five hours in the future.

"So the other you is over at Quickly's place right now, and has no idea you're here?" Robbie asks with amazement.

"Yeah, I never suspected anything this morning."

"That's crazy. It's so weird that we were just talking to you and now you're like a whole different person!"

"What is your plan now?" Mr. Cameron asks.

"I was hoping that I could just lie low for a few hours, and then when we get close to the time when I disappear off the roof, you can drive me over and drop me back off. I don't really want Blake to be stuck on that roof waiting for me for too long."

"We can certainly do that."

"I could use a bite to eat too."

Mr. Cameron gets up to get something for me but I gesture for him to sit back down. "I can get myself something." I stand up and go to the refrigerator. "I don't want to screw anything up by changing your day. I may have already I suppose, but I'm not trying to. I suppose it would be best if you two carried on as best you can like I'm not here. I'm just going to go upstairs and try to stay out of the way."

Robbie and Mr. Cameron seem agreeable, though Robbie is still incredulous, so after I finish a yogurt and another banana, I make my way upstairs. I take a shower and wash my dirty, cut arms, but climb back into my jumpsuit afterward. I find an extra pair of flip-flops to wear and set them by the bedroom door, then stretch out on Carson's bed. I stare at the ceiling with my head reeling with possible things I might be screwing up, but before long my eyelids start to droop, and before I really notice time has passed, I feel myself being shaken awake by Robbie.

"Hey. We should probably get going."

I'm sluggish and half awake in the back of Mr. Cameron's car, but as we near Quickly's neighborhood, my apprehension starts to build. *What if Quickly is upset with me for screwing up the time jump? I've never seen him get angry yet.* He's been a patient teacher so far, but until now, none of us has screwed up quite this badly.

"It's the next street down," I say, guiding Mr. Cameron toward our destination. "We should probably take it slow from here. I don't know exactly what time we left." I direct Mr. Cameron to an intersection a couple blocks down the street from where we were working with Quickly. As we cruise through the intersection, I look down the street and see the group of us standing around a mailbox. "It's almost time."

Mr. Cameron parks the car along the next block and the three of us get out of the car. I creep back to the corner and peek around a tree. Mr. Cameron and Robbie linger along the side yard on the sidewalk. Through a crook in the trunk of the tree, I watch the group break up and head in different directions. Blake and I disappear beyond some trees to go climb the roof of the rancher.

Francesca and Carson cross to the opposite side of the street and head toward me. They make it almost to the end of their block before walking into a driveway and climbing into a person's aluminum boat that is parked on a trailer. I watch with interest as they arrange themselves along the bow of the boat. I can see them gripping the bow rail. I gesture to Robbie and Mr. Cameron to look around the corner.

"This is going to be cool to watch."

The two of them join me by the tree and I point out Francesca and Carson off in the distance. Mr. Cameron raises his glasses and squints toward where I'm pointing.

"You have much better eyes than I do. I can't see much of anything that far."

"Carson and Francesca are in a boat down there," Robbie explains.

I keep my eyes fixed on them and watch as first Carson disappears and then a few moments later Francesca follows. The boat is empty.

"That is so wild," Robbie says.

We stare at the boat a few more moments before I straighten up.

"I guess we should be pretty much in the clear now. As long as Blake and I are gone by the time we walk down there, I think things will be back to normal."

"Want to just take the car?" Robbie suggests.

"Yeah, I guess that will work too."

We get back in the car and go around the block. As we pull up to the stop sign nearest our jumping off point, I slouch down in the back seat and peer around Robbie's headrest to glimpse the rooftop of the rancher. It's empty. I see Dr. Quickly lingering around in someone's driveway, still jotting notes, and point him out to Mr. Cameron. He pulls the car over again and parks. I watch Dr. Quickly's face as I get out of the car. His reaction is far less surprised than I had imagined. In fact, he doesn't seem surprised at all.

"Messed that one up a bit," I say, walking up to where he is on the sidewalk. He looks at his watch.

"You're a bit early. What happened?"

"I went backward instead of forward."

He looks a bit more concerned.

"By twelve hours."

"Oh my. That is a mess," he replies. "You successfully survived until now though, so that's something. Did you log your jump?"

I nod.

"Let me see your logbook."

I hand it over to him. "I think I may be missing some information still."

When he flips to the page I've been using, his eyebrows raise in surprise. "You made five jumps?" His eyes have an avid interest now as they look into mine.

"Yes, counting the mess up, I guess it was five."

He's studying my entries. "A toilet railing and some monkeybars?"

"Um, yes sir."

A broad smile breaks across his face. "There may be some hope for you yet!" He slaps me on the shoulder.

When Blake arrives on the roof of the ranch house, I'm standing in the front yard. It takes a few moments for him to see me. "Hey!" he yells down. "Did you chicken out?"

"Not exactly."

I wait for him to climb down, and when he emerges from the backyard, he's holding a slightly battered flip-flop.

"You lose something?"

"Ha. Yes. Can I see that?" The flip-flop has some teeth marks on the heel but otherwise is not too chewed up.

"That shows what I know," I say. Blake follows me as I walk around the corner to the alley trashcan where I deposited the other one. I lift open the lid and it's still sitting atop a black plastic trash bag. Blake watches me pull the flip-flop out of the bin with curiosity.

"Ben, I sense you have a story to tell me."

I smile. "It's a good one."

Chapter 12

"I lost track of my age some years ago. Now when people want to know, I simply ask them how old they think I am, and then congratulate them on their accuracy."
-Excerpt from the journal of Dr. Harold Quickly, 2105

The light from the star chandelier is gleaming off the table between my friends and me as I tell my story in the main study of the lab. Mr. Cameron has come with us and is browsing around the upstairs shelves. Dr. Quickly is seated a few feet back from the table in a brown leather armchair, dividing his time between staring out the window at the darkening clouds and listening as I fill my friends in on my adventure.

"So this whole time we were right about it being Stenger who killed those men in the van," Francesca says. She's settled herself into an armchair while the rest of us mount stools around the table.

"We don't have any specific evidence that it was him, but it sure fits," I reply. "He's definitely here."

"So if we're not the only ones who got sent back in time, does that mean there could be more of us? How many other people might have been made into time travelers?" Robbie asks from across the table.

I look to Dr. Quickly. He exhales slowly, then crosses his fingers in his lap. "I've been working on that issue myself. Malcolm is still watching the Temporal Studies Society for me. It's the most likely point of contact. You five and Mr. Stenger were very fortunate to survive this jump at all. There may have been others who were less fortunate and were shot into space, or worse. I imagine that when you finally make it back to 2009, you'll find a number of people in the area have gone missing." He scratches under his chin briefly.

"Checking it there would most likely be the only way to find out for sure. It's not necessary that they all arrived this far back either. If people were affected by various amounts of gravitites or voltage, they may have ended up traveling different amounts of time. They could be scattered across the next couple of decades if they were lucky enough to survive."

"There might be more like the lady in the storage unit?" I ask.

He stares through us briefly, his eyes locked on a non-existent horizon. "Yes. Unfortunately. Also, the effects of the gravitites are relatively permanent as far as I can tell. They come with their fair share of hazards. I would imagine that even if more victims survived, the lifespan of an uninitiated, involuntary time traveler is not likely to be long. The woman in the storage unit may only be one of many fusion events. I don't know that we'll ever know the whole toll of that accident."

"How much more training do you think we're going to need to make it back to 2009?" Blake asks. "We've made some successful jumps now. Couldn't we just ratchet up the intervals and do our training as we go? I mean, we could be doing this training later on just as easily right?"

Quickly's eyes slowly focus back to us. "I have a few reasons of my own for being in 1986 right now, but I could see about relocating soon. It wouldn't be a bad idea to lengthen your jump intervals. You may want to see how that works for your host however."

I watch Mr. Cameron on the second level balcony, holding a leather-bound book at arms length so he can read the title.

"We wouldn't necessarily all have to go, right?" Robbie asks. "I mean, we would all end up at the same place anyway."

"Yes, you could certainly take the normal timestream and end up in the same place. Usually." The last word trails off quietly, but Francesca still asks the follow up.

"What do you mean by, 'usually?'"

But Dr. Quickly gets out of his chair and heads for the stairs up to the second balcony, seemingly unaware of the question. He joins Mr. Cameron in his appraisal of the various items stashed in the array of cubbyholes.

"Did I just get dissed?" Francesca laughs as she watches him go.

"Maybe he just didn't hear you," Robbie responds.

"He is a little old," Carson suggests. "Maybe he's hard of hearing."

"Or has selective hearing," Blake adds.

"Would you not want to jump ahead yet?" I ask Robbie.

"I'm not in a hurry right this moment. I feel a little responsible for getting my grandpa into all of this. I'd hate to ditch out on him, especially now, when he could go any second."

"I didn't necessarily mean right away," Blake says. "I mean, it would be good to see that we'd gotten him through till your family makes it back, but we're going to have to leave eventually. I don't know that it necessarily does a lot of good to delay it."

Carson wanders around the table and leans his forearms on the back of Francesca's armchair. Francesca continues Blake's thought. "Also, I don't know if I'm the only one worried about this or not, but we're not getting any younger in the past. I know this may not be a big deal to you guys, because you are guys, but I don't really want to use up too much of my prime years in 1986. This girl has some things to get done in the present day, and I may need all my good-looking days at my disposal. Just sayin'."

"You don't want to date an eighties rocker?" Carson asks.

"Hey, I'm not saying I don't love a man who can rock a perm." Francesca laughs. "But I'm not sure I want to date a guy who has more beautiful hair than me. We might have problems. Plus, we have lives and careers there. I know we'll be making it back around the time we left, but there are a lot of things we left hanging when this happened to us. My cat will have no problem tearing a hole through the food bag if I don't make it home soon, but we have other people depending on us too. I don't really want to get fired from my job. I like it there."

Rain begins to pour outside and cascades down the glass wall of windows stretching up above us. My clouds from last night have finally decided to open up. I slide off my stool and wander over to the windows looking down on the street. I watch the cars splashing through a puddle growing from the runoff from a side street. A pair of umbrellas and a couple sets of feet pass below me on the sidewalk.

"Um, Carson?" Blake says.

"Yeah?"

"Are you okay, man? I think your arms are bleeding."

Francesca pivots in her chair. I look and see that Carson's arms are indeed red near his elbows. "Oh God, what is that!" Francesca springs from the chair and spins around.

Carson looks closer at his elbows. "It does look like blood, but it's almost like it's congealed."

"That's really gross," Francesca says.

"It's not me," Carson says. "It's on this chair."

Mr. Cameron and Dr. Quickly are descending the stairs together and Quickly points Mr. Cameron in the direction of the bathroom down the hall before walking our direction.

"Um, Doctor?" I say. "Your chair seems to be bleeding."

Dr. Quickly surveys the chair briefly. "Ah, yes. I was wondering if that might happen."

"You were wondering if your armchairs would start bleeding?" Francesca says.

"It's not the chair really," he says, walking closer and leaning in to have a look. "It's part of an experiment I have going on at the moment. I'm starting to get results back. Don't be worried, the chair will be fine." He grabs the back of the chair and drags it away to the corner. "I'll just move this and we can avoid sitting in that one for a bit."

"Does this sort of thing happen often?" Robbie asks.

"No. Thankfully not," Quickly replies. "The upholstery bills would get outrageous. I just happen to have a rather complex test going on at the moment. It's getting quite exciting."

"Can you tell us what it is?" I say.

"No. I'm afraid I don't want to share it yet. I'd hate for it to skew the results." He turns his eyes from the chair back to us. "I can however share, that I've had pizza delivered. It's in the kitchen for you. Though you will probably want to wash those arms off first, Carson."

"Yeah, I don't need some kind of chair disease," Carson says. He wanders toward the back.

Francesca continues to eye the chair in the corner suspiciously but finally pulls her gaze away. "You wouldn't think I'd have an appetite after seeing that, but it shows what I know. Pizza actually sounds amazing right now."

She and Robbie head for the kitchen. I turn back to the view of the rain. After a moment, I see Quickly's reflection next to mine. "No lunch for you today?" he asks.

"Maybe in a bit. I had breakfast twice today."

"Time travel can take a toll on your grocery budget," he replies.

"Doctor, can I ask you something personal?"

"I've always dressed this badly out of fashion, if you must know."

"Ha. I think tweed will never go out of style if you ask me."

He looks at me attentively.

"It's really a couple of questions. One thing I was wondering was why you never went big with this technology." I hold up the chronometer on my wrist. "This is amazing. The work you've put into this and the discovery of the gravitites must have been a guaranteed Nobel Prize. Haven't you been tempted to be rewarded for all of it? You would be famous worldwide."

Quickly looks out the window for a moment before responding. "I would say you've answered that question in part already. Fame is not for everyone. I had a partner working on this with me early on whom I know would have been thrilled to be on the cover of *Time* magazine. I think he had his interview already planned out in his head. We had very different motivations for getting into this research.

I did it partly for the achievement itself but also because I had strong motivation to succeed. There are things much more important and rewarding than fame."

"I know what you mean," I reply. "I don't know how willing I would be to share this either.

"Today, when I messed up my jump, it was a scary moment. Realizing how much harm I could have done was . . . sobering is the best word I can think of. But then later on, when I had to make that jump from the bathroom, and it worked, it was an amazing feeling. I mean, I was running and it was hectic, and I think the adrenaline had my heart going a mile a minute, but when I made it back and things worked out, I felt elated and excited about it all. I can see how it changes all of your perspectives on things.

"What you've done here, and how you've designed these chronometers, just blows my mind. I know we're headed home and back to our normal lives, but I've got to tell you, after an experience like this, I don't know how going back to fixing boats is going to stack up."

"You are at the tip of the iceberg, Benjamin. I'm not going to tell you that it is worth all of the risks, because I know I haven't told you all of the dangers. I'm afraid I've only just begun to tell you and your friends all the potential threats you face in doing this, but my years in the education system have taught me enough to know that scaring you all witless isn't going to help you learn, or help you get home." He slides his hands into his pockets and leans against the glass pane with his shoulder, facing me.

"That being said, I can say for me, that despite the innumerable dangers I have encountered to date, it has been incredible. I may not have seen my face on *Time* magazine but I have been amply rewarded."

The glass in front of me has fogged from my breath. I trace my finger through it in little swirls. "Do you regret leaving it all behind? Did you ever try to go back to your life?"

"I visited again a few times. There were people I cared about that I wanted to see. I haven't abandoned them. My disappearance was not total, like the media believed. Professionally I disappeared. Oddly enough it wasn't as hard as I had expected to leave that behind. My colleagues were a competitive bunch, and there were only a few that I really missed working with."

"I know what that's like." I turn my swirls into a sun and some planets.

"I'd known for a while that I was going to succeed with the gravitites. I was not rushing to get my results publicized because I always had other more practical intentions for this work. I rushed things a little obviously or I would never have involuntarily displaced myself, but I don't regret the result. On the contrary, getting lost in time was the best thing that ever happened to me, for more than a few reasons."

"So you don't plan on ever going back?"

"Not currently."

I finish drawing a comet on the glass and take a step back to look at my little cosmos. It's small, but it's growing. "How did you figure out these chronometers?" I fiddle with the dials on my wrist.

"Ah, well there I cannot take all the credit. After my first serious time traveling experience, I had the great fortune of meeting a marvelously talented watchmaker named Abraham Manembo, who worked with me on designing them. He was able to take my bulky equipment and streamline it into what you have on your wrist. His innovations are what have made time travel so much more efficient than anything I had previously dreamed up. "

A lightning bolt crosses the sky above us and it is only a few moments till the boom of thunder.

"During my experience last night, I realized what a fragile position I was in. Without the chronometer, I would've been in much worse trouble, especially if I ended up somewhere more dangerous. It made me wonder if you had any more specific survival type skills you could teach us."

"Survival skills are all I have been teaching you so far, if you think about it. It has all been about surviving."

"Well yeah. I see what you're saying, and that's true, but what I was thinking was more worst-case scenario type stuff. I mean, I spent most of last night either running away from people, or wandering around lost, or trying to get around barefoot in the city with no money. It was great exercise, I can say that, but I don't think I was very efficient."

"I certainly do have plans to get to some of those types of scenarios with you. I had not expected you to need them quite so soon, but I should have factored human error in better. That was my fault, and I hope you will forgive me. As a teacher of anything it is often difficult to remember that just because you have covered something does not mean it has sunk in properly, or really been processed to the point of understanding. Perhaps I shall have to devise some more quizzes or checks."

"My other question was . . . would you teach me how to build a chronometer?"

Dr. Quickly's eyebrows rise a little. "That's a big thing to ask, Benjamin. Having chronometers floating around unaccounted for has really never been a part of my plans for helping get you home. Time traveling is a serious business. All manner of chaos can ensue from careless use. What is your motivation for wanting to learn to build one?"

"Well, I had first thought that it would be good to know how to repair these in case one gets damaged. I wouldn't want to get stuck halfway back and not be able to contact you. The idea of being stuck somewhere in a time I don't want to be in really worried me, and it made me think it would be a good way to feel safer doing this if I knew how to get myself un-stranded. Plus, some of it is sheer curiosity. I think they're amazing. Working on one of these would be way more interesting than fixing boats."

"It's a fair thing to ask. There are a million possible scenarios where you might need to know. Yours could be damaged as you said, or lost, or stolen. It is a valuable item. The knowledge is an even more valuable commodity however. I have not really addressed this issue with your friends yet, but we're going to have to broach the subject soon. We're going to have to discuss your plans for what you will be doing once you make it back to your own time."

Quickly places his hands against the glass, to feel the impact of the rain beating against the other side. "I had intended that these chronometers would be a loan, and that you would return them to me once you succeeded. If you are starting to think you want to continue time traveling, then we are having a different conversation, and there are more concerns to bring up. One major one is the fact that there are a great deal of people who would go to possibly unpleasant lengths to get their hands on this technology.

"I have been around long enough to know that the amount of people who can posses this knowledge and not want to use it for illegitimate gains is smaller than one would hope. The more you know about this subject, the larger the target you may become for people who would like to gain this ability. I would say that you and your friends would already be quite valuable to a lot of people. A drop of your blood alone would now hold enough gravitites to keep innumerable scientists happy in research for decades. That is something you're going to have to live with now anyway, but the more you learn here, the more dangerous things may become for you."

"That sounds like more of a reason to have an escape plan to me. Couldn't having this ability be a great defense against those types of people?" I say.

Dr. Quickly smiles at me. "If you keep coming up with all these valid arguments I'm going to have no choice but to train you."

I grin back.

"We don't have to figure it all out right now," he adds. "Let's go get lunch. You may have had two breakfasts, but I missed mine this morning. I don't think my stomach will stand for much more of it." He puts a hand on my shoulder and we turn and head back to the others.

We spend the rest of the afternoon debriefing from our jumps. By the time we make it home to Mr. Cameron's house, I'm exhausted. I plop into one of the armchairs in the library and close my eyes for a few minutes, until I feel Spartacus lay his head on my knee.

"Hey, Bud. How are you doing?" His tail thumps the floor as I scratch behind his ears. Blake comes in and takes a spot on the loveseat.

"Hey, man."

"Hey."

"Sorry I almost left you hanging on that roof jump today. I was worried that if I didn't get back in time, you'd be stuck there not wanting to move, in case I appeared all of a sudden."

"No worries, man. I'm just glad you were okay."

"How are you holding up?"

"I'm all right. I'm glad we're getting to the point of making real jumps. It makes the waiting easier if I feel like there is progress at least," he says.

"You know if we manage to do this right, Mallory isn't even going to know you are gone. Do you plan on telling her about it all?"

"Yeah, definitely. We tell each other everything, so there's no way I could keep something like this from her. I might edit out the fact that I may have gone a little bit crazy with all the stress of waiting to get back to her." Blake pulls the ring box out of his pocket and opens and closes the lid a couple of times.

"I don't know. That is probably romantic. That might be the best part of the story as far as she's concerned."

"Yeah, maybe. I really won't care what happens once we get back. I feel like I could deal with anything just so long as I get back to her okay. I keep thinking I just want to find the most permanent thing I can, set this chronometer to twenty-three years, and zap myself back as fast as I can get there."

"I don't think these can go that far in one shot," I say, holding my chronometer up and checking my own dials.

"I know," Blake responds. "Ours don't go past five, and Quickly said they require external power for anything beyond one, even fully charged. I bet his could do it. Have you had a good look at his chronometer? His has all kinds of settings that ours don't have. I would bet it could go a lot farther too."

"We'll get there, man. I know you're anxious to get back, but this isn't something we should be rushing through. It sounds like we got pretty lucky, considering our alternatives."

One of the parrots flies into the room and alights on one of the curtain rods. I recognize it as Mercutio. "This place is pretty cool," Blake agrees, watching the bird pace back and forth on the open part of the rod. "I wish Mallory could meet Mr. Cameron. He's an interesting guy."

"Yeah."

Francesca walks past the library door, and after a moment, I hear clicking noises coming from the front door. "What are you doing out there Fresca?"

She reappears at the doorway. "I'm making sure all these locks work."

"Because?" Blake asks.

"Because there's a firebombing serial killer loose in the city! Are you not worried about this?"

"Oh. Yeah. But there's no reason he would be coming after us."

"He's a psycho serial killer. You really think you know who he's after?"

"That's a good point," I say.

"What are we going to do about him?" Francesca asks.

"Do about who?" Carson appears in the doorway Blake entered from, with a fork and a plate of blueberry pie in his hands. Robbie appears behind him a moment later, also bearing pie, and squeezes past him to take a seat in the other armchair.

"We're talking about what to do about Stenger," I say.

"That guy is crazy," Robbie garbles over a mouth full of pie.

"What can we do really?" Blake asks. "We're not the cops. And you were saying we should probably steer clear of them too, considering our circumstances."

"That is true. I'm not super excited about having to explain our situation to them, but we may be the only ones who know who he is and what he's capable of. I suppose we should probably warn somebody."

"What if we just call in an anonymous tip? People do that, right?" Francesca suggests.

"Yeah, we could try it," I say.

Blake frowns. "What are you going to tell them? 'Hey, you have a killer from the future loose in the city?' It's not likely to sound very convincing."

126

Francesca takes a seat in the other armchair, and as she sits, Mercutio flutters down from the curtain rod and alights on the back of her chair.

"You could tell them about the convenience store thing last night and hope they can catch him for that," Robbie suggests.

"Yeah, the store manager could back you up on what he looks like," Carson adds.

"Getting him arrested for something would be a start, but unless they find more on him, he won't stay in jail long. Especially if I'm the witness against him, and I'm anonymous, and we all disappear in a couple of weeks anyway."

"They might be able to connect him to the van murders. That would be more serious," Francesca says.

"That's true," I reply.

"So we need to contact the police without having to meet them, or explain who we are, but convince them we know who killed the guys in the van," Robbie says.

"Yeah, probably not easy, but they should at least listen to what we have to say. It can't hurt their chances, even if they don't believe us," I say. "But we should probably ask Mr. Cameron how he feels about us getting involved in this since we're living in his house."

"He's for it!" Mr. Cameron's voice carries through from the next room where he's obviously been listening. He appears in the hallway behind Francesca and leans on the doorpost. "I don't think there is really any choice in the matter. A criminal like that needs to be stopped. It is our duty to do whatever we can. It's our duty as good citizens."

"As long as good citizenship doesn't get us all locked up, then I guess I'm for it," Blake says.

Robbie and Mr. Cameron offer to make the anonymous call to the police the following day.

The morning's lessons with Dr. Quickly seem to drag by as I wonder what the police said in response. Quickly seems to sense my distraction and begins to give me more work. The four of us are working on researching jump locations. He has us planning multi-location jumps, using objects and photos from his array of cubbies along the second balcony. The goal is to find locations and items that exist not more than a couple of years apart, so that the amperage of the electricity required for the jumps doesn't have to be too high.

"We don't want to get you home but have your hearts stop," Quickly notes casually.

I look at my hand. Our singes and burns have mostly healed up from our original journey. Blake has a light-colored scar on the bottom of his right foot. Otherwise we feel okay, but I'm not anxious to repeat the process.

The balconies meet the staircase along the right side of the lab, but the left side holds a turn in the wall that runs away from the main room. It goes about twelve feet, seemingly to nowhere, but both sides and the back of the little hallway is lined with cubbyholes. The double rows of cubbies give me the feeling of being in library stacks or a long, narrow, walk-in closet. It's a little dimmer as I move away from the light of the main room.

Quickly has the cubbies labeled by months and years. Some I find are still empty, while others are packed full of unique objects and packets. I pull a pair of photos from a hole labeled, June 1989. One is a snapshot of a bowl of metallic fruit sitting on a table. The bananas, oranges and apples are copper-colored and piled together loosely in a stone bowl. One apple has fallen out of the bowl and it is lying on its side with its metal stem curving skyward. I look inside and find the apple, slightly tarnished and sitting straight up. I pick it up, surprised by the weight of it and then put it back gently. Quickly's scrawling handwriting on the back of the photo describes the scene succinctly as "Fiona's dining room. 6/11/89 shot 2002Z. Room cleared at 2004Z." Below, in a different pen, is an added note that says, "Mind the overhead lamp."

I look at the other photo. It's a well-lit scene that seems to have a more carefully artistic feel to it than Quickly's usual shots. It's a display of ladies' shoes in a department store. The center of the photo concentrates on a pair of purple shoes, with medium-sized heels on them. The back of the photo has a different handwriting that says, "Harrods of London 6/18/89. Clear from 2210Z to 2215Z, be ready to move right. Wall exit. Security guard's name is Paul."

Curious, I look into the back of the cubbyhole, and sure enough, at the back I see a pair of shoes. I reach in and pull them out. They have collected a little bit of dust, but I can still see their original sheen, and they seem to be in good condition. I turn to hold them up to the light and am startled to hear a woman's voice behind me.

"It's not polite to go prying through a lady's things."

I turn and find a petite young woman leaning against the wall at the opening of the hallway. The light from the chandelier is backlighting her short, curly blonde hair and making her head seem to glow. She is staring at me with a pair of bright blue eyes. She's smiling.

"I'm sorry," I say, trying to rapidly stash the shoes back in the hole they came from. "I didn't realize anyone other than Dr. Quickly had things in here."

"We tend to share."

I try to make up for the awkward beginning to our conversation by starting over. "I'm Benjamin." I walk the few feet toward her and extend my hand. She raises hers to mine and grabs it firmly.

"Mym."

"That's an unusual name," I say, now finally getting a good look at her. Her blue eyes are friendlier than her greeting had been and I get a sense of playfulness in them.

"I'm an unusual person."

"It's nice to meet you."

"Egualemente," she says.

"Feeling Spanish?"

"Maybe."

Her smile is contagious. I find myself grinning just looking at her.

"Where did you come from?"

She cocks her head slightly and considers me more seriously. "You know, I've wondered about this moment for a long time. It's different than I expected."

"You wondered about this? Catching me looking at your shoes?"

"I don't think you're doing a very good job so far."

What is she talking about?

"Not doing a very good job at what?"

"Meeting me." She leans her elbows back against a shelf behind her as she continues to appraise me.

"I didn't know there was a standard for that sort of thing," I say.

"Hmm. I was just thinking it was going to be more . . . obvious I guess."

"I'm sorry. I'm not following you. Are you suggesting we start over? I could go get your shoes again." I smile.

"No. It's just curious. You know that feeling you get sometimes when you first meet someone and it feels . . . significant?"

"Yeah. I know that feeling."

"I was thinking I would feel that."

"Are you suggesting I'm someone significant?"

"Don't you know if you are?" she asks.

"I'm significant to myself I suppose."

"Hmm. That might be the problem." She turns and walks to the railing of the balcony. I follow behind, wondering where she's come from and what on earth just happened. Looking down past her to the study floor, I see Dr. Quickly at the round center desk. After a few moments of shuffling maps, he looks up and catches sight of the young woman who has suddenly appeared in his sanctuary.

I had not thought of Dr. Quickly as ever being unhappy. His demeanor is always pleasant and cheerful enough with all of us. His expression now, at seeing the young woman leaning against the railing above him, makes me realize that I'm just now seeing him authentically happy. His face looks unapologetically elated. He doesn't say anything but his broad smile says it all. Moving to the side of Mym, I can see that Quickly's smile is matched on her face. She has the same unabashed grin.

Dr. Quickly moves swiftly up the staircase. Mym moves toward him as well. I stay put and watch as they meet at the top of the stairs. I can't make out what they say to one another. They embrace and the smiles continue. The others have noticed the new arrival also and are convening from other parts of the lab. Quickly smiles at me and waves me toward them. I follow them down the stairs toward Blake and Carson who are now at the center table. Francesca comes down from the third balcony to join us.

"I want you all to meet my daughter," Quickly says.

"Hi." Mym gives a low wave.

"Where have you been?" Quickly's voice has a tone of childlike curiosity.

"I made some new friends in '93. We did some exploring of the catacombs under Rome. Do you remember last time you took me to Rome and we met that bike shop owner named Gavino? I met his family this trip."

"Oh, Gavino is a good man. He's young in '93, no?"

"Somewhere around my age I think."

"Did you give him my regards?"

"He hasn't met you yet, Daddy."

"Oh, of course."

"He's still just as much fun as when he was older. He said he wants to build me a bicycle too."

"What did you tell him?"

"Well I wasn't going to refuse. His bikes are amazing. Can we gravitize a bike?"

"I suppose we could. I don't know where you would put it though. You may just want him to hang on to it for you to use there."

"Yeah. I guess. There are a lot of places I would like to have a bike for though. That road along those cliffs in Ireland would be fun again on a bike. It would be less scary than your driving."

"The wrong side of the road was harder than it looked. Also that car was rather obstinate if I recall." Quickly smiles. He turns his attention back to us. "I'm sorry. Mym, I would like you to meet Carson, Francesca, Benjamin and Blake."

"I'll do my best to remember all of those." She smiles at the others and turns her eyes back to me. "I already met Ben here trying to steal my shoes."

"Oh?" Quickly looks at me.

"Sadly they weren't my size," I reply.

Quickly gestures toward the armchairs near the windows. "Why don't we sit down and chat. It will be good for them to hear from another time traveler other than myself. I'm sure they're tired of my lectures by now. We've been learning a bit of navigation today."

"Oh, researching," Mym says. "My least favorite part of blinking."

"Blinking?" Carson asks.

"Oh, yeah. That's just what I call it. It always feels like blinking to me. I know Dad calls it jumping, or traveling or whatever. It has lots of names. I know a guy who calls it 'badooshing.' I think he just likes hearing himself say the word 'badoosh.'"

"I like blinking," Francesca says.

"I'm definitely going to make up my own word," Carson says.

"So you got to go to Ireland and Rome?" Francesca asks.

"Yes, Rome is great. We went before when I was younger, but it's nice to be back now that I actually look older than eighteen, so I can drink the wine. Not that the Italian guys really care."

"There was a lot more to do in Rome than drinking," Dr. Quickly chides.

"I know, Dad. It's just part of the experience. You don't want me to grow up without fully appreciating foreign culture do you?"

"As long as culture can keep their hands off my daughter, I'm fine with it."

"I love you, Dad. Don't worry, I have a really handy way out of awkward situations." She pulls at a thin gold chain around her neck and draws a shiny object out of her shirt.

Her chronometer is an orb-shaped pendant. It has a glass face that shows some of the inner workings of the device. The adjustment rings appear to be on the sides circumnavigating the face. There is a pin on top where a watch fob might be. It's smaller than our chronometers, but I can see even from a distance that it is intricately more complex.

"Why didn't we electrocute ourselves somewhere exotic like Rome?" Francesca says as she smacks Blake in the arm.

"Hey!" Blake rubs his arm. "I didn't pick it."

"I'm blaming you. I should have time traveled holding something cool instead of a stupid softball bench. I could have had dreamy Italian guys, but no, I got you guys in eighties St. Pete."

"Maybe we can stop by Italy on the way home," I say.

"Yes. And if you want to swing by Spain too while we are at it, I would be good with that. Doctor, do you have any good Spanish paraphernalia?"

"See if you can work that into your navigation practice," Quickly replies.

"I can find you a nice bull horn from Pamplona to land you on," Carson says. "See how you do at bull riding."

Mym lays her hand on Dr. Quickly's arm. "Dad, do you mind if I have a word in private?"

"Of course."

The two of them stand. Mym's eyes linger on mine for a brief moment, but then she turns and they head for the back of the lab.

"She seems cool," I say.

"Yeah, definitely," Carson says. "Cute too." His eyes have trailed her out of the room.

"Typical," Francesca says.

"What? I can say a girl is cute, can't I?" Carson says.

"I thought you were all into Tasha or Tisha, or whatever her name was from the bar the other night," Francesca says.

"It was Tanya," Carson says.

"Was she the one who sang the Elton John song?" Blake asks.

"No, that one was Tasha," Carson says.

"Oh good," Blake replies. "She was terrible."

My eyes stray to the back of the lab. "I wonder what she had to talk to him about."

"She probably just needed to chat with him without a bunch of random new people listening in. It seems like they were apart for a while," Francesca says.

When Quickly and Mym don't come back for a bit, we go back to our navigation planning. I collect the photos and items that I've gathered so far, and set them on the table on the second floor balcony. I have a doorknob, a portion of a trash can lid, a metal vise and a blue handle from a street-side mailbox. The doorknob photo is a long shot of a door inside the St. Petersburg Coliseum in 2002. The vise appears to be in someone's garage sometime in 1989. The trash can lid is in an alley in 1994. The mailbox handle photo shows a mailbox in my own neighborhood around 2006. I stare at that photo the longest. *So close to home.* I still need more.

IN TIMES LIKE THESE

Many of the cubbies that Quickly has labeled don't have any objects in them at all. They hold photos of objects that were much too big to collect. The backs of the photos include addresses where one can find them. I see flagpoles and old cars. There are a few statues and landmarks I recognize, but most are unassuming objects. There are fence poles, parking meters, stop signs and a myriad of other everyday items. While many are in Florida or in St. Petersburg specifically, I run across plenty of other cities and countries also. One of the cubbies that catches my eye holds a bronze spearhead, and the photo lists its location as a museum in Calcutta in 1945.

I wonder how far he's been back?

I learn to recognize Quickly's handwriting easily, his long lettered cursive flows across the backs of the photos in fluid strokes. As I keep searching, I also recognize more and more in the loopy feminine hand that I now know to be Mym's. Her object selection is distinct from Quickly's as well. Where his objects and photos are primarily simple functional items, I see that Mym has taken a more artistic approach to both the photos and the items she has selected.

I pick up a tarnished, silver knight chess piece. The accompanying photo shows it on the edge of a small stone table. A lone pawn sits next to it, but a few feet away, the remaining pieces still occupy a chessboard. I can see neither of the players, but in the background of the table is an immense stained glass window streaming multicolored light onto the game. The window is set in a stone wall that reminds me of a castle. The knight piece in the photo is polished and shining in contrast to the one in my hand, but the photo paper still looks new.

Did she bring the film back and develop it later? How old is this?

The back of the photo doesn't hold any clues to the location. It only states, "A great game in the making." There is no date listed.

I guess I'm not using that one.

I poke around a few more cubbies before rounding the corner of the shelf toward the early nineties. Some of the holes here are larger. I stoop to peer into some of the lower ones and my eye catches on an odd dome shape. I squat down and reach my hand into the hole and remove an empty tortoise shell. It's about eight inches in diameter and bumpy all over. The most unique thing about it is that there are two lines of faded red paint running from front to back on the shell. *What kind of tortoise has racing stripes?*

Curious, I look for the photo. When I pull it out, I see a shot of a wide expanse of desert populated by a few Joshua trees and some sparse vegetation. The tortoise shell in the photo is still occupied by a benevolent looking creature, munching on a weed in the shade of a large rock. There is nothing beyond it except rolling desert hills stretching to the horizon. I flip over to the back of the photo to read the description and immediately shoot to my feet.

That's my handwriting!

I back up into the light to read the two lines of writing more clearly.

"May 20th 1990, 2310:32 Z Ten minute window. For use when all hope is lost."

Holy shitballs. What am I supposed to do about this?

I take the shell and walk back to the main study. I hear voices above me and see Blake and Francesca chatting over items on the highest balcony. Carson is on the balcony above me browsing through a book. I consider calling to him but stop myself. *I need Quickly.* I trot down the steps to the main floor and turning away from the windows, head down the hallway that leads to the rear lab rooms. The first couple rooms I pass are empty, so I poke my head into the kitchen and dining area. Nobody. I continue down the hall to some of the practice chambers but they are likewise empty. I consider turning back to the study when I hear voices from behind one of the doors in the corner of the hallway. I'm about to knock, when I hear Mym shout, "You have to!"

I put my ear to the door and listen.

"Dad, we haven't come all this way to risk our lives now. I know you like them. I do too, but you also know what happens here. You know why we need to leave."

"They're not ready," Quickly responds.

"They're not supposed to be ready. They never were before, but that's how it works out. They have to be unprepared. He said it had to be that way." Mym's voice sounds closer than Quickly's through the door.

"I have worked so hard to find their original timestream." Quickly sounds more agitated than I have ever heard him before. "All the signs seem to verify that it begins there. The tests I've done are holding. The frequencies are right, all of it. I don't want to leave something undone and have it all unravel. This one will be too complicated to try to redo."

"I don't want to screw your tests up either, but some things are more important than experiments, Dad. You're the one who taught me the rules. Keep together. Avoid unnecessary risks. Never choose the unknown when the known is available. THIS is unknown AND an unnecessary risk."

"It's not unnecessary for them. It might be that the most necessary information is yet to come."

"We at least need to get you out. You gave them the basics. They know more than I did the first time I blinked. They definitely know more than you did. We survived," Mym says.

"We were incredibly fortunate. They have been too. I don't want to push the limits of that good fortune," Quickly replies.

"I don't want you to die! That's my motivation. You always told me to avoid witnessing natural disasters because they were too unpredictable. This guy is a natural disaster. He's the most unpredictable thing we've ever dealt with. That's why we should do what we always do and get the fuck out of here!"

"You know I don't like that language."

"Sorry, Dad, but you know I'm right. You told me to be back in time to get you. Here I am."

"Okay, I'll get them as ready as I can by—"

The rest of his words are drowned out by the ringing of the telephone in the room behind me. There are still snippets of talking behind the door, but I can't make it out over the persistent ringing. I do hear the footsteps however, and I back away from the door, uncertain of what to do with myself. The door swings open and Mym emerges with quick strides in my direction. She slows a moment at the sight of me, but then continues past.

"Your turtle fell out."

I'm too caught off guard to come up with a response. "Yeah," I stammer.

Brilliant comeback.

She disappears into the room with the phone and I hear her pick it up. I peek my head into the room she came out of. Dr. Quickly is standing with his back to me, facing a window that looks into an office space bustling with workers. I see professionally dressed men and women typing at bulky word processors and typewriters and milling about the office space, seemingly oblivious to Quickly's observation. I'm so captivated by the situation that it takes a moment to see that Quickly is actually observing me in the reflection in the glass.

"For them it's a mirror." His voice is calm now.

"Oh. Hey. That's pretty cool. So they have no idea your lab is over here?"

"I believe the night janitor might be on to me actually. He seems more observant than most. I saw him counting out steps along one of the hallways one night on the video monitor. I believe he was trying to figure out why the interior spaces don't match up. But he's the exception. These folks are too concerned with their own doings to notice mine."

I walk up beside Quickly and share his observation of the office.

"I almost envy them some days," he continues. "Ignorance has its perks. I've almost forgotten what it's like to have an uncomplicated existence." Quickly's eyes stray to the tortoise shell in my hands but he doesn't comment on it.

"Yeah," I begin. "About that. I was wondering . . ."

Mym reappearing in the doorway stops me. "Hey, sorry to interrupt, but it seems important. The phone was someone named Robbie. He said he's at the hospital and you should come right away. He said you would know what it was about."

Quickly hands me his car keys. "Take the Galaxie."

I take his keys in my free hand and head for the door. He calls to me as I'm about to walk out.

"And Benjamin!"

"Yes?"

"Do me a favor and check the air in the spare tire for me, would you?"

"Um. Okay."

"I'd hate for you to get left flat somewhere."

I think we have bigger worries than flat tires right now.

"Okay, I'll check it out," I say.

Mym steps aside for me. I catch her eye and for a moment she looks as if she's going to say something serious to me. The moment passes. She looks down at my hands. "I hope you find your turtle."

"Thanks."

I sprint for the study to find my friends.

Chapter 13

"I like to believe that my discovery of time travel was for the betterment of mankind, but I must be honest with myself. It has spawned its share of weirdos"
-Excerpt from the journal of Dr. Harold Quickly, 2088

The plastic chairs in the hospital waiting area are torture. I can feel the circulation being cut off in my legs after a few minutes in any one of them. No matter how I shift myself, there is no way to get comfortable. I give up and go sit on the floor, leaning my back against the wall opposite the chairs.

Francesca has found a way to nod off leaning on Blake's shoulder. Blake is awake but lost in his own thoughts. Carson had sat with us for a while but has wandered off somewhere now. Robbie has alternated between sitting and pacing the floor. He is back to his pacing phase. A muted television in the corner shows a pair of couples competing for a car in front of a bank vault. Without the sound, the game show makes very little sense to me.

Robbie checks the clock on the wall for the hundredth time, then walks over and slumps against the wall next to me. "The not knowing is killing me."

"Yeah. I'm glad you were able to get him here though."

"He just collapsed right in the middle of the yard," Robbie says. "I was lucky to be able to get him into the car. I drove like a madman getting here. Surprised I didn't run somebody over."

"You're a good grandson."

I don't really know what else to say.

"I hope it worked."

I pat him on the knee and we lapse back to silence. *I wonder if I could just jump ahead a few hours to see how things turn out, and then come back and tell him.* I ponder the possibility for a few minutes but realize that if Mr. Cameron doesn't make it, I'm not really interested in knowing it yet. *Quickly was right, sometimes ignorance can be better.*

My head is beginning to nod, when Carson reappearing out of the elevator brings me back to attention. "Guys, you need to see this." He heads for the television. Not seeing a remote anywhere, he reaches for the dial and twists it until he lands on a station showing a news report. As he hunts for the volume control, I see the shot of the news anchor change to a scene of firefighters and trucks battling a building fire. I get up from the floor and walk closer to the screen to get a better look.

"What is it?" Francesca fights a yawn.

"Whoa, is that what I think it is?" Blake asks.

The shot widens out to show the reporter in front of a large, glass-fronted building with a massive hole in the side of it. The building is engulfed in smoke as firefighters discharge multiple hoses into the flaming breach.

"That looks like the lab!" Francesca exclaims.

"It is the lab," Carson says, as he dials up the sound.

We stand incredulous as the reporter describes the catastrophic damage to the building.

"Quickly" Francesca whispers.

Mym.

I check the clock on the wall. "How long have we been here?"

"Three, four hours now?" Robbie replies.

"One of us should get over there," Blake says. "See what's going on."

"We should make sure Dr. Quickly and his daughter are okay," Francesca adds.

"I'll go." Carson seems eager to have a reason to get out of the hospital.

"I'll go too," I say. "We can come back soon, Robbie, and let you know what happened."

"I'll stay here with you." Francesca grabs Robbie's arm.

"Blake?" I ask.

Blake is hesitant. He looks from the screen to Robbie and Francesca, and then says, "I'll stay. You don't need me there."

I pull the car keys from my pocket and Carson and I head for the hallway. "Be careful," Francesca calls after us.

"We will," I say. "We'll be back soon."

Ninth Street is completely shut down with emergency vehicles as we get close, and traffic is being detoured through the residential neighborhoods to either side. I park the Galaxie a couple blocks west of the lab and we work our way toward it on foot. Other curious pedestrians from the neighborhood have also gathered to check out the spectacle.

By the time we get close enough to see the building, the fire is out. A single ladder truck is still spraying a stream of water into the hole that stretches from the second floor to the fifth.

"All of our planning has been destroyed," Carson says. "Whatever wasn't burned is sure to be water damaged."

"Do you have your logbook?" I ask.

"No. I left it in the study when we left. You have yours?"

"No. Mine is in there too."

Ash from the building is floating down out of the sky around us and settling on cars and observers alike. I brush some of it out of my hair as I walk toward the nearest firefighter. A police officer steps into my path with his hands raised. "Please keep back."

"Do you know what caused the fire?" I ask.

"Please just keep the area clear and let the fire department work."

He doesn't know.

"We have some friends who were in that building," Carson says. "How do we find out if they've gotten out?"

The police officer considers Carson for a moment. "You can try phoning the department. Information will be made available to family members as necessary."

"Do you know what time the fire started?" I ask.

The officer seems to consider whether giving that information would do any harm and apparently decides it won't. "I got the call around seven."

"Thanks. Come on Carson," I say, tapping him on the arm. We turn and walk back toward the car. "I have an idea. Do you remember what time we left the lab to get to the hospital?"

"I don't know. Sun was still up. Five, five-thirty maybe?"

"Right. We were definitely already at the hospital by the time the sun went down. So how about this? We find somewhere safe to make a jump. We go back to just after we left for the hospital, get ahold of Quickly or Mym and get back into the lab, and we can get our stuff. We might even be able to figure out what causes the fire in the first place, and stop it."

"Would we want to stop it though?" Carson asks. "How would we have ever gotten to this point if the place never burns down?"

"Oh. True. That might make one of those paradoxes Quickly has talked about." *No way I want to end up lost somewhere.* "We can at least check it out. Wouldn't hurt to know why the place burned down."

"I'm game," Carson says. "I've been wanting to try some more outdoor time jumps. Way more exciting than the lab. Do you think we should tell the others first?"

"As long as we don't screw it up, we should be back before they ever realize we're gone. I guess we could leave a note or something just in case."

We walk back to the car and I rummage through the glove box for a slip of paper to use. Finding nothing, I try the pocket in the door and find a receipt for gas that will work. I think for a second, then scribble out our message.

"Gone back a couple of hours to get our stuff. Left at . . . "I check the clock on the car dashboard, "10:25. Should be back by 11—Ben and Carson."

I shove the slip of paper under the windshield wiper and shut the door. I see my tortoise shell rock back and forth on the floor in the passenger side where I left it. *Shouldn't need that. Not losing hope yet.*

"So now what?" Carson asks.

"I guess we need a place to blink from." I look at the neighborhood around us. "Maybe we could try that mailbox?" I point to a nondescript house across from us.

"Couldn't we just use the car?" Carson asks. "We know where it was a few hours ago."

"I don't see why not," I say. "As long as we don't get hit by traffic or something." I assess the car and try to visualize the clearest place to be around it. "I think we should get on top of it."

"Better not scratch Quickly's paint job," Carson says. "He loves this car."

"Considering his lab just exploded, I don't imagine a few scratches will fluster him," I reply.

I'm careful anyway as I climb onto the back of the trunk. I dangle my feet off the back of the car as Carson positions himself next to me.

"So what are you thinking? Five hours maybe?" Carson asks.

"Yeah, sun has been setting around six these days. Gets dark maybe an hour after? Sun was definitely up when we left so we need to land on the car at least before five-thirty, otherwise we risk ending up on the car at the hospital, or worse, we land on the back of it while we're driving to the hospital. That would suck."

"Ha. I hadn't even thought of that. We should probably shoot for earlier. We can always watch ourselves leave. That would be cool," Carson says.

"That's a weird experience," I say. "All right. Let's aim for five o'clock." We both dial in our chronometer settings. *Switch the slider to back. Not going to screw this one up.* I triple check my settings before I'm confident.

"Ready?" Carson asks.

"Ready."

"Let's do it." Carson straightens up briefly, looks straight ahead and disappears.

Wow, that's still crazy. Here we go again.

I push the pin.

We're on Ninth Street. Traffic is light, so no one is shocked by our sudden arrival. I look diagonally across the street and realize that we're in view of the large windows of the lab. "We need to move. Fast."

We slide off the trunk and head south down the sidewalk, past the car and away from the lab. The first available means to get out of sight is a walkway between two storefronts. We step around the corner into the walkway and stop near an air conditioning unit.

"So we just need to wait for the other us's to leave and we should be good, yeah?" Carson asks.

"Yeah. I think so. I guess we can just wait here. I don't think we're going to bother anybody. They might see us when they drive past though."

"Let's just head around back when we see them coming out," Carson says.

I look down the walkway to where it connects to the back parking lot. "Should work."

"So we get in, grab our stuff, and Blake's and Francesca's," Carson says. "Are we going to take our practice navigation stuff, or do we need to look for more?"

"All of our stuff should be useful, since we were trying to plan for the real trip anyway," I say. "I know Quickly never got to review any of it, but hopefully it can get us there. Maybe if Quickly is in there, we can get him to help us check it."

"Yeah, that's true. Unless he left too," Carson adds.

"Let's hope he got out at some point. That fire looked awful," I say.

"Hey, how are we going to get into the lab? Does he have a lab key on that set of car keys he gave you?"

I grab at my pocket for the keys but don't feel them. I check my other pockets. "Shit. I must have left them in the car." I move toward the car for a moment, then realize it won't help me. *Damn it. That's hours from now.* Movement catches my eye beyond the car. Carson's red hair suddenly stands out, and I see that he and Francesca have just walked out of the side street next to the lab onto the sidewalk.

"No worries, I got this," the Carson next to me says, as he moves the dials on his chronometer and sprints to the front end of the Galaxie, twenty yards ahead of us.

"Wait, Carson, we're coming!" I call to him, but I can't tell if he hears me. He slides smoothly up onto the hood of the car and instantly disappears.

A hundred yards farther on I see my friends and myself crossing the street.

No! No no no. This is not good.

The group passes out of view behind some vehicles. I hold my breath. I see Blake and me step onto the sidewalk past the parked cars and instinctively jerk my head back behind the corner, but then there's Carson, back on top of the Galaxie.

He slides off the front of the hood and walks casually toward me, his back to the other versions of us. He smiles and jingles the keys in his hand as he cruises right past me and heads for the back parking lot.

Of course. He's good at everything, why wouldn't he be great at this?

I sneak one more peek around the corner at the earlier versions of us, walking obliviously toward the car, and then turn and follow Carson.

"Nice job, man. That was smooth," I say, as I join him in the parking lot.

"Thanks. It may have bumped back our return a smidge. I didn't leave there again till ten-fifty. Took me a few minutes to double-check my settings for coming back. I've never tried to hit such a small window of time before." He smiles.

"You did great. They never noticed you at all. A few more seconds and who knows what would have happened."

The dumpster behind the building smells like stale coffee and something dead. We move away from it and exit the parking lot into the alley, taking it back to the street to look for the car.

"It's gone. We're in the clear," Carson says.

I glance up at the shining reflective windows of Quickly's building and wonder who might be watching us as we dash across the street. We move around the side of the building till we find the door that leads to the lab. Some of the other side doors along the alley are labeled with business names or "No Soliciting" signs. Quickly's entrance is a steel door, painted a rust red with no markings whatsoever. The two locks on the door appear to have different mechanisms, so I scour the keychain for possible candidates. I find the key to the doorknob lock on my third try. The deadbolt takes me longer, but after going through each of the keys on the ring, the last one fits. The satisfying click of the bolt sliding back heralds our entry.

I wonder if Quickly has a security system? I survey the outside wall of the building but don't see anything that looks like a camera. *Doesn't mean he doesn't have one though.* We slip inside and proceed down the short hallway to the stairwell. There are a couple of other doors in the hallway that I've not paid much attention to before. Now they are a mystery I will never get a chance to solve. *No time for exploring in a soon to be burning building.*

"You have a key to this one?" Carson asks after he tries the handle. The stairwell door is steel as well, but painted a sky blue. I fumble through the keys again and this time I get it on the second try. The stairwell is dark and I see no switches. We walk a few steps and are soon engulfed in darkness. Ten steps up we hit a landing and I navigate the turn with my hands sliding along the walls. It's another ten steps till the second landing.

"I think the door is here somewhere," I say.

"Got it," Carson says from beside me.

This door isn't locked. The fluorescent hallway lights illuminate us as Carson opens the door. The hallway is empty. We take it left and then left again out to the study, and emerge under the second balcony. The study is silent and the orange light of the setting sun is streaming through the window.

"Dr. Quickly?" I call to the upper balconies. Silence answers.

"Maybe they're in one of the back lab rooms," Carson says.

"Yeah. Could be. Let's grab our stuff and then see if we can find them."

"We're going to need something to carry this stuff in," Carson says.

"Okay. See if you can consolidate everybody's things. I'll look in the back and see what I can find. I think I saw some backpacks in the jumpsuit lockers."

Carson starts climbing to the upper balconies as I walk back down the hallway toward the kitchen. The hallways in the lab still confuse me. It takes me a few wrong turns before I remember that the lockers were on the next floor up. I locate the stairway and head up to the next floor. The second level of the lab is a combination of jump rooms, lab spaces and some classrooms. I pass the room where I first saw Quickly disappear. Three turns later I find the hallway with the lockers. Scanning the contents of the first locker, I slide the jumpsuits aside and check the floor. I see a pair of Francesca's flip-flops. I open a few more lockers to see what I can find. I come up with some socks, a couple of blank logbooks, and finally what I'm looking for, four canvas backpacks. I snag the flip-flops and the logbooks and stuff them into a pack. I consider for a moment, then grab the socks and one of the jumpsuits too. It feels a bit like stealing. *The place is going to burn down, Benjamin. If anything, you're doing Quickly a favor by saving things.*

143

I take the four packs by the straps and carry them like luggage around the corner. I make a couple more turns before I hit a dead end. Without any windows to the outside, I have a hard time knowing which direction I'm facing. *I just need to find the stairs.* I backtrack to the lockers and am going the other direction, when I hear a door slam.

"Carson?" I call.

Carson is up in the balconies in the study. There aren't any doors through to here, are there?

I walk back to the lockers and turn down a side hallway of blue jump room doors. It's quiet. I open one of the doors and see nothing but an empty anchor stand in the center of the room. I walk inside past the anchor stand to the green door on the far side, and as I twist open the doorknob with my free fingers, I glimpse someone's backside walking past the door. I swing the door open with my foot and poke my head out into the hallway, spying the figure of a man walking away from me.

"Dr. Quickly?"

The man turns and I see that it is Dr. Quickly, but he looks younger than I've ever seen him. There is only a sprinkle of gray on the hair that protrudes from under a baseball cap.

"Hello," he says with a smile. "I wondered when I might meet some new faces around here. "I don't believe I've had the pleasure." He takes a couple of steps toward me and extends a hand.

"Oh, hi. I'm Benjamin." I drop two of the packs and shake his hand.

"What's your last name, Benjamin?"

"Travers."

"I'm Harry. Though you seem to know that."

"Yes. Well . . . I've met you before, or later I guess. I'm not sure how phrasing that works."

"Ah. Future me. Please say no more. Still not sure how much I should know about my own future, though I have run into myself a couple of times now and seem not to have hurt anything. It's not an exact science yet, this time traveling, by any means."

"What are you doing here?" I ask.

"Just passing through, currently," he says, smiling. "I use these jump rooms to come and go. It's a relatively secure location the way I've got things worked out. Has the future me explained the use of these rooms to you?"

"We made some short blinks in here."

"Blinks?" he says.

"Oh, yeah, time jumps? Blinks is just the name your . . . um . . .one of your associates made up." *Does he know he has a daughter yet?*

"Ah. I see."

"But we only stayed in the rooms. We didn't really come and go."

"Oh, well the color-coded doors are my system of knowing which door to leave from and know how not to run into myself. I usually set up the anchors and leave out the blue door. When I arrive after using an anchor, I leave out the green door so I don't run into the other version of me. There are tunnel exits that lead to different areas around town."

"That makes sense," I say. "I saw the ladders on the way in. Does that mean the other version of you is close by somewhere? Maybe in the tunnel? Because I was actually hoping to talk to him."

"Oh. I don't know. This was one of the anchors I set up a while back. Would have been a younger version of me that set that up. I'm afraid I have no idea where this older me has wandered off to."

"You might want to be careful. Something bad is going to happen here soon," I say.

"Oh, you probably shouldn't tell me," he says, and puts his hands in his pockets. I can tell he is thinking about the possibilities. He gazes past me a moment before his eyes come back to mine. "How bad are we talking?"

"The building is going to catch on fire in a few hours," I say.

He looks at the four backpacks in my hands. His eyes grow suddenly serious. "It's not you burning it down, is it?"

"No! I would never want to hurt this place. I just know that it's going to happen soon. I'm trying to get our stuff out before it happens. My friends and I are trying to get back to 2009. You were helping us, but I'm not sure where you are now."

Quickly takes off his hat and runs a hand through his hair. "This is getting complicated again, as always. I'm headed toward the past, so I should be safe for now, though I suppose I ought to adjust my jump plan for heading forward again, if this place is going to be on fire, like you say. What time does this happen?"

"Before seven. Not exactly sure," I say.

He consults his wrist and I notice he has a regular watch strapped next to his chronometer. He draws a leather bound notebook out of his back pocket and makes a couple of notes in it. Quickly looks at my wrist next. "What are you working with there?" I hold out my arm so he can have a look. "Oh, that looks like a later model than mine. Manembo must be working on some modifications. I will have to check in with him soon. Want to trade?" He smiles.

"Um, I kind of need this one," I say.

"Ha, I'm just kidding. I will get my own at some point it seems. No use rushing things."

"Yeah. Yours is much more advanced than this later on, I think. These are just our training models," I say.

"It certainly looks like it will do. I wouldn't have minded having that as my first device. You should have seen all the clutter I had to lug around in the beginning. I must have looked like a hobo. I even had a shopping cart involved for a bit."

"That must have been tough," I say.

"Ah well, there's a lot of trial and error in science, no matter how far in time you go. Luckily I'm still here to tell about it. It sounds like we ought to be moving along if we would like to stay that way." He extends his hand. "It was a pleasure meeting you Benjamin Travers. Till we meet again."

"Good to meet you too, sir."

Quickly gives a nod and walks back down the hall. He's about to walk into the next jump room when I call out to him. "Oh hey, Doctor Quickly?"

"Yes?"

"Can you point me to the stairs by chance?"

"Indeed." He points to the hall behind me and crooks his finger to the left. "East down that hall, second door on the right."

"Thank you."

Then he is gone.

I walk to the corner he was pointing to, pull out my pen, and reaching up under the trim, draw an arrow with the word "East."

That should help if I get lost again ... at least till the place burns down.

I find the second door on the right, and sure enough, the stairwell is beyond it. As I'm about to head through the door, I look to my left and spot a door across the hall hanging open. Through the open crack I can see an oak desk with photos on it. Even from this distance, I recognize one of them as Mym.

Curious, I cross the hall and swing open the door the rest of the way. It appears to be Dr. Quickly's private office. Behind the desk are an oak credenza and a Van Gogh painting. I inch closer to it and see the texture of the paint. *Oh God, is that an original?* I scan the office for any clues to Quickly's whereabouts. I stop at the desk and pick up the photo of Mym. She's standing in a wide-open expanse of land with a hot air balloon basket in the background. For a moment, I consider stuffing the photo in my bag.

No. Don't be a creeper, Ben. You just met this girl. I set the frame back down.

I slide open a couple desk drawers but just find stationary and pens.

I open the doors on the credenza and take a step back in shock. On the shelf inside the credenza, in neatly ordered rows, are stacks and stacks of hundred-dollar bills. The edge of the shelf has sticky labels fixed to it, telling the year the stacks of bills belong to. The years range from 1965 all the way to 2050. *There must be millions of dollars sitting there.* I stand in front of the credenza, debating for a moment, then start stuffing stacks of bills into the backpacks. *Now this really feels like stealing.*

After I have a couple dozen stacks deposited in the backpacks, I stop, because I realize I still need to fit so many anchors in there too. It's hard to leave all that cash sitting there, knowing the place is about to burn down. *We have more important things than money to worry about, Ben.* I leave the rest and walk back out of the office.

I push through the stairwell door and head downstairs, emerging on the floor below, in the hall across from the kitchen. I know my way from here and don't have any trouble making it back to the study.

"Took you long enough," Carson says as I walk out from under the balconies. He has shuttled our anchors from the upper balconies and placed them on the table in the middle of the study.

"I ran into Dr. Quickly," I say.

"Oh cool, is he going to help us with this stuff?"

"There was a complication there." I fill Carson in on my encounter with the younger Quickly as we stuff items into the backpacks.

"That's nuts," Carson says. "So different versions of Quickly are coming and going through this place all the time?"

"I guess so. He said he was headed for the past, so this must have been a sort of pit stop."

Carson wrestles a portion of chain link fence into an already stuffed backpack. "I don't think I could handle a life that complex," he grunts, finally getting the pack to close. He grabs the next pack and notes the stacks of bills in it. He holds one up. "What's this?"

"A little traveling money," I say.

"Sweet." Carson thumbs the stack and then stuffs it back into the bag.

I check the clock on the wall. *Almost six.* I scan the walls of cubbies above us. "What else do you think we should grab?"

A crash from somewhere in the back of the lab startles me into silence. It's followed by a couple of shouts. "What was that?" Carson says.

"I don't know."

147

We start to move toward the hallway when a pair of loud bangs stops us. "That sounded like gunshots," Carson says. "We should get out of here."

"What if someone is shooting at Quickly?" I say. *Or Mym.*

"We didn't bring a gun to this party, so I don't know what good we can do." Carson picks up two of the packs as I slip over to the entrance of the hallway and peek around the corner. The hallway is empty but I can still hear noises. "Ben. Come on!" Carson whispers.

I grab the other two packs off the table. I sling one over my shoulder and carry the other. "That's our way out anyway, if we're going to get this stuff outside."

I walk back to the corner and peek around it again. It's still clear. We move quietly toward the adjoining hallway that runs in front of the kitchen and make a right. The exit stairwell door is just ahead of us on the right when at the far end of the hall, a figure walks backward into view from the left. He's aiming a gun down the hallway he's just come from. We freeze. The man still has the gun aimed down the other hallway when he turns his head and sees us. Confusion contorts the face of the last person in the world I want to encounter. Stenger.

He swings the gun toward us and scowls. In his other hand, he's holding something colorful. I recognize it as a Rubik's Cube.

"I've had enough of your tricks."

I raise my hands. "We don't want any trouble."

"Ha! A little late for that. Give me the watches." Stenger takes a couple of steps toward us. We're trapped. There's a door to the left of Carson but it leads to a classroom. The door to the stairs is between Stenger and us on the right. *I could sprint back out to the study and try to get out the stairs to the tunnel, but in the small hallway with no room to maneuver, he'll probably just shoot me in the back.*

Carson sets his two packs on the floor and puts his hand to his chronometer.

"Toss it here," Stenger says.

Carson gives me a quick look, and I get the sense he's trying to convey something to me but I don't understand what. The next moment he grabs the doorknob of the room to the left, and vanishes.

Why didn't I think of that?

Anger burns in Stenger's eyes as he swings the gun from where Carson has disappeared and points it at me.

"You know it's probably easier just to take it off your body—"

I've been holding the backpack in my hands in front of me as a shield between us. I toss it at Stenger's face. He reels backward a step but stays standing. He's about to aim the gun at me again when Carson reappears behind him and tackles him. The gun and the Rubik's Cube both hit the ground and skid past me as Carson and Stenger crash to the floor. I jump after the gun and go down on one knee as I grab it. I spin and aim it at Stenger's head as he lashes backward with his elbows at Carson who is holding him down with a knee in his back.

"Stop moving!" I yell.

Stenger sees me pointing the gun and stops. He holds his hands up ahead of him, a few inches off the floor. Carson relaxes his grip on him. Pounding footsteps echo from the hall that Stenger came from. I can't see anything but it sounds like multiple people.

Did Stenger bring friends?

"Come on, Carson. Let's get out of here!"

Carson grabs the pack I threw at Stenger and we move hastily toward the stairwell door. I keep the gun aimed at Stenger's head till we're through. The moment before the door slams shut I see him sneer. We plummet down the stairs, jumping as many steps as we dare, and crash out into the lower hallway. Carson kicks open the alley door and we sprint for the street.

"Shit. I forgot the car is gone," I pant, when we reach the other side of the street.

"What now?" Carson says.

My hands are shaking. I find the safety on the gun and set it, then stuff it into one of the packs Carson is carrying. "Let's get out of sight." We cut back down the same path between buildings we used earlier. Passing the smelly dumpster, I turn left and head for the cross street. We keep up a steady jog till we reach an alley to turn down, and then I slow to a walk. "God, that was scary. Thank you for tackling him."

"No problem," Carson pants.

"Where did you go?" I say. "Before you came back."

"Not far. I just jumped back to about ten minutes before. I'm guessing you were still upstairs, and I would have been in the balconies. It took me a minute to figure out what to use to get behind Stenger, but finally I just used the wall. I was worried it wasn't going to be conductive enough, but it worked out."

"It was brilliant." I walk over and give him a quick hug. "You saved my life, man."

"No sweat, dude." He pats me on the back. "You would have done the same for me."

"That was some quick thinking." I shoulder my second pack.

"So what's the plan now? We still have a couple of hours till we can get the car back."

"I vote we stash this stuff somewhere safe, blink back to eleven o'clock and retrieve it. We can go get the car then and get back to the hospital. They're probably worried about us."

"They aren't yet, we haven't even left the hospital," Carson says.

"Oh yeah. Well they ought to be worried after what we just went through. I can't wait to tell them this one."

We continue down the alley, keeping an eye out for good hiding spaces for our stuff. We finally settle on an old 1950s truck that we find behind someone's garage. The fabric cover over the truck is mildewed and dirty and one look under the canvas shows us that the truck is not likely to be moving anytime soon. We make sure no one is watching, then stuff our packs into the bed of the truck, careful to replace the cover how we found it.

We find our jump location only a couple of houses down.

"Boats work great." Carson points to a center console fishing boat on a trailer next to a garage apartment. The layer of leaves on the floor of the boat gives away that, like the pickup truck, the boat hasn't seen much action recently.

"Should be good for a few hours," I say. I climb into the back of the boat and initially sit on one of the cushioned seats but then think better of it. I move to the bow and position myself so I'm balanced on the two rails. "Be careful not to be anywhere a leaf is likely to fall in the next few hours," I caution.

Carson heeds my advice and perches on the stern rail near the motor.

"I'm going to plan for five after eleven." I set my chronometer for 0305 Zulu.

"Ready?" Carson says.

"Ready."

A scent of smoke reaches me and I turn in the direction of the lab. Looking over the garage across the alley, I can make out the top of Quickly's building. An orange glow is emanating from the middle windows.

I turn back to my task at hand. This time it's me who blinks first. I push the pin and watch Carson disappear.

Chapter 14

"I once met a time traveler who insisted on only traveling to his own birthdays. He claimed he was over a thousand years old. I found the idea rather ridiculous, but I have to admit, he did get a lot of free drinks that way."
-Excerpt from the journal of Dr. Harold Quickly, 2115

The parking garage at the hospital is quiet as we pull in. The hospital lobby is likewise subdued. The gift shop is closed and a janitor has a buffer working on the floors. Carson and I take the elevator to the third floor. The waiting room where we left our friends is deserted. I find the charge nurse at her desk.

"Excuse me. We're here visiting Robert Cameron."

The white-haired woman looks up from her paperwork. "Visiting hours are over."

"I think our friends might already be in there," I say.

"Are you with the group that was waiting earlier?" the nurse asks.

"Yes, we just had to step out for a bit."

"Okay, your friends are still back there. Room 328. Just try not to make too much noise. Most of the patients are sleeping."

"Thank you."

She buzzes us through the double doors. We're passing room 316 when I see Blake and Francesca emerge from a room ahead. They turn our direction, still talking to one another, but after a moment Francesca spots us.

"Hey," I say.

"Hey," Blake responds.

"Good news." Francesca smiles. "He's going to be okay,"

"What happened?" Carson asks.

"The doctor said he had a minor stroke," Blake replies. "Apparently it could have been a lot worse if Robbie hadn't rushed him in."

Francesca gives me a hug.

"Is Robbie still in there?" I gesture toward the room they came from.

"Yeah. What did you guys find out?" Blake says.

"That's a pretty crazy story."

"Stenger must have burned the lab," Carson says.

"You saw him?" Francesca asks.

"Carson actually tackled him. He tried to kill us and take our chronometers."

"Where was this?" Blake asks.

"Inside the lab," I reply.

"You guys went into a burning building?" Francesca says.

"No. Not exactly." I tell them the story of our plan to get our stuff back and how the night unfolded. We walk back through the doors and take seats in the waiting room again as I'm talking. Carson interjects whenever I leave something out.

"Wow," Francesca says. "You guys are really lucky."

"Yeah. Glad you're both okay," Blake adds. "So no sign of Quickly? Other than the younger one you ran into?"

"No. Hopefully they got out okay. I think they were planning on leaving anyway." I tell them about the conversation I overheard before we left for the hospital. Carson leans forward to listen to this also. "It sounded like Mym was back to get Dr. Quickly and leave."

"He did say he was only going to be in 1986 for a little while," Francesca says.

"He didn't even say goodbye though?" Carson asks. "That's kind of odd.'"

"No. He just asked me to check the spare tire," I say. "It was very odd."

"Did you check it?" Francesca says.

"No, we didn't really have a chance. We were kind of busy."

"What if it was a clue?" Francesca says. "What if he was trying to tell you something?"

"Why the secrecy?" I say. "Why not just tell me if he was trying to tell me something?"

"I still think you should check it," Francesca says.

"Yeah, I suppose so."

Robbie emerges from the double doors and we get out of our chairs. "Hey guys."

"Hey. Is he doing okay?" I ask.

"Yeah, he's sleeping. The doctors have him on some medication to help him sleep through the night. They said we can come back in the morning."

"Want to head back to the house?" Blake says.

"Yeah." Robbie nods. He looks exhausted.

As we make for the exit, Robbie inquires after our trip to the lab and I give him the condensed version of the story. "You guys are ballsy going in there like that," he says. "Not sure I would have gone back in, knowing the place was going to burn."

"Yeah, thanks for doing that," Francesca says. "I'm glad you got our stuff out."

In the garage, I grab the packs out of the back seat of the Galaxie and have Carson pop the trunk. As the trunk lid yawns open, I see nothing but carpet inside.

"Where's the spare?" Francesca says.

"Under this maybe?" I drop the packs on the ground and tug at the edge of the carpeting. I pull it back part way to reveal the tire. It's white-walled like the others and appears to be in good condition. I press hard on the sidewall of the tire with my thumb. "Looks like it's decently inflated. Not sure what else he wanted me to check."

"Maybe you should pull it out," Francesca says.

"That's what she said," Carson mutters. Francesca takes a swing with the back of her hand and smacks Carson in the shoulder.

I grab the wheel and remove it from under the carpet. As I do, I hear something fall off the back and land in the wheel well. Leaning the spare tire against the bumper, I pull the carpet back the rest of the way.

"What's that?" Blake asks, peering over my shoulder. I reach in and extract a small leather bound journal. It has a thin cord tied around it.

"This looks like the book Quickly was taking notes in when I ran into him earlier. The young Quickly." I untie the cord and pull open the front cover. There is a quote handwritten on the front page. I read it out loud. "To everything there is a season, and a time for every purpose under heaven. Ecclesiastes 3:1."

"Never would have pegged Quickly as the religious type," Carson says.

"I think there are a lot of things we might not know about that guy," Blake replies.

I flip through a few more pages. Each is full of handwritten notes and occasional drawings. I see sketches of chronometers, both the watch type like ours, and pendants like Mym's. I even see versions incorporated into other objects like hats and belts. There are journal entries listing activities and dates. On one page I see a list of objects he notes as having been treated with gravitites. I pause when I notice there's a groundhog on the list.

"Apparently there's a time traveling groundhog somewhere."

"He would make better weather predictions than Punxsutawney Phil," Francesca says.

I skim to the last few pages of the journal where I find a list of names and addresses. Along with each name is a list of date ranges. Some of the date ranges are not consistent, but jump around and skip years.

"Who do you think they are?" Francesca says, leaning in close to read the names.

"I think they might be other time travelers." I read out loud. "Martin Sambo. Anchorage Alaska, June 2002—March 2018. Valerie Terraveccia, Port Hyacinth, D76 April 10th 2072. Wow, some of these names are pretty far into the future."

"That's a pretty decent list," Blake says from behind me. "Must be a dozen names there. You think there are that many other time travelers bouncing around?"

"There are five of us just right here," Carson says. "It figures there'd be more."

"That's kind of exciting," Francesca says.

I slap the book shut and stuff it into my back pants pocket. "Let's get this stuff back where we can get a proper look at it." I drop the spare tire back into the wheel well and replace the carpet. Blake and Robbie load our packs into the trunk. Robbie meets us at the house with Mr. Cameron's car and we unload them again in the driveway, each guy taking a pack into the house. Spartacus bounces up and down as we enter the back door. The parrots are squawking too.

"You guys missing out on some attention today?" I scratch the dog behind his ears. Spartacus follows us with tail wagging as we file upstairs to Blake and Carson's room.

"Mind if we use your bed a minute?" I ask Carson.

"Go for it."

I set the pack I'm carrying down on the bed and unfasten it. I ease a few of the items onto the bed.

"What are you doing?" Francesca says.

"Looking for something."

After emptying the first pack, I grab a second one and repeat the process. I'm a third of the way through it when I find the gun. I double check the safety and hand it to Blake. "Can you unload that?"

"I'm not much of a gun guy," Blake says.

"I can do it," Robbie says. Blake hands him the gun and Robbie removes the clip. He then smoothly pulls the slide back and ejects the bullet in the chamber.

"Didn't want that thing accidentally going off in one of the bags," I say.

"That was Stenger's?" Francesca asks.

"Yeah. We're lucky we didn't get taken out with it," Carson says.

I keep unloading the bag I have on the bed. The bedspread disappears beneath a layer of knickknacks and odd pieces of junk.

"Do you guys remember which stuff was yours from your planning? We probably need to organize all this." I shake the last envelope of photos out of the pack before tossing it on the ground.

"Think we have enough to get back with?" Blake asks.

"Oh. My. God." Francesca holds up a stack of hundred dollar bills from the pack she's holding. "Are we rich now?"

"Oh. Yeah. I snagged that from Quickly's lab before it burned down. It's his money, but I thought we might need traveling funds. It looked like it was meant for time traveling. He had it all organized by dates."

"Oh wow," Francesca says, squatting down and unloading stacks of bills onto the floor in front of her. "How much is this?"

"I don't know."

She sits down to count it while I unload more items onto the bed. It's full before the third pack is empty, so I start using the floor.

"If you guys remember what stuff was yours, maybe we can sort out into years and see what we have to work with."

"That conch shell is mine," Carson says.

"That's my trophy." Blake reaches across the bed and picks up a figure of a golfer.

We begin to sort our items into piles and then into lines on the floor. Robbie doesn't have any items since he wasn't there for the planning lesson, but he helps read out dates from the photo packets and organizes them. After about twenty minutes, Francesca finishes counting the money. Her face is flushed. "We have one hundred and forty thousand dollars." She considers the piles in front of her. "I've never seen this much money in one place before."

"We should probably give it back to Quickly at some point. I wouldn't get too attached to it," I say. Francesca stares at the money for a few more moments and then scoops it back into the pack.

Once we have all of our items laid out in chronological order, I survey the results of our work. We've laid out the objects in four parallel lines on the carpet. I stand up and step to one end of the rows.

"So this is 1986. What's the first item we can jump to? I know I have this door knocker in June of '87." I point to my line of items with my toe. "Anybody have anything closer?"

"My bike handle grip is from December of '86," Carson says.

"Okay. That's less than a year away. That's good," I say. "Blake, what's your first jump point?"

"I actually don't have much till about 1988. I hadn't gotten to that yet. I have a bunch of stuff from the nineties though. Did we figure out if we can all use the same object at the same time?"

"I don't know," I say, "I know we can definitely use the same objects but I still don't know about the 'at the same time' thing."

"Maybe Quickly has something about that in his journal," Francesca suggests.

"Yeah. He might." I pull the journal out of my back pocket and page through it.

"How soon are you guys thinking of trying to go?" Robbie asks. "We still have some time to plan, right?"

I look up from the journal. It's Blake who responds. "I really want to get a move on. From what Ben said, we don't even know if Quickly is coming back. It sounds like they were leaving 1986 all together. I don't know that we're going to get much more help. I think we have enough to work with though. I want to get home."

"What about my grandpa?" Robbie says. "I'm not just going to leave him in the hospital. Plus I know you guys have been doing classes with Quickly every day, but I was hoping we'd get a bit of time so you guys can catch me up to speed. I'm definitely not ready for this yet. I've only made a half dozen jumps."

Blake stands up and looks at his line of jump objects. "I'm just not sure how much longer I can wait. Things are getting pretty crazy around here. I really don't want to get stuck."

"Yeah, you know I love Mr. Cameron too, Robbie," Francesca says. "But the fact that there is a fire starting serial killer that has run into you guys twice now . . . that's starting to freak me out. I want to make sure your grandpa's okay of course, but I would really like to get back to my normal life too."

We are quiet for a few moments.

"I can stick around with you for a bit Robbie," Carson says. "I'm not that worried about Stenger, and I can teach you some of this stuff." He shakes his arm and the chronometer wiggles around on his wrist. "It doesn't really matter what time we all leave right? We could all still get there at the same time."

That's true.

"Yeah that makes sense," I say. "As long as we plan to meet up at the same point we'll all be getting back to our lives around the same time. Some of us will be a little older than the others, relatively speaking, but that won't matter too much. A couple of weeks aren't going to be noticeable."

"So we go first, and they meet up?" Francesca asks. "You're coming with us, right Ben?"

I look from her questioning eyes to Robbie's. I turn to Carson. "You think you would be okay showing Robbie the ropes?"

"Definitely," Carson says. "It'll be fun. Carson's backyard school of time travel. I may have to charge for my superior expertise though." He winks at Robbie.

Robbie looks relieved.

"So we'll need to divide this stuff up into two trips' worth then," Blake says.

I look at our lines of anchors. "Yeah. We can try to divvy it up so it's fair."

"Can we divvy tomorrow?" Francesca yawns. "It's late."

"Yeah. I'm bushed," Carson says. "Saving all of your asses took it out of me today."

Francesca lobs a pillow at him. "You're so humble about it too."

I say goodnight, and after brushing my teeth, make my way downstairs. Spartacus follows, and climbs on top of me when I lie down on the couch. I try to avoid his awkwardly placed paws until he finally settles down, wedged between me and the couch cushions.

"Don't worry, buddy. Your master will be okay." He lays his head on my chest and I scratch him behind the ears for a bit before drifting off to the slow rhythm of his breathing.

Spartacus is gone when I wake up. I find him in the kitchen intently following Robbie's hand as he moves it from his cereal bowl to his mouth. Robbie gently nudges the dog out of his way and makes his way to the table and sits down. "You already had breakfast, you mooch."

"I guess he knows we're suckers and thinks he might get more out of us without Mr. Cameron around," I say as I open the refrigerator door.

"I think he has Grandpa wrapped around his finger too. Or paw. Whatever you would say there."

"Anybody else up?" I ask.

"I heard someone moving around up there recently. I've been up for a bit. Didn't sleep very well. I think I'm going to head back over to the hospital pretty soon to see how things are going."

"You want the keys to the Galaxie?"

"No. I still have Grandpa's car."

"We'll probably join you in a bit. I might try to do some more organizing. You sure you're okay with staying here without us for a bit? I don't want you to feel like we're ditching you."

"No. It's okay. Carson will be a big help. He seems like he's pretty confident he can teach me what we need to know to get back. Plus, you never know. Quickly may show back up and I might be able to get some more lessons from him."

"That's true."

"Do you know if Malcolm went with them?"

"No, I haven't heard anything from him lately. I don't think he would have gone with them." *Constant Malcolm.* "I might give him a call at the Temporal Society and see if he knows what's going on with Quickly and Mym. They may have filled him in on more details. He'll probably want to know what we saw with Stenger too. That should finally convince him I was telling the truth about that guy."

By the time I've finished my breakfast, the others have made it downstairs. I feed the parrots and let them fly around the house for a bit. I take a seat in the library and browse through Dr. Quickly's journal. Mercutio lands on the back of my chair after a few minutes and starts chirping at me.

The journal entries are not in chronological order. It occurs to me after a few minutes that it might be Quickly's life that is out of order, and the journal might be chronological according to him. I skim through a few drawings of chronometer parts and then find an illustration of what appears to be a black hole. The next page shows a sketch of some sort of vessel on the front of a wave. The drawing is labeled "The Alcubierre Drive." I flip through a few more pages and find a section describing jump methods.

That's interesting.

"Hey guys," I say, poking my head into the dining room. "We can jump simultaneously using the same object. He says it's even possible to jump more than one person with only one chronometer." I walk in and set the open journal down between Blake and Francesca as I read it. "As long as both people are infused with gravitites and the chronometer has enough power to compensate for the additional mass, it can still conduct the jump."

"Speaking of power, I haven't charged mine in a couple of days," Blake says. "Did you guys grab the chargers?"

"Yeah, I grabbed 'em," Carson says.

"Cool," Blake says. "I'm gonna go plug mine in."

Robbie stands up also. "I'm going to head over to the hospital."

Francesca gives Robbie a hug before he leaves. "Tell him good morning for us too."

Carson, Francesca and I clean up our dishes and join Blake in his bedroom. "How soon do you guys want to leave?" Carson asks.

I look to Blake. "I don't know. As soon as practical I guess."

"I was kind of hoping we could go tomorrow," Blake says.

"That soon?" Francesca frowns.

"Well, if we're going to go, I don't really see the sense in putting it off. Plus Stenger found the lab. How long till he finds this place?"

"That's not really cool of us to leave Carson and Robbie here alone to deal with him then. And Mr. Cameron is sick. They're not going to be very safe," Francesca says.

"I don't think he's going to show up here," Carson says. "He would have no reason to."

"We're leaving you the gun in any case," I say. "I'll hope you won't need it, but it can't hurt your odds."

We organize a bit more of the jump anchors and I put in a call to the Temporal Studies Society. The secretary claims to have not seen Malcolm in a couple of days however, and says she doesn't know when he'll be returning. A little before lunchtime, we're walking out to the Galaxie to go visit the hospital, when Robbie pulls into the driveway. Mr. Cameron is in the right seat. I walk up to his window to say hi.

"I've escaped!" Mr. Cameron smiles. He looks pale but seems in good spirits.

"Wow, that was fast," Francesca says.

I open Mr. Cameron's door and Robbie holds his cane out for him. I grip Mr. Cameron's forearm and help him get out of the car. Once he's on his feet, Francesca gives him a gentle hug.

"They said he could go home, but he needs to rest," Robbie says. "He couldn't wait to get out of there though."

"My nurse last night smelled like an ashtray. And she was a little too interested in my business," Mr. Cameron says. He mutters behind his hand to Francesca. "My man business."

Francesca laughs and blushes slightly. "Well you can't fault her taste in men."

I take his left arm and help him along the walk to the house. When Robbie opens the door, Spartacus rushes out to lick Mr. Cameron's hand and squirm around his legs. I help him to the library to his armchair.

"I hear I'm not the only one who had an exciting night last night," Mr. Cameron says as he settles into his chair.

"Yeah, we had a couple of thrilling moments too," I say.

He pats me on the arm. "I'm glad you're okay."

"I'm glad you're okay too."

We hang around the kitchen and library most of the afternoon, making lunch and spending time with Mr. Cameron. As the sun is beginning to sink, I decide it's time to fill him in on our plans to depart.

"I can't say I won't be sad to see you go," he replies. "You have all brought a much needed ray of light into my life. It's been a most enjoyable experience."

"Carson and Robbie are going to keep you company a while longer, assuming you can still put up with them."

"I've gotten pretty used to Carson's guitar strumming in the evening. I'm glad I get to keep that a little longer," Mr. Cameron says. "And Robbie is family. I can't very well kick out my own family."

"Tell that to Mom when I turn eighteen." Robbie smiles.

"Will you be okay getting back without your scientist friend?" Mr. Cameron asks.

"We hope so," Blake says. "We had some pretty solid practice in the lab, and around town."

We chat for a while longer, but before long, Mr. Cameron's head starts to nod. We leave him alone so he can rest, and go upstairs to finish our planning. Robbie opts to take the dog out.

"So, Carson, we're leaving you most of your anchors you had from planning," I say. "We divided out the anchors as evenly as possible. I traded you my doorknocker for your bike handle though. We needed something we could jump to in one shot. I figured you might be able to find another decent first jump point to replace it, since you'll have a bit more time here to work on it."

"That's fine," Carson says.

"I gave you a bunch of my nineties stuff," Blake says. "You had a bit of a gap in between '95 and '99. That's filled in now."

Carson surveys the two groups. "What about that one?" He points to my tortoise shell, sitting by itself against the wall.

"I'm keeping that one. It technically goes in the early nineties I guess, but I'm keeping it as a last resort kind of thing," I say.

"It looks okay to me. Robbie and I can probably scrounge some more if we need to. Are we aiming to get back to the same day we left, or after?"

"We don't have any anchors from that same day, but we can get close. I'm hoping to be able to do a couple of short blinks once we're in the vicinity," I say. "Let's plan on meeting on the same day we left in any case. After the game obviously."

"Works for me," Carson says.

"Do you guys need some money?" Francesca says.

"Oh yeah, I guess we can divide that up too," I say. We divvy out the stacks of hundreds. Francesca and I each take a backpack and begin loading it with our items. I save my tortoise shell for last and stuff it in the top. I take another glance at the photo wedged inside the shell. "*When all hope is lost.*" *Maybe I won't ever need that.*

We round up the items of clothing Quickly treated with gravitites for us and stuff those in as best we can. I wiggle my logbook into the front pocket of my pack and have trouble getting the flap closed. "I don't think we can fit anything else in here."

With nothing else to pack, we wander downstairs to socialize. When dinner is ready, we eat it out on the veranda on the second floor. We watch Spartacus chase lizards from under potted plants as we share some wine and a dish of enchiladas Francesca made. When the stars come out, it makes me wonder where I'll be the next time I'll see them. I watch Mr. Cameron chatting with Blake about the state of the garden in the yard and get a sudden pang of sadness. *I'm going to miss him.*

The melancholy makes me feel like being quiet the rest of the night, but I make a point to chat cheerfully with Mr. Cameron whenever the opportunity presents itself. The evening ends too soon. After I've showered, I say my goodnights to everyone upstairs and make my way down to the couch. Spartacus hangs out with me briefly but doesn't climb onto the couch this time. "You have your buddy back now, huh?" I say to the dog. He cocks his head at me as he listens and his tail begins to wag. "I wish you were a time traveling dog."

He pads over and nuzzles me on the couch and lets me scratch behind his ears for a bit. I give him a hug and tussle his fur, but after a while, he wanders toward the stairs and makes his way up them. I follow him with my eyes as he goes. "Okay, bud. I guess we all have our priorities." I lie on the couch staring at the ceiling for a bit. I half hope that I will hear Malcolm climbing the front porch to drag me out on another investigation.

No one shows.

Last night in 1986. I wonder how far we'll have made it by tomorrow night.

Chapter 15

"If you post your used concert tickets on Craigslist and someone actually buys them, you know you've found yourself a time traveler."
-Excerpt from the journal of Dr. Harold Quickly, 2013

"Where are we going to do this?" Blake is standing in the kitchen, holding Carson's bike handle and the corresponding photograph. The photograph shows a child's bicycle propped on its kickstand on the sidewalk in front of a blue house. The description on the photo lists the bike handle as being 38 1/2 inches off the ground. Mr. Cameron has loaned us his tape measure since we didn't bring any of Dr. Quickly's.

"I guess we could do it anywhere really," I say.

"Let's use the backyard," Francesca says. "It's nice out."

I pick up my pack and carry it out the back steps. The mid-morning sun feels good on my skin. Mr. Cameron and Robbie are already out there watching the dog foraging through the garden. Francesca is carrying the other pack.

"You want me to carry that for you?" Blake asks.

"No. I got it," she says.

We congregate in the middle of the walkway to the garage and find a cement paver that looks level.

"I guess we can measure from here. As long as we have the handle down lower than thirty-eight inches, our feet will show up higher than ground level."

"You know which way is up on that handle?" Francesca asks.

"Yeah, it's got these little finger grip things on it," Blake says, pointing to the picture. "This way is down." He twists the bike grip so the finger bumps point at an angle toward the ground.

"Okay. Just checking," Francesca says.

"That's good," I say. "We should check each other's work a lot, just to be sure."

Once we've figured out the details of our jump, Blake sets the bike handle down and we turn to our host. Robbie helps Mr. Cameron out of the lawn chair, but once up, Mr. Cameron seems to be doing okay on his own. We meet them in the middle of the grass.

"I guess this is it," I say.

"You have everything all set?" Mr. Cameron asks.

"As ready as we're going to be."

"It's going to be exciting to see it. I've never had any time travel activity in my backyard before. I probably should have sold tickets to the neighbors."

"Maybe you can set that up for Robbie and Carson." I smile.

"It has been a pleasure having you here, Ben." Mr. Cameron steps forward to embrace me. When he steps back, he pats my shoulder. "You're a good man."

"Thank you, sir. Thank you for . . . everything."

Francesca is next. She wraps her arms around his neck and gives him a quick kiss on the cheek.

"It was great having a lovely young woman in the house again," Mr. Cameron says. "I wish Abby could have met you. I think she would have loved getting to know you."

"It was really great being here," Francesca says. "Thank you so much for being so kind to us. I'm really going to miss this place." Francesca steps back and brushes a tear away with her finger.

"Blake." Mr. Cameron gives him a hug as well. "I wish you all the best in getting back to your future fiancé. She's lucky to have a man like you fighting for her."

"Thank you, sir," Blake says. "Thank you for all your generosity. I don't know where we would be without you."

Robbie gives my hand a shake. "See you in a bit, huh?"

"Yeah." I smile. "Take good care of them."

Francesca hugs Robbie as Carson extends me his hand. "Be careful, dude."

"We will. You too," I reply. "Don't linger too long. We'll need you back throwing batting practice. Big game next week."

Carson smiles. "Yeah, no worries. Those guys are chumps. We're gonna crush 'em." I pull him in for a hug.

Francesca and Carson stand apart for a moment.

"Later gator," Carson says.

Francesca hugs him and lingers a moment before stepping back. "After a while crocodi—" She turns her head and wipes away more tears.

"Don't worry, kid. We'll see you there," Carson says.

Francesca nods, still holding her hand under her nose. Mr. Cameron offers her his handkerchief. Blake exchanges handshakes with Carson and Robbie also.

"Now get outta here," Carson says. "We've got shit to do today."

I smile and we make our way back to our bike handle. Spartacus comes by and sniffs it before Mr. Cameron calls him. "Leave that alone, you menace. They need that."

Blake picks up the bike handle and Francesca and I huddle around him. "Let's see that picture again," I say. Blake pulls it out of his back pocket with his free hand and I take it. I extend Mr. Cameron's tape measure back to the ground. "So thirty-eight inches is here." I hold my hand out and Blake lowers the handle a few inches below it. "We're going to have a little bit of a drop when we get there."

"That's great. I love immediately falling on my ass whenever I show up somewhere," Francesca says.

"Shouldn't be that bad," Blake says. Francesca and I crouch down and put out our chronometer hands to touch the bike handle, making sure to stay clear of where the rest of the bike will be.

"You guys all look ridiculous by the way," Carson says from behind us.

"You're not helping, Carson," Francesca replies.

I toss the tape measure back toward Robbie's feet. I see Blake feel for the lump in his pocket that is Mallory's engagement ring.

"You guys ready?" I say.

Francesca nods.

I look back over my shoulder at Mr. Cameron and Carson and Robbie. Robbie smiles and gives me a thumbs up.

"Bon voyage," Mr. Cameron says.

"Okay, let's do it," Blake says.

"On three," I say. "One . . . two . . ." One last glance at our home. "Three."

I push the pin.

I sway for a moment on the landing, but stay standing. Blake and Francesca manage to keep their feet too, though Francesca grabs my arm to steady herself. We're on a sidewalk under an iron gray sky. My breath catches from the cold.

"We did it!" Francesca says.

In place of Mr. Cameron's backyard is a residential neighborhood on a cul de sac. We're standing in front of a home three houses from the end of the street. Its blue vinyl siding is stained rust-colored around a hose reel in the front yard. The grass looks unhealthy, but I realize that's just because it's winter. The neighborhood is silent.

It only takes a few seconds till Francesca complains.

"God it's cold." She crosses her arms and holds her shoulders. "Why don't we go anywhere when it's summer?"

"Working with what we've got," Blake says as he walks up the driveway and picks up a newspaper lying on the porch. I study the bicycle in front of me. It's a pink-and-white Huffy with red dice and some beads on the spokes.

"December 15th, 1986," Blake reads.

"Well we got that right," Francesca says.

"Oh shit," I blurt out.

"What?" Francesca says, her eyes alert.

"I forgot about the space shuttle."

"What?"

"The Challenger explosion was going to happen in January. I was going to see if we could stop it from exploding."

"Oh wow," Francesca says.

"I'm glad you didn't," Blake says as he walks back to us. "Probably would have screwed up a bunch of shit. The only thing I'm interested in changing about the past is the fact that we're stuck in it."

"Hey, Ben?" Francesca asks.

"Yeah?"

"Does your pack feel lighter?"

I jostle my pack on my back. "Actually, yeah."

I swing it off to look at it. Instead of being stuffed tight, the edges now hang loosely around the contents. "Shit. What happened?"

Francesca takes her pack off as well.

"What are you—" Blake looks at our partially filled packs. "What did you do?"

"It wasn't me!" Francesca says. I open my pack on the ground and see my tortoise shell inside on a pile of clothes, and a few other anchors.

"Damn. We're missing a lot of stuff," I say. I peer into Francesca's pack. Hers has likewise been depleted.

"We just lost a ton of shit!" Blake pulls Francesca's pack toward him and rummages through it.

"What happened?" Francesca asks.

I pull a notched silver dollar out of my pack and then throw it back in as I root around. "We still have some of our anchors."

"Do we have our next one?" Francesca asks. "Next was the piece of rain gutter right?"

I look through the pack. "I don't see it."

"It's not in here either," Blake says.

"What was next on the list?" Francesca grabs her pack to look in the front pocket. "Damn it. My list is gone too."

"That makes sense actually," I say. "Your list was written on paper from Mr. Cameron's house. That never had any gravitites in it. I copied the list into my logbook though."

I pull my logbook out of my pack and see Francesca's in there also. "May as well log this jump," I say, handing her book to her.

"So you knew this was going to happen?" Francesca says.

"No. Well I knew your paper wasn't going to make it, that's why I wrote it in here, but I figured all the anchors would be fine. They all came from Quickly's lab. They must not have all been treated with the gravitites though."

Blake is frowning down at us as we squat over the packs. "Nice if he would have stuck around long enough to tell us that." He kicks over the bicycle.

"Hey!" Francesca says. "That's not very nice. That's some girl's bike."

Blake glares at her for a second as if he's going to respond, but doesn't. After a moment he picks the bike back up.

"So what are we going to do now?" He pulls out his logbook and starts angrily flipping to the right page. I finish jotting my entries and hand him my pen.

"Let me see if there's anything about this in Quickly's journal." I pull the journal out of my back pocket. "Wait!" I spin around and search the area around us.

"What?" Francesca looks up from her logbook.

"Dr. Quickly!" I say. "He was here! He wrote on the back of this photo." I pull out the photo of the bike and show her the back. "That's Quickly's handwriting, so it means he took the picture. He has to be around here somewhere!"

I dash out into the middle of the street and look around. There's no sign of anyone except a postman a few blocks down delivering mail. I trot down to the end of the cul de sac and continue looking, but see no one. A Dalmatian barks at me from behind a chain link fence. Disappointed, I walk back to my friends.

167

"He had to be here recently or that photo never would have been taken."

"Well, he's not here now," Blake says. He and Francesca have finished with their logbooks and Francesca is pulling a couple of T-shirts out of her pack. She layers them over the shirt she's wearing. One of them is mine, but she doesn't seem to care.

"Where are we?" she asks.

"I don't know actually," I say. The back of the photo doesn't list a city. I look around at the neighborhood but see no clues. *Quickly was right, American suburbia does pretty much all look the same.*

"The newspaper was *The Boston Globe*," Blake says. "We must be somewhere in New England." He walks to the mailbox and pops it open. He reads an envelope he finds inside. "We're in West Bridgewater, wherever that is."

"So what now?" Francesca says.

There's a trashcan sitting at the edge of the curb of the house next to us. I walk over to it and toss the photo of the bike handle inside.

"What're you doing?" Blake asks.

"I read in the journal that you're supposed to dispose of your used photos immediately, so that you don't accidentally reuse one that you've used before." I flip open the journal and thumb through it till I find the page I'm looking for. "It says, 'Maintain a careful and accurate inventory of used and unused jump anchors to avoid duplication of use.'"

"Well we already screwed that up," Blake says. "We left half our inventory on Mr. Cameron's lawn."

I keep reading. "It also says as a precaution we need to 'exit the vicinity of the jump area immediately, to avoid potential collisions with other time travelers accidentally using the same location.'"

"So I shouldn't have been still standing here the last five minutes?" Francesca says. "Is that what you're telling me?"

"Yeah." I start walking.

"Great. Another way I could have died." Francesca picks up her pack and follows me.

"Does it say what to do if you find yourself suddenly stranded in Boston? Because we're kind of screwed," Blake says.

"Hey, it could be a lot worse," I say. "We could have died or . . . wait a minute. I actually did see something about Boston in here."

I flip to the back of the journal and turn back a few pages. "Here. Look." I show the journal to Blake and Francesca. "On this list of people we think are time travelers, there's one listed in Boston. Guy Friday. Green Dragon Tavern. Marshall Street, Boston. Fridays from August 1984-1988."

"The guy's address is a bar? And his name is Guy Friday?" Francesca says. "Well, how could that go wrong?"

"It's something at least," I say. "I mean, we can research our own jump points from here to the next one we've got left. The research is going to take some time though. Maybe this guy can help us. He's in Quickly's book."

"What day is it today?" Francesca asks.

"Monday," Blake says.

"So we need to find this bar and get there on Friday," Francesca says. "Cab?"

"Yeah, I guess so," I reply. "Don't think we're likely to see one in this neighborhood though. We should probably find a payphone."

We find our way out of the neighborhood in short order but my hands and toes are already numb by the time we reach a main road. When we finally locate a payphone, we realize that all we have for cash is hundred dollar bills. Francesca talks a laundromat attendant into breaking her hundred and scores us some quarters. We shiver on the sidewalk waiting for the cab, and huddle happily into its warmth in the back seat when it arrives.

The ride to downtown Boston takes the better part of an hour. The cabby assures us, that while he doesn't know the exact bar we're looking for, that most of the good pubs are in one area and easy to find. We have no real choice but to believe him.

"You ever been to Boston before?" Francesca asks me as we get out of the cab.

"Yeah, but not in the eighties obviously."

I scan the street of bars we arrive on. The buildings are mostly brick architecture layered over historic sites from the 1700s. The street is narrow and bricked as well, with little room for cars. The daytime pedestrians appear to be predominantly tourists.

"God, New England girls even dress better in the eighties." Francesca frowns. "I might need to go shopping."

"Won't do you any good, unless you want to leave a nice pile of new clothes where we jump from, and show up at our next spot naked," Blake says.

"I mean, we aren't going to complain if that's what you really want." I smile.

Francesca shoves me in the arm. "Darn it. I should have had Dr. Quickly gravity zap me a pea coat."

169

"I've got a nice brown jumpsuit in my pack you can wear," I say.

"Ugh. Maybe this time traveler we're meeting will have a girlfriend who has some cute clothes I can borrow."

We find the Green Dragon Tavern by asking a couple of pedestrians. The tavern has a wide exterior of small paned windows in the front with a doorway in the center. A hanging wooden sign advertises that it has been in business since 1773. As it is Monday afternoon, we find the bar area nearly deserted. The hulking bartender immediately detaches himself from his conversation with his two patrons at the far end of the bar as we walk in.

"You all want menus?" he asks as we take stools.

"Actually we have a question," I say.

The bartender lays out a few coasters in front of us. "Whatcha got?"

"We're looking for someone named Guy Friday," I begin. "We were told we could find him here."

"Oh. Yeah. I think I know who you're talking about. Young blonde guy? Kind of . . . different?"

"We aren't really sure," I say. "We haven't met him before."

"Well there's a guy named Guy, and he only ever comes in here on Fridays, so I figure that's how he picked up the name. I don't know what his real last name is though."

"Okay. Do you know how we find him?"

"On Friday, yeah. He usually sits over there at that booth by the front, unless we've kicked him out. He can get a little mouthy with the girls sometimes. Mostly he's all right though. Comes in with another big guy sometimes. Dark hair, that one."

"Are you going to be working Friday?" Francesca asks. Her eyes are admiring the bartender's muscled arms and Celtic tattoos. She smiles at him.

"Actually yeah, I think I am. I could probably point him out to you."

"That would be great," I say.

"Well I'm going to have a beer," Francesca says. "Can I have a Guinness please?"

The bartender looks to Blake and me.

"I'm okay right now," I say. Blake shakes his head also.

"So what, are we just going to sit here and drink till Friday?" Blake says.

"I'm okay with it," Francesca replies, watching the bartender pour her beer. "That accent is so sexy."

"I was assuming we were going to just skip to Friday," I say.

Francesca frowns. "Just when I found somewhere I like. It's warm in here . . . there's good scenery . . ."

"We're skipping," Blake says.

"How about you guys blink ahead and I'll stay and get to know the locals." Francesca smiles.

"I really think we ought to stay together," I say.

Francesca pouts. "Fine. But I'm going to drink this beer reeaaallly slow. And we're definitely stopping somewhere for me to get something to wear. I'm certainly not coming back in here looking like this now." She gestures to her triple T-shirt ensemble. She beams at the bartender as he sets her beer in front of her. Blake and I cave in and order beers too.

An hour later, we reemerge into the fading afternoon light of wintertime Boston.

"We need an anchor," I say, as we look around.

"We could shimmy up a light pole," Blake suggests, gesturing to the stoplight at the intersection. "No one will be going up there."

"I don't shimmy," Francesca says.

"Yeah, we could use a roof or a locked room or something," I say, still scanning around.

"Fire escape." Blake points to the side of one of the neighboring buildings. "The odds of that being in use when we arrive are pretty slim."

"I like it," I say.

"How do we get up there?" Francesca asks.

We cross the street to the side alley of what appears to be an apartment building, and crowd under the fire escape.

"I bet you could reach it if I boost you up," I say to Francesca.

Blake eyes the passersby. "We should probably get set up first, in case someone says anything."

"Good idea." I set my pack down and concentrate on my chronometer. "We could do four days and get here around the same time Friday, or we could do a time and date specific jump."

"Let's just do four days," Blake says. "We can get here this time Friday."

"I still need time to shop," Francesca says.

"You should have a couple of hours."

Once we have our settings dialed into our chronometers, we compare with each other to double check. "We have enough power for this?" Blake asks. "That last one was a long one."

"Yeah, hopefully," I say. "We should definitely charge them up after this one though."

Blake takes the packs from Francesca and me, and turns to keep an eye on the pedestrians. "You look clear."

I intertwine my fingers and cup my hands atop my knee to give Francesca somewhere to step. She grabs my shoulders and places her right foot in my hands.

"Please don't drop me."

"I got you."

"Go for it," Blake says.

I boost Francesca up and then wrap my arms around her knees to lift her higher. She latches her hands onto the bottom rung of the fire escape and I slowly lower her down, dragging the fire escape ladder with her. Blake grabs it when it gets low enough and I set her back down. I check the area, but no one is paying attention. Blake hands me one of the packs and we clamber up. Francesca leads the way up the ladder, and once she's on the first platform, I gesture for her to keep going.

"Let's go up a couple and get out of people's eyeline."

Nobody ever looks up.

Blake eases the ladder up behind us and it clanks back into place. He joins us on the third floor landing. Francesca peeks into the window of the apartment we're adjacent to.

"Looks like no one's home."

The wind feels stronger three floors up. "Let's make this quick. My toes are getting numb," I say.

Flip-flops were a poor choice.

I squat down and grab one of the vertical rails of the fire escape, hoping to make myself less obvious to passersby. Francesca copies me. Blake stays standing but extends his chronometer hand and touches the tips of his fingers to the railing. "On three again. One, two, three!"

Pin in.

Blake recoils from the railing in pain. The buildings and streets around us have been blanketed in white.

"Agghh," Blake moans, holding his hand and staring at his fingertips. I look to where his hand had been and see the half-inch of snow that has managed to linger along the top of the railing. There are two indents where Blake's fingers were.

Shit. He got fused with the ice crystals.

I grab Blake's wrist and dial his chronometer for him. "You gotta jump again! Here!" I drag his arm back toward the railing and touch his hand to the vertical rails. "Just a couple of seconds." Blake's eyes are full of pain as he looks in mine. I step away. He pushes the pin and disappears. The finest mist lingers momentarily where his fingertips were. I look down at the diamond-shaped holes in the metal floor of the landing that prevented snow from settling on it. *Thank God for that.*

Three seconds later, Blake is back. He's still gripping his wrist as he pulls away from the railing.

"God, that hurt," he says through gritted teeth.

"Is it better?" I ask.

"Yeah. A little." He examines his fingertips.

"I'm so sorry, dude. I never even thought about snow."

He hisses through his teeth a little as his touches his fingertips together. "It's okay. It's not your fault."

Francesca has her hands over her mouth. "Are you okay?" she says, staring at his hand.

"Yeah." Blake shakes his hand. "I think I'll be all right. Let's just get down from here."

The temperature is even more bitter than the day we left. I rub my arms as we descend the fire escape. The streets are busier despite the cold. The Friday afternoon pedestrians are bundled in colorful scarves and hats. I'm happy I chose to wear pants, but standing shivering in my flip-flops and short-sleeved shirt, I'm eager to get indoors.

"I think Francesca is right about the shopping," I say. "Let's find a clothing store, quick."

We draw innumerable stares from store patrons and tourists as we make our way south on Union Street. A cab pulls up to the stop at the next block and I'm elated to see it vacant. Blake flags the driver with his good hand and Francesca opens the back door for him. Blake slides across the seat and I sandwich Francesca in the middle.

"Where to?" the cabby says, eying our unusual outfits.

"We could use a department store," Francesca replies. I slam the door shut and shiver.

"Well there's Filene's." The cabby scratches his salt-and-pepper whiskers. "That's a nice one. Got about everything."

"Sounds perfect." I unbuckle my pack and pull the last T-shirt out of it. It's too cramped to attempt to put it on, so I simply drape it over my bare arms and hold the pack close to my chest for warmth.

"You having some clothing difficulties?" the cabby asks.

"Stupid airline lost our luggage," Francesca says.

I nod. *That's a pretty good one.*

"I had that happen to me and the wife once. They had a big snowstorm in Cleveland on our way out to California for a nephew's wedding. Boy, they had things all screwed up. I thought my wife was going to murder that baggage agent." He chuckles to himself. "Not that I'm saying your situation is funny."

"No. It's okay," I say.

It's a very short drive to the Filene's. We probably could have walked it if it wasn't so cold.

"Wow this place is huge," Francesca says, leaning her head back to look out the rear window at the ornate multistory stone building. The cabby deposits us on the sidewalk in front of the main entrance, and Francesca pays him.

"Hope your trip gets better." He waves as I shut the door behind us.

I take a quick glance skyward at the columns and decorated stone of the façade. A stately green clock with a white face is perched above the sign saying Filene's. The clock reads 5:25. The last bits of sunlight are reflecting in the glass doors as we file inside among dozens of other holiday shoppers.

"How's your hand?" I say as we step into the warmth of the store. Tinsel sparkles above the escalators as overloaded shoppers glide upwards.

"My fingertips are turning purple." Blake holds out his hand. "Feels kind of like a blood blister."

The skin under the nails on his index and middle fingers has darkened. "Ouch," I say.

"It's not hurting that much anymore," Blake says. "Just looks bad. Hope I don't lose my fingernails."

"You guys just want to meet me in the women's department when you're done?" Francesca asks.

"All right."

The men's department has been relegated to the second floor. We ascend behind a mother holding her two children's hands. The older girl is probably three. She peers shyly at us from behind her mother's thigh. She reminds me of my niece. The slightly younger boy keeps grabbing for the railing but the mother pulls him back against her leg at each of his attempts. The trio turns right off the escalator and the little girl follows us with her eyes as she's dragged away around a display of custom Filene's Christmas ornaments. I get a sudden pang of homesickness as we veer left for the menswear.

I find myself a basic zip-up, collared black jacket made of some type of synthetic. It's quilted on the inner liner and I feel instantly warmer as I slide it on. I grab a bag of athletic socks and a dark red, button-down shirt. I look down my thrift store jeans to their slightly damp pant legs and debate grabbing new pants, but opt to head to the shoe department instead. Blake meets me there.

"I got us socks," I say, and show him the bag. A salesman helps Blake pick out a pair of dark, ankle-high boots. I settle for some comfortable lace-up blue sneakers. I keep the shoes laced up as I walk to the sales counter. Yanking the tag off the sleeve of my jacket, I set that on top of the slightly reduced bag of socks. "We're just going to wear this stuff out."

The salesman nods stiffly with a look of thinly veiled disdain as Blake lays his acquisitions down also. I see Blake has found himself some gloves. *That was smart.*

"Will this be cash or charge?"

"It'll be cash." I pull a stack of bills out of my backpack and lay it on the counter in front of me. The salesman gives the wad of hundreds a long look before snapping back to his duties at the register.

"Very well, sir." His disposition improves. "And, might I interest you in some of our holiday gift sales items?"

"Just the clothes for now."

I take our change and stuff it into the pocket of my jeans. We find Francesca sitting at the makeup counter in the women's department, having a saleswoman apply eye shadow for her. She's wearing some nearly knee-high boots and leggings under a purple cotton dress. She has several large bags piled around her already.

"You've been busy."

She glances from us to her bags, and then gives her attention back to the saleswoman. "Decision making gets a lot easier when you don't have budget constraints."

Blake watches the saleswoman put the finishing touches on her eyelids.

"You know that stuff isn't going to stay on either as soon as we have to make another jump," Blake says.

"I know," she replies. "Why do you think I'm not bothering to buy makeup remover?" She gives Blake a wink.

After the saleswoman finishes tallying her bill, Francesca hands her a couple of hundred-dollar bills. "You can keep the change." The saleswoman smiles and bows slightly. "Thank you miss."

"Hope your burly bartender friend appreciates the investment," I say.

Francesca smiles. "It's Friday night. Who knows what can happen?"

I stop near a fake Christmas tree and put my button-down shirt on over my T-shirt. I slip my jacket back on and adjust my pack before we head for the doors. Francesca unloads one of her bags and slides her arms into a grey pea coat. She dons a wooly hat with it and wraps a scarf around her neck.

"That was probably a good idea," I say, eying the snow flurries that have begun to fall outside the glass doors.

"One of these years we should actually stick around for Christmas," Francesca says.

We emerge back onto the sidewalk and I zip up my jacket to keep out the chill.

"You guys want to walk back?"

"I'm okay with it," Blake says.

Francesca's mouth and nose are now covered with her scarf but her green eyes are showing and she nods.

I stuff my hands in my pockets and we make our way back north to Union Street. The Green Dragon is glowing bright and bustling with patrons as we walk in. As Francesca unwraps her face, I see the cold has given her cheeks a rosy glow. I scan over the throng of patrons trying to get to the bar, and spot our bartender.

"Do you see Cole?" Francesca asks, trying unsuccessfully to see past the crowd.

"Is that his name? Yeah. He's back there." I remove my pack and hand it to Blake. "I'm gonna try to squeeze through. You want a beer while I'm up there?"

"Yeah. That would be good," Blake says, as Francesca hands her shopping bags to him as well, leaving him looking a bit like a bellman.

I feel Francesca's hands holding my waist as I navigate us toward the bar. The young bartender at our end is not one I recognize, but I task her with our drink order while still trying to catch Cole's eye. He's busy figuring a customer's tab but as he hands it to them and waits for his payment, he scans past the taps and catches sight of me leaning on the bar.

Francesca is squeezing through under my right arm. He gives me a nod and then turns back to his customers to collect their cash. Once he deposits the money into the register and tosses the extra into the tip jar, he strides over to us.

"Hi!" Francesca beams.

Cole peers around the taps to get a good look at who's speaking. "Hey there. Wondered if you'd be back." He smiles. "You guys get drinks yet?"

I gesture toward the other bartender. "She got us." I start to open my mouth to ask about Guy Friday, but Cole reads my mind.

"Your man is in the back tonight." He points over the crowd to a booth in the back corner. I spot the back of a blonde head and three or four pint glasses on the table.

"Thanks. I appreciate it."

He gives Francesca a wink and departs to deal with a middle-aged man with three chins who is waving bills with both arms from the other end of the bar.

Francesca smiles at me. "See, totally worth it."

She does look good.

I stand on tiptoes to catch Blake's eye and I point him toward the back end of the bar area. I forge through the crowd and meet him midway, to take one of the packs off his hands and trade him his beer.

"He's here?"

"Yeah, in a booth in the back."

Francesca has followed me through the patrons, carefully guarding some sort of dark mixed drink with a slice of orange rind in it. I make it to the end of the line of booths and cross to the far side of our target's table before turning around.

The sandy haired man looks up from his beer and a doodle he's been drawing on a bar napkin. He looks to be about Blake's age or possibly younger.

"Excuse me, are you Guy?"

The young man looks from me to Blake and considers our packs and bags before responding. "Could be."

"Hi. I'm Benjamin." I set my beer down and extend my hand. Francesca squeezes her way in between Blake and me and smiles. Guy ignores my hand and looks Francesca up and down, stopping unapologetically to stare at her chest. He looks back to me.

"This one yours?"

Francesca's smile quickly fades. "I'm mine."

Guy holds his palms up and gives a small shrug. "Just asking."

He gives his head a small toss to get his floppy hair out of his eyes and takes a sip from his beer.

I already don't like this guy.

Blake has a go. "We were hoping to talk to you about something rather important. Do you have a few minutes?"

Guy gestures vaguely at the other side of the booth while still holding his beer to his lips. As he pulls the glass away, he gives a grin to Francesca and pats the seat next to him with his free hand.

Francesca ignores him and slides into the opposite side. I take her pair of shopping bags from Blake and hand them to her to stuff beside her. Guy seems less enthusiastic to be sliding over for Blake, but does so after a moment.

"Thanks," Blake says.

"So what's the big important issue that needs my attention so badly?" Guy says.

"Well . . . we're—" I pause and start over. "This is Francesca, and this is Blake. We're traveling together and we've gotten into a situation where we could use some help."

Guy makes no response, but simply stares at me. I get the impression he's not even really looking at me.

"We understand you're a time traveler," Blake says.

Guy sits up a little straighter and his eyes narrow as he looks from Blake back to me.

"You Journeymen?" he asks. His right hand has strayed off the table to somewhere I can't see.

"No. I don't think so," I say. "What are Journeymen?"

Guy's face relaxes a little and his hand reemerges to the top of the table. "So who are you then?"

"We're just passing through," Blake says. "We're looking for some help. We were referred to you by a friend, sort of."

"He sort of referred you, or he's sort of a friend?"

"Both, I guess," Blake says. "We're trying to get back to 2009."

Guy pauses for a moment, then his eyes widen slowly. "Wait a minute." He points to Francesca and then me and Blake in turn. "Francesca, Benjamin, Blake."

I nod.

"Oh shit, my little brother is going to flip. Don't tell me, you were stuck in the beginning of 1986, for what? Two weeks was it? Ha!"

Francesca is taken aback. "How do you know that?"

Guy drains the rest of his beer and clunks it back down on the table. "For that answer, you will need to buy me another beer." He waves toward the bar. I turn and see that Cole has been watching us. He looks to me and I nod.

Guy is beaming at all of us. "Of all the things to happen to me tonight, I would not have expected this." He slaps his hand down on the table and the empty pint glasses jump. I pick up my beer to keep it from sloshing over. I'm too late and my fingers get soaked.

"So you can help us?" Blake asks.

A server appears, bearing a beer for Guy, and he stretches across the table to grab it.

"You might just have found your lucky day." He slurps the foam off the top of his beer and then looks at Francesca. "And you might just get lucky."

Francesca's eyes narrow.

"Hey, so can we talk about you for a second?" I say. "Who are you, and how did you manage to end up a time traveler?"

"Manage to end up a time traveler?" Guy says mockingly. "I was trained for this. I was born for this."

"How did you get trained?" I say.

"The best school money can buy, my friend," Guy says. "Oh man, Lawrence is so going to wet his pants when I tell him who I found." He places his hands on the table. "Oh we should go get him! We should totally go blow his little mind." His eyes roll back a moment as he smiles.

He's drunk.

"You guys want to meet my little brother?"

"Yeah, I guess," I say.

"Then drink up!" He takes his beer in hand and starts chugging it. Much of it leaks past his mouth and trails down his chin. He slams the glass back down and belches. Francesca recoils slightly across from him.

"Oh, I'm sorry there, angel. That must have been rude of me." He turns sideways and gestures with a shooing motion toward Blake. "Let me out. I need to use the head. Then we'll go!"

Blake slides out of the booth. Guy sways a moment as he exits, but steadies himself on the edge of the table. Then, locking his eyes on the restroom hallway, he staggers into the crowd.

"Wow," Francesca shakes her head. "I mean, wow."

"Yeah, he's a piece of work," Blake says.

"So what now?" Francesca asks. "We aren't actually going with him, are we?"

I look from her to Blake as I consider our options. It's Blake who speaks first however. "He does know something about us. You heard what he said."

"Maybe his brother won't be so difficult," I add.

"Won't be an alcoholic douchebag you mean?" Francesca says.

"Yeah, basically. But at least he's a time traveler."

"This is not how I saw this night going," Her gaze travels to Cole pouring pints behind the bar.

"We have to at least find out what he knows," Blake says.

"Okay." I down another swallow of my beer. "I'll go get our tab."

I press through the crowd to the bar and after a few moments Cole sidles over.

"I guess we're closing out early. Just the three of our drinks and the one of his beers."

Cole starts drying out the inside of a glass. "You going to take him off my hands for the night?"

179

"Yeah, looks that way."

"Don't worry about it then. They're on the house."

"Really? You don't have to do that."

"No problem, man. Just bring that one around sometime again without your new friend." He nods toward Francesca and I see her smile.

"Thanks, man. I'll try."

Cole drifts off to another customer. I tuck a twenty under the edge of the container of limes and go back to my friends. I've just reached the booth when Guy collides with me.

"Let's do this!"

He sways past me and works his way toward the door. A girl with a kilt and thigh-high socks jumps suddenly as he walks past her, and I see her glare at him as he makes for the exit. He manages to keep his hands to himself the rest of the way outside and we catch up to him on the sidewalk. Francesca snakes her scarf around her neck again and scrounges around her bag for her hat.

"This way," Guy says, and jolts off to the right. The cold seems to sober him up a bit and we have a hard time keeping up with him as he plunges down alleys and side streets.

He comes to a stop near the steps of a brick apartment building. He looks from the front entrance down to the next building and back.

"Pretty sure it's this one." He trots up the steps and fumbles with his keys for a few minutes before he finally gives up and pushes the button on a call box next to the door.

"Lawrence, let me in!"

A moment later, the door buzzes and Guy jerks it open.

"Come on." He waves us through. Francesca gives him a wide berth as she slides past. The interior of the hallway we enter is warm and stuffy. The stairs are carpeted with a shag in a variety of browns that may have once looked good before the years of foot traffic wore it down. We ascend behind our host to the third floor.

The landing holds two doors. Guy pounds on the door labeled 3B, and a few moments later, it swings open.

"I brought you a present," Guy says to the face that appears behind the door.

Lawrence is dark-haired and large. He's shorter than his brother but easily twice as wide. He scans us skeptically but his gaze lingers a moment on Francesca.

"Who are they?"

"They're some fellow titties. Aren't you proud of me?" Guy drawls, and pushes his way past his brother into the apartment.

Lawrence stands in the doorway appraising us for a moment, but then opens the door wider. "Well, come in I guess."

I step cautiously into the kitchen area of what appears to be a two-bedroom apartment. Guy staggers around the right side of a kitchen island. The living room space beyond the kitchen's linoleum is dominated by a bank of computer monitors and an L shaped couch that Guy drops himself onto. I notice the office chair in front of the largest computer screen is littered with wrappers and some crumbs that match the ones on Lawrence's T-shirt.

"I'm Benjamin." I extend a hand to Lawrence, and he takes it. "These are my friends, Francesca and Blake."

"I'm Lawrence." He shakes the others hands also, and gestures toward the living room where Guy is lounging on a corner of the couch with his feet up. We follow him in.

"You like my titties, Lawrence? That's three more than you were likely to see tonight."

"Why is he calling us that?" Francesca says.

"Oh, yeah. Sorry," Lawrence says, "It's not you. He calls lots of people that." He scratches behind one of his ears. "One of his school professors used to abbreviate, 'Travelers in Time' to T.I.T. He's been calling all time travelers, 'titties' ever since. Although usually it's just when he's drunk."

"Which is often, I take it," Francesca says.

"He's not always like this," Lawrence replies.

"What? You don't like my charming personality?" Guy calls from the couch.

"We're actually looking for some help," I say, ignoring Guy. "We got your brother's name from Dr. Harold Quickly. We thought you might have—"

"Whoa. Wait. What did you say your names were?" Lawrence backs up a step and looks at each of our faces.

"I'm Benjamin, this is Blake and Frances—"

"Francesca Castellanas?" Lawrence asks.

"How did you know that?" Francesca replies.

"Oh holy shit! My friend Cassandra wrote a paper about you in like first term."

"Someone wrote a paper about me?" Francesca asks.

"You're the original '86ers," Lawrence says in awe. "Wow. That's crazy. I didn't expect to run into you back here. I mean I knew it was theoretically possible but—"

"What are '86ers?" I ask. "Why do you know about us?"

"We all study you at the Academy. I mean, we study all the early time travelers, but you guys especially. It's like required reading and shit."

"Told you he'd wet himself," Guy says.

"What's the Academy?" Blake asks.

"Time Travel Academy," Lawrence says, "Well, it's The Academy of Temporal Sciences, or ATS if you want to be specific. Guy was class of 2157. Or . . . would have been."

"That school blew," Guy comments from the couch. "You could learn more about time travel from a fly on a pile of dog shit."

"So they have a school for time traveling in the future?" I say.

This is getting wild.

"Yeah, they did anyway," Lawrence says. "It's shut down now. Or at least it will be. That's what we heard anyway. Sometime in the 2160s."

"So you guys are from the future?" Francesca asks.

I look around the apartment. The computer monitors definitely outclass anything that ought to exist in the eighties, but otherwise, nothing looks especially out of place.

"That's right, baby," Guy says, and puckers his lips at her. "I'm your future."

"What's it like being you?" Francesca says, staring him down. "Do people just punch you in the face all the time?"

Guy grins and flips her off.

"Please ignore him," Lawrence says.

"So you are from 2160?" Blake asks.

"We came back from 2155," Lawrence replies as he plops down into his office chair. Blake and I set our packs down and Blake takes a seat on the far end of the couch from Guy.

"Wow. What's that like?" Francesca and I lean against the countertop of the island.

"Spacemen and flying cars, bro," Guy says in an affected surfer voice. "It's gnarly."

"It's not that different," Lawrence says. "Technology is way better of course. And we've got the grid, but that has its downsides too."

"The grid?"

"Yeah, satellite system programming for time travelers. Makes it a lot safer."

"Time travel is a regular thing there?" Blake asks.

"Not exactly. It's pretty regulated. And unauthorized usage is definitely frowned upon."

"Nice lethal frowns," Guy adds. He sticks his fingers in his mouth and pulls his cheeks down in a sort of snarl, then laughs.

"Who regulates it?" I ask.

"Oh, there are a couple of different factions."

"What are you doing in 1986?" Francesca asks. "Why come all the way back here?"

Lawrence looks away to his computer screen. "We have our reasons."

"It's okay, brother. I'll tell them." Guy sits up straight on the couch and wags a finger back and forth at us. "I'm going to tell you the whole . . . amazing . . . story. But first, I need a beer."

He pushes himself off the couch and I can't tell if it's walking, or simply trying not to fall, that propels him into the kitchen. He makes it to the refrigerator and pulls out a can of Old Milwaukee.

"See, the problem with the future," he says, as he pops the top on the beer, "is that they just can't take a joke." He looks from me to Francesca. "Too serious."

"So . . . you got in trouble?" Francesca asks.

"Trouble is a relativistic term." Guy sips his beer. "You would know that if you ever went to the Academy. Like me." He sways sideways and collides with the back of the couch, but tries to play it off and just leans against it.

"So you went to time travel academy, but you got in trouble, and they . . . kicked you out?" Blake asks.

"I didn't get in trouble with the Academy."

"Well you kind of did," Lawrence says.

"Hey, this is my story." Guy points to the back of Lawrence's head. "He wasn't even in the Academy. He was still in Academy Prep." Guy's face contorts into a look of disgust. "Little prepper shits." He swallows a burp.

"At least I didn't get kicked out," Lawrence mutters under his breath.

"A lot of good that did you, Tubster. Let's see if they take your fat ass back now."

Lawrence ignores him.

"But as I was saying, we didn't leave because of the school. We left . . . because of the Journeymen."

"You mentioned them earlier," I say. "What are Journeymen?"

"They're thugs," Lawrence says. "Mob hit men."

"There is a mob in 2160?" Francesca asks.

"There's always a mob," Lawrence replies, still fiddling with the computer. Guy weaves his way around the end of the couch and plops down into the corner again. Lawrence continues. "They were the ones that started it actually, the crackdown on the time travelers. They had the most riding on it."

"I don't follow you," I say. "Why would the mob be involved with time travelers?"

"Because they get their panties all in a bunch when you clean out their casinos," Guy says. He leans his head back and speaks toward the ceiling to no one in particular. "It's only money, guys." His head lolls back onto the cushion but he tilts it toward us. "They burnt down our mansion . . ."

"You had a mansion?" Francesca says.

"Yeah, baby. I'll give you the private tour sometime."

"You said it burned down."

"Details, baby, details." He rolls his head back and resumes his contemplation of the ceiling.

"So you guys had your house burned down by casino hit men from the future. Am I getting that right?" Blake says.

Lawrence nods. "Yeah, more or less."

"And you came to the eighties because . . ."

"We've never met anyone who knew Journeymen to come this far back. They're pretty thick in the early part of the twenty-second century. We've never heard of one going pre-millennium though. We figure this is as good a place to lie low as any."

"What happens if they catch you?" Blake asks.

Lawrence shrugs. "I don't especially want to find out."

"How much money did you steal?" Blake asks.

"We didn't steal it. We won it," Lawrence says. "They just didn't see it that way."

"Can we come back to this thing about your friend writing a paper about me in school?" Francesca asks. "What did she write about?"

"Oh, I don't know. She probably just made up some B.S. about your life to impress our history teacher. He was an idiot."

"But people have heard of us in 2155?" I say.

"Everybody knows about you because they know about Harold Quickly. You all got famous by association. Famous with time travelers anyway; I don't know that anyone else has ever heard of you."

"Quickly is a big deal then, too?" I ask.

"Oh yeah, he's like Grandfather Time. He started it all. Of course there are some guys who claim to have gone farther into the past, so they say they're, 'The first time travelers.' But that's all horseshit. Everybody knows it was Quickly who started it all. His dissertation on the nature of temporal gravity is pretty much the first thing you read when you get into the Academy. Every major temporal physicist to come after him basically just stole his original theory and just made tweaks to try to get attention. He blew them all out of the water when he came to the Fuller Hall debates."

"Quickly's been to the Academy?" I say.

"Oh yeah. Well, he will. Maybe."

"Maybe?" Francesca says. "Aren't you sure?"

Lawrence holds his hands up and wiggles his fingers around. "Wibbly wobbly, timey wimey."

"Excuse me?" Francesca asks.

Lawrence looks from her face to mine and then to Blake's. "Really? Nobody got that reference?"

We stare at him mutely.

"*Dr. Who*? . . . Nobody?"

"*Dr. Who*?" Francesca says. "Is he another scientist?"

"Ha. No. He's a TV alien. You guys really are babes in the woods aren't you? Twenty-first century time travelers and you've never even heard of Dr. Who? If the Journeymen hadn't torched my digital media library, I'd make you sit and watch every episode till you were properly ready to have intelligent conversation on time travel culture."

I look to the couch and notice Guy has fallen asleep. His beer is leaning precariously on the couch cushion in his loose fingers. *At least the conversation has gotten more intelligent there.*

"So you seem pretty knowledgeable. Will you help us out? We're trying to get back to 2009."

"I might be talked into it," Lawrence replies. "What's in it for us though?"

"We could pay you," Francesca says.

"With what? Smiles?"

"We've got money," Francesca says. She reaches down into her pack and holds up one of the stacks of hundreds.

"We're time travelers. We can always get money. What do you have to offer that we can't already get?"

Francesca straightens up. "Well I don't know what you're suggesting . . ."

"What have you been using for anchors?" Lawrence cuts her off.

"Oh," Francesca says.

"We've been using items from Quickly's lab," I say.

Lawrence swivels his chair to face us directly. "Got anywhere good?"

"Depends on where you want to go I guess."

I pull my pack up from the floor and lay it on the counter. Popping open the latch, I begin pulling out a few of our anchors. Francesca does the same. Lawrence gets out of his chair to come look. He picks up the photo of the notched silver dollar and sets it back down. Next he picks up a photo of a toolbox in a barn and reads the description.

"Oh, you have Montana."

I notice it's one of the ones with Mym's handwriting on the back.

"We actually need that one," I say, and take it out of his hands. He gives me a suspicious glance but then moves on to another packet of photos.

He lingers over an antique hourglass and then again on a picture of a pewter mug on a bar in Germany.

"Okay. I think I could possibly help you," he says.

"How would you be able to help us?" Blake says. "If we trade you some of our anchors, what would we get in return?"

"You can use our time portal." He nods toward one of the doors along the wall.

"What's a time portal?" Francesca says.

"I'll show you." He leads us around the couch to the wooden door and cracks it open. He meets some resistance in the form of some clothes on the floor but once he has it open, he flips on the light and steps back so we can have a look. I lean in to see. The bedroom is a mess for the first few feet of space. There's a small twin bed jammed against the wall in the corner that's littered with clothes and random magazines. Taking up the majority of the rest of the room, is a floor-to-ceiling cell made of cinderblocks, with a steel door.

He elbows past me with a set of keys and unlocks the three deadbolts on the steel door. The hinges complain slightly as the door swings open. Francesca peers cautiously past me to see inside. We inch closer.

Lawrence illuminates the cell with a switch that turns on a set of fluorescent overhead lights. Inside are two metal chairs and a table with some straps and diodes on it. A tangle of wires on the table leads onto the floor and over to a pile of car batteries that have been linked up in series with each other. A single computer monitor sits on the table with the wiring.

"What do you think? I built it myself."

I try to think of something complimentary to say. *It looks like an interrogation room.*

"Looks . . . efficient."

"The batteries are just back-up power in case the electric were to fail. The room is totally impenetrable once you're inside. Makes for a super safe travel environment."

It smells like feet.

"How far can we get in this?" Blake says.

"Guy only likes to go from weekend to weekend in it, but it'll do ten years at a pop, easy."

"You only go to weekends?" Francesca says.

"Yeah, Guy doesn't really like weekdays much."

"Mondays are for suckers." Guy's voice reaches me from the bedroom doorway. He has found his feet again and is leaning on the doorpost with half-lidded eyes.

"It has fringe benefits too," Lawrence says. "You only age like a hundred days per year that way. Keeps you young."

"You have enough room for all of us in here?" I say.

"Yeah, I'll rig up some more straps," Lawrence says. He flips off the light. "I'll do it in the morning." He passes through us and leads us back to the living room. "You guys are welcome to crash here tonight. The couch is pretty comfortable."

"My bed is really comfortable," Guy says to Francesca.

"Ugh." Francesca turns to me and whispers, "We aren't really going to stay here are we?"

Blake leans in. "I'd do about anything if it gets us ten years."

Francesca stews for a moment. "Well, you're not leaving me alone with either of these guys."

"Don't worry. We aren't going anywhere," I say.

I turn to Lawrence. "We actually need to charge our chronometers. Do you have a wall outlet we can use?"

"Yeah, sure. Not that you'll be needing those antiques anymore, but I don't mind." He points me to the wall past the couch. "I can grab you guys a couple of blankets if you want."

"Thanks."

Lawrence and Guy disappear into the other bedroom and don't immediately return.

"You trust that thing?" Francesca gestures toward the jump room.

"It looks a little sketchy, but these two obviously use it okay. Neither of them are missing arms or anything," I say.

"It will only take three jumps to get home if it can really do ten years at a time," Blake says. "We could be home in our own beds tomorrow night. If the chronometers were charged, I'd just skip to tomorrow morning and say 'strap me in.'"

"I just don't know how much I trust these guys," Francesca says. "Dr. Quickly at least evoked confidence, and it was bad enough doing jumps with him. The idea of traveling with these guys ... it actually makes me nauseated just thinking about it."

"It's just three jumps," Blake says.

I plug two of our chargers into the wall and Blake hands me his chronometer to plug in. I slip mine off my wrist and hook it up as well. I leave them near the baseboard and lay my pack down next to them. I look around for another outlet for Francesca's and have to settle for one in the kitchen. Lawrence emerges from the bedroom with an armload of blankets as I'm plugging it in.

"These should help."

"Thanks." I take the blankets and set them on the couch.

Lawrence begins shutting down his different computer monitors. One large flat-screen, mounted higher up than the others, shows a dense web of diverging lines. Each thread seems to have a thousand little threads branching off it. In the center of the web on the screen is a flashing blue blip.

"What is that one showing?"

"That? That's us. It's showing our location in time."

The little blip seems almost buried by all the threads around it. Lawrence merely gestures with his fingers and the screen zooms in. As the blip grows larger, information begins to appear alongside it. It lists the date in 1986 and shows a frequency oscillation. The frequency is labeled LVR17. Each thread branching off our thread shows a different frequency.

"So it's like a map?" I say.

Lawrence looks from the screen to my face. "Did Dr. Quickly explain the fractal universe to you yet?"

"Um. I don't think so. We talked a bit about the timestream and paradoxes and such, but I don't really recall anything about fractals."

"Huh. That's interesting." He flips off the monitor and the map disappears.

"Why? What's interesting?"

"Just thought that would probably have come up. No problem though. Plenty of time to fill you guys in tomorrow morning."

Lawrence walks to the room with the time cell in it and begins to shut the door behind him. "Oh, bathroom's over there if you need it." He gestures toward the door next to the computer monitors and closes his door.

Blake checks his chronometer's status near the baseboard, and then grabs one of the couch cushions and throws it on the floor next to the wall.

"You guys want me try to squeeze down to one end of the couch, so we could have two on here?" Francesca says.

"No. Don't worry about it," I say. "I don't think we'd fit." I sit down near the chronometers and rearrange the clothing in my pack to be soft enough to use as a pillow. I lie down and try to get comfortable. Francesca picks up one of the blankets gingerly with two fingers and gives it a sniff. Her nose wrinkles and she sets it back down. She lays her pea coat over herself instead as she gets comfortable on the couch. After a few seconds on the couch cushion, she pops back up and grabs a T-shirt out of her pack. She lays that over the cushion and then rests her head back down.

"I'll be really happy to be out of this place."

"Yeah. I'm sorry this night didn't go like you planned," I say. "I'm sure you would much rather have been hanging out with nicer company."

"Maybe you can look up your bartender friend when we get back," Blake says. "He might be a little old though."

"That's okay," Francesca says. "Let's face it. In twenty-five years, that man is still going to be gorgeous." She smiles at me, then rolls over toward the couch cushions. I contemplate the ceiling. *Another night in 1986 after all.* I reach my hand over to where my chronometer is charging. I can feel a slight hum inside as I rest my palm on it. It's not long before I drift off.

There is the faintest hint of predawn light shining over the top of the blinds as my eyes pop open, but the rest of the room is dark.

"I'm telling you, it's not there." Francesca's voice is coming from the far end of the bank of computer screens. As my eyes adjust to the darkness, I make out Blake's silhouette near her.

"Did you feel along that inside wall?" he whispers.

"Yeah, of course I did. You try if you like."

"Hey. What are you guys doing?" I ask.

"Looking for the bathroom light switch," Blake replies.

"I can't find my backpack," Francesca says.

I rise up to an elbow and peer into the darkness near the couch. "Didn't you have it right by you?"

"Got it," Blake says, as light from the bathroom streams in over the couch. "It was a pull cord."

The pack isn't near the couch. I sit up and realize I'm still holding my chronometer, so I set it down.

"See. Told you," Francesca says to Blake. "I had it right there. I was going to get another shirt because I was cold, but it wasn't there."

Climbing off the floor, I walk over to the couch and look behind it. *Nothing. But why would it be . . .* I look to the corner of the kitchen counter where I left Francesca's chronometer charging.

"Oh shit."

"What?" Francesca says.

I rush around the island and grope at the area near the refrigerator in the half-light. "It's gone. Your chronometer is gone."

"You've got to be shitting me," Blake says. He strides to the kitchen and then immediately walks over to Guy's bedroom door. The door swings open easily as he turns the knob. Tangled sheets and a pile of dirty clothes are all we see when he flips on the light. I move to the other door. This one doesn't move.

"You're kidding," Francesca says. "They're gone?"

I pound on the door. "Lawrence!"

Nothing.

I grab the handle with both hands and shoulder the door. I feel it bend slightly but it doesn't open. My heart begins to pound. I step back and kick the door hard near the knob. This time it gives way. The room inside is dark. Blake is the first through.

Francesca finds the kitchen light switch and light streams into the vacant bedroom. Blake tries the door of the cell but it's locked and unyielding. The sound of his fist on the steel door echoes hollowly on the inside.

The words taste like vinegar in my mouth. "They're long gone."

Chapter 16

"I used to think thirty minutes was a reasonable amount of time to wait for a pizza. Then I discovered you could have food delivered by time traveler. My standard for freshness has been raised."
-Excerpt from the journal of Dr. Harold Quickly, 2157

"I'm gonna kick them both in the teeth. I'm gonna pull his stupid floppy hair out and . . . and . . . kick that too." Francesca is storming back and forth from the kitchen to the living room. She reaches the couch again and spins around. "I'm going to . . . wait!" She stops mid-stride. She looks from Blake to me. "You guys can get them! They said they only go to weekends. You can just go to next Friday, be there waiting, and get my chronometer. You can just kick both their asses and get our stuff back!"

I've resigned myself to the long end of the couch during her tirade. Blake is stewing in the office chair. The sunrise gleams through the window beside me.

"I don't think it's that easy, Fresca. Believe me, I wish it was."

Her face is flushed with anger. "Why not?"

"If they have any sense, they won't go to next Friday. Most likely they would have gone to the past. In fact we don't know which direction they were traveling in the first place. They said they went to weekends, but they didn't say they did them in any order. They could very well be traveling backwards."

"But Quickly's book said Guy goes to that bar for years," Francesca argues.

"He never said it was done in any particular order though," Blake says. "Ben's right. They could be anywhere by now."

"This could have been the last Friday they were there," I say. "They could have done all the other one's before this from their perspective. I know I wouldn't come back now if I was them."

Francesca slumps onto a barstool. "Damn it. You mean they're going to get away with this? They just stole like fifty thousand dollars, and a bunch of our anchors. Not to mention my chronometer. I'm really screwed without that."

"I know," I say. "I just think the odds of us catching them are pretty slim. We have no idea where they got to, and if that machine of theirs can jump ten years, they could outrace us anywhere."

Blake sits up a little straighter. "What if they went backward and then came back here? That could be even worse. If they wanted our chronometers, what's to keep them from coming back with guns and taking the rest? They have all the time in the world to make it back here." He stands up and grabs the few items of clothing he has left, and unplugs his chronometer from the wall. "I think we should get out of here."

He's got a valid point.

I slide off the end of the couch and grab my chronometer too.

"What about me?" Francesca says. "Now I'm stuck."

"We can still jump more than one person with these," I say. "It was in the journal. I'm not exactly sure how that works, but we know it can be done. We can figure it out."

"I don't want to end up the victim of some experiment, like Quickly's mice." Francesca says. "He said some of them never made it back."

I look her in the eyes and see her fear. I rest a hand on her shoulder. "We're gonna figure it out. Don't worry. We're not going anywhere without you."

We stuff all of our possessions into our remaining pack and don our jackets. "I hate them," Francesca mumbles. "It's too bad they live in an apartment with other people. I would totally burn this place down." Blake opens the door, cautiously peering down the stairwell before stepping into the hall. Despite our worry, the walk downstairs and outside is uneventful. I pull my jacket closed and zip it up against the cold.

"Where are we going?" Blake asks.

"Let's just get away from here to start," I say.

"I need coffee," Francesca grumbles.

We wander a few blocks through the waking city until we find a coffee shop tucked between a closed bar and a newsstand. A few early rising customers are already reading newspapers in the cozy interior. After I get a warm chai in my hand, we retreat to the back corner of the café to a table and a few cushioned chairs.

"What now?" Francesca says.

192

IN TIMES LIKE THESE

I pull Quickly's journal from my pocket and page through it till I find the section I saw about jumping multiple people. "It says doing tandem jumps is really not that much different. You have to have a chronometer that is charged enough to go the distance. And you have to have a good connection between the people. Looks like skin-to-skin contact is what it's showing here in the drawing." I hold up the journal to show Quickly's sketch of a person with both hands on another person who is activating a chronometer.

"The second person has to be infused with gravitites too, obviously. Oh. And it says you can usually only go about half as far on a charge. That makes sense I guess. You have to make up for all the additional mass."

"Watch it, talking about my additional mass," Francesca says. She's smiling behind her coffee.

It's good she can still smile through all this.

"Where are we going to jump to though?" Blake says. "What have we got left?" I set the pack on the table and rummage through it to pull out our remaining anchors. Francesca helps line them up in chronological order on the table as I pull them out.

When I'm certain I've retrieved everything out of the bag, I drop it back to the floor and survey our results. We have about a dozen items.

"That doesn't look like much to get us twenty-five years," Blake says.

"Yeah, some of these are clumped together pretty closely in time too," I say. "The soup ladle and the beer bottle cap are only like a month apart."

"Hey, there's something I don't get," Francesca says.

"What's that?" I shift in my seat a little, and take another sip of my chai.

"A bunch of our stuff got left on Mr. Cameron's lawn, right? Because it didn't have any gravitites in it. But these things did, so they came with us." She picks up the silver dollar. "They obviously can move through time. How can we use them as anchors then? Won't they just try to come with us again?"

I pause to consider what she's saying. "Yeah. That's a good question. I never really thought about it like that."

"So wait. We can't use this stuff?" Blake says. "This just keeps getting worse and worse." I thumb through Quickly's journal looking for something related to this.

"I just don't want to get us zapped into outer space," Francesca says.

"No. I'm glad you said something," I say. "I wish this thing had an index." I flip to a page that has a sketch of someone making a jump while still plugged into the wall charger. *That could be useful.* A guy in a blue beanie bumps my chair on his way to the bathroom. I wait for him to squeeze by and then go back to the journal. Three pages later, I find what I'm looking for.

"Found it. 'Carrying jump anchors.'" I skim down the page briefly before I begin reading. "Anchors can be transported for use in times other than their original location, if they are treated with gravitites. The gravitite treatment must be reversed prior to use however. Transported anchors must be thoroughly purged of gravitites before use or the resultant jump may be negatively impacted."

"You can de-gravitite something?" Blake says. "I thought Quickly said the effects were permanent."

"Well he said they were permanent on people," I say. I flip to the next page. "Oh. This is probably why." A drawing on the next page shows an object being zapped by a complex looking device. A note is scribbled near the sketch. "While I have been able to successfully purge metal and some durable organic and inorganic matter, purging of biologically living matter still eludes me. Trial results so far remain discouraging."

"So how do we de-gravitite these?" Blake says, holding up the ladle.

"We need one of these things." I show him the drawing.

"That looks . . . involved," Francesca says.

"Yeah. There are a couple more drawings of it. Component parts maybe. Couldn't tell you what any of it is though. I think we are out of our depth with this one."

"So we're back to being screwed," Blake says. "All this stuff is useless." He gives my tortoise shell a spin and it twirls around on the table, wobbling and knocking.

I pick up the photo of the toolbox and flip it over. It's the one with Mym's handwriting. *May 2nd, 1989. Montana. She's going to be in Montana.*

"Maybe they're not completely useless," I say.

"Why?" Francesca says.

"We still have the pictures of these things. And we know that Quickly and Mym were there to take these pictures at these times. What if we could find them and ask one of them for help? They helped us before. Why wouldn't they help us again?"

"You want to find Quickly again somewhere else?" Francesca says.

"Yeah, well, either of them. Malcolm said we shouldn't bother the one at the Temporal Studies Society. He never said anything about finding Quickly somewhere else. We need help from someone."

"Someone who won't rob us blind," Francesca says.

"Yeah, and who knows? Maybe they'll have another chronometer for you to use."

"Oh, that's a conversation to look forward to. Hey, I know you loaned me a priceless piece of technology, and I let some sleazeballs walk off with it, but do you mind giving me another one?" Francesca frowns.

"I'm as much to blame there as you," I say. "I'm the one who left it on the counter."

"It's the fault of those guys being assholes," Blake says. "Well, I wouldn't mind finding someone trustworthy to help us this time. How do you plan to find them though? These dates on these photos are all still pretty far away. That one you've got there is probably the closest, and that's still a couple of years out."

"I was thinking about that. This toolbox looks pretty well used, and it's not an object people usually throw away. Whoever owns this toolbox is probably using it right now somewhere. If we find the toolbox, we can use it to jump ahead to this date in the photo. Mym was there on that date, taking the picture. If we can find her before she leaves, we can get her to help us."

"How do we find the toolbox?" Francesca says.

I flip over the photo and show her the address on the back. "We go here."

"You want to go to Montana?"

"Do we have any better plans?" I look from her face to Blake's.

"How are we going to get to Montana, if we don't have any other anchors from there?" Blake says.

"Well, we can't blink our way there." I reach into my pack and then lay one of the stacks of hundreds on the table. "But we can fly."

Francesca looks from the stack of bills back to my face. Blake slurps the last dregs of his coffee and tosses it into the trashcan.

"Let's do it. Anything beats doing nothing." He grabs the photo from Francesca. "Let's go to . . . Scobey?"

The ticket agent at the counter at Logan International Airport is not having it.

"You can't fly to Scobey." Her fingertips are slightly orange between her index and middle fingers. Her teeth are yellowed too. Despite her obvious habit, I get the impression that she hasn't had her cigarette fix in a while. "Nobody goes there. You'll have to pick somewhere else."

Francesca steps in front of me, and smiles at the woman. "Brenda. You mind if I call you Brenda?" The woman narrows her eyes slightly but doesn't respond. "People live in this city, yes?" Francesca waits for a response but doesn't get one. "So these people have to get there somehow. How do they make that happen?"

Brenda gives Francesca a cold stare but then begins checking a list of airports in a black binder. "You could fly into Minot, North Dakota. You would probably have to drive from there, but we have a flight leaving in an hour that goes to Minneapolis. You could connect to Minot there."

"How far is the drive once we get there?" Blake says.

She flips to a map of the area and considers it a moment. "Looks like it's probably five or six hours, depending on the weather."

"Weather?" Francesca says.

The ticket agent smirks at her. "I believe the average temperature in that area this time of year is about five. Bad snowstorms too."

"Five?" Francesca blanches. "Degrees?"

"Sounds great. We'll take 'em," I say, before Francesca has time to back out. I hold my wad of hundreds up to the counter.

Francesca still has not forgiven me by the time we're ready to board. She sulks behind Blake and me as we walk down the jetbridge. She has pulled her scarf up over her face again and keeps it that way even after we take our seats, as if trying to store up the warmth for later. By the time we make our connection in Minneapolis to our smaller flight to Minot, the situation has not improved.

"Cheer up, Fresca. Did you know that Minot is the geographic center of North America?" I hold up the brochure I've found and try to hand it to her. She has her hands buried under her coat. I settle for setting the brochure in her lap.

Blake smiles beside me. "So, you think we can find Mym before she leaves, once we get to the right spot? It didn't really work that way with Dr. Quickly last time."

I think about my fruitless search in the cul de sac. "Yeah, but this is out in the prairie of Montana, not a Boston suburb. Maybe she won't be able to disappear so quick."

"Yeah. That's true I guess." He settles into his seat and closes his eyes. "We certainly are due for some good luck for a change."

The balding man at the rental car stand in Minot takes one look at the date on Francesca's driver's license and slides it back. "You think I was born yesterday?"

I slip a pair of hundred dollar bills out of my pocket and place them on the counter. I set her license on top and slide them back. He considers me from over top of his glasses, before reaching his hand up and grabbing the bills.

"I guess even the government makes typos every once in a while. What year were you really born, honey?"

Francesca is ready. "1961."

"Good answer." He smiles and scribbles her ID number on a rental form. "Sign here."

"You have any maps? I ask.

"Yeah. Where are you headed?"

"Scobey, Montana."

He leans over the counter and notes our single backpack. He straightens back up and hands Francesca the keys. He smiles at me. "Hope you have a warmer coat."

When we get to the parking lot, Francesca takes one look at the snow piled up near the exit, and holds the keys out toward Blake and me. "I've never driven in snow before. I don't think I'm going to start today."

Blake and I trade off driving and navigating duties for the next few hours as we head west on Highway 5. The expansive plains around us are seas of white, but I occasionally make out tracks and paw prints in the snow. At one point, we pass a small herd of buffalo grouped together near a fence. Their beards are gleaming with ice crystals and large swaths of snow have been cleared around them as they've foraged for grass. Francesca is huddled miserably in the rear seat but her eyes follow the buffalo as we pass them.

The other vehicles on the road are infrequent and most of the miles consist of long, straight expanses of nothing but snow and highway stretching toward the horizon. The few drivers of other cars we do pass, tend to wave at us.

"At least they're friendly out here," I say, as I wave back to the tenth pickup truck we see. Blake keeps his hands on the wheel. "This address is right off the highway somewhere. These roads don't seem well marked," I say.

"Yeah. I noticed that. I don't know if we are supposed to be looking for the road on this side of town or the other side," Blake says.

We come upon some buildings, and cruise through an intersection where I see a couple of men pulling an old Ford truck onto a flat bed. A few minutes later we're back to prairie.

"How far are we from town?" Francesca says.

I look out at the expansive plain stretching ahead of us and then pivot in the seat to view what's behind us. I double-check the map. "Actually, I think we just passed it."

Blake slows down and pulls off into a dirt side road that looks like it was recently plowed. Chunks of dirt and frozen gravel litter the drifts along both sides of the road.

"I thought you said Scobey was a town," Francesca says.

"Yeah. It is," I say. "They might have a broader definition of the term out here."

Blake turns us around and heads back the other direction. The men with the flat bed truck have successfully strapped down the Ford by the time we cruise back into the intersection. Blake pulls the car up next to a man bundled up in a thick, tan, Carhartt coat.

"Excuse me. We're looking for an address and we could use some help."

The man crunches through the snow and leans down to take us all in. He has snow in his beard too. He looks a lot like the buffalo. I hand the photo with the address across Blake, and the man reaches out a gloved hand to take it. "Where you all from?" he asks. His dark brown eyes glide from Blake and me to the pile of clothing that is Francesca in the back seat.

"We're from Florida," Blake says.

"Oh. Long way from home, eh?"

"Yeah. Very," Blake replies.

The man reads the back of the photo. "This is the Parsons' place. Used to be Hank Parsons' ranch. I think his son's got it now. Don't see much of him lately, but the ranch isn't far." He squats down a little and points west. "You're gonna wanna go about five miles. You'll see the grain silo on the Farnsworth farm. It's on the right. Can't miss it, they painted it blue last summer. Two roads past that, you'll hit the road to the Parsons. Just stay on it going north. You'll find the house eventually. Hopefully they've got around to plowing it. Do they know you're coming?"

"No. Not yet, we're a little early," Blake says.

"If you can't make it out there in this thing, come back and use the phone in the diner. They can probably come down and get you."

"Thank you, sir," Blake says.

The man gives us a thumbs up and climbs into his truck.

"People are really nice here," Francesca says.

"I hope that's true of the Parsons too," I say.

Blake heads us west again until we spot the blue grain silo. We creep along more slowly after that and find the second drive that heads north. A mailbox sticking out of a snowdrift across the street from the entrance is the only sign of a residence. We turn north and bounce ourselves along a dirt road that makes its way over gentle hills that would normally present little trouble, but covered with ice, make the tail end of our rental slip and slide.

Many of the potholes are frozen over, which improves the bumpiness slightly.

We've traversed a dozen small hills before I catch sight of some outbuildings up ahead. We pass a small shed and an old farmhouse that appears to have been abandoned for many years. The road continues on, and a couple of hills later, I spot a larger group of buildings in the distance. The sight is lost to me however, because as we descend the next little valley, the tires of the rental slide on a thick patch of ice. Blake tries to steer us out of the skid to keep it straight, but we slide sideways off the edge of the road and stop with a thump, nosed into a snowdrift. The front end of the car is in a ditch to the right side of the road and partially buried in white. Blake shifts into reverse and tries to back out, but the angle of the car gives the rear wheels very little traction on the icy road. The wheels spin futilely for a few moments.

"Try going forward a bit and then back again," I say.

Blake attempts to move the car forward but it won't budge. He tries backwards again with no luck.

"Well this sucks," Blake says.

"I think I saw the house from the top of the hill. Maybe we can just walk the rest of the way," I say.

"Don't they say not to leave the car in these situations?" Francesca says.

"I think that's in blizzards and stuff. I don't think that counts if it's not snowing."

I pop open my door and the blast of cold air assaults my lungs. I stuff my hands in my armpits and shuffle carefully around the back of the car. Blake joins me.

"They should issue winches with all these rental cars," he says.

Francesca slowly emerges from the driver's side as well, and mumbles something I don't catch under her scarf.

"Let's hope they have a fireplace," Blake says.

My sneakers slip and slide on the patches of ice on the road. I stick to the areas with gravel showing through as much as possible as we climb the little undulating rises in the terrain. Francesca mumbles something again at the top of the next hill.

"I don't know what you're saying," I say.

She pulls her scarf away from her mouth and points her finger ahead. "I see smoke." I look where she's pointing, and sure enough, little patches of smoke are drifting out of the chimney on a distant building.

"That can't be more than a half mile," Blake says.

With renewed enthusiasm, we trudge and slide our way over the next dozen rises. The first building we come to appears to be an old equipment barn. A rusting tractor hides in the shadows as we make our way past the dusty windows. The next outbuilding is also dilapidated, but is more encouraging, as there is a fluffy, gray cat perched on the edge of a hay bale, watching us with pale, gold eyes as we walk past the open door. The interior of the oversized shed is filled with tools and a riding mower.

"How are we going to get these people to help us?" Blake asks.

"I guess we need to see if they even have the toolbox, and go from there," I say.

Turning the next small bend in the road reveals the main house of the ranch, but to my surprise, the chimney of the house is not the one that's smoking. The smoke is rising from the top of a long, narrow building about twenty yards past the main house. An immense barn sits across from it with an empty paddock behind it. The split rail fence of the paddock is draped with snow and dead vines. Other than the subtle movement of the smoke from the chimney, the ranch is eerily vacant.

My toes have gone numb in my sneakers but I attempt to wiggle them as I walk toward to the low porch of the smoking building. It looks like it holds multiple units, and I suspect it may have been used to house ranch hands in more vibrant times. The room with the smoking chimney is at the farthest end of the building, away from the main house.

Once we reach the porch, Blake and Francesca use the edge of the step to knock the snow off their boots. The wooden door has a fan of glass windows at the top. I can make out a ceiling light through the cloudy glass.

My knock on the door inspires movement inside. A chair scrapes the floor and a steady footstep follows until a shadow appears beyond the frosted glass. The shadow pauses at the door and contemplates me. I fear it's not going to open the door at all, but a moment later, I hear the deadbolt slide back. As the door opens a crack, a set of wrinkled fingers and a sharp blue eye belonging to a leathery brown face appears. The man has a thick crop of grey hair sprouting behind his ears but the top of his head is rather wispy. His jaw works the tobacco in his lower lip and he looks like he is in need of a spit. I worry from his expression that he's going to spit it at me, but he contains himself.

"Hi there," I say. The weathered face doesn't respond. "How are you?" The man's blue eyes appraise Blake and Francesca behind me and then come back to my face. "We're looking for the person who owns this toolbox." I hold up the photo for him.

He glances at the photo for a quick second, then garbles in a voice that sounds rough and out of use. "That's mine. What's it to ya?"

"Well, sir, we were wondering if you might let us see it?" I say.

"What for?"

"Uh . . ." I falter.

"We think it might be valuable," Francesca improvises. "Um, there were some special boxes that were made that year . . . that are now collectors' items."

The man steps out of the door and strides to the edge of the porch. He has on a green-and-brown flannel shirt and his battered jeans are held up with suspenders. He spits into the snow bank along the porch. I notice there are multiple brown stains in the drift from previous outings.

"Got that toolbox off a shelf at Sears. Probably had a dozen more just like 'em sittin' on the shelf next to it. You trying to tell me that's what goes for collectors' items these days?"

"Well . . . there's a market for everything," Francesca says.

"Do you mind if we have a look at your box?" Blake says.

The man slips back inside. As he crosses his threshold, I notice he is only in socks. The heat from his home feels heavenly on my face.

"It's not for sale." He begins to shut the door.

"Sir do you mind if we at least see the box?" I say. "So we can determine if it really is one of the rare ones. It would really help us out if we knew just how many of them are still around. We could compensate you for your time."

He considers this a moment. His eyes linger on my arm, and I notice my chronometer is showing past the sleeve on my jacket. I move my sleeve and cover it back up.

"I'll get my boots."

He turns his head away and I get a glimpse of the fire burning in the hearth and a rough-spun blanket draped over the back of a leather couch in front of the fireplace. The room looks cozy and well lived in, right until the door shuts in my face.

We could have waited for you to put your boots on in there.

I stuff my hands into my pockets and shiver.

"You think he buys it?" Blake says.

"I don't know. It is a pretty flimsy story but it's the best we've got," I say. "No offense, Fresca."

"None taken," Francesca says. "You weren't exactly wowing him with your eloquence there."

"No, it was great thinking," I say. "I had nothing."

I stomp my feet a few times to get feeling back into my toes. The door clicks behind me and the weathered man reemerges in a wool coat and a hat with fuzzy earflaps. He's carrying a set of keys. He spits into the snowdrift again as he passes by and leads the way across the yard toward the barn.

The late afternoon sun finds a gap in the overcast sky and for a few moments the pasture gleams a blinding white. I shield my eyes until we reach the barn.

"I never got your name," I say, as the man fiddles with the lock on the barn door.

"I never gave it."

I wait for him to offer it now but he only jerks the lock open and unlatches the door. Snow and dirt rain down from the top edge of the door as he swings it open. He kicks at a few chunks of ice to get them out of the way, and then pushes the door into a drift till it sticks. He pulls a locking rod up from the ground on the other half of the door and it swings open with a moan.

The interior of the barn has been cordoned off into stalls, but I see no animals. The man strides into the open center, and as we follow him in, my attention is drawn upward to a dome of multicolored fabric strung from the ceiling. The fabric looks to be synthetic and it encompasses the entire center section of the immense roof.

"Oh wow. Is that a parachute?" Francesca asks.

"I don't know," I say.

One of the stalls we walk past has an elaborate metal object on a table that reminds me of a jet engine. It has a perforated grill and a couple of flexible hoses coming from the center of it. Away from it in the corner of the stall, sitting on a metal shelf, are two ten-gallon propane cylinders.

The weathered man pays none of the stalls any attention until he reaches the back left corner. That stall has been made into a work area with sawhorses and a workbench. Along the floor under the workbench are four large fire extinguishers and a stool. The toolbox from our photo is sitting atop the workbench next to a leather tool belt.

The man turns to face us and gives his head a jerk to the left. "That's it there."

Francesca puts on a serious expression and steps up to the box. She runs her fingers over the top and sides, and then with some effort, turns it around on the bench to view the back.

The toolbox has no exceptional markings or labels. The corners of the steel lid have begun to accumulate some rust and I recognize the handle as being the same one I have riding around in my backpack.

"Hmm," Francesca says. "I think this does look promising. Do you mind if I open it?" The man says nothing, but she takes that as a yes and begins to fiddle with the latches. The interior of the lid has a Craftsman sticker on it with some ID numbers. "Ah. Here we go." She turns to me. "Benjamin, do you want to check the numbers against our list?"

"Um. Okay." I pull my pack off my back and rummage around in it for a moment, before pulling out my logbook. I flip through it, and after settling on an arbitrary page of my jump entries, I pretend to be reading numbers on it. I step up and read the model and serial number of the box. "Uh huh."

Does she want it to match or not? I hold the page up to Francesca at an angle that obstructs it from the man's view. She pretends to check it. The man's face is stone. He spits in the corner and resumes glaring at us.

"I think you might have a winner here," Francesca says. "Do . . . um, do you mind if I have a few moments in private with my associates?"

The man's jaw works and he spits again.

"Also, do you happen to have an electrical outlet nearby?" I say.

He looks like he wants to murder us.

He jerks his head toward the ceiling of the stall that is also the floor of the loft above us. A bare bulb has been wired through with two electrical outlets at the base. "I'll have to turn on the generator for you," he grumbles. "You need me to dial in them chronometers for you too?"

He turns and steps back into the main barn area. "'We could compensate you for your time.' Ha! You just tell Bob I want a raise when you see him." He spits one more time for emphasis and walks away. I watch him go in amazement. The barn door bangs shut as I turn back to Blake and Francesca.

"Wait, he knew?" Francesca says.

"Yeah, I didn't see that one coming either," Blake says.

"Apparently we aren't the first time travelers to come calling," I reply.

A motor coughs and rumbles outside the barn wall and the light bulb above us flickers to life. Francesca has turned red. "God, I feel like such an idiot. He must think we're complete jerks."

"It's okay." I toss my logbook back into my pack. "I get the feeling he doesn't like much of anybody."

Blake holds his arms out to the toolbox. "So it's here."

Francesca flips it shut to look at the handle. "Looks like the one in the picture. So what now?"

"Now we figure out how to blink ourselves to 1989." I pull out Quickly's journal. "I was reading up on this on the plane. Apparently what we need to do is plug in our chronometers to a power source using our chargers, and then we can blink a lot farther. Our chronometers only go up to five years, but that's plenty for us."

"Does it say that you can do that with multiple people?" Francesca asks.

"It says you can do multiple people, and then it says you can do it plugged in. I don't see why you can't do both."

"But it doesn't say that specifically?"

"Well . . . no, but he just sort of scribbles things in here, it's not really all that organized . . ."

"Oh God. I'm going to die."

"If you want to have the chronometer and I can hold on to you instead, we can do it that way," I say. "I feel confident about it."

"No. That's okay," Francesca exhales nervously. "I'm not gonna make you do that. I would feel terrible if you got left floating in outer space. I'm not sure I could handle that."

"Ben and I would feel terrible too," Blake says.

"Yeah, but if it happens to somebody, I don't want to be the one feeling guilty about it forever," Francesca says.

"You'd rather be the one launched into space, than to have to feel guilty?" Blake asks.

"Yeah. I don't want that on my conscience," Francesca replies.

"Nobody is getting launched into space!" I frown and pull the chargers out of the pack, handing them both to Blake. "See if you can reach that outlet."

Next, I pull out the envelope with the toolbox handle and its photo. I extract the photo, and after considering the handle for a moment, stuff that back inside. "Okay. The box is sitting on a table in this picture. Is this the same table?"

Francesca steps over to look. "No. I don't think so. See that background? It actually looks like it's out there, in the picture." She points to the main area of the barn.

"It doesn't have a height dimension on this one," I say. "You can see the floor though. I would guess that's like three and a half feet or so, wouldn't you?"

"I don't know. I'm terrible at guessing stuff like that," Francesca says.

Blake reaches past me and flips open the toolbox. He hands me a tape measure and flips the lid shut again without saying a word.

"Oh. Yeah. Glad one of us is thinking." I walk out into the barn, look up at the multicolored canvas again, and turn to face the back wall. "Looks like it's facing this way. There's no table here now, but we can find something to use."

"That's not gonna work," Blake says. He points to the light bulb above him with our chargers sticking out of the socket.

"Oh. Yeah. You're right. We'll have to do it in there to be plugged in. We're going to end up out here though."

"We won't end up hitting that table whenever there is one?" Francesca says.

"No. Not if we do it right."

I walk back to the toolbox and pick it up, then set it back down. "This bench it's on is too high, unless we all had something to stand on."

"What if we set it on this?" Blake reaches under the workbench and pulls out the wooden stool.

I measure the height. "Yeah. That should work."

"Okay. So May 2nd, 1989 right?" Blake says, starting to dial his chronometer. "What time?"

I consult the back of the photo. "1800 Zulu. So that's what? 6 pm? But we're in Montana so . . ."

"Mountain time. That's minus seven hours," Blake says. "That's 11 am."

"Except May is daylight saving time," Francesca says. "That makes it noon."

"Okay. It shouldn't matter for the settings," I say. "We can just set Zulu time." I set the tape measure down and start to dial my chronometer settings.

"Doesn't hurt to know what time of day you're arriving though," Francesca says.

I nod.

"So we get there around noon, and then we immediately look for Mym?" Blake says.

"Yeah. Hopefully she hasn't gotten far. I don't know how she usually sets up her anchor shots, but how far could she get out here in the middle of a prairie, right?"

"Unless she blinks away using something else," Francesca says. "Then we'd never find her."

"Let's hope that doesn't happen." I frown.

"We should get a move on in any case," Blake says. "Before this generator runs out of gas, or he shuts it off on us."

I finish my chronometer settings and compare them with Blake's. I center the toolbox on the stool and then set the photo down in front of it. "Okay, the box is going to be about a foot back from the edge of the table, so that edge should be about here." I gesture to our imaginary table edge and we all step away a bit to have plenty of clearance. I extend my left hand with the chronometer to touch the toolbox and make sure I have enough room. Blake hands me the charging cord to my chronometer.

"Oh shit!" Francesca blurts.

"What?"

"My clothes!" She immediately drops down to my pack and rummages through it.

"Oh yeah. I forgot about that." I look at my outfit and pull the waistband back on my jeans to double check my boxers.

I'm not too bad off. Need to lose the shoes and the jacket though.

Francesca grabs her small armful of clothes and disappears around the corner into one of the empty stalls. I lean down to look through what's left of the items in my pack. I pull out my flip-flops.

"My flip-flops got stolen," Blake says as he lays his coat on the workbench and begins pulling off his boots.

"Yeah, that sucks," I say, looking at the rough-hewn boards of the floor. "You can use one of mine if you want. We can share. That way neither of us is totally barefoot."

"Okay. That might help actually," Blake says.

I slide him one of my flip-flops and toss my jacket on top of his. A few moments later, Francesca reappears in her wrinkled short-sleeve top and jeans, and her flip-flops. She shivers as she lays her pea coat, hat and scarf on the table with our jackets. She gently sets her boots on the floor, then folds her arms and shuffles over between us. I toss Quickly's journal back into my pack and sling it onto my shoulders.

"Okay. Now we're ready," I say.

"Where am I holding onto?" Francesca says. I extend my arm. She looks from me to Blake. "How about I be Blake's backpack."

Blake looks at her and then shrugs. "Okay."

He stoops down, lets Francesca wrap her arms around his neck, and stands up with her piggyback.

"If you suggest anything about me being heavy, I'll knee you in the kidney," Francesca says.

I plug in my chronometer and lift up my shoeless foot. Blake sways a little as he tries to balance on one foot with Francesca on his back.

"Carson was right," I say. "We do look ridiculous."

"Let's get this over with," Blake says.

I stuff the photo back in my pocket and touch my hand to the top of the toolbox handle, next to Blake's.

"On three. One . . . two . . . three."

206

We drop about six inches. Blake plants his other foot but still goes over backward. The chronometers' charger plugs rain down on my head. Francesca rolls off with a thump and tries to get free, but Blake lands between her legs and the two of them end up in a tangle. It has to be sixty degrees warmer.

My one bare foot has landed in a pile of brown mushiness that I really hope is just mud. Blake struggles to his feet and I give Francesca a hand up.

"Thank God it's warm," she says, as she brushes off her backside.

I scan the barn around us. I don't see her. "Spread out. Let's see if we can find Mym."

I hobble on my one flip-flop and muddy foot toward the barn door while Francesca and Blake fan out inside the barn. I scan the loft briefly and notice the color of the canvas in the rafters has changed to a vibrant blue and green. I open the barn door to bright warm sunlight.

Oh that feels good.

The barnyard has a pickup truck parked in front of the house and a Palomino horse is leaning its head over the paddock fence, chewing tufts of grass. It lifts its head to consider me as I stumble out of the barn into the yard.

I hear a loud whoosh and a crackle like a dragon's breath. A woman laughs from somewhere behind the barn. I turn and look back to the distant interior wall of the barn and see movement through the thin spaces between the boards. Vibrant colors are shifting and changing.

"What is that?" Francesca says, as she and Blake exit the doors.

I back up a few steps to try to see the top of the barn. The roof looks like it's moving. A massive dome of a dozen different colors is blooming from beyond the sheet metal roof.

"No way . . ." I mumble.

"What is that?" Blake says.

I lose the flip-flop as I sprint around the left side of the barn. As I round the rear corner, I slow to a stop to take in the sight before me.

Floating twenty feet off the ground and slowly rising, is the biggest hot air balloon I've ever seen. A burly, bearded man with muscular arms is letting out rope from the massive wicker gondola hanging below the balloon. Looking down from his side is a petite young woman with curly blonde hair. I wave to her.

She smiles.

Chapter 17

"I frequently lecture on the dangers of misusing time. People often ask me afterward about what I feel is the biggest waste of time, suspecting that I will say something like television or arguing politics. I think the biggest waste of time is feeling sorry for yourself. That and traffic. Thankfully I found a way out of that one."
-Excerpt from the journal of Dr. Harold Quickly, 1972

The man in the balloon confers with Mym about our sudden appearance. She touches his shoulder and speaks something into his ear. He pulls on a cord and the balloon stops rising, then slowly begins a descent back to earth. Francesca and Blake join me as I duck under the fence rail and walk toward the balloon through the tall grass of the pasture.

"Look at the size of that thing," Blake says.

The balloon is immense. The gondola looks as though it would hold ten people. A metal cable connecting it to a big iron hoop in the ground grows taut as the wind attempts to push the balloon away from the barn. As it sinks close to the ground, the man gestures for me to come closer, and tosses out another cable.

"Tie us off over there!" He points me toward another iron hoop on the far side of the balloon, partially buried in the grass. I pick up the end of the cable and trot to the iron ring. The end of the cable has an oversized carabineer clip on it. I snap that over the ring and stand back. As soon as I've completed that, he tosses another one out and points to an identical hoop on the opposite side. I repeat the process there. He moves to a winch on the railing of the gondola and begins cranking. He signals to Mym, who gives periodic pulls on the cord to lower the balloon as he cranks the cables tighter.

After a few moments, the gondola settles to the grass with a thump. The man gives a few more cranks of the winch and locks it in place. He gives

Mym a hand climbing over the rail and she drops into the grass. Francesca, Blake and I convene in front of her and she smiles at us with curiosity. Something the bearded man is doing is causing the balloon to wilt rapidly behind her.

"Hello," she says.

"Hi, Mym."

She tilts her head a little as she considers me.

She looks young.

"Have we met?" she asks.

Damn. She has no idea who we are.

Francesca holds out her hand. "Hi. I'm Francesca."

"Mym," she replies, giving Francesca a warm smile.

"I'm Blake." Another handshake.

She turns to me.

"Benjamin."

She takes my hand and shakes it firmly while looking me in the eyes. "It's nice to meet you." She turns and gestures back to the bearded man climbing over the edge of the gondola. The balloon now lies horizontal in the field. "This is Cowboy Bob."

The man walks over to us and extends Francesca a hand first. "Bob is fine. This one loves to embellish." He gives a jerk of his head toward Mym.

"There are a lot of Bobs in the world," she replies. "So you're Cowboy Bob. Makes you sound more eccentric when I tell people about you." She gives him a grin.

Bob's handshake tells of years of manual labor. He's a little shorter than me, but more broad-shouldered. I had thought him older from a distance because of his beard, but on closer inspection, I realize he's likely only in his late twenties. His close-cropped beard is neat and tidy compared to the buffalo man from town, but his dark eyes are just as friendly.

"We're sorry to barge in on your ballooning," I say. "We just needed a little help."

"It's all right," Cowboy Bob replies. "I would have waited anyway if I'd seen you driving up."

"Oh. We didn't drive," I say.

Mym has been observing my chronometer and nudges Cowboy Bob with her elbow. He looks down where she's gesturing.

"Ah."

"We actually came from your barn," Francesca says.

"We may have left a rental car buried in a snow drift in your driveway," Blake adds.

"Oh. Haha. You're who did that!" Cowboy Bob grins. "That gave Levi fits when he found it." He looks at Mym. "You should have heard him complaining. It snowed the next day and buried the car before he found it. He tried plowing through the lump without checking what it was first. Made quite mess of things from what I hear."

"I'm sorry to cause so much trouble," I say.

"Oh, no. It's fine. Levi is never happy unless he has something to complain about."

"So who is he?" Francesca asks.

"He's my ranch hand. He lives here full-time and takes care of the place while I'm gone."

"He knew right away that we were time travelers," I say.

"Oh, yeah. He's seen me vanish out of this field enough times. And he's met Mym over the years, so it's probably getting to be old hat for him now."

"You can time travel in this?" Blake gestures to the balloon.

Cowboy Bob smiles. "It's the only way to go, if you ask me."

"It's really nice," Mym says. Then she smirks at Cowboy Bob. "Not always nice for the birds."

"Oh. Yeah. But that's rare," Cowboy Bob replies.

"What's rare?" Francesca asks.

"Oh. This last time through . . . the balloon is really safe. Probably the safest way you can go if you ask me. There's hardly ever anything in the sky you can run into . . ."

"He had just gotten through bragging about that." Mym smiles.

"Yeah, of course. Having just said that, we moved, and there happened to be a flock of swallows flying through where the top of the balloon arrived . . ." He looks at Francesca's horrified face. "Most of them were fine, mind you."

"Except for poor Pokey." Mym frowns.

Cowboy Bob gives her an exasperated smile. "Yes." He looks back to us. "One bird didn't make it. He got fused into the fabric of the balloon up top."

"With just his little head poking out," Mym adds, pouting her lower lip.

"Yeah. And it was sad, I'll give you that, but it could have been worse. I don't think it was a bad way to go."

"He had his poor head stuck in a hot air balloon! What's worse than that?" Mym chides.

"Well, he could have ended up in the burner, or the gondola, or us. At least he still had a nice view at the end."

Mym shakes her head. "I think you still owe him a better apology."

"I'm not apologizing to the dead bird. Again."

Mym tries to maintain her frown. "He wouldn't even say anything at his funeral . . ."

"So enough about the darn bird," Cowboy Bob says. "Where are you all from? Other than my barn."

"We're from 2009," Blake says.

"Florida," Francesca adds.

"Oh!" Mym says. "Saint Petersburg?"

"Yes," Francesca replies.

"What brings you out here?" Cowboy Bob nods toward the road.

"My Dad probably sent them," Mym says. "You know my Dad?"

"We do actually," I say. "But he didn't send us. It's kind of a long story."

"Would it be a better, long, inside story?" Cowboy Bob asks. "We could get out of this field if you like."

"Yeah, I think something just tried to crawl up my leg," Francesca says.

"I'll show you the house." Bob guides us to a paddock gate that he unlatches and swings open for us. The horse whickers as we pass and plods over to Cowboy Bob as he closes the latch. He gives the mare's face a quick rub and then leads the way across the barnyard toward the house.

Unlike the last time I saw it, the house looks open and inviting. The curtains have all been drawn back and most of the windows are up. The front door is open also, with just a screen door for keeping the occasional bug out. As we climb the porch steps, I hear a clatter of dishes from inside and realize someone else is home. Bob stops to take off his boots by the front door. Mym leaves hers there too; only then does she notice that Blake and I are barefoot. Blake is holding the flip-flop I lent him.

"You guys were prepared for this, huh?"

I scratch behind my neck. "Yeah, we've been having a few clothing and footwear mishaps." I set my backpack down just inside the door.

The front doorway leads into a spacious living room full of natural light that allows a great view of the ranch. It's decorated in a western style with leather furniture and a massive stone hearth. Much of the light is streaming in from above, where the high, wood-beamed ceiling has allowed room for extra windows. We pass under a loft balcony through a hallway lined with framed black and white photos. Among scenes of cattle branding and hay baling, I notice a photo of a younger Cowboy Bob cradling a baby goat. The photo looks old but it's hard to tell.

We pass into a dining area that's likewise well lit with sun. The rough-hewn table would seat a dozen people. The room adjoins the kitchen, and as we round the corner, a woman appears. Stout, gray-haired and perhaps sixty-five, she brushes her hands off on an apron as she turns to greet us.

"Not leaving yet after all, Mrs. A," Cowboy Bob says.

"Oh, you brought me some more visitors!" The woman smiles.

"Yes, these are . . ." He turns to us.

"I'm Blake." Blake is closest and extends a hand.

"Francesca."

"I'm Benjamin."

"How do you do. I'm Connie," the woman replies. The edges of her green eyes have a lot of smile lines. "Are these friends of yours?" she asks Mym.

"Um. Possibly." Mym smiles. Her eyes find mine. "Hard to tell what people are right at first sometimes."

"You all lead the most interesting lives," Connie says. "I don't know how you keep anything straight." She turns back to us. "Are you all time travelers too?"

I nod.

"We try not to be," Blake says.

"I'll tell you, things just keep getting more fun around here. The ladies in my quilting circle never believe a word I say about this job. I'm sure they all think I've gone senile. When did you all get here? Are you hungry?"

"Um. Yeah, we just got in. I don't want to impose or anything, but I could eat," I say.

Francesca and Blake murmur agreement.

"Okay. I'll fix you something up."

"Mrs. A makes an outstanding lasagna," Mym says. "I feel like I gain about ten pounds every time I visit."

"Why don't you all go sit on the back deck. It's so lovely out. I'll bring you out some iced tea."

"Yes ma'am," Cowboy Bob replies, and opens the screen door off the kitchen. The back deck is shaded by a tall, flowering tree. Its thin leaves are silver and it's covered with white blooms.

We gather around a picnic table. Francesca squeezes in between Blake and me on one side, while Cowboy Bob and Mym take the other.

"I really like your house," Francesca says.

"Thank you," Bob replies.

"What kind of tree is that?" Blake asks.

"That's a Russian Olive," Bob says. "My dad planted that years and years ago."

"I noticed there aren't many trees out here," I say.

"Yeah, if you want a tree, you pretty much have to plant it yourself or truck one in. Nothing much grows out here naturally. Scrub brush and grass. We have plenty of that."

"It's beautiful here though," Francesca says. "Now that it's not freezing."

"Ah that's right, you were here in the winter," Bob says.

"Yeah. We came from December of '86." I brush a leaf off the table.

"Man, it wasn't too fun around here then. What made you decide to visit in December?"

"We were actually looking for Mym," I say. "We didn't know how else to find her." I pull the photo of the toolbox out of my back pocket and lay it in front of her.

"I just took that," Mym says. "I haven't even printed it yet. Where did you find it?"

"I got it out of your dad's lab in 1986."

"Oh. I should probably make a note of that." She reaches into her pocket and pulls out a device.

"Is that an iPhone?" Francesca asks.

"Um. No. Not exactly. It does look like one though," Mym says. "It's a multi function device for time traveling stuff. They just call them MFD's. I brought it back from the future and one of dad's friends helped customize it for me. It's pretty handy." She taps the screen a few times, takes a scan of the back and front of my picture, then slides the MFD back into her pocket. She pushes the photo toward me. "You probably want to get rid of that."

"Okay."

"So what is dad up to in 1986? Anything exciting I should know about?"

I look at Francesca and Blake.

"Do we tell her?" Francesca says.

"We're still pretty new at this," I say. "We don't really know much about what you should and shouldn't know about the future or past. Do you want to know what happens then?"

Mym considers me. "This was two and a half years ago, right?"

"No. We actually came from January of '86 originally; at least that's where your dad was anyway. So that's more like three and a half. He was helping us get home."

"What happened? It's okay. You can tell me. The universe isn't going to explode or anything."

Connie appears with pitchers of lemonade and iced tea and some glasses. We make room to help her navigate the tray onto the table. I give Bob and Mym an abbreviated account of our experiences in 1986. As I reach the part about meeting Stenger with Carson in the lab, Connie returns, the tray now loaded with tuna melt sandwiches. I take one eagerly.

"So where was Dad in this situation?" Mym asks between bites.

"That's the thing. We really don't know. You and he just sort of left, I guess."

"He left you the journal though," Francesca says. "Show her."

I reach into my back pocket and pull out Dr. Quickly's journal. Mym stops chewing when I lay it on the table. She swallows and sets her sandwich down. She traces the front cover of the book with her fingertips, but doesn't open it.

"Wow. I've never known him to even show that to anyone other than me before, let alone give it to someone."

Bob has been listening quietly until this point, but now leans in. "This Stenger person. What happened to him?"

"I don't really know," I say.

Blake interjects. "We had our friend Robbie tip off the cops about him. So we're hoping they picked him up eventually."

"That doesn't seem very conclusive, if you don't mind me saying so," Bob replies.

"We aren't the cops," Blake says. "I'm not really sure what else we could do."

Bob's eyes linger on the chronometer on my wrist for a moment, but then he picks up his plate and stands up. "Yes. I suppose not." He opens the screen door and goes back into the kitchen.

"We really are just trying to get back to 2009," Francesca says. "That's been our goal this entire time. We could really use some help though."

"Things haven't been going great," I add.

Mym chews another bite of tuna melt and then replies, "I'm sure Cowboy Bob can help you out without too much trouble. We were just going to take a quick blink up to 1993 and back today, but we could probably talk him into going farther if you want. He's kind of a push-over if you ask nice enough."

"That balloon of his will go that far?" Blake says.

"Oh definitely, that is one of the best distance time machines ever. Not a lot of people know about it because he's pretty private, but other than some of the transverse wormhole gates they come up with later, his is the best. The gates are always fixed points too, so even though they can travel farther, the fact that his balloon is portable and actually flies makes it way more versatile."

"What's the farthest you've been?" Blake says.

214

"With Cowboy Bob? Or in general?"

"Either I guess."

"Dad took us all the way back to the 1860s when I was a kid. He said it was part of my history lessons. We were in the crowd when Lincoln gave the Gettysburg Address."

"Wow," I say. "That's awesome."

"Were you tempted to go find John Wilkes Booth and kick his ass?" Francesca says.

"No. I was only thirteen then, and dad was doing one of his 'paradox free' trips. He tries not to mess with historical events at all. He was really intent on my education being thorough. It was mostly pretty great. I had a hard time when I was young though, because my parents put me in regular school sometimes, so that I could have that experience. I never got along very well with any of my history teachers. We argued a lot."

"I guess they don't get a lot of grade schoolers with firsthand knowledge of history," I say.

"You'd be surprised how wrong textbooks can be too. I've realized that people are happier thinking what they know is true. Telling them the actual truth doesn't always improve things."

Cowboy Bob returns with Connie and she snatches up our plates of crumbs. I notice he has his boots back on. "We can help you with the dishes," Francesca offers.

"Nonsense, honey," Connie replies. "You just sit and visit. I know you all didn't come all this way to scrub pots and pans."

Bob stays standing at the end of the table. "So what's the plan?"

"They need to go to 2009," Mym says.

Bob considers us. "You need to get there right now?"

"Is that an option?" Blake asks.

"Well, I was going to make some other stops. I could get us most of the way today, if you like. I'll probably need to stop and recharge the batteries somewhere. I could probably get you there by tomorrow though."

"Really?" Francesca says.

"That would be amazing!" Blake's hands go to his head. "I can't believe it. Thank you!"

"That's awesome," I say.

"We should take them to the meteor shower," Mym adds.

"Yeah, we could do that." Bob nods. "Which ones have I already taken you to?"

"We did a couple Leonids, and we did Haley's Comet."

"Okay. We could hit another Leonids on the way. They're always good."

Mym turns back to us. "The meteor showers at night here are amazing. The sky is so huge and dark. I like to watch the Space Shuttle go by a lot when I'm here. You can see it pretty easily on a clear night."

"That's really cool," I say.

"When do you want to go?" Bob asks us.

I glance at the others. "Um. Whenever, I guess."

"All right. I'll tell you what. After lunch we'll do a big move to maybe the late nineties or early two thousands, since the balloon is already set up. Then we can stop and relax. I'll charge the batteries overnight, and we can go the rest of the way in the morning."

"That is so great," Blake says. "Thank you so much."

"It's no problem," Bob replies. "I'll go finish prepping the balloon. Just come out to the field when you're ready." He gives Mym a nod and strides off around the side of the house for the barn.

"I can't believe it." Blake smiles. "We can be home tomorrow!" He stands up. "I'll go get our shoes."

"One of mine is by the barn," I say.

As he disappears inside, Francesca turns to Mym. "Speaking of shoes, is there any chance you have any extra clothes I might be able to borrow? We have been wearing the same things for what I guess is years now, and I feel kind of gross."

"Oh definitely." Mym smiles. "My stuff is already packed up in the balloon, but once we get through the trip and stop for the night, you can look through what I've got and see what you like."

"Oh thank you. That would be amazing."

Mym looks to me. "Cowboy Bob could probably hook you guys up with some clothes too, if you need them."

"Okay. That would be cool. We've been having a lot of difficulties there. That reminds me. I want to ask you something. How do you get around with the anchors? We brought some with us, but then we realized we couldn't use them because they have gravitites in them. How do we fix that?"

Mym tilts her head slightly. "Dad didn't give you guys a DG?"

"What's a DG?" Francesca says.

"It's what we call the device. I guess it's called a 'de-gravitzer.' We always thought that sounded cheesy, so we called them DGs."

"No. We never got one of those," I say. "Aren't they really big? I saw some pictures in your dad's journal and it looked really complicated."

"Oh yeah, the ones in his lab are. Those are for doing lots of items simultaneously, or for really big items. Those work better and faster, but if you're just doing anchors and stuff, the portable ones work okay. I have a spare one actually, I can loan it to you till you get home."

"That would be fantastic," I say.

"I wonder why he never told us about that?" Francesca says.

"We missed out on a lot of things apparently," I reply.

"How long did Dad train you for?"

"About a week I guess."

"Huh. Yeah, that's not a very long time, considering . . . but don't worry. Cowboy Bob is a pro. He can get you home okay."

"How did he become a time traveler?" Francesca asks.

Mym smiles. "I'll let him tell you that story. Come on. Let's say bye to Connie."

She picks up the pitcher of tea and heads for the kitchen. I grab the lemonade and follow. As I get through the door, Mym grabs Connie from behind as she's trying to wash dishes and gives her a hug. Connie pats Mym's arms and turns around.

"You all set to go now?" she asks.

"Yep. We're going to show our new friends one of the meteor showers around 2000. Bob says they're great then."

"Well, Bobby would know." Connie smiles. "You all have a good time." She turns and extends her arms to us. "It was great to have your company."

Francesca steps in for a hug. "Thank you for lunch, it was delicious."

"Thank you," I say, getting a hug also. "It was really great meeting you."

"So . . . does this mean you won't see Cowboy Bob again for . . . twelve years?" Francesca asks.

"Oh, no. I'm not worried about that. I know how you time travelers are. You might be cluttering up my kitchen again tomorrow for all I know." She smiles at us. "Bobby always finds his way home before too long. And he's never once missed my birthday. He's a sweetheart like that."

Francesca grins. "I'm glad he has you. I'm pretty jealous."

"You just come back anytime you want, honey. There are lots of good times to be had out here." She pats Francesca on both her arms.

"Thank you." Francesca smiles. "I'll try."

"Okay, now get going. I want to see that pretty balloon do some flying."

She shoos us out the front door, where we find Blake returning from the barn with my other flip-flop. I tell him to keep them for himself and I snag our backpack from inside the door. Connie waves from the porch as we cross the barnyard through the pasture gate. The horse has migrated across the far side of the pasture, but she lifts her head and gives us a contemplative stare as we enter, before going back to her grazing.

Cowboy Bob is inside the gondola, adjusting the gas on the burner. Little flowers of flame shoot up with pops and spurts. The balloon is upright again and shifting gently in the light breeze.

"This is so cool," Francesca says. "I've never been in a hot air balloon before."

Me either.

"Um. I'm not super great with heights," I say.

Bob smiles. "Don't worry. The sky never hurt anybody. It's hitting the ground that gets you. Go ahead and climb in. Levi is going to release us."

I look past the burner and see the ranch hand on the far side of the balloon, near one of the iron rings. He doesn't appear to have changed a bit. From his expression, you would think he was staring at a blank wall and not a massive, multicolored, flying time machine.

I climb over the wall of the oversized basket and drop inside. I take a firm grip on the metal frame of the burner assembly.

"Sorry about the lack of a door," Bob says.

The interior of the gondola has been divided up. While the overall shape of the basket is a rectangle, two diagonal opposing corners have been made into storage areas. The remaining passenger space is made up of the two other corners and the space directly below the burner cans. There are four burners total, mounted to the frame above the gondola.

Once we're all in, Cowboy Bob lights off the burners in earnest and I feel the balloon pop up and settle back down on the grass momentarily. Bob gives Levi a thumbs up and he begins unclipping the winch lines. Cowboy Bob reels the cables in as the balloon drifts slowly upwards. The moment we leave the ground is silent and smooth.

That wasn't so bad.

Francesca grips the edge of the basket with both hands as she watches the pasture dropping away from us. The balloon rises fast, and in a matter of seconds, we can see over the barn to the front of the house. Connie waves to us from the porch and I pry one hand loose to wave back. Levi disappears into the barn.

We are still tethered to the ground, but the one remaining cable is long and thin and runs away toward the center of the pasture. As we rise, it rises with us. I lean forward and look down to watch, as the breeze pushes us over the anchor point for the line, and away from the house and barn. We traverse perhaps a hundred yards of pasture before we reach the end of the tether's length.

"How high are we?" Blake asks.

"A little under a thousand feet," Cowboy Bob replies.

Mym is in the opposite corner of the gondola, looking away from the pasture at prairie hills stretching to the south. I squeeze past Bob to join her.

"This is pretty awesome," I say. I try to look casual, but I take a firm grip on the railing.

She glances at me, and smiles. "Yes. This is my favorite part of my visits. Sometimes we cut loose and drift for hours before we blink."

"How do you get back?" I ask.

"I guess normal people drive," she says. "Bob usually has some anchors from the ranch that he has set up beforehand for whatever time he wants to get back. You degravitize one and attach it to the anchor line and you're ready to blink home. It's pretty painless really."

"Is that what he's going to do this time?" I ask.

"I can't yet," Cowboy Bob says from behind me. "I don't have any anchors set up from the ranch in 1999. We're going to have to use the tether or just use local anchors."

"What are local anchors?" I say.

"Usually other people's involuntary contributions," Mym says.

"They're not always involuntary," Bob says. "Well I suppose mostly they are, but what you do is this." He leans down and picks up a metal ball with a ring sticking out the side that has been lying at the inside edge of the basket. "You take something like this and attach it to the end of your cable. You lower that down till it touches the ground. You make your move and you end up in that same spot at your target time just using the ground as your anchor."

"And sometimes you get stuck in a gymnasium," Mym says.

"You see what she's like?" Bob gestures toward her. "You take her on adventures, and she likes to bring up your every little mishap."

"What did you mess up?" I say.

"Nothing really. My end went fine. But it turned out that the empty field I dropped my anchor into, got developed into a middle school while I was gone, so when I arrived, my anchor cable got fused through the top of the gymnasium. It wasn't a big deal."

Mym laughs. "They just had a hard time figuring out why they had a stainless steel cable running through their foundation, and out onto their roof the next day."

"Yeah." Cowboy Bob scratches his beard. "In hindsight, I could have tried to let the wind push me away a bit, dropped another shorter anchor and zapped the other cable out of there, but it may not have worked. I just cut it loose and drifted away and then avoided the area for the next few years."

"There weren't any little kids in the gym at the time, were there?" I say.

"Oh no. Luckily I showed up during the summer. That kind of stuff is rare though. Most of these fields have been fields for a hundred years. Hopefully they will be for hundreds more." Bob drifts back to the burners and lets off another burst. "You guys ready to see 1999?"

"Sounds good to me," Blake says.

Cowboy Bob steps to the controls near the tether winch and dials in some specifics. The instrument cluster reminds me of an airplane, only with a lot more clocks involved.

Mym opens a trunk in one of the storage areas and hands each of us a wool blanket. "You might want these."

"November 17th, here we come." Cowboy Bob declares.

Francesca looks at me as she unfolds her blanket. "November? How cold is it going to be in Novem—"

The next moment, we're in fading twilight and the night air sends a chill right through me.

"—ber," Francesca finishes.

"Wow that's brisk." Blake shivers.

I promptly wrap myself in my blanket, and as Bob sends up another burst of flames into the balloon, I find myself stepping forward to take advantage of the radiant heat.

"Actually not bad out." Bob shines a flashlight at the gauges. "Temp gauge is showing forty-one degrees. That's pretty balmy for this time of year."

I look over to Francesca and see her clenching her blanket to her chest in silent argument. Mym is snuggled in a blanket also, but her eyes are happy. She looks at me, and smiles.

That smile again.

I lean out of the basket to look up at the sky. To the east, stars have already begun to appear. Cowboy Bob tugs on a line and I feel the balloon sink. He cranks at the tether winch and draws us back toward our anchor point. The breeze has shifted and it helps move us closer to the barn. He eases us back down into the pasture and we land with a gentle thump.

"Go ahead and get your things out before I collapse the top," Bob says.

Mym moves to the storage areas and begins handing us suitcases and a couple of boxes. Blake vaults over the edge of the basket and we relay the items out to him. I boost Francesca over the side, and after all the gear is moved, follow her over. Mym glides over the edge easily and slips down next to me.

"Here's where we could use the horse I guess," I say, surveying the luggage.

"Hey. It's not that bad," Mym retorts.

"I'm just messing with you. I'm sure you left a couple of things at home."

"At least I was smart enough to bring shoes."

"Hmm. Touché."

We carry the bags and suitcases over to the long ranch hand building, while Cowboy Bob opens a cupboard that's mounted to the outside wall of the barn. He pulls a handful of paper scraps from a coffee can and begins reading them.

I nudge Mym with my elbow as we walk. "What's that about?"

She looks. "Oh, he's checking his notes. He likes to leave himself messages so he knows what has changed since he was here last. It's been a long time, so he probably has a lot of them from future versions of himself to read."

"Huh," I say. "That's cool."

Mym opens the door of the guest room closest to the house. I look to the windows of the main house, but there's no sign of Connie. A door slams behind me and I see Levi stride out of his room and across the barnyard to assist Bob with the balloon. He doesn't look at us at all. The room Mym has opened is small, but tidy, with two beds in it. It contains a kitchenette and a bathroom. It doesn't have a fireplace like Levi's end of the building, but there's an electric heater. She sets her bags down and turns it on.

"You can stay in here with me if you want," she tells Francesca.

"That would be great."

Blake and I open the room next door and find a nearly identical space inside, minus the extra window.

I turn on the heater and stand with my bare feet as close to it as I dare. A few minutes later, Cowboy Bob and Levi find us.

"Will this work out for you?" Bob leans in at the doorway.

"Definitely. Thank you," Blake replies.

Levi looks at my bare feet and smirks a little. "Looks like you shouldn't a left them shoes lyin' in the barn."

Bob looks from my feet to Levi. "Oh. That's right. I forgot. We still have your things."

"You do?" Blake says.

"Yeah, you left a pile of clothes in the barn your first time through. I never knew whom they belonged to then, but we kept them in a closet in the house. You'll probably be wanting them back."

"That would be phenomenal," I say, rubbing my bare arms.

Bob leads us through the house to a back bedroom that has been converted into an office. He rolls aside a track door to the closet and shows us the shelves inside. There are a few different piles of clothes, but I recognize my blue sneakers sitting atop my department store jacket, looking slightly dusty. Francesca's pea coat and scarf are next to it. As I collect our things, I can't help but wonder whom the other piles belong to.

"You get a lot of people leaving stuff here?"

"Looks that way," Bob says. "I must have gotten some additions along the way, because I've never seen most of these before. I'm sure I'll meet their owners eventually."

"You have a pretty interesting life."

"Yeah." He closes the closet door. "Can't argue with you there."

My toes feel infinitely better when I meet back up with the girls. Francesca is elated to see her coat and scarf again. She finds her hat stuffed in one of her pockets as well, but she positively swoons over getting her boots back. Mym admires them too.

We leave the girls alone to change, and once they reemerge from their room, we turn off all the lights. Bob has retained the blankets from the balloon and we each carry one as we walk behind the house and into the open expanse of prairie. Bob guides us through the darkness and the tall grass. The stars have come out in force. We reach the top of a small rise that offers a panoramic view of the prairie and sky. Bob has obviously grown accustomed to the sight, but the rest of us keep our eyes skyward, taking in the immense array of stars.

"This is better than any observatory," Francesca says.

"I've never seen a view like this anywhere," Blake adds.

We lay down the blankets and sprawl out in a circle. Cowboy Bob points out the constellation Leo and it's not long till we spot meteors.

"It's usually most active toward the morning, but this isn't bad either," Bob says.

Mym is lying to my left and Blake to my right. Francesca and Bob have aligned themselves facing the other direction. We point out meteors until our arms get tired; then there are long periods of just lying in the quiet, appreciating the night.

After a while, I hear Francesca roll over and address us. "I know it's technically only a bit after lunch for you guys, but we haven't slept since 1986, so I'm pretty tired."

"I'll walk you back," Bob says.

Blake rises slowly as well. "You coming back too?"

"I think I'm going to lie here for a bit," I say.

Blake looks from me to Mym and then nods. "All right. I'll see you back there."

Once their footsteps have receded into the distance, Mym and I are left with just the sounds of the breeze through the grasses. I point out a pair of especially bright meteorites, but when I turn to look at her, I realize she's not looking at the sky, but rather at me.

"You're an odd one, Benjamin Travers."

"What makes you say that?"

"There's something up with you, but I haven't figured out just what it is yet."

"Am I doing a better job at meeting you?"

"What do you mean?"

"The first time I met you, in 1986, you seemed to think I wasn't doing a very good job of it."

"Hmm. I think you're doing okay. Future me might have higher standards though." She looks back to the sky.

"Does it get really hard to keep all your relationships straight with all this time traveling?"

"It's different with different people." She pauses a moment and then continues. "You have to pick the ones you want to stick with."

"What do you mean?"

"You just don't have enough time to keep up with everyone. You might think that time travel would make it easier to keep up with friends. It really doesn't. It makes it harder, because you end up with friends in different times. Sometimes it's multiple versions of the same friend. There's only one of you to go around, so you have to pick. You have to decide which relationships you are going to keep working on and make them great. It's the only way I've found that works."

"So Cowboy Bob is one of your relationships you keep?"

She nods.

"Are you and him . . . a thing?"

"A thing?"

"Yeah, you know, are you . . . romantically involved?"

Her smiling eyes meet mine and then go back to the stars. "No. Bob and I . . . we just both like to float around. He's a great friend. He always has been."

I look back to the sky and stay quiet for a few minutes.

"You have somebody waiting for you back in 2009?" She's watching me again.

"Hmm, no. Not really. I've been in a bit of a dry spell recently. My last relationship didn't end very well. I've been just waiting."

"Waiting for what?"

"Something different I guess."

"You gonna try playing for the other team?"

"Not that different."

She smiles again. "Well now when you get home, you'll be a seasoned time traveler. You can impress all the girls."

"Does that work for you? Playing the time traveler card?"

"I haven't really had to," she says.

"Ah. I see."

"I don't mean it like that. I'm not saying I don't need to. I just don't usually get into that with people. Most guys aren't really interested in being with a girl who can go look up their past behavior in person."

"Ha, yeah, I guess you would be pretty hard to lie to. Maybe you just need to find guys who have less to hide."

"Maybe."

"You seem like you have a pretty awesome relationship with your dad. Does he usually approve of your friends?"

"He's really great. I think he knows that I know better than to let myself get mixed up with the wrong people. I had a bit of a rebellious phase when I was a teenager. It didn't really pay off though."

"What do you mean?"

"You really have to stick together as time travelers, if you want to keep the people you love. You have to be pretty close, so you can't really get too much distance from each other. I did do little things to try to assert myself sometimes." She smiles. "One time when I was about fourteen, I went and got my tongue pierced at this little stand at the Santa Cruz Beach Boardwalk. It was going to be my way of acting out, because I knew Dad would hate it. I was so excited. I completely forgot to treat it with gravitites though, so the very first time I blinked out of there to go show him, it got left behind. Probably the most short-lived rebellion ever."

"Ha. At least it makes a good story."

"Yeah. I laughed at the time too. It made me realize how ridiculous I was being. I just went home and gave my dad a hug instead. He still doesn't know anything about it."

The constellations creep through the sky above us as we lie there and share stories about our lives. The conversation comes easy. It's the wee hours of the morning when I finally gather up our blankets and head back to the house. Blake is snoring softly as I crack open the door to our room. Mym gives me a wave and a smile as she disappears into her doorway.

I know I ought to be exhausted, but as I lie on the bed, staring at the ceiling above me, my mind won't stop thinking of infinite future possibilities, and the way starlight reflects in blue eyes.

My late hours don't seem as great of an idea when Blake shakes me awake. The morning sun is already bright as we step off the porch into the barnyard. Cowboy Bob waves us over from the front of the barn and Blake and I help him carry three car batteries to the gondola. Once he's satisfied with the way they're wired into the jump circuit, we head back to the house and find the girls in the kitchen. Mym dishes scrambled eggs onto plates, while Francesca turns strips of bacon and some sausages in a pan.

"That smells amazing," Blake says.

"I'm no Connie, but hopefully I can't screw up bacon," Francesca replies.

"Where is Connie?" Blake says. "Is she okay? She didn't . . . die or anything did she?"

"She's okay," Bob replies. "On vacation. I left a note about it."

"That's a pretty handy system," I say.

"Yeah, it cuts down on the worry."

The clink of forks on plates is the only sound when we first sit down to eat, but then Cowboy Bob broaches the subject of the next trip.

"What time are you looking to get back home? You have a specific date and time?"

"We need to get back to right after our softball game, preferably," Blake says.

"It was June 10th, around sevenish," I say.

"Okay, we probably can't get you there exactly on time but we can get you close. We'll get to June of 2009 by balloon and we can probably find you something that will work as an anchor to get you back to St. Pete. We both go there often enough. If Mym doesn't have an anchor that will work, I might even have one."

"Actually, I think I do have one that will work for 2009," Mym says. "I have the piece of that bank clock."

"Oh yeah. That thing's there for a long time," Bob replies.

Mym wipes her mouth with her napkin and explains. "There was a bank downtown that they demolished sometime around the millennium, but they left this free-standing clock on a wooden pillar still there, so for years and years there's just this empty parking lot and a clock. I have a whole packet of photos of it from different times. I've free jumped it without a photo too, and been fine. I don't really recommend that as a general rule, but realistically, the odds of you hitting something are pretty slim. Hopefully we have some time close, but worst case scenario, you could free jump it."

"Or we could get you to the day of, or perhaps the day before, right here, and you can just fly home by airline again," Bob says.

"This is going to be a great day." Blake grins. He slaps his hand down on the table and the silverware jumps.

"Whoa," Francesca says.

"Sorry," Blake replies. "I'm just really excited." He pops up from his seat and takes his plate to the sink.

"He's got a girlfriend waiting at home," Francesca explains to Cowboy Bob.

"Sounds like a lucky girl," Bob replies.

Blake smiles. "I'm the lucky one. I just need to get back. Almost there."

After we get the dishes cleaned, Blake and I convene with Mym and Francesca in their room to look through Mym's photos. She locates a small square of wood with an envelope taped to it.

"I cut this piece out the day before the clock got demolished. But it had a good long run before that, including all of 2009. Hopefully I have a photo of something close to your date." She untapes the thick envelope of photos and hands out a small pile to each of us.

I sit on the floor and flip through the backs of mine. I notice some are yellowed and are dated as far back as the seventies. Some are slightly grainy like still shots taken from a surveillance video.

"I've got November of 2008 as my closest." Blake lays his pile down and holds up one shot.

"I have September 2009, but we'd be three months late," I say.

"Jackpot!" Francesca says. She slaps a photo down on the bed. "June 10th, 2009. Looks like it's a window from 4:30 to 6:30 pm once you convert it. It's Dr. Quickly's handwriting. How's that for right on the money?"

"Nice! It's about time we catch a lucky break," Blake says.

I grab the photo off the bed and look at the scene of the dusty parking lot.

Home. We're almost there.

"Do you guys want to take those clothes home with you?" Mym asks.

"Yes," Francesca blurts out immediately.

"Come on then. We can use Bob's gravitizer quick before we go."

We follow her back to the house and she leads us upstairs to the loft. There is a bedroom and an office. Inside the office is a device about the size of a photocopier. It has a shape more along the lines of a microwave however, with a large hinged door on the front. We strip off our winter clothes and shoes, and Mym shoves them inside the machine. She shuts the door and latches it, then moves to the control panel. She checks to make sure it's plugged in, and observes a graduated sight gauge full of blue fluid.

"Looks like we have plenty left," she says.

"What is that stuff?" Francesca asks.

"It's actually liquid gravitites. Well, it's in a base solution to stabilize them, but it's mostly just gravitites."

She punches a button and flips a lever. The machine vibrates. A couple of seconds later, a chime dings.

"All done." Mym smiles and opens the door.

"If only we'd known it was that easy . . ." Francesca says. "I really need one of these."

Cowboy Bob and Levi have the balloon upright again as we carry Mym's luggage and my pack out to the gondola. Levi consents to give me a nod as I walk past him.

That seemed downright friendly.

Bob helps us stow the luggage and we climb aboard.

The sky is clear as we loft upwards. This time, Levi releases all of the cables and we drift up and away from the pasture. The breeze carries us northeast.

"Looks like we might be going to Canada today," Bob comments.

Farmhouses and fields pass beneath us. A pair of children wave to us as they ride bicycles around their driveway. Bob lets us drift for about half an hour before spotting a handy landing spot. He fluidly guides the balloon lower and lower till we're about a hundred feet above a grassy hillside. He tosses a cable overboard and its weighted end thuds into the grass below. Moving to the controls, he checks his settings and connections to the batteries, then puts his hand on the lever.

"Ladies and gentlemen, I give you . . ." He flips the lever. "June 10th, 2009."

The sun has moved. It's warm out again. I look over the edge of the gondola and see that the anchor is buried under a pile of healthy grass. I can see the shadows of our silhouettes on the ground below us. I strip off my jacket and roll it into my pack. Blake and Francesca hand me their winter things as well, and I stuff them in as best I can.

Bob depletes the lift in the balloon till we settle to the ground with a thump. He hands Mym the cord as he vaults out of the gondola with some corkscrew stakes in his hand. He screws the stakes into the ground and Blake and I toss him cables to tie off. I swing over the basket edge and bring him the last one. The others follow me out.

Blake is smiling. He slaps me on the back. "We made it!" He turns and hugs Francesca. She's smiling too. We gather in a circle.

"It's just one more short hop and you're home," Bob says.

I reach out and shake his hand. "Bob, you're a lifesaver. Seriously. How can we ever repay you?"

He smacks me on the shoulder. "It's no trouble. Any friends of the Quickly's are friends of mine. You don't owe me anything. I've gotten plenty of help along my way too."

Francesca steps up and gives him a hug. She then turns to Mym and hugs her too. "Thank you so much for helping us."

Blake shakes both of their hands as well. "You've both been so amazing. Thank you so much."

"I've got something for you," Cowboy Bob says. He walks to the gondola and leans over the edge into one of the storage areas. When he returns, he hands Francesca a small crystal fob and an envelope. "I found this anchor for you last night when I was going through my stuff from 2009. It's off the ceiling fan chain in the office. It's not till about two months from now, but if you guys run into trouble for some reason, come back and see me. I'll make a point of stopping back by 2009 on my return trip."

"Where are you off to now?" I ask.

"Since we're up this far anyway, I might go farther and check out the London Olympics in 2012, or maybe Rio in 2016. I heard that one is a great time."

"Bob is a big Olympic badminton fan, in case you were wondering," Mym says.

"Who isn't?" I smile. Bob grins back. I turn to Mym. "And will we be seeing you again, ever?" I try to sound casual.

"I'll get your addresses." Mym pulls out her MFD and speaks to it. "Catalog addresses." She holds the device up. "Here. Just say them out loud and I'll have them all."

We each speak our contact info and she records it and stuffs the device back into her pocket.

"Do you have your anchor?" Cowboy Bob asks.

"Yeah, I have it," Francesca says. She holds up the piece of wood from the clock.

"It's about this high up," Mym says, and holds her hand in front of her chest. "I can hold it up for you. That works the best."

"You need to de-gravitize that sucker," Bob says.

Mym reaches into the back pocket of her jeans and pulls out a cylindrical device about the size of a mini mag-light. Instead of a flashlight bulb, the tip has an open, cupped end. The device is silver but has a clear sight glass built into the handle.

"I'll show you how to use this," Mym says. "It doesn't really get rid of gravitites, as much as relocates them."

"It basically just yanks them out, so you don't want to do it to anything living or organic," Bob says.

"Yeah, dead wood like this is okay, since you aren't that worried if the interior cells get a little damaged. It's bad news for living cells though. Gravitites really don't like to come back out of stuff," Mym says. "So don't leave it on in your pocket."

I smile. "You sound like your Dad."

Mym takes the piece of wood and sets it on the ground. She points out two small lights on the side of the device. One is red, the other is green. "The device has a built in temporal spectrometer of sorts. It won't read frequency, but it will read gravitite concentration. You hold it up to your potential anchor and push the test button." She demonstrates it on the wood. The red light comes on. "Red light shows the object still has gravitites in it." She aims the device at a rock sitting near the chunk of wood. The green light comes on. "Green means it's gravitite free. So the goal is, turn on the de-gravitizer function, and keep sweeping the outside of your anchor until all the gravitites are transferred. It basically just collects them into the chamber inside."

She shakes the device and I see the blue solution in the sight-glass slosh around. "Once it starts getting full, it takes longer to get stuff out because of how dense the gravitites get, but this one still has plenty of room. Eventually you can find a gravitizer to store them in, for when you want to reuse them on more stuff. That gets a little complex though, so you're gonna wanna get some help with that." She hands Francesca the de-gravitizer. "You want to try it?"

"I just point it at the wood?"

"Yeah, you have to put it right up against it for the removal part. You can test it after from a few inches away though."

Francesca puts the cupped end of the device against the smooth surface of the wood. Mym squats down to help her. "You just move the safety cover over with your thumb and press that button."

The device hums quietly when Francesca pushes the button.

"Ooh, I can feel something happening."

"That's probably the solution inside reacting to the new gravitites," Mym says. "So just move it around the surface of the wood. Try to cover each area and then we'll test it again."

Francesca slowly sweeps back and forth over the wood, still keeping the cupped end touching it. When she pulls away and pushes the test button, the red light flickers a few times.

"Looks like you're almost there. Must be a few left," Mym says.

Francesca repeats the process on the back side of the wood and then hits the front again. This time, when she pushes the test button, the green light shines brightly.

"Nice job," Mym says.

Francesca stands back up and nudges me. "I get a gold star in degravitizing."

"You can keep that one," Mym says.

Francesca smiles and double-checks the safety on the DG before she slips it into her pocket. "Thank you."

"So that's ready for use now," Cowboy Bob says. "You guys ready to see home?"

"Very," Blake replies. He's grinning again.

Mym holds up the piece of wood with her fingers on the edges, a little lower than chest high. I set my chronometer and compare it to Blake's, then step up next to Francesca. Blake sandwiches her on the other side. We both extend our chronometer hands to touch our fingertips to it. Francesca grips my right arm as I extend it toward my chronometer.

Bob and Mym are both watching us from beyond the board. "Tell St. Pete I said hi," Bob says.

"Thank you for this," I reply.

Mym looks me in the eye and smiles. "Be good."

We push the pins.

Chapter 18

"When you run into yourself from another time, don't worry too much about what you're going to say. The universe won't collapse if you fail to say exactly the right thing at the right time. Feel free to give yourself a few nice compliments too. It's not every day that you can surprise yourself with some sincere admiration."
-Excerpt from the Journal of Harold Quickly, 1997

The clock says 6:30.

"We did it!" Francesca screams.

We're immersed in the sounds and smells of urban daytime traffic again. Blake spots a woman on the street, opening her car door a couple dozen yards away, and sprints over to her. Francesca wraps her arms around me and hugs me with vigor. "We made it!" She leans her head back and looks me in the face. "We really did it!"

We're back.

Blake returns from his brief conversation. "June 10th, 2009." He beams. "We're home!"

"Wow. We're really here," I say. *We got it right.*

"I've never been so happy to see downtown St. Pete in my life," Francesca says. "I'm sorry for anything I ever said bad about you," she yells with her arms wide open to the buildings around us.

Blake's arm shoots up, and he points to the street. "That's a cab." The next moment, he's sprinting into the street, heedless of the speed of the oncoming maroon mini van.

"Blake!" I shout. *Oh God.*

"You're gonna get run over!" Francesca shrieks.

I break into a run to get to him. Blake holds his arms out to stop the oncoming traffic. The driver of the van blares the horn but slows and stops. Cars in other lanes continue to speed past.

"You fucking crazy, man? What're you doing?" the driver yells, sticking his head out the window.

"I need a ride," Blake says.

"Use your damn phone and call like everybody else!" the driver says. "I already have a fare." I reach the curb and see two middle-aged women in the back of the van, peering around the driver's seat to get a better look at Blake.

Blake walks around the side of the van and looks past the driver's head to address the passengers. "I'll give you . . ." He reaches into his pocket and grabs out his wad of cash. " . . . four hundred dollars for your cab."

I can't hear their response, but the next moment the sliding door opens and the two women emerge. The heavyset woman who descends second slings her purse onto her shoulder. "You don't have to ask me twice!"

Blake meets them around the passenger side of the van and hands them a stack of bills. He then opens the passenger door and climbs in next to the cabby.

"I guess we're going," Francesca says from behind me, and climbs into the sliding door. I throw my backpack on the floor at her feet and then follow her in and slam the door.

"Thirteenth Avenue North and Twentieth Street," Blake says. "Hurry, and I'll make it worth your while." The cab driver has found his motivation, and says nothing more as he gets moving.

The clouds grow darker as we approach the area around the softball fields. I eye the clock on the cabby's dash. 06:38.

"We were at the field till what? 7:15 maybe?" I ask.

"If that," Francesca says.

"We should be safe to get to Mallory's as long as we don't go by the field," I say.

"I honestly don't even care right now," Blake says. "I just want to get there."

Blake's left leg is bouncing up and down in anticipation in the front seat. Francesca leans back into the cushions of the bench seat next to me. "I can't believe we're back. It's so surreal." She holds her hands to her face. "I can't wait to see my own house again."

"No one is going to believe us," I say.

"It doesn't matter," Blake says. He leans forward to look at the stoplight, willing it to turn green.

"I wonder if Carson and Robbie are here yet," I say. "We never really decided on a specific place to meet."

"Maybe they'll be waiting for us when we get home," Francesca says.

"We could go by their places after Mallory's to see if they are there," I say.

"I don't think I'll be going anywhere after Mallory's," Blake says, pulling out the ring box from his pocket.

Francesca's eyes widen. "Oh my God, are you going to propose to her right now?"

"I'm not waiting a single second longer than I have to," Blake says.

"I think that's your cue to drive faster," I say to the cabby.

"You guys been gone a while?" the cabby replies.

"Yeah, you could say that."

I catch a glimpse of the softball field light poles as we cruise down Ninth Avenue. They are already illuminated because of the darkening cloud cover. One of the clouds lights up from a flash of internal lightning.

When we pull up to Mallory's house on Thirteenth Avenue, the clock on the dash reads 06:52. Blake is out the door before the van even comes to a complete stop. He heads for Mallory's door without looking back. I give Francesca my hand as she steps out of the van and then lean down to address the cabby. I pull a hundred dollar bill out of my pocket and hand it through the window to him. He looks at it and nods, and then glances at Blake pounding on Mallory's door. *Maybe he's wishing I were Blake. He's still not getting four hundred dollars.*

"Here, give my card to your friend there," the cabby says. "I'm Roger. You guys ever need another ride, you give me a shout."

I take the business card and turn in time to see Mallory's face as she answers her door.

That's a good smile.

Blake is frozen for a moment as he looks at her, but then grabs her with both arms and pulls her to his chest. Francesca and I walk closer, stopping near the front of Mallory's car in the driveway. Blake's face is buried in Mallory's hair, but she has her head toward us. She opens her eyes and smiles at Francesca and me.

"I thought you guys had softball," she says, looking from me back to Blake as he loosens his arms.

"We did," I say. "Bad weather."

"Mallory. I have something to say to you." Blake locks his eyes on hers.

Francesca leans toward me and whispers, "Should we be standing here for this?"

"Too late now." I smile.

Blake drops to one knee and shows her the ring box.

"Oh my God." Mallory puts her hands to her face.

"Mallory, I've loved you since the day I first met you," Blake begins. "I should have told you a million times a day. There's not a single place on this earth I would rather be than with you. I've been through a lot the last couple of weeks, and the thing it taught me, is that I don't want to spend a single minute more of my life without you."

"Aww," Francesca murmurs next to me.

He opens the box. "Mallory Watson. Will you marry me?"

Mallory's mouth is hanging open slightly as she takes the ring box from Blake's fingers. It takes her a couple of seconds to respond.

"Yes . . . Yes, yes, I will. Oh my God. When did you—"

Blake is up and kissing her. After a few moments, I realize they're not coming up for air anytime soon.

"Maybe we should give them a minute," I say to Francesca. She nods and turns toward the street. We make a left at the sidewalk. Francesca uses the back of her hand to wipe away a tear. "Are you crying?"

"What? I'm a woman. Of course I'm crying." She sniffs. "That was really sweet."

When we get a couple of houses down, I glance back to Mallory's porch. They're still at it. "Let's walk around the block."

"How are we going to get home?" Francesca says.

"Maybe once all the mushiness has died down, Blake and Mallory can give us a ride," I say.

"Oh. Wait." Francesca stops walking. "Aren't our cars parked over at the softball field?"

"Oh yeah," I say. "That's not too far to walk . . ." At that moment we start to get hit with a few large raindrops. I look down the street and see heavier precipitation moving toward us. "Damn. I guess we should have packed an umbrella in this backpack."

"I don't really care. I'll get soaked," Francesca says.

We turn toward the softball fields and have made it about a block when the rain starts to catch up to us. Squinting against the droplets, I watch a vehicle approaching.

"That looks a lot like Blake's Jeep," Francesca says.

"Yeah, it kinda does," I reply, hoping we don't get splashed by it.

Not that it's going to matter. Rain or puddles do the same job.

The Jeep draws closer and I see a dark-haired man behind the wheel and recognize the surf shop sticker on the windshield.

No. This can't be happening.

"Holy shit!" I blurt out.

"What?" Francesca says.

I don't have to explain. The Jeep slows down and comes to a stop next to us. Blake has the Bimini top on the Jeep, but the sides are open and the doors are off, so I see he's starting to get wet too.

"What are you guys doing, walking in the rain?" Blake asks. He's wearing his softball clothes and I see he has shoved his bat bag between the seats to shield it from the rain.

Francesca's mouth is hanging open. I turn and grab her by the shoulders. She looks at me but her eyes drift back to Blake sitting in the Jeep. Rivulets of rainwater are running down her temples. I touch her face and bring her eyes back to me.

"Get back to the house. Get him out of there. I don't care what you have to say, just get him out! I'll be back for you."

Francesca's eyes focus on my mouth as I'm talking but she remains speechless. I drop my hands from her shoulders and take a step back. I swing the backpack off my shoulders and push it into her hands.

"We will fix this. I'll come back for you." I leave her standing there and dash around the back of the Jeep to climb into the passenger side. Francesca has backed away a couple of steps and is staring vacantly past the back of the Jeep.

"Is everything all right?" Blake asks, looking from me back to Francesca.

"Yeah, keep driving. We have to go."

Blake shifts into gear and starts rolling, still keeping his eyes on Francesca.

"We need to get away from this street," I say.

"I was headed for Mallory's," Blake says.

"Yeah, you can't do that right now."

"Why? What's going on?"

"Um, it's . . . supposed to be a surprise."

"A surprise?" Blake looks over to me and then into the rearview mirror, where the figure of Francesca is slowly dwindling in his vision. "Why is Francesca acting like someone just shot her puppy?"

"She was just upset the plan isn't going right."

That's not really a lie.

We make it to a stop sign. "So where am I going?" Blake asks.

"Do you trust me?" I ask.

"Yeah, of course. You're kind of weirding me out right now, but yeah. I trust you."

"Let me drive."

Blake looks at my face for a moment, and then unbuckles his seat belt. "Okay." He slides out into the rain. I scoot over into the driver's seat. As soon as he's in, I start rolling.

I cut out to the main street and head north. *Why are there two of him? And what am I going to do now?*

"Can you at least give me a clue about what the surprise is?" Blake says.

"It's kind of going to blow your mind," I say. I turn right and head for Fourth Street. I need something to do with him. "Are you hungry?"

"Starving actually," Blake says.

"Okay good."

"This surprise is food-related?"

That could work.

"Yeah, Mallory has something special in mind, but the rainout sort of messed up the timing. She called me and asked me to divert you. Francesca was freaked out that you got there so fast."

I pull into a smoothie store parking lot and let the Jeep idle in the handicapped space in front of the door.

"I think you should wait in here for a bit. I'll come back and get you."

Blake eyes the building. "You aren't coming in?"

"No. You should probably get yourself a smoothie to hold you over. I wouldn't eat too much though."

"I actually don't think I brought any cash," Blake says, feeling his pockets.

"I can spot you." I rummage in my pocket for my wad of bills.

Shit. All I have is hundreds.

I keep my hand out of sight from Blake as I gingerly extract a single bill from my pocket, trying to keep the rest from falling out.

"Here you go." I hand him the bill.

"Whoa, high roller." Blake smiles.

"Yeah, sorry. It's all I got. Just bring me the change later."

"Okay, so you'll be back in a bit?"

I look at the Blake next to me. *He looks so stress-free. No sign of devastating loss on that face. Blake is going to be destroyed. My Blake.*

"Yeah, man. Maybe a half hour or so. Oh, and don't call Mallory. She'll know I botched the job," I say.

"Okay."

He glances at my pants as he's about to get out. "Hey, how'd you change so fast?"

"I'm ridiculously talented," I say.

He shrugs and hops down. He gives me a quick two-fingered wave and dashes for the cover of the smoothie store awning.

I pull the Jeep back out to the street. As I sit at the stop sign waiting for traffic to clear, the rain slants into the Jeep and soaks my left leg.

I hope this lets up. I'm going to need a change of clothes.

The implications of what has just happened start to dawn on me.

Shit. There could be another me too . . . I should have told Blake not to call me either. I'm going to need to move fast.

I rev the gas pedal and pull out into traffic. Racing back to Mallory's house, my tires spray huge arcs as I blast through the rivers of rainwater pooling in the intersections.

Francesca, Blake and Mallory are huddled in the doorway of the front porch, watching for me as I pull up. Francesca tugs on Blake's arm and sprints out to the Jeep, carrying my pack. Blake takes Mallory around the waist for another long kiss and then dashes out after Francesca. I tilt the passenger seat forward so Francesca can squeeze into the back. Blake is smiling as he climbs into the Jeep.

"If I wasn't so happy right now, I would seriously question your choice of vehicles. With all of our cars there, you chose mine?"

I shift into gear and pull away from the curb. Mallory waves to us from the porch and Blake blows her a kiss in return. She pretends to grab it and stuff it into her back pocket.

This is going to suck.

I drive a few blocks north and wind my way into the Euclid neighborhood. I find a section of street where the heavy foliage from the trees is blocking most of the rain, and pull over.

"What's so important that it couldn't wait?" Blake says.

I switch off the ignition and turn to face him. "Okay, man. This isn't going to be fun to hear, but I have some really bad news."

Blake searches my face. "I'm flying pretty high right now. It would take a lot to bring me down. What's going on? Did something happen to Robbie or Carson?"

I look back to Francesca. She has tears rolling down her face. I face Blake. "We're not back."

He narrows his eyes at me. "What are you talking about?"

"Something is screwed up. We're not back to our lives. I didn't get your Jeep from the parking lot at softball. I got it from you. Another you."

Blake leans away from me. "You're messing with me, right?" He looks at Francesca's face and back to mine. "This isn't funny."

"Blake, you know I wouldn't joke about something this serious. I know how badly you wanted to get home."

"I am home!" Blake says. "We made it."

I look at the clock on Blake's dash and point to it. 07:48. "Something's different. The power line should've zapped us by now. I don't know why, but that didn't happen to you this time. We ran into you driving back from softball."

"How is that possible?" Blake says.

"I don't know. Maybe you left earlier, maybe we didn't all hang around when it started raining at the field. Maybe the power line never struck the bench this time. I don't know."

"Did you and Francesca still go back?"

"I don't know. I just know you definitely didn't, because you're sitting in a Tropical Smoothie right now, waiting for me to come pick you up."

"Why am I still sitting here then? Why haven't I disappeared or something?" Blake says.

"It doesn't work like that, remember?" I say. "Quickly said time is not strictly linear when—"

"I don't believe you. This can't be happening." Blake raises his hands to his head and grabs his hair. He turns and slides out of the Jeep.

"Blake—"

"No. This is not happening." Blake paces back and forth next to the Jeep, still fidgeting with his head. "You're sure it was me?"

"Yes." I climb out of the Jeep and join him by the tailgate.

He looks at Francesca. "Mallory. What about Mallory?"

"I don't know," I say. "I don't know what's going on. I just know there are two of you."

"Quickly did tell us about this," Francesca says. She's staring out the windshield of the Jeep. "He said there can be alternate timelines. Paradoxes."

"That was an alternate Mallory?" Blake asks. "And the alternate me . . . so he's going to . . ." Blake stops moving. "I gave her the ring. We're in the wrong life and I gave her the fucking ring?" He spins away from me and yells at the sky. He turns back and grabs me by the shoulders and shakes me. "Where is she Ben? Where's MY Mallory?"

"I . . . I don't know," I say, putting my hands to his shoulders. He brushes them away and forces his way past me to the back of the Jeep. He reaches across the back seat and pulls his bat bag toward him. He jerks his bat out of the bag and takes a firm two-handed grip.

"Blake, what are you—"

He doesn't look at me as he strides toward the curb. A "No Parking" sign has the misfortune of being in his path. He unleashes his fury upward, smashing the left face of the sign backward to a ninety-degree angle with one swing. He recoils and smashes the other side as well. The bat clangs and reverberates as he takes fierce swings at the post.

Somebody is going to call the cops.

When he finally lets up, the No Parking sign is lying on the ground, missing a corner, and the post is dinged and notched. He lets the bat dip and touch the ground as he stares at the wreckage. He turns to us, walks to the back of the Jeep, and hands the bat to me. Standing still for a moment, staring at the ground below the back bumper, he closes his eyes and grabs the back of the tailgate with both hands, then leans his forehead against his knuckles. "This just can't be happening."

Francesca's eyes are red. She sits silent.

"I think you cracked your bat," I say.

Blake lifts his head up and looks at the bat in my hands. He snatches it from me, and with a two-handed swing, hurls it across the street. The bat just clears a parked car on the other side before bouncing off the sidewalk with a clang and crashing into a fence. He turns and starts walking away down the middle of the street.

"Blake. We need to figure out what to do next," I say.

He turns around. "You figure it out, Ben. You're the one who's having such a great time with all of this. You should just keep hooking us up with more of your time traveling buddies, cause that's worked out sooo well."

"Blake. You know that's not—"

"It's fine, Ben. Do what you want. But just because you don't have anybody in your life you care enough about to get back to, don't drag us along with you. You should just take your little diary, and your little gizmos, and go find your time traveler girlfriend, and leave. I've got a life already. I've got my family waiting for me. I'm going home."

He turns and walks away.

I watch him reach the end of the block and turn left.

You're my family, you stupid jerk.

"He's just upset," Francesca says. "He didn't mean it."

"I know," I say. I turn and see her watching my face. "I know."

I climb back into the driver seat of the Jeep and start it up. The rain has lessened to a light drizzle. I make a U-turn and then follow Blake. When I pull up alongside him, he continues to stare straight ahead. "Hey, I know you need some time or whatever," I say. "I'm going to go over to Mr. Cameron's house and look for some sign of Robbie and Carson. If you need a direction for your walk, maybe head that way." He doesn't say anything, but I can see from his eyes he's listening. "We'll meet you over there." I shift into second and pull away. He still says nothing, but I know he'll go. *What choice do we have except stay together?*

Francesca and I cross Fourth Street and splash through the brick streets of Old Northeast. "Where are you going?" she asks. "This isn't the way to Mr. Cameron's."

"I want to check something first."

Turning north on Oak Street, Francesca identifies my destination. "We're going to your apartment?"

"Well I'm not. I was hoping you might check it out for me though. I really want to know if all of us are still here, or if it's just Blake." I pull up to the curb across the street from my second story apartment. The blinds are down but I see lights on.

Did I leave my light on?

"I look a mess," Francesca says, pulling down the sun visor to check herself in the mirror. She tries to straighten out her hair and rubs away the tearstains from under her eyes.

"It's just me," I say.

"Well yeah, but what if the other you is hotter?" She grins. "Never hurts to look good."

"Hey! Not possible." I smile. *It feels good to smile. At least Francesca seems to be taking this okay. Haven't screwed everyone's life up yet.*

She decides she's done the best she can and unbuckles her seat belt. "What should I say?"

"I don't know. I guess just be friendly. See if he had any weird experiences at softball tonight."

"Okay." She steps down from the Jeep.

"Oh hey, do you still have your phone?"

"Yeah. Should be in the backpack."

"Do you mind if I use it?"

"Sure, if you think it will work."

"Okay, thanks."

I rummage through the pack as Francesca makes her way toward the apartment. I find the phone and power it on as she's knocking on the door. From my angle, I can't see the person inside as the door opens, but I see her smile, and after a moment go inside.

The cell's battery is low but not completely depleted. It has a decent signal. I dial the number into her keypad and wait three rings till someone picks up.

"Hello?"

"Hey, Mom. It's Ben."

"Oh hi! This is a nice surprise! Is everything okay?"

"Yeah. I was just calling to say hi." *Just needed to hear your voice.*

"Oh, that's very sweet. I was just talking about you to one of the neighbors. Do you remember the Hammersteins? Their oldest is back from college. Rachel, or might have been Carly; I think Rachel is the younger one. Very pretty girl though. I told Deborah that next time you're visiting we'll have get you two together."

I remember the Hammerstein girls taking prom pictures in their yard the last time I was home. Hard to believe they could be graduating college.

"Have you been seeing anyone lately in Florida?"

"No. Not right now." *Met a cute time traveler from 1986. Not sure that counts.*

"Well I'm sure she's out there somewhere," she says.

She tells me about the latest trip to the vet with the dog and how my dad sprained his ankle coming down the steps from the attic. In a few minutes I see Francesca reemerge from the apartment. I catch the glimpse of an arm hugging her as she leaves but I don't see the other me.

"I have to get going, Mom. Tell Dad hi for me."

"Oh I will, sweetie. He'll be happy to know you called. He'd want to thank you for your package you sent too."

I don't know what she's talking about.

"That will make a great gift for Father's Day. I peeked, but I won't tell him what it is."

"Okay, thanks, Mom." *Father's Day. At least this other me is staying on top of things.*

"I love you."

"I love you too, Mom, very much. Talk to you again soon."

I hang up the phone as Francesca climbs back into the Jeep. She's struggling a little because she has a cup in her hand.

"Who were you talking to?" she says, finally making it into the seat.

"My mom. Well, wrong mom I guess. Still felt good to talk to her. What's that?" I point to the cup of pinkish something in her hand.

"Oh. Yeah. You were making smoothies, so you gave me some."

"You took his cup?"

"What? You're a nice guy. What do you want me to do? Apparently you really like smoothies after softball. Plus, don't look at me for stealing a cup, you stole a whole Jeep!"

Blake.

"Yeah, he's going to be so pissed at me. Well, he'll probably be pissed at the other me."

"What did you do with him?"

"He's still over at Tropical Smoothie waiting for me to pick him up for his surprise." I frown.

"Ah. See? Smoothies!" Francesca points at me. I shake my head. "So, what? You're just going to leave him there?" Francesca sips her drink as I put the Jeep in gear.

"I don't know what else to do. I know it's kind of mean, but I already have one angry Blake to deal with. I don't think I can handle two." I pull into the street and drive us west toward Mr. Cameron's house. "Did you learn anything interesting from the other me about the softball game?"

Francesca nods and finishes a gulp of her drink. "Yeah, he said they left early because of a rainout. No sign of anybody getting hit by lighting, or power lines breaking. It sounded pretty routine."

"That's interesting," I say. "At least we know why they never left. No power lines breaking means no power surge, so no gravitites, and no time traveling. These versions of us won't be going anywhere unless they randomly get exposed to gravitites some other way. That's not very likely."

"It's so weird talking to another you, by the way. I mean, it's you, so that part isn't weird, but him not knowing anything that has been happening to me the last few weeks is just surreal."

"I know what you mean. I felt the same way with the other Blake."

"So what do we do?" Francesca says. "We can't go back to our lives if someone else is already living them."

"Yeah. I know. I want to find out what happened to Robbie and Carson. If they made it back, then they might be as confused as we are, but maybe they know something we don't."

The lights are on in Mr. Cameron's house as we pull into the alley driveway. "Do you think his family is living here?" Francesca says. "How old would Mr. Cameron be if he's still alive?"

"Pretty darn old," I say.

The yard gnomes are still on the back porch, watching me as I knock on the door.

"Feels like déjà vu," Francesca says.

The black woman that answers the door is a stranger to us. Middle-aged and pear shaped, she's dressed in colorful floral scrubs and white Velcro sneakers.

"Hello. Can I help you?" Her greeting is friendly, but I note she hasn't opened the door very far.

"Yes. We're looking for Robert Cameron."

"Are you selling something?" she asks.

"No ma'am," I say, "We're friends of his."

She gives us both an appraising stare and then opens the door wider. "I'll see if he is awake and willing to have visitors. Who shall I tell him is here?"

"I'm Benjamin and this is Francesca," I say. "We've been his houseguests before."

"I don't remember you," she says. "I've been working here eight years."

"It was a while before that."

She nods and shows us into the library. The birdcage in the corner sits still and vacant. The house is quiet with the exception of the sound of raindrops dripping off the gutters outside. The library is much how we left it, though dust has settled on most of the books, and a flat screen television has been installed on the wall opposite a recliner.

We are sitting for only a couple of minutes when the nurse comes back in and gestures for us to follow her. She leads us upstairs and down the hall to Mr. Cameron's bedroom door.

"He's pretty tired, and none too strong, so try not to get him worked up."

"Okay. We won't. What's your name, by the way?" I offer my hand.

The woman takes her hand off the doorknob and accepts my handshake. "My name is Delilah, but everyone calls me Dee."

"Thank you, Dee," Francesca says.

She opens the door for us and we enter. The door closes quietly behind us. I set my pack down near the dresser. Mr. Cameron is propped up against a stack of pillows in his four-poster bed. The curtains have been pulled back and the windows are open so the sounds of the dripping rain come through. Mr. Cameron smiles at us as we walk to opposite sides of his bed. His green eyes are still bright, though age has taken much of the substance from his body. His hair is only wisps of white, and the bones of his hands protrude sharply through his pale skin. He smiles at us as we draw closer however, and I see he still has all of his teeth.

"Hello, Mr. Cameron," I say.

"When Dee told me you were here, I almost didn't believe her." He pats the edge of the bed. "Come. Let me have a good look at you." Francesca sits down on his left and I do the same on his right. "Robbie always said you would come back. He never lost faith, that one."

"How is Robbie?" I ask. "Have you seen him?"

"Oh yes," Mr. Cameron says. "He left just a while ago, said he was going to the softball fields. He said that was the most likely place he would find you when you arrived."

So Robbie beat us back.

"When did he get here?" I ask.

"He came over this afternoon and had dinner with me. He was excited of course. Excited to see you."

"It's really good to see you," Francesca says. "You look great."

"Thank you, Francesca. I know I look like a withered prune, but it's nice of you to say. You're the one who is just as beautiful as the day I last saw you, more beautiful even. Where is the other one? The other tall one."

I wonder if he's forgotten my name.

"Blake is here too. He's out walking around right now, but he'll be by."

"Good. It will be like old times." He smiles.

An orange cat emerges from under the bed and hops up next to me. He rubs against my arm briefly and climbs into Mr. Cameron's lap.

"Hello, Samwise," Mr. Cameron scratches the cat's cheeks. "Have you come out to meet my friends?"

Samwise purrs contentedly and begins kneading the comforter over Mr. Cameron's stomach with his paws. After a few moments he crosses the bedspread and head-butts Francesca's elbow. She brushes his tail away from her face. "He's no Spartacus, but he seems sweet," she says.

"Oh poor Spartacus." Mr. Cameron smiles. "He was a good dog. I don't think he was ever as happy as when he had all of you living in the house though. Once I got too decrepit to go for walks, I had to switch to feline friends. I never could get into small dogs."

The cat settles down in Mr. Cameron's lap, still purring. There's a knock on the door and I turn, expecting to see Dee returning, but a man enters the room. He's middle-aged and bald and wearing a still-dripping windbreaker. He breaks into a smile as soon as he sees us.

"I was wondering if I was going to find you here," he says. "I saw Blake's Jeep in the driveway."

"Oh my God," Francesca says. "Robbie?"

It takes me a moment but then I realize what she's saying. I take another look at the man and see the smiling eyes of my friend. Francesca leaps off the bed and wraps her arms around him.

"I can't believe it!" she says.

"It's been a long time," he replies.

It's only been a few days.

"You're all mature now!" Francesca says. "Oh wow."

"I got old, you mean," Robbie says.

Francesca picks up his left hand. "And this?" The gold ring on his finger looks well worn.

"I figured you would catch that pretty quick," Robbie says.

"Wow, man. This is crazy," I say. I give Robbie a hug.

He's spread out a little in the middle.

"What happened?" Francesca says, covering her mouth with her hands. "I mean, look at you. You're so grown up!"

Robbie leans around us and addresses Mr. Cameron. "Hey, Grandpa. I'm going to take them downstairs and tell them the story."

Mr. Cameron nods and extends his arms toward Francesca. "Only if I get a hug first."

Francesca gives him a hug and a kiss on the cheek. He extends a hand to me as well and I hold it for a moment.

"It's really great to have you back under my roof again." Mr. Cameron smiles.

"It's good to be back," I say.

Robbie leads the way downstairs and we find chairs in the sewing room. Francesca takes the couch.

He looks like a different person, but that's really my friend.

"You took the slow road to get here, I guess." I say as I sit down.

"That's one way to put it," Robbie replies. "It's had its perks though."

"What is your perk's name?" Francesca smiles.

"Her name is Amy. We have a couple of little perks too." He pulls out his wallet and hands a plastic sleeve of photographs to Francesca. "The youngest is Micah, the older one there is Dominic. They're older than this now."

"Oh wow. They are precious," Francesca says. "And is this Amy?" She holds up a photo of a blonde woman with a Rays baseball cap on.

"Yep. That's her. Guess it shows there's someone for everyone. Even I found somebody."

"She's really pretty, Robbie," Francesca says. "You did good. I can't believe this. You're so grown up!"

"It seems like you have a pretty great life," I add.

"I really do. I couldn't be much happier," Robbie says. "And Grandpa has been hanging in pretty well. My kids love him."

"Wow. Is that awkward with the rest of your family?" Francesca says. "What about the younger version of you? He's grown up now too."

"Yeah. That is a little weird. I wasn't really sure how that was going to go. I mean, he's me, so I've tried to have a pretty hands-off approach to being around him." Robbie scratches his head. "But . . . he's not me. The thing is, I don't know how bad this is, but I know some stuff got changed. He's had some experiences I don't remember ever having." He looks from me to Francesca. "He even had a girlfriend that I obviously know I never dated. I didn't know what to do. I made sure he still was on the softball team, but that didn't work out either. I was by there tonight. None of us time traveled. The game got rained out, but everybody just went home. I was freaking out for a bit. I kept thinking any second I was going to get erased or disappear or something.

"When nothing happened, I waited a while to see if you guys would show up, but when you didn't, I headed back here. I knew I needed to tell you quick that you're all still here."

"I know. We saw the other Blake," I say. "Have you seen Carson? Where is he?"

Robbie furrows his eyebrows. He exhales slowly and looks me in the eyes. "Carson is dead."

Francesca draws her breath in sharply. I look over to her and she has her hands up to her mouth.

His words are slow to register. My chest feels like someone is crushing it.

I must have heard him wrong. We just left Carson. He was smiling in the backyard. He can't be dead.

"How?" I choke out. "What happened to him?"

"It was about ten years ago," Robbie begins. "Initially we'd planned to follow you guys like we discussed. Grandpa was a little slow to recover though, so I kept putting it off. Plus, not having had all the training you guys had, I was pretty unsure of myself. Carson was sure he could get me through it, but I wasn't as confident. We had the planning all laid out, but I procrastinated. I found more and more excuses for not leaving. Carson wasn't really in a hurry either. He met a girl, started getting some regular music gigs."

Carson playing the guitar. That part is true. I can see him. Not dead though. Dead people don't play guitars.

Robbie stands up and begins pacing the room as he talks.

Not Robbie. Some old man. Who does this guy think he is? Why am I listening to this?

"One day a guy came into the bar where Carson was playing. He'd found himself some bandmates by then. This guy offered them a recording deal. Carson, and I think her name was Jeanna, they decided to move out to L.A. and pursue the recording offer."

This guy gestures funny when he talks. Robbie doesn't gesture like that when he gets agitated. Robbie doesn't get agitated. He's always calm. The calm little center of our group.

"After a while, Carson actually made it pretty big. He didn't record that much himself but he started writing and producing. He'd compiled a huge portfolio of songs. Some of them were actually his. A lot were covers of stuff we all knew growing up, he just always came out with it a couple of years before the original artists did."

Carson did want to do that.

I scoot forward to the edge of my seat. "That idea worked?" My voice is not my voice.

Why can't I breathe? I need to remember to breathe.

"Yeah, some of the stuff was great, maybe even an improvement in some cases. Some things weren't too good though. He got into screenwriting too. He totally screwed up *Independence Day*. I don't think it even had Will Smith in it this time. Or maybe he left out Jeff Goldblum. In any case, it wasn't very good." Robbie sits back down and pauses. "Problem was, I wasn't the only one who noticed the changes."

"Another time traveler?" Francesca asks.

"Yeah. The worst one who could have noticed," Robbie says.

"Stenger?" I ask.

"No one ever caught him after those murders here. I tried finding Malcolm and Quickly to see if they knew anything about him early on, but I never could find them again. The cops never found any sign of him either. But Stenger found Carson. He showed up in L.A. after one of the albums Carson produced went platinum. I don't know what he wanted. He never said apparently. He traumatized Carson's girlfriend at the time pretty bad. She's still screwed up. He kidnapped her, and when Carson came to save her, he killed him."

"I can't believe it," Francesca says.

"Yeah, it was really messed up. She said he kept ranting about how he was going to be the only one. She didn't know what he was talking about, but I think he may have meant time travelers. I think maybe he didn't want any others to find out about him. He knew Carson was a time traveler from meeting him at the lab. I think that was part of why he went looking for him."

"No. No no no." I put my hands on my head.

Carson dead. Two Blakes. Stenger loose. This is just a nightmare. We must not really be here. I'm dreaming. When did I go to sleep? The ranch house after the stars. Why does that seem so long ago? I just need to wake up.

"What did you do?" Francesca says. Her eyes are tearing up.

"What could I do, really?" Robbie says. "It was three thousand miles away. I flew out there, but there wasn't a lot to do. Carson made a lot of friends, but no one knew his family. The young Carson was still here, growing up, oblivious to it all. I saw him tonight. Still plays shortstop."

Our Carson is dead.

"Stenger is still out there?" I say.

I should have shot that monster when I had the chance. This is my fault.

"I don't know. The cops found very little evidence except the surveillance video showing Stenger entering Carson's building the night he died. The police showed me the video. That's how I know it was him. I couldn't very well tell them anything about the time traveling though. Not if I wanted them to believe anything I said. I told them the same guy killed a bunch of people here in St. Petersburg in the eighties. They did follow up on that. Problem was, they matched those prints to the younger Stenger. The one who never time traveled. He had a pretty good rap sheet by that point anyway. They convicted him of Carson's murder, along with some other things. He went to prison, but it wasn't the right guy."

"They caught the younger Stenger?" Francesca says.

"Yeah. It was no good for me to tell them they had the wrong one though. The guy that killed Carson is still out there. And there's one more thing."

He stops altogether for a second and looks at the floor. When he looks back up his jaw clenches. "He has Carson's chronometer."

Chapter 19

"Many erroneously believe that time travel is a way to fix their past mistakes. You can't undo what's been done. Revisiting past pain only lets you relive it, not prevent it. One's time is better served crafting the future. It's a commodity too valuable to be squandered on repetition."
-Excerpt from the journal of Harold Quickly, 1980

My mind is on fire. Nothing is connecting anymore. The house, the man who claims to be Robbie, even Francesca. Their mouths are moving but I don't hear the words. Francesca is in tears. *She shouldn't cry. None of this is real.*

I stand up and move out of the room into the hallway. I pass through the library with its empty birdcage, empty chairs, empty existence. *Mr. Cameron's house should be alive. There should be something alive in here. Why is there no Spartacus? No. He wouldn't belong here now. Not in this dying place.*

I veer through the dining area and fumble with the knob on the back door. I finally get my hands to do what I want and wrench the door open. The blackness of the backyard yawns out to reach me through the porch. *No. There's nothing out there for me either. Why bother? There's nowhere to go.* I lean my head against the doorpost and stare with one eye out into the dark.

Carson was great at everything. Great at living. How could he be the one to die?

The images in my mind shift and churn till I see Stenger on the floor. Carson holding him down, and the gun in my hand. *This is my fault. I could have stopped him. I could have ended him right then. I ran.* My vision is blurry from tears but I see movement beyond the screen door. *Who's out there? Malcolm?*

I step onto the back porch and move to the screen door. Blake is sitting on the porch steps, staring off into the night. I wipe the tears away from my eyes and open the screen door. *I owe him an apology. This is all my fault.*

I let the screen door slam behind me and slump down next to Blake on the steps.

"I know what I have to do," Blake says. "You aren't going to like it, but I'm going to need your help." His voice is somber but his eyes still look wild. He doesn't look at me. He just keeps staring into the darkness. "I'm going to have to kill him."

Who is he talking about? Does he know about Stenger?

"There can only be one of us. I know I can't live my life without her. She won't have to know."

"What . . . what are you talking about?" I mumble.

"We're going to get rid of him. She won't have to know. It's not murder. It's okay. They'll never be able to say he's even missing."

"You want to kill . . . yourself?" *What is wrong with this place?*

"I don't think it even counts as killing. I'll still be alive. There will just be one of me. It's more like suicide, only not self-inflicted. Well, another self . . ."

I try to wrap my brain around what he's saying. "Blake. I saw him. I talked to him. He's you. We can't kill you."

"That thing is not me," Blake says. His voice is cold. "He's just living my life."

"Dude. He's you. And it's not just you," I say. "I'm here too."

Blake is quiet for a moment. "We'll just have to get rid of him too."

The image of me facing another version of myself takes me aback. *Could I do that? Could I fight myself? I couldn't even shoot that monster who deserved it. How could I kill myself, or Blake or . . . Francesca?* The image of Francesca screaming on the softball bench fills my mind."

"Francesca," I say out loud. "I would never hurt Francesca."

Blake finally takes his gaze away from the darkness of the yard and looks me in the eyes. His eyes are red. *He looks lost in there.*

"No." He lowers his eyes. "Not Francesca."

A breeze moves through the yard and makes the palms rattle. *More killing won't solve this problem. This isn't home.*

"Carson is dead."

Blake lifts his head back up and looks me in the eyes again. "When?"

I breathe the night air deep into my lungs and then let it out. "He never made it here. He never came home. Stenger found him."

Saying it out loud makes it real.

Blake looks into the porch toward the back door. "And Robbie?"

"Robbie is here," I say. "Robbie never left. He's old now. He's okay though. Mr. Cameron is still here too."

Blake holds the back of his head with both hands and stares at his feet for a few moments, then turns to look at me. "What are we going to do, Ben? How are we going to live like this?"

"I don't know." *I don't want to live here. Not in this place. Even if there weren't two of me.*

"How'd everything get so screwed up?" Blake asks.

"I think it might have been Stenger, but I don't really know. Robbie says things in his life have changed too. Well, the other him's life."

"What kind of things?"

"Life experiences. Girlfriends. That sort of thing."

"So we screwed stuff up when we went back," Blake says. "We screwed something up so bad that we never time traveled." He pauses a moment before he continues. "But then how are we here? If we never went back, how can any of this have ever happened?"

We broke something. How do you break time? Can something so bad happen that you fracture the world? I stare into the dark yard and think about the mess my life has suddenly become. *It certainly feels broken. I picture myself in a mirror with a million little cracks spreading through the glass till the whole mirror crumbles apart.* The image lingers in my mind. *Nothing but cracks.*

"Hey, do you remember the screen that Lawrence had up on his computer? The one with all the diverging lines?" I say.

"Yeah."

"He said something about 'the fractal universe.' He said he would explain it in the morning, but of course he never did. It seemed like something to do with time being a bunch of different threads. He seemed surprised that we didn't know about it."

"I feel like there's a lot of stuff we don't know about," Blake grumbles.

"I do too. It's almost like we were deliberately left in the dark on certain things."

"Why would Quickly do that though? Why help us, but then leave out information that was important?" Blake says.

"I don't know. Maybe he was going to tell us, but never got the chance. Maybe he planned to but couldn't after that night when the lab burned. I sure want to know now."

"You think our lives are still out there somewhere? The right time? You think we can fix this?"

"I'm sure willing to try."

"So you think I might still find Mallory? My Mallory?"

"It's the only thing that makes any sense to me," I say. "We came from somewhere. There has to be a way back." *And there has to be a way to save Carson. Please let there be a way to fix this.*

"I guess we're time travelers. I suppose if anybody can do it . . ." Blake straightens up. His eyes look a little clearer. He stands. "If she's still out there, waiting, I owe it to her to get home." He extends his hand and grabs my arm, pulling me to my feet.

"I'm sorry I got us into this mess," I say.

"How was it your fault?"

"Stenger. I could have shot him. I had the opportunity. If he's the reason things got screwed up, we could've been home by now. And Carson would still be alive."

"Stenger being a psychopath is not your fault. I don't know what caused him, but I am sure it wasn't you. I'm the one who should apologize. I was pushing us so much to get back and to not worry about him . . . I could have listened . . . and I shouldn't have said what I did earlier about—"

"It's okay."

He nods and reaches an arm out and we give each other a brief hug.

"I'm glad you came back," I say.

"Me too."

I open the screen door and head back inside. Blake follows.

When I make it to the sewing room, Robbie is still sitting on the armchair where I left him, but Francesca is gone. Robbie stands when Blake enters behind me.

"Hey, Blake."

"Hey, Robbie." Blake gives Robbie a hug. "Glad you're okay, man."

"You too."

"This is surreal," Blake says, taking in Robbie's appearance.

"It's pretty crazy for me too," Robbie replies.

"Where's Francesca?" I ask.

"She went upstairs. She's pretty upset."

I make my way upstairs while Blake stays to catch up with Robbie. The hallway is dark except for a gleam of light coming from the first bedroom doorway. It's opened a crack and I see Dee at the far side of the room, reading in an armchair by the light of a single overhead lamp. She looks up for a moment and our eyes meet, but then she goes back to her reading.

Moving to the door of the farther bedroom, I hear muffled sobs. I give the door a couple of raps with my knuckles and wait. The sobs grow silent, but I hear no response. I try the knob slowly and peer around the door into the darkness.

"Francesca?"

I hear a sniff in reply. Francesca is a darker lump in the corner of the dark bed, shaking slightly. I move to the bed slowly so I don't collide with anything in the darkness, and sit down on the edge. Reaching my hand out, I find what I think is her thigh. After a few moments, my eyes adjust enough to make out the rest of her curled in a fetal position around a pillow.

"Hey," I whisper.

Another sniff.

"It's going to be okay."

"I was mean." Her voice is slightly muffled by the pillow.

"What?"

"The last thing I said to him. I don't really remember what it was, but I think it was mean."

"Oh. I don't remember you being mean. And I'm sure Carson would have known you were joking anyway."

She turns her head toward me. "I was always mad at him."

"Well, sometimes he deserved it." I smile and rub her shoulder.

"I should have been nicer. I can't believe he's dead. It seems like a bad dream."

"I know. I feel that way too."

She sniffs again. "I've known Carson since second grade. How will we ever explain this to his mom? What are we going to do?"

"I was talking to Blake about that. He's downstairs. We want to try to fix it."

"Fix it?"

"Yeah. Somewhere out there is the world we came from. The one where we got struck by a power line at softball and left our lives behind. We came from there, so it has to exist. We just somehow got to the wrong 2009."

"We can find the right one?"

"There has to be a way. These other time travelers zip around and change stuff all the time. We just need to figure out what we did wrong."

"And Carson? What about him?"

"We save Carson."

"How?"

"We need to stop Stenger. If we stop him, we can keep Carson from dying."

"Stenger. I really hate that guy. I've never even met him."

"You don't want to."

"I do now," she says. "I want him to meet my boots with his teeth."

"I think that's a fantastic idea."

Francesca's tears have stopped. She sits up, but still hangs onto the pillow. There is a rap on the door and Blake pokes his head in. "You guys okay?"

"Yeah. Come in," I say.

"You can turn the light on," Francesca says.

Blake flips the switch. The room hasn't changed much. The little cat statue still guards the closet door. Francesca has tearstains down her face.

I probably look terrible too.

Blake takes a seat in the armchair. Robbie appears at the door as well. "Hey."

"Hey, man."

"How are you guys holding up?" Robbie asks.

"It's been kind of a rough night so far," I say.

"Yeah. Rough," Blake echoes.

"I know Grandpa would be happy to let you stay here as long as you need to. I have to get home, but I want to make sure you're going to be okay . . . I don't know what happens now."

I straighten up and look him in the eyes. "We've actually been talking about that. I don't think we're going to stay long."

Robbie drops his eyes a moment, but then nods and looks back to me. "What are you going to do?"

"We have to try to fix this," I say.

"How do you mean?" Robbie says.

"Carson," I say. "We want to stop Stenger, find Carson and get home. Our real home."

Robbie shifts his feet and considers this. "You're going back? Back to 1986?"

I nod.

"How?"

"We haven't figured that part out yet," I say.

"I have." Francesca reaches into her pocket and removes the crystal fan fob. She dangles it from her fingers. "He said he's coming back. I vote we hitch another ride."

I explain our adventures with Cowboy Bob and the Fridays in Boston and how their machines can make long-distance jumps.

"I wish I would have known that," Robbie replies. "It wouldn't have been as many jumps as I thought."

"You can come back with us," Francesca says.

"Hmm. I appreciate the offer, but I think a few people here might miss me. I never planned it this way. I always thought that eventually I would get back to my old life, but as the months, and then years went by, I realized it stopped being realistic. I remember one conversation I had with Carson on one of our meet-ups after he went to Hollywood. We were in our mid-thirties then, and we joked about what it would be like to go back and try to pretend we were twenty-six again." Robbie runs a hand over his balding head. "I think we both knew at that point that it wasn't going to happen. We'd missed our window of opportunity."

"Do you miss it?" Francesca asks.

"Sometimes," Robbie muses. "There are times when I think about friends I missed out on seeing, and of course my family. But I had my family here in a different way. It wasn't exactly the same, but I never felt alone. And Grandpa. He's been amazing. He was the only one I could really talk to about all this stuff after Carson was gone. I eventually told Amy too. Some days I still wonder if she really believes me."

"How did she handle finding out?" I say.

"She didn't walk straight out the door, so I guess that was a good sign. Grandpa helped there too. I had at least one person to back me up."

"What are you going to do now?" I say.

"I'll be okay. I like my life here. My kids are here, and Amy. I have a pretty comfortable existence. What with the money you guys left us and some good investments, I'm doing pretty well. Carson was really generous too when he made it big. He never forgot about Mr. Cameron and me. I coach soccer now for the school. I really can't complain."

"Sounds like a good life," Blake says.

"It's a great life. I mean, I was really looking forward to having you guys back in my life. It's been so many years though. It was stressful when nothing happened tonight at the field. I wasn't sure whether you were going to make it at all, but I was also relieved in a way. The idea of something happening tonight that was going to screw up my life, worried me a lot."

"I think you should be okay now," I say.

"But we're going back to change things," Francesca says. "Is that going to screw up Robbie's life?"

"We need to find our own time. I don't know if that affects this one or not," I say.

"If we successfully stop Stenger, that has to change things here, right?" Blake says.

"I really don't know."

255

"You have to try," Robbie says. "I owe Carson that. I love my life here, and I wouldn't want it to end, but if there's a way you can save Carson, and stop that psycho from killing more people, then I think you have to try. I'm not going to make you stay just so my life can go uncomplicated."

"That's pretty brave of you, Robbie," I say.

"Yeah. It is," Blake adds. "If I had my life the way I wanted it, I don't know how I would feel about anyone attempting to screw it up."

"You won't screw it up," Robbie says. "I trust you guys."

Francesca slides off the bed and rummages through the top dresser drawers. "They used to keep notepads in here." She locates one and comes back to the bed. "You have a pen?" I hand her my logbook pen and she sits down. "So this is us, right?"

Blake and Robbie step closer to see what she's drawing. She traces a line back from her first point and marks the other end 1986. "We go back here to stop Stenger and save Carson, but this timeline is here right now still. We're sitting here and Carson is dead and the other ones of us never left. Does that mean we failed?"

"You mean, since it turned out this way anyway, maybe it doesn't work?" Blake asks.

"Yeah. If the future versions of us are going to stop Stenger in the past, then why hasn't that happened yet? It was twenty-three years ago." She turns to Robbie. "Have you ever seen any other older versions of us? Have we ever stopped in before or anything?"

Robbie shakes his head.

"So we could die back there," Francesca says. "What if Stenger kills us too?"

"There could be another option," I say. I take the pen back from Francesca. "We could end up somewhere else. A new timeline, or our original one." I draw an offshoot from the 1986 marked on the paper. "It doesn't necessarily mean we die . . . we just never come back here."

Robbie looks grave. Francesca pauses a moment, then steps over to him and wraps her arms around him. She stays that way. *No matter how this turns out, we won't see him again. Not this him anyway.*

"Hey, it's okay," Robbie says, giving Francesca a squeeze. "You never know what can happen. It's time travel right?" She just hugs him harder.

"We're going to go back to Montana first," I say. "A couple of months from now. Francesca has the photo. If anything happens between now and then that makes you think we need to change this plan, will you let us know?"

Francesca lets Robbie go.

"Yeah, I can definitely do that. Leave me the address."

"Okay. I hate to leave you again so soon. I know we just got here . . ."

"You don't want to stay the night at least?" Robbie says. "I could bring the kids by tomorrow."

"We have a lot of questions that need answering," I say. "I don't know how much longer I can wait." *I want out of this place.*

"I don't think I'll be sleeping anytime soon," Blake says.

Francesca looks from Robbie back to us, and nods.

I wish there was a way to keep Robbie and Mr. Cameron and just move them to our time. They don't belong here either. My mind goes back to the conversation with Mym in the grass. *"You have to choose the ones you are going to stick with." If we ever get back to our own time, there's no older Robbie, no Mr. Cameron . . .*

"Well," Robbie says. "I'll see if Grandpa wants to say goodbye." We follow him across the hall into Mr. Cameron's room. Samwise raises his head from Mr. Cameron's lap as we enter, but he is asleep. My pack is still leaning against the dresser. Robbie presses a hand to Mr. Cameron's shoulder to wake him up. The cat stands up and stretches. The old man's eyelids flutter open and he turns to look at us. Recognition takes a moment, but then he smiles.

"Grandpa, they decided they can't stay."

"Hmm. No?" Mr. Cameron straightens himself up on the pillows with Robbie's help.

"We have to fix some things," Francesca says.

"If anyone can do it, you can." He smiles.

This would be easier if he wasn't always so kind. We move toward the bed.

"We'll come back someday if we can," Francesca says. She takes Mr. Cameron's hand.

"I'm not worried, darling," Mr. Cameron says. "You'll see me again, and I'll get to see your magic act one more time."

"Hopefully we make less of a mess of it," Blake says.

"You had to leave room for improvement," Mr. Cameron says.

The cat is purring loudly and rubs its face under Mr. Cameron's chin. He pushes its head away from his face. Robbie picks it up and gently tosses it off the bed onto the floor.

"Thanks again for all your hospitality," I say. "We owe you so much."

"Nonsense. I've had a wonderful time. I owe you."

I pick up my pack and sling it over my shoulder. "We'd better get going."

Francesca pulls the photo of the fob out of her pocket and hands it to me.

"Where is the next adventure?" Mr. Cameron asks. Francesca squats down and pulls the de-gravitizer out of her pocket and aims it at the fob.

"We're going back to Montana," I say. I look at the back of Francesca's photo. "In August."

"Let me get that address," Robbie says. He grabs a pad and pencil off the nightstand and copies down the info on the back of the photo. "This Cowboy Bob sounds like a useful guy to know."

"Definitely," I say. I dial my chronometer for the afternoon of August 20th as he scribbles. The light on the DG turns green and Francesca stands back up.

"You have everything you need?" Mr. Cameron asks.

Blake's hand instinctively reaches for the jeans pocket where he's been carrying the ring. His hand connects with only fabric. He sets his jaw but says nothing. I reach into my own pocket and remove the keys to Blake's Jeep.

"Robbie, do you mind doing us a big favor?"

"Sure."

"We made a pretty big mess of Blake's life. The other Blake. You think you could try to explain things to him? I'm sure he'll be looking for that Jeep soon."

"You going to get me arrested for auto theft?"

"Let's hope not." I toss him the keys.

"I can handle it."

"Thanks, man."

"And tell Mallory," Blake begins, "Tell her that everything I said was true. Just because I was the wrong guy . . . she still . . . well, just tell her I don't regret it."

"Okay." Robbie nods. "I will."

"Okay, how tall is this thing?" Blake eyes the ceiling and the fob in Francesca's hand.

I'm not the only one eager to get out of here.

"It says seventy-three inches," Francesca replies.

"I'm 6'3", so that's seventy-five inches," I say. "It would be about here." I hold my hand to my forehead. Francesca hands me the fob.

"I'm just going to be holding onto you, so you hold it."

I hold the fob lower than it is in the photo.

"Let's not hit our heads on the ceiling fan," Blake says.

"Yeah. That would suck." I raise it slightly.

Blake reaches his chronometer hand up and touches the crystal as well.

"Good luck, guys," Robbie says. "Tell Carson hi for me. Tell him we miss him."

"We will," Francesca says.

"And tell the younger me . . . tell him that everything will be okay," Robbie adds.

Mr. Cameron puts his hand out and pats Robbie's arm. "That goes for me too."

"You got it." I smile.

I watch their faces as Blake counts off. "One, two, three."

We drop an inch onto the carpeted floor of Cowboy Bob's office. The crystal fob swings back and forth on the chain from the fan as we release it. I move to the window and look out onto the waving grasses of the prairie behind the house.

August 2009. So this is what the future looks like.

Francesca is staring past the gravitizer microwave in the direction we last saw Mr. Cameron's bed. "I'm really starting to hate goodbyes."

I expected Cowboy Bob to be surprised to see us, but when we file into the dining room and find him seated at the head of the table, he continues chewing his Belgian waffle as if we'd been standing there the whole time. He gestures toward the other seats around the table with one hand while still holding his fork in the other. I look around the kitchen and down the hall toward the laundry room, but he seems to be alone.

Damn. I wonder where she is.

"Hi," Francesca offers.

He swallows, and I think he's about to greet us, but then he takes a swig of orange juice instead. Once he sets it back down, he finally addresses us. "Good morning."

I check the clock on the wall. It says three o'clock. "Isn't it afternoon?"

"For some," Bob replies. He gestures again to the other seats, and this time we find places and sit.

"So we're back," Blake says.

"I can see that."

"Things didn't go according to plan," I say.

"Can I offer you a waffle?" Bob replies.

"In this case I'm not sure that's going to help," I say.

Cowboy Bob considers me a moment while wiping his mouth with his checkered napkin. "The syrup is from Vermont."

"Be that as it may, I think we'd rather talk about some of our more pressing issues," I say.

"There's your first mistake." Bob stands up and takes his plate to the kitchen and sets it near the waffle maker. "You should never pass up good food just to deal with your personal problems." The counter top is dusted with flour and batter drippings. He scoops a measuring cup into a bowl of waffle batter and pours it onto the griddle. "But since we have a minute anyway, what seems to be the dilemma?"

"We're in the wrong 2009," Francesca says.

Cowboy Bob pauses in the act of putting a finger full of batter to his mouth and then lowers it back down. "Where are you supposed to be?"

"Well, 2009, but not this 2009," Blake says.

"Yeah, but which timeline are you navigating?" Bob wipes his finger off on a paper towel.

"That's the thing. We don't know," I say.

Bob looks at each of our faces, seemingly to verify the truth of my statement. "You don't know which stream you are trying to navigate?"

"No," I say.

"No wonder you got to the wrong time. You mean you didn't even know the first time through, when I brought you up this way?"

"Nobody told us we needed to know that," Blake says.

"Oh wow. I had no idea." He runs his non-battered hand through his hair. "Man. Now I feel pretty bad. I should have asked you when you first showed up. I assumed when you said you wanted me to take you to 2009, that you meant in the stream we were in. Switching streams would have been a whole different process."

"So you can do it?" Blake says. "You can switch timestreams?"

"Of course. You did it, obviously."

"I don't think we noticed we did," I say. "Whenever it happened, we didn't do it deliberately."

"Maybe you guys should remind me again just how much training Harry gave you."

"How long has it been for you since we talked last?" Francesca asks.

"A couple months or so," Bob says. He opens a cupboard and pulls out three glasses. He walks over and sets them on the table in front of us and then moves the pitcher of orange juice to the table as well. "How long has it been for you?"

"It's still the same day," Blake says. "Still the same bad day."

"Must not have liked home too much, huh? What's different? Did they vote in the wrong president or something?"

"We're still there. Other ones of us," I say. "We never left."

"Ah." Bob nods. "That'll do it." He sits back down at the end of the table and continues to pick at his food. "So do you guys know which timestream you originally came from?"

"Not really," I say. "We know stuff that happened in it I guess."

"Is that bad?" Francesca says. "Are we going to be able to figure that out?"

Bob waves his hand. "Oh yeah, that's no problem. We can always figure that out pretty quick from doing a spectrometer test. That's not an issue. Getting you back there could be tougher, depending on how far away you're from."

"So what happened?" I say. "How did we end up in a different timestream?"

"That happens easy enough," Bob says. "You just went back and changed something significant enough to alter reality as you know it."

"That's easy?" Francesca asks.

"Yeah. Happens all the time. Trying to predict the consequences is a lot tougher though. Knowing where that branch of the stream is going to take you is a big gamble. Sometimes it's somewhere good, sometimes it isn't."

I pour myself a glass of orange juice.

"So how do we get back?" Blake asks. "Back to where we originally came from."

"You have to get back to before the stream branched off and then follow the original stream," Bob says.

He makes it sound so simple.

"So how do we do that?" I say.

"This would probably be easier to explain with a spectrometer," Bob replies.

Francesca looks to the kitchen. "I think your waffle is burning."

Bob pops out of his chair and trots back into the kitchen. He mutters curses as he tries to pry the waffle free of the waffle iron with his fingers. He grabs another fork and then finally manages to flip it out onto a plate. He snags the glass bottle of syrup as he passes the counter, and sits back down.

"So the universe is a fractal. Did Quickly cover that with you?"

"No," Blake says.

"Okay. That's a lot of your problem then. I'll start at the beginning. You can't think about time as a line. It's only linear in places it's never been changed. And it can potentially be changed anywhere. It's better if you think about it as a sort of spider web, or a snowflake."

He picks up the bottle of syrup again. "Okay. Let's say you start in the middle." He begins pouring syrup on the center of his waffle. "You go straight for a bit, but then something happens." His syrup trail moves up one of the crevasses before cutting right across a quarter of the waffle. "See, I left my original path and started down a different one. I never noticed because it all felt like a straight line to me." His syrup trail stops. "It turns out that I could possibly have made all manner of turns along the way too." He begins to fill in some of the other waffle squares off the first line with syrup. "I could divide up each one of those little lines too. It just depends on how many changes I want to go back and make."

"So you're saying we're off course somewhere?" Blake says.

"Yeah. But don't feel bad about it. Most time travelers are."

"What do you mean?" I ask.

Cowboy Bob leans back in his chair and looks at me. "Most time travelers you meet are so far from their original timestreams, they couldn't tell you the first thing about how to get back. Most of them never get back. Some don't even realize they're lost."

"Are you in your original timestream?" Francesca asks.

"Oh no. Definitely not."

"So where are you from?" Blake says.

Bob forks some waffle into his mouth and then stands up. "Crrm on." He wipes his hands off and signals for us to follow him. I carry my glass of orange juice with me. He leads us back upstairs to the office. The crystal fob is still swinging gently in the wash of the ceiling fan.

Walking past the gravitizer, Bob reaches into a wicker basket full of cardboard tubes and pulls one out. He slides a drawing out of the tube and spreads it open on the desk. The drawing is a blueprint with an array of little dark blue lines intersecting dots with identifiers. I recognize it as the same type of map Lawrence had on his computer monitor but without the depth.

"Here's one of the Zeta stream. A fair amount of known fissures to work with. You can see how the streams have identifiers based on numbers and letters. That helps I.D. what you are working with. You can trace your way backward or forward that way."

"What are all these little symbols?" I point to some little marks that resemble hieroglyphics along some of the lines.

"Those are special notes of events and persons, kind of like shorthand for references. You can't fit all the info on one page, so it pays to have symbol references."

"You catalog all this stuff yourself?" I ask.

"Me? No. Well . . . some of it. Most of it I got from Harry. He did all the major work. The rest of us just mooch off his good graces."

"What timestream are we in right now?" Blake asks.

"That's an excellent question to ask," Bob says. "And often." He reaches into a cupboard next to the gravitizer and pulls out what I recognize to be a temporal spectrometer. Like Malcolm's, it has a handle coming from a box with a screen. This one is larger and gray, however, and seems to have a few more dials. Cowboy Bob points it at the wall and squeezes the trigger on the handle. The green light flashes and a squiggly line graph appears on the screen.

"Okay, so you see this squiggle? That's the frequency of this timestream. When you get down to a sub-molecular level, and start dealing with things like string theory, everything vibrates. The whole universe is vibrating. The good news is, if you look hard enough and small enough, in any given timestream you see it's all vibrating at the same temporal frequency."

He points the spectrometer at Francesca and pulls the trigger. The light flashes red this time and another squiggly line appears.

"Only thing is, when something gets changed in the universe on a scale that is no longer capable of being contained by a simple paradox, the frequency can change. A time traveler's activities can be a good example. They change something and then our interaction with the universe changes."

"It makes another universe?" Francesca says.

"No, not exactly. It's the same universe. We're not duplicating matter or energy or all the other things the universe is made of. You're just operating on a different frequency of that universe. It's like another facet of the same diamond, if you will. You might be in the same place, but the way you see it and interact with it has changed."

Bob looks at his frequency reading from Francesca. "Hmm. Interesting." He points the spectrometer at me and takes another reading.

"What's interesting?" Francesca asks.

"It looks like you three are from one of the primes."

"Prime?" Blake asks.

"It's one of Quickly's earliest timestreams. He cataloged the first twenty-six major divisions he discovered after letters. Those became the primes. He started adding numbers to the various branches off those streams as things changed. That structure became the basis of our time mapping system."

"What does that mean for us?" I say.

"Nothing really." Bob rummages around in the cupboard some more. He pulls out a thick binder and lays it on the desk. "It just means that the timestream you originally came from, and the one Quickly came from, are not that far apart."

"Could he be from the same one?" Francesca asks.

"Let's see." Bob flips through the first few pages of the binder and runs his finger down an index. He then turns to a section in the back that shows various frequency graphs and letters. He flips through a few pages, comparing the images to the one on the spectrometer. "Looks like . . . you're a November Prime."

I lean in and see the graph he's looking at. "November?"

"Yeah, it's the phonetic name for the letter N."

"So which one are we in now?" Blake asks.

"This is an L branch. LVR17, to be precise." Bob grabs another cardboard tube out of the basket, and after extracting a couple of drawings, finds the one he's looking for. He lays it over the Zeta drawing and spreads it out for our inspection. He points a finger to the centerline. "Okay. Here's Lima Prime. That's broken up by letter codes of its own. You trace that up from its origin point till you hit its V branch, follow that till you hit the R branch of that line and then seventeen breaks later, you find us. Approximately here."

"It's like a road map," Francesca says.

"Yeah, more or less," Bob replies.

"So how do you move around?" I ask. "You said you can get from one stream to another?"

"Yeah. It can be challenging at first, but you can do it fairly routinely once you get the hang of it. What you have to do, is one of two things. The most basic option is to backtrack. All the different branches stem from a prime somewhere. You can backtrack down the branch till before the offshoot you're looking for. It's like you put your car into reverse on the interstate and back up till you get back to the exit you missed. Then you need to find a way to take that exit instead of going forward on the interstate again."

"What does that involve?" Blake asks.

"You need to use something as an anchor to jump forward that exists on that offshoot, but no longer exists on the interstate. Usually you just destroy something on your way back."

"Destroy something?" Francesca says. "This is sounding complicated."

"It's really not that bad," Cowboy Bob replies. "Look." He reaches into the cupboard and pulls out a glass ball anchor of the same type we used in our lab training. "Let's say I want to get to a branch of time that diverged off of this one a few minutes ago. Maybe Francesca here punches me in the eye half an hour from now and I cry about it. You guys laugh at me. I decide I don't want to keep on living in the timestream where a girl made me cry, and everybody made me feel bad. Well, no problem. I channel my anger and smash this anchor into tiny useless bits. Then I go back to an hour ago, right before this timestream exit I know about. I find my glass anchor there, still intact, and jump forward with it again, going past the point in time where I smashed it.

"The anchor doesn't exist in that form here anymore at that specified time. You can't get here at that time anymore, so where do you go? The anchor takes the exit, and you arrive at that same parallel point in time on the nearest timestream where it didn't get smashed."

"Hang on though." I say. "I thought for sure Quickly said we shouldn't ever use things that could get destroyed. He said something about not using paper and such cause you could die or something."

"Yeah," Francesca straightens up. "He said that happened to some mice."

Bob scratches his beard. "Quickly said that? He said you'd die?"

"Yeah," I reply. "Maybe he didn't say die exactly. I think he said some lab rats got lost or something. I'm not really sure now."

"Maybe it was in a different context. You could certainly get lost that way. No doubt about that."

"That's not how I took it." Francesca says. "I like the part where we get to destroy things though."

"I figured," Bob says. "I knew you were violent from that time you punched me in the eye."

Francesca smiles.

"But wait a minute," Blake says. "If you go to another timestream that's parallel to yours, aren't you already there?

"Yes, that's true," Bob says. "There would be two of me there, and none of me in the timestream I left from. You guys would just have to go on living your life knowing you laughed at me and hating yourselves for it, and you would never see me again. I would just have to have a great time with myself and the other versions of you, who are hopefully nicer. You can't ever leave a time without leaving a hole or adding something to somewhere else. Things that happened, happened. You can't undo that. But you can choose to live somewhere else."

"Okay, so you said there were two ways," I say. "What's the other way?"

"Yes, with the other way you get to skip all the backtracking business and just go straight to the point on the other timestream you're aiming for. The trick is, that only works if you already have something from there. If you have an object you can use as an anchor that is from the time you want to get to, the anchor has no choice but to function there."

"We have some things from our time we brought with us, like some of our clothes and my phone," Francesca says. "Could we just use those?"

Cowboy Bob scratches his beard. "Yeah, that could possibly work, if you de-gravitized it. Do you have any specific times you remember where you have a safe location of your phone that's accurate enough to get to? You can't be seen by your other self either, or you'll instantly branch off into a new timestream. Unless you have a memory of meeting yourself in your bedroom one night."

Francesca shakes her head. "Wow, that's kind of hard actually. I had that phone with me pretty much all the time. Mostly it was just in my purse or maybe on my nightstand. I can't think of any time when I could sneak three people around it without noticing."

"Yeah, that's where stuff gets complicated," Bob says.

"But if we were to find something, something from our time, we could use it to get home?" Blake asks.

"Yeah, provided you were in range of your chronometer," Bob replies. "And provided you don't change your home timestream by your arrival."

"And there won't be two of us there?" Blake asks.

"Not if it's the timestream you originally left from. You're still missing there. It will stay that way unless you make it back."

"Good," Blake says. "I've had enough of my other selves already."

Cowboy Bob straightens up and puts away the charts. "The bad news is, I'm not headed to the November Prime in 2009 anytime soon, or I could give you a lift. I might pass the N on the way back, but it wouldn't be till wherever it intersects the L. I think that happens decades back."

"We're actually planning to go back to 1986," I say. "We left some things undone there that we need to fix."

Bob nods. "I could probably get you there without much trouble. I'll be going that way anyway. Any day in particular?"

"We need to get back to the day the lab burned."

"I see."

"Where are you going?" Francesca says.

"I'm actually going back to 1910 or so, if I can make it."

"Wow. That's really far back," I say.

"Yeah, but for me that's home."

"You're from 1910?" Francesca's eyes widen.

"More or less. I was a kid then. I was actually born in 1899."

"Seriously?" I say. "That's so cool. How did you end up here?"

"That's a long story, but Harry and Mym found me when I was a kid. Life wasn't going too great for me at the time when they picked me up. Mym was a little kid then too. They were on the way back from a trip to the mid 1800s. I guess Harry had a soft spot for orphans. He treated me like family."

"The Parsons, who owned this ranch, weren't really your parents?" I ask.

"No. Hank was an old school friend of Harry's. Hank and his wife never had any kids but always wanted some. Harry thought Montana would be a good place for me to grow up without too much culture shock while he trained me. Things around here haven't changed all that much in the last hundred years."

"Why are you going back to 1910?" I ask.

"Just need to figure some things out." He closes the cupboard door and leads us out of the office. "Come on. I've had enough of the house."

A barnyard cat is lounging in a patch of sun at the end of the porch and looks at us sleepily as we emerge from the house. The crunch of dry dirt under our feet changes to hollow thumping as Bob leads us onto the porch of the ranch hand apartments. Reaching Levi's door, he gives it a few raps with his knuckles. There's no response.

"He's probably out checking the livestock in the north pasture. I guess you guys get to help me with the balloon."

It takes us over an hour to get the balloon and gondola out of the barn and ready to be inflated. Bob takes care to show us the different burner settings and how the parachute release valve works. We help move his storage bins into the basket and Bob grabs some last minute things from the house. I throw our pack into the basket as well.

An enormous fan, run by the barn generator, channels air into the balloon, to get it in a position where we can fire the burners. Bob is patient with us as we ask questions and generally slow down his progress. Once we have the balloon upright and the gondola loaded with our necessary belongings, Bob has me untie the last of the anchor lines. I have to sprint to make it to the gondola before it floats too far off the ground, but I make it in time, and Bob and Blake help pull me over the side. I tumble awkwardly to the floor of the basket.

"Onward and upward," Blake says.

"Or upward and backward." Bob smiles.

I scramble to my feet and grip the burner mount railing breathlessly. My heart is pounding. *No problem. I got this.*

We drift over the town of Scobey with a lazy southerly breeze. I join Bob at the side of the gondola and peer cautiously over the edge. "So where's Mym?"

Bob is leaning on his elbows watching the horizon. "She hopped off in 2020. She had some things she wanted to do up there."

"Oh. Did you get to the Olympics?"

"Yeah, we did actually. Rio was a great time. We ended up skipping London though."

"So . . . she just took off after that?"

Bob turns to face me. He considers me a moment. "Mym's not one to be pinned down."

"Yeah, I kind of got that impression." I look down at a red-and-yellow combine making its way through a field of grain. The driver gives us a wave. I wave back. "So . . . how do you get a hold of her? Like if you want to call her for some reason."

Bob plucks a toothpick out of a box in his pocket and begins working it through his teeth. "Do you have a tachyon pulse transmitter?" His laughing eyes already know the answer.

"Must have left that in my other pants."

"Guess you'll just have to wait till she finds you then." He smiles and returns to contemplating the horizon.

Cowboy Bob moves us back to May of 2001 on our first jump. The second gets us to June of 1993. Blake and I help him switch to a spare set of batteries at that point. We've drifted pretty far south, but on our last jump of the day, Bob de-gravitizes an iron ring and secures it to the cable before lowering it to the ground as his anchor. When we jump, we find ourselves back in the field behind the barn, anchored to one of his tie-down points.

We're back.

"Voila," Bob declares. "1986. As you commanded." He moves to the instrument cluster and double checks the indications. "It is now May 3rd, about two in the afternoon. We're still a couple months ahead of when you left, but the last bit should be comfortable enough to do by chronometer."

Bob signals Blake to pull on the cable to start our descent. In a few minutes we're back on the ground. Blake and I vault over the edge of the basket to tie off the balloon, but Bob doesn't get out of the gondola.

"No need to tie me off, this is where I leave you fine people." He slaps the frame of the burner rig. "I think she's still got one more good move in her before I have to stop and charge the batteries. I'm going to see if I can make the seventies tonight."

"Will we see you again?" Francesca asks.

"Oh, I'm sure you will," Bob replies, offering his hand to help her over the side. Francesca slides over into the grass. "I do have something for you before I go." He leans over into one of the storage areas, hands a cardboard tube to Francesca, and then tosses something small and colorful at me. I catch it with both hands and open them to reveal a completed Rubik's Cube.

"That will get you to the time you want to go. Keep the red side up. It'll put you in Quickly's lab in one of the jump rooms."

"Thank you," I say.

"We really appreciate everything," Blake says. "You've been a life-saver."

"It's been a pleasure," Bob replies. "Feel free to come back and see me anytime."

"I hope you have a good time in 1910," Francesca says. "I hope you find what you're looking for."

Cowboy Bob nods to us and ignites the burner. We back away from the tether line and watch the balloon climb. As the tether cable grows taut, Bob leans over the edge of the basket and gives us a salute. We wave and he vanishes.

I stay looking at the sky for a few moments, just watching the vacant space he's left behind. Francesca breaks the silence. "You know that scene in *The Wizard of Oz* when Dorothy climbs out of the balloon to chase Toto, and the wizard can't take her home because he floats away without her?"

"Yeah."

"I think we're Dorothy."

"That's okay." I lower my gaze to the ranch around us. "We're not going home yet. We still have our witch to melt."

269

Chapter 20

"Time travel is a very effective way to sober up. It does however involve trying to make precise calculations while inebriated. I have visited some unexpected new places that way, but I can't say I'd recommend it as common practice. "
-Excerpt from the journal of Dr. Harold Quickly, 1975

"We need a plan," Blake says.

We stride through the grass toward the barn. The mare in the corner of the paddock eyes us suspiciously as we make our way through the gate into the barnyard. We stop in the shade of the barn to consider our options.

"We know where Stenger is the night the lab burns," I say. "And Carson and I got his gun, so after that point he should be unarmed."

"You want to try to get to him then?" Blake asks.

"Seems like the best time to find him."

"And then what do we do with him?" Francesca says.

"I don't know. I think we probably need to kill him."

Francesca frowns. "I've never plotted to kill someone before."

"Me either, but I don't know what else to do. I figure it's like self defense, because we're saving Carson."

"Even if he's unarmed?"

"He was unarmed last time and I let him go. That was obviously a mistake."

"Yeah." Francesca nods. "We owe it to Carson."

"We're going to need some kind of weapons then," Blake says.

"And we're going to need to use Bob's gravitizer," Francesca adds.

"We should have asked him if he had a gun we could borrow." I shift my pack on my shoulder.

"We could try to buy one?" Blake suggests.

"We don't have any ID," Francesca says. "Or a car."

The screen door on the house slams and I look around the side of the barn to see Connie on the porch, feeding scraps to a pair of cats. As she tosses them bits of food, a few more materialize out of the bushes until she's feeding half a dozen. When we walk toward her, she looks up. "I hoped I might see you all again." She tosses the last of the scraps to the cats and wipes her hands on her apron. She comes down from the porch to greet us.

"At least you didn't say I told you so," I say.

She smiles. "You young people seem to run off a lot, but I like it better when you come back. Is Bobby with you?"

"He actually just dropped us off."

"He was going back farther to see some family, I think," Francesca says.

"Oh. Okay. I'm glad he brought you three back. Did you have a good time?"

"Um. Well . . ." I mumble.

"It was educational," Blake says.

Connie seems satisfied with that. "Why don't you come inside, and I'll fix you up a snack."

"That's nice of you," I say.

The kitchen is full of baking supplies and fruit. The oven is on and something smells delicious. Francesca slides up onto a stool at the counter. Connie checks on the oven and I glimpse two pies inside before she shuts it again.

Pies are great, but we need a gun.

"We actually could use some help with something a little more serious today," I say.

"Oh? What's that dear?" Connie gives us her attention.

"We actually really need to borrow a gun."

Connie's smile fades. "A gun?"

"Yeah, we have something to do a couple of months ago that might involve some shooting."

"Oh." Connie fidgets with some spoons on the counter. "I know Levi has a rifle for the coyotes, but I don't know if he'd be willing to loan it to you. What is it you are trying to shoot?"

"One of our close friends got murdered by a really bad man," Francesca says. "We need to keep that from happening."

Connie watches Francesca's face with concern. "Well that is terrible . . . I don't know if we have anything . . . I think Bob has his dad's gun upstairs, but I don't know how he would feel about it being used for something like that." The conversation seems to have drained the joy out of her face. She moves an eggbeater to the sink and straightens her apron front.

This was a bad idea.

"It's okay," I say. "We can figure something out. We don't mean to bother you with it."

"Okay. I can talk to Levi about it," she says.

"Your pies smell amazing." Francesca sits up straighter on her stool.

"Oh, thank you." Connie brightens a little. "I have an apple and a . . . a peach. I have a book club meeting later, and Bob's kitchen is so much bigger than mine at home."

We won't be able to fit a rifle into the gravitizer upstairs. Levi's gun won't work. I wonder what Bob has?

"We were also hoping we could use Bob's gravitizer, if it's not too much trouble," I say.

"Oh, yes. I think that would be all right," Connie replies.

"Why don't we take care of that real quick while you're baking." I nudge Blake with my elbow and gesture with my head toward the upstairs.

"Okay, I'll see if I can find you all something to snack on." Connie opens a pantry door and begins pulling things out.

"Okay, we'll be back down shortly." I lead the way upstairs to the office. It looks essentially the same as we left it in 2009. Cardboard tubes of maps still lean against the desk.

"Which map did Cowboy Bob give you?" Blake asks.

Francesca looks into the tube in her hand and pulls out the drawing inside. She lays it on the floor. The drawing looks like a spiderweb with the major lines labeled with letters. "It's all the primes," Francesca says. She points to the N branch. "There's ours."

A map to get us home. But not yet.

"We're going to need to de-gravitize this." I toss the Rubik's Cube to Francesca, then begin rummaging through the cupboards and desk drawers.

"What are you looking for?" Blake asks.

"She said there's a gun up here somewhere."

"You're going to get it, even though she said not to?" Francesca asks.

"Good idea." Blake begins to help me search. "I'd rather face the anger of an elderly woman than go up against a serial killer unarmed."

Francesca frowns but sets to de-gravitizing the Rubik's Cube. I'm closing a drawer full of paperclips and staples when Blake finds it.

"Whoa. This should work." He turns from the cabinet and displays a wooden box with two revolvers in it.

"Oh wow. Those are cool." I admire the polished wood handles and shining stainless steel. "Are there bullets for them?"

"Yeah." Blake reaches back into the cabinet, pulls out a small box labeled "Barnes," and gives it a light shake. It sounds full.

"Do you think they have gravitites in them?" Francesca asks.

"I guess we should check." Blake lays the gun box and the box of ammo down on the floor in front of Francesca. She aims the end of her degravitizer at it and pushes the test button. The light turns green. "Nope."

"I guess we'll have to throw them in Bob's machine," I say. "Is there anything else we need to take with us?"

"What do we have to work with in that pack right now?" Blake asks. I grab our pack and dump it out on the floor. Our winter clothes tumble out, followed by my tortoise shell, a few other miscellaneous anchors we have left, and multiple envelopes of photos, along with our logbooks.

"Do we need to take all this stuff?" I ask.

"I'm way behind on logging our jumps." Blake picks up his logbook.

"Mine is gone," Francesca says.

"We should probably plan out this next one. I can add your entries into mine." I pick up my logbook and flip to one of the empty pages. "Bob said the Rubik's Cube is in one of the jump rooms the day the lab burns. That was January 9th, right? We need to figure out what time we want to show up."

"What time did you get Stenger's gun away from him?" Francesca asks. "I don't want to show up till then."

I think about my trip into the lab with Carson. "I remember we were stuffing things into the packs around six o'clock. We ran into Stenger right after that. I'm guessing it wasn't much later, 6:05 maybe?"

"When did the lab start burning?" Blake asks.

"I saw the smoke before I jumped back, I think that was probably around six-thirty or so, maybe a little after. I don't remember exactly."

"Did you write it in your logbook?" Francesca points to the book in my hand.

I flip through the pages. "Um. I think I forgot."

Blake stares at his logbook. "I'm starting to understand why these things are important."

"Okay, so we're trying to get to Stenger between the time he loses his gun at 6:05 and when he lights the place on fire a half hour later? Is this really our best option?" Francesca asks. "It sounds unnecessarily dangerous."

"We could try to find him later, but I don't know where he'll be, and he could end up with another gun for all we know," I say. "This is the only time we know of, where we know where he is, and we know he doesn't have a gun."

"I want one of our guns at least," Francesca says.

"You know how to use it?" Blake hands her one of the revolvers.

"I think I've seen enough Clint Eastwood movies to figure it out," Francesca replies. "Plus my brother took me to a gun range once. I've killed my share of paper targets."

"So we get to the lab jump room, find our way near the hallway where Stenger is when he loses his gun, shoot him and get out of there, yeah?" My stomach churns a little at the idea of being in the hallway with that psycho again. *It has to be done. Carson needs us.*

I toss our other anchors back into the pack and leave out the socks and my extra shirt. I pick up my tortoise shell and extract the photo from inside it. *When all hope is lost.* I put the photo back inside and toss the shell into the pack. "You want your coat?" I ask Francesca.

"Yes. It's January there."

I hand it to her. I cinch up the pack and start dialing my chronometer for January of 1986. "What's the Zulu conversion for winter? Five hours?"

"Yeah. No daylight savings." Blake starts dialing his as well.

"Wait, we're going right now?" Francesca asks. "What about Connie? She's downstairs making food for us."

"I think the snacks can wait."

"That's kind of rude," Francesca says.

"We're going to the past," I say. "She won't notice. We can always stop for cookies or whatever on the way back. I really want to get this over with before I have to think about it any longer."

Francesca frowns again. Blake is stoic. "Fine," she says. "But I need to pee first." She sets the revolver on the desk and disappears into the hall.

"That's probably a good idea," I say.

"So what did we decide on? Six?" Blake asks.

"I think we should get there a little earlier to give ourselves time. We'll just have to be careful to not run into me or Carson before they get the gun away from Stenger. The lab is a big place. We should be able to hide out and get ourselves some prep time. Let's go with 5:25. That should be plenty of time."

Blake nods and finishes his chronometer settings. I do the same. Blake stuffs the box of ammo and the revolver in the gravitizer, then grabs Francesca's gun and puts that in as well. I move to the control panel.

The blue vial on the side is still full of gravitites. There is a button labeled "gravitize" and one labeled "de-gravitize". The gravitize button is already illuminated. *Simple enough.* I flip the lever, and it's only a matter of seconds till the chime dings. Blake opens the door and pulls out the guns. He hands one to Francesca as she walks back in. I put the box of ammo in a side pocket of my pack.

"Where's the bathroom up here?"

Francesca points. "First one on the left."

As the water from the sink flows over my fingers, I look my reflection in the eyes. They look the same as they always do. Maybe a little more tired. *You're going to have to kill somebody. Are those the eyes of a killer?* I shake off the thought. *You're going to save someone. Killing Stenger is just the only way to make sure he won't hurt anybody else. The families of all those people he's hurt over the years would probably thank me.* The face in the mirror doesn't look convinced.

My heart has begun to pound as I rejoin my friends in the office. Francesca and Blake both have the unloaded guns tucked into the fronts of their pants. I join them in the middle of the room and pick up the Rubik's Cube, holding it a little lower than the height of the lab anchor stands. Blake touches his chronometer hand to it as well. Francesca hesitates a moment, then turns and darts out to the railing of the stairs in the hallway. She leans over and yells down, "Miss Connie? We'll be right back!" She doesn't wait for a response, but promptly rejoins us and puts her hands to ours.

"Feel better?" I say. She gives me a nod. I count off. "One, two, three."

The fluorescent lights of the lab jump room seem harsh and uninviting after the warm afternoon sun of Montana. *Jump lessons feel like forever ago.* We move away from the anchor stand and I stuff the Rubik's Cube into my pack.

Francesca pulls her revolver from her waistband. "Bullets, please." I slide the ammo box out of the side pocket of the pack as Blake unhinges his revolver. I open the box and hold out six bullets. "How did you get it open?" Francesca asks.

Blake hands his revolver to her and takes hers. I hand the bullets to her instead.

"It's this thing on the side." Blake shows it to Francesca.

"I thought you said you didn't know much about guns," she replies.

"I can get them open. That's about the limit of my knowledge."

I fish out six bullets for Blake.

"Um. Why aren't these fitting?" Francesca asks.

I watch her trying to slide the bullets into the various holes in the gun. "Let me see." She hands me the gun.

"She's right," Blake says. "They don't fit."

I try to slide one of the bullets into Francesca's gun and the brass casing is just slightly too large for the holes. "Shit." I look at the flap on the box. "Are these the wrong kind of bullets?"

Blake takes the box from my hands. "It says 0.45 caliber. What are these guns?"

"I don't know." I turn Francesca's gun over in my hands and read the engraving on the barrel. "Shit. It says 0.38."

"You've got to be kidding me," Francesca says. "Seriously? They won't work?"

"Oh God. I'm so sorry," Blake says. "I just grabbed what was next to the gun box."

"Does that one say the same thing?" I point to Blakes gun.

He nods. "Thirty-eight."

"Why would Bob have the wrong bullets in there?" Francesca asks.

"He must own a forty-five somewhere too," Blake mumbles. "I never bothered to look for more guns. I thought those were the only ones."

"Oh God. We're in a building with a serial killer and we have no weapons at all now? We've got to get out of here," Francesca says. She moves to the blue door and swings it open.

"No! Francesca, I'm out there!" I say. She's midway out the door when she freezes.

"Son of a bitch!" She jumps back into the room. The doorknob slips out of her grip and the door slams shut behind her. She cringes at the noise.

"What?" Blake says.

"I just saw you," Francesca says. She looks to me. "You were looking the other way, but I just saw your back."

"I had to have heard that." I shove the box of shells back into the pack. "Come on!" I move toward the green door and crack it open. We hurry out the door and across the hallway into a classroom. I gently close it behind me till there's just a sliver of space to look through. A moment later I see a door open farther down the hall. The man emerging from the room isn't me however. I touch the door closed gently.

"What is it?" Francesca whispers.

"It's the young Quickly."

"Is he going to come in here?"

"No. We're okay. He talks to me in the hall for a few minutes and then goes into a jump room."

"What do we do now?" Blake whispers.

"I think we just need to wait it out. I end up going into Quickly's office in a few minutes and finding the money. We should be able to sneak out of here and make our way toward the hallway where we run into Stenger."

"How do we get rid of him now? Our guns won't work," Francesca says. "Are we just going to throw bullets at him and hope he gives up?"

"Well, we do have the guns. He doesn't know that there aren't any bullets in them," I say. "Maybe we can still get him to surrender."

"Surrender?" Francesca glares at me. "That's a terrible plan. We were supposed to shoot him, not keep him as a pet."

"If we capture him, we can give him to the police. At least he'll be locked up, and maybe we can get rid of him later."

Francesca is breathing heavier. "I'm not facing a serial killer with an empty gun. I can't even lie at *Balderdash*. This isn't going to work. We should just get out of here and come up with a better plan."

"What if he gets away?" I ask. "Robbie said the cops never catch him. Well . . . they catch the wrong one, but they never find the Stenger we're after. How much of our time are we going to have to waste tracking him down later, when we know where he is right now?"

"I've wasted enough time," Blake says. "I'll club him with a fire extinguisher if that's what it takes to stop him now. I've had enough of this place. I want to go home."

I hold my index finger to my lips and crack the door open again with my other hand. I can hear myself telling Quickly about the impending fire. We wait for the end of the conversation before cracking the door open slightly farther. I see myself scribbling the word east on the wall.

"Okay. I'm headed for the stairs, but I'm going to go into Quickly's office to get the money first. We should be okay to move."

"Where are we going?" Francesca asks.

"We need to find the other staircase and get downstairs," I reply. "That's where Stenger will be."

"I can get us to the other stairs," Blake says. "Let's cut back through the jump rooms." He swings open the door and moves across the hallway at a half-crouch. We follow him as quietly as we can, crossing a different jump room than the one we arrived in. The hallway on the far side is empty. Blake leads us down the hall till a left turn leads us to the back stairwell. He slowly cracks the door open and listens.

"Carson should be in the front balconies," I whisper.

"Where does Stenger come from?" Francesca asks.

"I don't know. I only know it's the hall near the alley stairs where we get his gun."

"Then we need to be really careful," Blake says. "He could be anywhere."

We slink down the stairs as silently as we can and Blake cracks the door open on the first floor. He peers through for a few moments before opening it wider. Francesca is gripping her empty gun. Blake slips through and we creep along the wall till we reach the first doorway. Blake opens it and we enter one of the lab experiment areas. A half-dozen rows of stainless steel workbenches divide the room, while various pieces of lab equipment and a few cages line the walls.

"You ever wonder why this laboratory is so big for one guy?" I whisper.

"Apparently more than one version of him uses the place," Blake says.

"This room reminds me of Mr. Pellegrini's biology class," Francesca says. "Did you have him for Bio?"

"No. I had Sanderson," I say.

"Oh, that guy was perv." Francesca makes a face.

I slide my hand along one of the countertops as we walk toward the door at the far side. "I remember I had this one lab partner who tried to stick the pickled frog's legs into—"

The sound of the door opening behind us freezes the words in my mouth. I turn to see a black-haired, thirty-something woman in a ragged, off-the-shoulder sweatshirt, staring at us from the doorway. She smiles, revealing yellowed teeth.

"Well, look what we have here."

Her slightly pocked marked face isn't familiar. *Does she know us?*

I'm about to greet her when she raises the gun. We stand like statues. My mind is racing to catch up to what's happening.

"Hey Baby!" she yells. "I think I found 'em!" Her eyes gleam as she smiles at us. She takes a step into the room. A moment later, Stenger steps into view from the hallway behind her. He is likewise holding a gun.

His eyes are cold but as he looks at me, I see a flash of recognition. "You . . ." He raises his gun.

I come unfrozen and dive behind the nearest workbench, hitting the floor with a thud. One of the guns goes off with a bang and a set of beakers shatters around me. I look up to see Blake pulling Francesca behind the next countertop. I scramble on my hands and knees to get out of the glass shards and move to the other end of the workbench. I poke my head up just slightly to see where Stenger and the woman are. Another gunshot ricochets off the steel bench. I sprawl backwards onto my rear with my heart pounding. Something crashes off a bench farther down and I catch a glimpse of Francesca's feet disappearing behind one of the benches two down from mine. Without thinking, I roll to my toes and fingertips and then dive diagonally across the open space between me and the next set of benches. I tuck my feet around behind me as I scramble up against the bench on the other side. Blake is leaning against the cabinet doors of the workbench parallel to me, holding his useless gun. Our eyes meet.

"Who the fuck is that chick?" he exclaims.

"I don't know!" I peek around the corner and instantly jerk my head back. Stenger is still near the door.

"Come on out now!" he taunts. "You can't hide in here. There's nowhere to run."

Blake gestures to me and mouths silently, "What do we do?"

I shake my head. "I don't know. Can you see Francesca?"

He points to the benches beyond me toward the door. *She's much closer to the exit than we are. If we distract them, she can probably make it out.*

Slow, deliberate footsteps echo off the wall beyond Blake. Blake pokes his head into the center aisle and then slides across to my side, moving away from the footsteps. We're close to the stack of cages along the wall now. I peer around the end of the workbench closest to the wall and see no one. I slip around the corner and Blake follows me. We press our backs against the end of the workbench cabinets, trying not to be visible from either aisle. I hear the footsteps stop at the end of our row along the opposite wall. They begin moving in our direction.

What now?

Francesca screams. I jolt to my knees and see the black-haired woman pulling Francesca up from behind a workbench near the door, by her hair. She has a gun to her head. Francesca is grimacing in pain. The woman sees me. "They're by the cages!" she yells.

The footsteps stomp closer and I duck down with my fists clenched. Blake clamps his hand on my forearm. He slams his chronometer hand up against the cabinet in front of us. "Push the pin!"

I press down on his chronometer with the fingers of my free hand. We blink.

Chapter 21

"Being a time traveler is not great for your longevity. Ways to perish increase with use, and natural hazards are only a fraction of them. I would love to say that the centuries ahead are full of open minded, generous souls. In reality, many of the citizens of the future will exert great effort to kill you."
-Excerpt from the journal of Harold Quickly, 2135

"How far did you send us?" I whisper.

"Just a couple minutes," Blake whispers back, looking at his chronometer settings.

I poke my head up cautiously above the edge of the countertop. "Forward or backward?"

"Forward. Are they still here?"

The room appears to be empty. "I think they left." I stand slowly, still ready to dive back down. Blake climbs to his feet with assistance from the edge of the bench. "They have Francesca," I growl.

"What do they want with us?" Blake says. "That woman said they were looking for us."

The clock on the wall says 6:04.

"How many minutes did you say you jumped us?"

"Just two."

"We can still make it!"

"For what?"

"Stenger loses his gun. It happens any minute now. Come on!" I sprint for the door. Blake scrambles to follow. I throw open the door and dash into the next hallway. I spin around, trying to get my bearings.

"What about that bitch who has Francesca?" Blake says.

"She's not going to be there." I run for the end of the hallway and Blake races to keep up. When I get to the end, I slow down and peek around the corner.

"But what about . . . Francesca?" Blake pants.

The hallway is clear. "If we get Stenger, she'll have to trade her for him!" I rush down the next hallway.

Rounding the corner, we find him. He's climbing to his feet, still watching the exit door to the stairs. He turns to see Blake and me running toward him, and a wave of confusion washes over his face. He looks to the exit and back to us, scowling. The Rubik's Cube lies on the floor just past him.

It must have fallen out of my pack when we blinked, and he found it . . .

"You think this is a big joke, huh?" he yells.

I skid to a stop. Blake steps up next to me, aiming his gun at Stenger's head. "Where is she?" he snarls.

Stenger smirks. "If you shoot me, you're never going to see your friends again."

Friends? Who else is he talking about?

"Shut it!" Blake says. "Put your hands up and turn around."

Stenger raises his hands but he smiles. "Really kid? You think you've got what it takes to shoot me?"

Blake takes a step forward. "You want to test me?"

Stenger's smile wavers for a moment but then he leans forward and grins. "Your gun better have more in it than your girlfriend's did."

The moment his words register on Blake's face, he knows we're bluffing. He turns and sprints away from us. I tear after him, with the contents of my backpack bouncing up and down on my back. I chase him around the corner and into the main study. The star chandelier is reflecting in the wall of windows. Stenger dashes around the back of the big center table and stops to face me. I feint to one side and he moves the other way.

"You think you can get away?" I say. Blake catches up and moves to my right to cut off Stenger's escape. We both have a good six inches of height over Stenger and probably twenty pounds. He looks fairly muscular, but not enough to beat two of us.

"You must think you're pretty funny," Stenger says. "Playing with people's lives."

"What are you talking about?" I say.

"You flit around with your fancy little watches, sending people to the past without so much as a thought. You ruin people's lives like it's a big joke. Well, I'm not amused."

"You think we sent you back in time?" I say, incredulous.

"Don't try to deny it, your little foreign friend told me enough."

"Who—" I begin.

Blake cuts me off. "Listen, asshole. Even if we were the ones who caused this, you were shackled to a van on your way to an eternity in prison. If anything, all this did you a favor!"

Stenger glares at him across the table. "So I'm supposed to be happy to be left on my ass in the eighties, without a single person who knows my name? Happy to have to shack up with some dumb bitch just to eat? Happy to be just scraping by, like a sucker?"

"You were going to prison," I say.

"I was famous!" Stenger screams. "There wasn't a person in the country who didn't fear my name! You could see it in their eyes."

"God, you'd think you'd be happy to be somewhere where no one knows you. You were free." I say.

"Oh, I'm free now. Or I will be. With Judge Waters dead and that fucking bitch prosecutor smeared all over her dorm room, I'm on my way back. When I'm done, my first run will look like play school."

"Dude. Why are you such a dick?"

Stenger reaches around his back and pulls out a large survival knife. He slides his thumb along the back edge and points it at me. "Why don't you come find out?"

The knife gives me pause. *Shit.* I look to Blake. He's standing ready on the other end of the table.

"Or maybe you won't get to." Stenger smiles. He's looking up to the back balconies. I spin my head to look, and see the black-haired woman stepping to the rail of the third-floor balcony. The gun muzzle flashes, and Blake staggers forward as a mist of blood sprays out the front of his collarbone.

"No!" I scream.

Blake crashes into the armchair ahead of him and it tumbles over, sending him sprawling on the floor. I look back to the balcony and the woman is aiming the gun at me. I lunge toward the back of the lab as the bullet misses somewhere behind me. A second shot hits the floor just as I make it under the overhang of the first floor balcony. I turn to see Stenger in pursuit with his knife. I only have time for a quick glance to the chair where Blake was lying. There's a smear of blood on the cushion but I don't see him. I turn and sprint down the south hallway.

Even with the pack on my back, my long legs rapidly outdistance Stenger by the end of the hall. I glance back as I turn the corner to see him midway down the hallway, still running with the knife. *Shit. I missed the door to the stairs.* I sprint down the corridor to the kitchen and turn right. *Gotta get away and find a weapon somehow.* I see a phone hanging on the wall in the kitchen. *I can call the cops, but they're going to be here soon anyway. This place is going to burn.*

I hear Stenger's footsteps and keep running. I cut through some storage rooms and pause briefly at some brooms and mops piled in the corner. *Plastic pieces of shit.* I crash through the next doorway and stagger into the hall. I've reached a corner of Quickly's lab where it butts up against the office next door. *I'm trapping myself.*

I run down the hall toward the front of the building. I make it a dozen steps when I reach a door on my right. I recognize its proximity to the kitchen and slip inside. I'm back in the room where I last saw Quickly. The trick glass mirror still shows a view of the interior of the office next door. I keep the light off and move toward the window. An exit sign beckons from the distant wall.

It's a way out. My hands grip the desk chair. *I could throw it through. No. The fire. I have to find Francesca and Blake before this place burns. If Blake is still alive he might be able to blink his way out. Francesca won't have that option. If I don't find her . . .* I block the thought from my mind.

That woman was up on the third floor when she shot at us. Francesca is probably up there too. I look through the office window. *Could I get through and get upstairs through the office? There's no guarantee there would be any more of these double mirrors to get back into the lab. Stenger might hear me breaking the glass too.* I release my grip on the chair and return to the hallway door. I crack it open and peer through. It's quiet. Slipping into the hall, I walk as silently as I can into the kitchen. I gently open a couple of drawers, flinching at every rattle of the contents. Finally, I find a butcher's knife. I check the edge on it with my thumb. *Better than nothing.*

I move toward the far door with the knife poised to defend myself. The swinging doors at the far wall squeak a little as I squeeze myself and my backpack through. I reach the stairwell in the next hallway without any sign of Stenger. *If he's searching for me, he must be on a different floor.*

I climb the stairs with my eyes on the floors above. When I reach the third floor of the lab, I approach the wooden doors cautiously. I've never been in this part of the lab before. I open the door slowly and find myself in a living room. With the exception of a small square of linoleum near the door, the floor is carpeted. A couch and a pair of recliners face a television and some bookshelves. There's no sign of the occupants.

As I tiptoe through the room, I pass a low table of photographs. The faces of Quickly and Mym beam at the camera from exotic locations. I see pyramids and jungles; one photo shows Quickly in front of the Golden Gate Bridge that is still under construction. *Quickly must live up here.*

I creep past a hallway bathroom and glimpse the kitchen, when I hear a thump from a little farther down the hall. I raise my knife. The apartment is silent again. I inch forward. A hallway just past the kitchen leads left toward a door to the main study balcony. *That must be how the snaggle-toothed bitch got out there. Francesca has to be up here somewhere.*

There are three more closed doors at the end of the hallway. I reach the first one on the right and lean my head close to the doorframe. From beyond the door, I hear another thump and a muffled grunt. *There's someone in there.*

I square myself up with the door and hold my knife ready. My heartbeat is thudding in my eardrums as I reach for the doorknob. I take a deep breath, and as I exhale, I shove the door open.

On the floor of the bedroom, a figure is sprawled sideways, duct-taped to a chair. His dark eyes are wide with fear and a muffled shriek comes from his gagged mouth. A few books lie on the ground around his head near the bookshelf where he has been struggling.

"Malcolm?" I gasp. I rush into the room. Malcolm begins to thrash around, shaking his head. His eyes grow even wider. "Malcolm it's me, Ben!" I lower the butcher knife as I drop to one knee near his prostrate figure. He shakes his head violently and garbles something through his gag. His thrashing suddenly stops as I hear the door click closed behind me. Malcolm shuts his eyes and droops his head.

I spin around and look at the door. The inside of the doorknob has been removed. In its place is a mass of wires and a six-inch metal box with an antenna sticking out. A light on the top of the box is blinking red. I pull the gag down on Malcolm's face and stand back up, looking at the door.

"What the hell is that thing?"

Malcolm spits a wad of fabric and drool from his mouth. "It's a trap!" The little red light on the device starts blinking faster. "He's trying to kill Dr. Quickly," he moans.

"He was using you as bait?" I climb over Malcolm and start cutting away the ropes that are binding him to the chair. He grunts as he tries to pull his hands free. "What is that device going to do?"

A low hiss coming from the doorway is my response. A strip of black gel along the base of the door erupts into flame. A similar strip around the window combusts simultaneously.

"Oh shit!" I drop the knife and leap back over Malcolm to the door. The flames race up it and engulf the entire face of the door. The perimeter of the ceiling erupts as well, joining the lines of flame spreading from the window. The substance that has been spread into the joints of the ceiling burns with a fierce white flame. The paint immediately starts to blister and peel away. I spin helplessly around, looking for a means of escape. Malcolm frees himself from the remains of the ropes and gets to his feet.

I reach for my chronometer dials. "We've got to blink out of here!" Malcolm shakes his head. "What? Come on!" I reach out my hand to him.

"It won't work," he replies. "I'm not a time traveler. I'm a constant."

"Damn it!" I look around wildly. The flames are catching on some of the furniture and the smoke is starting to get thick.

"What's out that window?" I yell over the roar of the flames.

"It's four stories to the street," Malcolm says. He crouches down to get away from the smoke. "You have to go!"

"No! I can't leave you here!" I swing my pack off my back and dump it on the floor to get to Quickly's journal. Anchors bounce off the carpet as they fall out of the pack. The journal lands on the floor and I drop to my knees to read it. I scan wildly through pages, trying to find anything about transporting someone without gravitites.

"You can't take me with you, but you can still save me!" Malcolm says. "But you have to leave me here to return!" He moves to the desk and grabs an object off of it. I recognize it as his temporal spectrometer. He flips open a compartment on the side of the box and removes a DG, slightly smaller than Francesca's. He begins pointing it at some of the anchors. The red test light illuminates. "Choose one now! I can de-gravitize it for you."

The smoke is making my eyes water and it's getting difficult to breathe. I look at the objects littered on the floor. Next to my foot lies my tortoise shell. I pull out the photo. *When all hope is lost.*

"This one!"

Malcolm works the de-gravitizer over the shell in smooth, efficient strokes. He flips it over and repeats it on the other side. I crouch lower and lower as the flames begin to engulf the walls. The heat is getting unbearable. Looking at the photo, I dial the time into my chronometer, while squinting through the tears in my eyes. *Shit. That's really far.*

I pull aside a dresser near the bed to get to a wall outlet. I scramble back to my pack and grab my charger to plug it into the wall. The test light on the DG turns green and Malcolm shoves the shell into my hands. I stuff the photo and Quickly's journal into my back pocket, then lay the shell on the floor and place my hand firmly on top. I plug the charger cord into my chronometer.

"I'll be back in a minute!" I yell.

Malcolm coughs. "Better make it sooner!"

I push the pin.

I'm crouched in bright sunlight on a dirt road. I blink the tears out of my eyes and see a vast expanse of desert stretching away from me in every direction. Scrub brush and Joshua trees dot the landscape but there's not another living person in sight. A thigh-high boulder sits directly in front of me. I look down at my chronometer hand and see that the tortoise shell is now occupied. A pair of scaly, clawed feet are protruding slightly from under the lip of the front end. I collapse onto my butt on the road. My hands are shaking. I look at my chronometer readings. May 1990. I sprawl onto my back in the dirt and stare at the sky.

Malcolm. Blake. Francesca. That was four years ago. What have I done? I hold my palms to my forehead. *Did I just let my friends die?* The sky is blank and holds no answers. I close my eyes and feel tears trickling from the corners of them. The heat of the sun beats down on me, but after the fire, it's a relief. My sweat makes my clothes stick to me. I can still hear the roar of the flames in my ears and Malcolm's racking coughs, despite the silence of the desert around me. The last image of the brilliant flames still floats across the inside of my eyelids. I notice I don't smell of smoke anymore though. I no longer have the urge to cough either. I lay my arms back down at my sides.

No gravitites in smoke Benjamin. You only take what's a part of you. Not smoke. Not your useless weapon. Not your useless plan to save Carson. Not your friends. What have you got left, Ben? My fingers clench at the dirt. *Nothing. That's what you've got left. You get dirt and a desert. And you get a tortoise.*

I open my eyes again slowly, and roll my head over to look toward the boulder. The shell is still sitting in the shade of it, but a scaly head has now emerged and is regarding me suspiciously. We stare at each other for a bit. I roll my head back and look at the sky again. *This was a horrible idea. What on earth would possibly make me think that a tortoise shell would solve my problems? I should have chosen one of the anchors that Quickly catalogued. He might have been there to help me when I showed up. Instead, I chose the one with a barren desert. Now I've got no one.*

The sky is empty. There are no clouds or even birds to be seen. For a few minutes I just stare into that blue void. Eventually I look back to the tortoise.

"Hey." The tortoise watches me and eases his feet out just slightly. "Some place you got here. I like your boulder."

I ease myself up onto my elbow. The tortoise retracts his head back into his shell but keeps his legs slightly extended. I can still see his eye watching me from the interior of the shell. I wipe a little bit of snot away from my nose with the back of my hand.

"Huh. Yeah. I don't blame you. I wouldn't want to be my friend either."

I look over the tortoise's shell. The stripes on the shell are brighter than they were on my anchor. The paint looks fresh. "You have a big race coming up, buddy?" I lean closer to him. He pulls his feet in a little. "How did you end up with those racing—" As I lean closer still, I realize there are more than two lines on his shell. I get up to my knees and peer down at it. The two stripes that run from the back to the front are joined near his head by another V-shaped mark. "Hey those aren't stripes, it's . . . an arrow."

The arrow on the shell points at the opening for the tortoise's head. *Or it points to something beyond it.* I look in the direction of the arrow. It points along the road that trails off into the horizon of dusty hills. I sit back and cross my legs under me. "Are you trying to point me somewhere?"

I lean forward, pulling the photo and Quickly's journal out of my back pocket. I lay the photo on the cover of the journal and study it. I look from the photo to the tortoise and then down the road again.

"Well you're definitely still sitting in the same spot as when this photo was taken. Other than you munching on the grass, it's identical." The tortoise has poked his head back out and is eyeing me again. "Apparently I ruined your lunch."

I tap the photo with my finger. "So if you were sitting just like this, someone had to be here to take your picture a short enough time ago that you haven't moved." I look back to the tortoise. "Though it's not like you seem highly motivated to go anywhere . . ."

The tortoise opens and closes his mouth briefly. "So then who the hell was here to take your picture?" I flip over the photo. "Oh that's right. It was me. I got me into this mess. So tell me this, tortoise. Why on God's green earth was I in the middle of a desert in 1990, taking pictures of tortoises? And where the bloody hell did I go?"

The tortoise and I ponder each other in silence for a few minutes. The desert horizon around me seems to undulate in the waves of heat. I can already feel my forehead starting to burn. "I don't know about you, tortoise, but I can't hang out here much longer. It's gotta be like a hundred and five. I don't have a nice shady boulder like you, and I'm wearing jeans." I get to my feet. The tortoise retracts himself a little bit again, but not as far. I unplug the chronometer charger cord that's still dangling from my wrist and wad it into my pocket. I look down at the arrow on the tortoise's shell. "It looks like I'm going that way." The tortoise cocks his head to look up at me. "What about you tortoise? Do you live here? Is this what you do all day? You hang out by roads, munching on dried up grass, and pointing people places?"

The tortoise opens his mouth again. "Okay. It's been good talking to you." I give him a wave and start down the road. I make it a dozen yards and stop, staring at the hazy, distant horizon. I look back to the tortoise watching me from beside the boulder. I stride back and stand over him. He retracts himself completely inside, with his scaly arms blocking off his head hole.

"I feel bad leaving you out here, and let's be honest, I could use some company for the walk." I stretch down and pick it up by its sides. I make it a few steps when a sudden jet of fluid bursts out sideways from the bottom of the shell.

"What the—"

I hold the tortoise out in front of me as a thick stream sprays out onto the ground. I wait for the torrent to stop and then tilt the tortoise upwards until I can look down into the front hole. "I try to save you from this blistering hot desert, and you pee on me? Not cool, man!"

The tortoise is unapologetic.

The puddle of urine is seeping rapidly into the parched earth. *Shit. That was probably most of this thing's bodily fluids. Now I really feel bad. He's going to dehydrate because of me.* I stare down into the tortoise shell. "I'm sorry. You're still coming with me. You're the only friend I've got left right now."

The dirt road gradually deteriorates as I walk farther into the desert. It traverses small hills and dunes of sandy desolation. I spot a few lizards in the sparse vegetation, and once I pass what I believe to be rabbit tracks near a gulley of dried-out mud. The heat is unbearable. I set the tortoise down and roll up the pant legs on my jeans. The tortoise tries to make a break for it once it's back on solid ground, but after I'm done adjusting my pants, I scoop him back up. He gives me a hiss this time, but keeps his head and arms out for a while as I plod along. My bare forearms are starting to burn. The tortoise must feel the same thing, because after a while, he regresses to a mostly retracted state. I feel grateful when I notice the sun is beginning to edge closer to the horizon ahead of me. The dirt track bends and turns from time to time but keeps me heading generally west. I start counting my footsteps for something to do, but once I reach eight hundred, I lose interest.

"You'd think if I was going to be out leaving directional reptiles in the desert, I could have left a mountain bike or something too, huh buddy?"

I plod onward. My eyes begin to droop and before too long my feet are scuffing the ground with each step. *How long have I been awake? It feels like forever. I haven't slept since Montana. How many hours ago was that?* I track backwards through time in my mind. *I have to have been awake for at least twenty-four hours by now. Could be more.* I look at my chronometer as I walk. It still shows the settings from my last jump. *Shit. I still never logged my jump.* I stop walking. *I don't even have my logbook.* I stand there for a moment and then set the tortoise down. I step past him to give him some shade and then pull Quickly's journal out of my pocket. I find a blank page near the back and get out my pen. I scribble down the time I left from the recessed inner dial. It shows my hour of departure down to the second. *I'm going to need to be exact if I want to get back to Malcolm in time. If that's even possible now* . . . I write everything I can think of about my departure point, then look around to assess my arrival location. I write what I know. *Middle of nowhere.* I shove the photo into the journal with my entry and stuff it back into my pocket.

The tortoise hasn't moved this time. I pick it up and keep walking. The sun is touching the horizon when I climb over a small rise and finally see a destination. In the distance is a small valley made by the surrounding hills. In the center is a wooden shack near a dried-out riverbed. I break into a trot, invigorated momentarily by the sight of habitation. My pace gradually fades again as I see no activity. As I approach the shack, I make out some blue plastic rain barrels along the side, connected with PVC pipes to the gutters. The corrugated tin roof has been painted white and there's a narrow covered porch. The whole building looks homemade, with rough-hewn boards assembled with effective but imprecise measurement. Right now, it looks like a palace.

I've developed a sort of drunken stagger by the time I reach the front of the shack, and my arm muscles are complaining from the miles of holding up a tortoise. There's no sign of life nearby. I clomp blissfully up the couple of steps into the shade of the porch and slump against the doorframe as I rap on the door. There's no response. I try the door handle and the door swings open easily.

"Hello?" The interior of the shack is quiet and vacant, though there are clear signs of it being inhabited. A kettle sits atop a gas camp stove and a cup and plate are in the basin sink. A low single bed is made up along the far wall. "Doesn't look like anyone's home, buddy."

Stepping inside, I kick the door shut behind me. I set the tortoise on the floor and rub my arms. Moving into the kitchen area, I open a couple of cupboards. I find a cup and look around for a source of water. There's an icebox sitting on the floor near a small table. I open the door and smile to see a large glass pickle jar full of water. The jar is as warm as the ambient air but I don't care. I pour some into my cup and gulp eagerly as it courses down my throat. Once I've drunk two glasses, I remember my friend. I find a saucer and pour some of the water into it. The tortoise has crawled into the corner under the single dining room chair. I set the dish of water next to him but he only stares at it.

"Okay. Well it's there if you want it." I fill up another glass for myself and put the jar back before I begin browsing around the room. The accommodations are sparse and decorations near non-existent. A few books line a shelf near the bed. A solitary lamp occupies a stand next to them. I walk over to the sleeping area and notice a handmade quilt folded up at the foot of the bed. I pull open a layer and notice the pattern. *My grandmother made a quilt for me just like this.* I run a finger along one of the patches. *This looks exactly like it.* I pull it open all the way to be sure. *This is definitely my quilt.*

I consider the rest of the shack. *Does that make the rest of this mine too? Do I own a shack in a desert?* I set my cup on the nightstand and sit down on the edge of the bed. *My bed? I like the sound of that.* I look out the windows at the barren landscape stretching into the late afternoon sun. *I'm not ready to go back out there yet. Maybe I can just rest here for a bit.* I slump over horizontally on the bed and lay my head on the pillow. The tortoise is still watching me from the corner. *We're just going to rest a minute, buddy. It won't be long, don't you worry.* I close my eyes.

Chapter 22

"One unusual fringe benefit of time travel is the ability to visit your own grave. Personally I find the practice a tad morbid, but I do get some satisfaction from the fact that the disproportionate dates on my tombstones have confounded many a passerby."
-Excerpt from the journal of Harold Quickly, 1897

"Get out of my bed." The voice is stern and gravelly. My mind tries to fit the voice into the fractured puzzle of my memory. *It sounds like my dad.*

"Yo. Get up." This time the voice is accompanied by something prodding me in the abdomen. I open my eyes and see the toe of a thick-soled boot near my stomach. The boot is attached to a leg in khaki. At the other end of the leg is a tall grey haired man with bristly stubble on his face. The face is weathered and tan.

"You're not my dad," I mumble into the pillow.

"No. I'm not," the man replies. "Get up."

I prop myself up to a sitting position as the man crosses the room to the camp stove. My tongue feels like sandpaper. Dim light is filtering through the threadbare curtains. "How long was I asleep?" I ask.

"A while." He turns around and walks back to me, carrying two steaming mugs.

"It's like four hundred degrees in this desert and you want me to drink hot tea?" I realize as I'm speaking, that it really isn't that hot at the moment. The night air has cooled things off considerably.

"I need you awake. Drink it."

I take the mug and blow on the top to cool it down. "I'm Ben." I extend my hand.

The man ignores it. "I know."

I wait for him to give his name, but it doesn't come. I drop my hand back into my lap. "Where are we?"

"This is the Mojave desert. Northwest of the Kelso Sand Dunes."

"Oh." I sip cautiously at my tea. "I brought your tortoise back." He grunts. I consider him as he settles into the chair by the table. He looks in pretty good shape for his age. Sixty? Sixty-five maybe? "It was pretty far," I add.

"You fishing for a thank you?" The man's eyes are hard.

"Well it wouldn't hurt. You could have lost your tortoise."

"I knew you'd bring him."

"How could you know that?"

The man pauses his mug on the way to his mouth and stares at me. "You once tried to give mouth-to-mouth resuscitation to a rabbit that you hit with your car. You were definitely going to bring the tortoise."

"I've never told anybody about that," I say. I look at the man's face closely. "If you know that, then that means WE once tried to give mouth-to-mouth resuscitation to a rabbit."

The man sips his tea and sets his mug back down on the table. "No comment."

I lean forward. "So that's it? You're me?"

"No."

"No?"

"No." The man stands and pours the rest of his tea into the sink. He sets the mug down and walks to the door. He swings it open and gestures for me to leave.

"That's it?" I set my mug down on the floor and stand up. "Have some tea and now get out?"

"Just walk outside, will you?" The man jerks his head toward the porch. I stride past him and off the porch to the front of the shack. The sunrise is just dawning over the distant hills. I walk a few yards and then spin to face him. He sidles out of the shack and closes the door behind him. He descends a step, and leans against a roof support as he considers me.

I put my hands to my hips. "So what now?"

He looks me up and down. "I forgot what an impatient little shit I was."

I scowl back. "So you are me."

"No."

"No? That's it? No? You care to elaborate on that a bit, man?"

"You know, you should be more polite to the people whose beds you steal."

I look down at the ground for a moment, considering my response before I look back up at him. "You know? Okay. Yes. Thank you for the use of the bed. But you should understand why I'm a little tense. I'm not exactly having a great life right now. I just had what is unequivocally the worst day of my life and my only hope of salvaging it was a photo you left in a tortoise. I walked forever in a God-forsaken desert to try to find some help, and you were nowhere to be found. So I'm sorry if I dirtied up your bed sheets or whatever, but I didn't exactly have a lot of options."

The man straightens up and steps the rest of the way off the porch. "I know."

"You know? That's right, but you're not me, so I can just figure out how you know from the complete lack of sense you're making, right?"

"We're the same person," the man says. "I am Benjamin Travers."

"Okay, so you are now," I say.

"But I'm still not you."

I cock my head and stare at him. *He's not making any sense.*

"The life you've had and the life I've had were the same up to a certain point," he says.

"So what happened?"

"Some of the decisions I made were . . . different."

"When?" I ask.

The man walks toward me. "You're here because you have a problem to solve. Let's concentrate on you." I look into his serious brown eyes. My eyes. *This is so surreal.*

"Okay." I drop my hands to my sides. "So you can help me?"

"Yeah. Come on. We're going for a walk."

"Um, okay." I hesitate. "You mind if I use your bathroom first? You'd think I'd have sweat out all my fluids yesterday, but my bladder begs to differ."

"Outhouse is around back."

I find the wooden outhouse to be tidy and clean with a half-moon vent hole in the door like old west cartoons. There's no faucet to wash up with, but there's a plastic gallon jug of water, a basin with a towel, and a mirror. I look at the young man in the mirror. My face is smeared with dirt in vertical lines from sweat. Another smear of dirt angles across my cheek from where I must have wiped my nose at some point. *You're looking pretty rough, Benjamin.*

I pour some of the water into my hands and splash my face. It takes three attempts till I approach any form of cleanliness. Even then, my face leaves brown stains on the hand towel. I look myself over again. *Better than nothing.* Those eyes stare back at me. *Not the eyes of a killer after all. The eyes of a failure.* I see Francesca with a gun to her head, the spray of blood spattering the chair as Blake gets shot, Malcolm coughing smoke as he's surrounded by flames. *Is there anything you didn't screw up?* I think about

Dr. Quickly and his encouraging smile as we'd master new lessons. *He wouldn't be very happy with me now. I burnt his lab down with my blundering attempt at a rescue mission. And Mym . . . how would she feel if she knew I was the one who cost her father everything?*

I stop myself and shove open the door, taking in the rickety building and the desolate landscape. *No wonder I end up alone in a desert.*

The older me is waiting around the front of the shack with a pair of canteens. He hands me one to carry.

"So what do I call you?" I ask. "Do we both just refer to each other as Ben?"

The man looks at me and shrugs. "People started calling me Benji later on in my life."

"Benji?" I say. "I always despised being called that. Sounded like the dog."

"It grew on me after a while," he says.

"What was her name?"

He grunts, and continues walking.

"Okay. Better you than me, I guess." *She must have been a looker.*

He leads the way into the trackless desert. I dodge around tufts of scraggly brush and other low sparse vegetation that's too stubborn to just wither and die. After about the fifth dune, we descend onto a flat expanse of hard dirt that's free of vegetation. From the structure of the hills around the perimeter, I realize that it was likely a lake at some point. Half a dozen fifty-five gallon drums sit rusting, spaced seemingly at random around the perhaps hundred yard circle. Benji sets his canteen down, then turns to face me. "Why didn't you kill Stenger?"

I'm taken aback by his question. "Um. Well, there were lots of reasons." My mind flashes back to the lab. "I wasn't armed, for one. He had this woman with him who had a gun."

"You could have stopped him, but you didn't."

"No. I couldn't. I mean we tried . . . Blake and I had him cornered, but that's when the woman with the gun showed up. She shot Blake. And they had Francesca. They somehow got the drop on us and grabbed her."

"And you didn't save her."

"Look, I tried! I went up to search the third floor, and I found Malcolm, but it was a trap. They had the whole room rigged to burn as soon as someone went in there. There was no way out."

"So you just left." Benji's expression shows no sign of mercy.

"No! I mean I left, but I left to get help. If you just brought me out here to remind me how awful of a job I did, and that I failed miserably, you could have saved your breath. I know I screwed up. I know I failed. My friends were counting on me and—" I feel tears coming on. I stop talking and stare at the ground. My body is shaking again.

Benji takes a step toward me. "Why didn't you stop Stenger?"

"I couldn't . . ."

He steps closer and puts his index finger to the center of my forehead. He pushes my head up till I'm looking him in the eyes.

"You didn't stop Stenger because you didn't believe you could."

I sniff. "How could I?"

He looks me over. "You say you were unarmed. What's that thing on your wrist, decoration?"

I look at my chronometer. "Well I use it, but it's not a weapon."

"Isn't it?" Benji stares into my eyes again. "Your problem is you need to readjust your concept of 'possible.'"

I consider my chronometer. *Does it have some sort of function I don't know about?*

"So what do I do?"

"You learn to use that thing like it's meant to be used." He walks past the drum and picks up a rock the size of a baseball. Setting it on the drum, he then reaches into his pocket. He pulls out a chronometer and fastens it to his right wrist. The sun glints off the stainless steel as he dials the settings. He's holding something else small with the fingers of his left hand, but I can't make out what it is. He picks up the rock with his chronometer hand and strides forward a few steps toward the open expanse of lakebed.

"I want you to see something." He holds his arm back to hurl the rock, does a quick crow-hop and then throws, but just as he's releasing the rock, he vanishes. I watch the rock sail through the air. It arcs upward and then plunges downward about forty yards from me. It gathers speed. It never hits the ground. Six feet before impact, Benji reappears with his hand around it, and drops onto his feet with a light thump.

I realize my mouth is hanging open, and close it. Benji walks back to me, giving the stone a casual toss in the air and catching it again. When he gets to me, he's smiling at my shock. "That was a little sample for you."

"That was incredible," I stammer, as he hands me the rock. "How—"

"That is what you need to learn. Well, not the rock throwing trick. That one takes years to master. But you're going to learn the 'how.'" I turn the rock over in my hands. It's nothing special. "So what did you notice about that little maneuver?" Benji is watching my face for my response.

"Um, for starters, your anchor was flying through the air . . . and you never actually touched your chronometer."

"Good. I was hoping you'd pick up on that." He extends his left hand and shows me a tiny white tube with a button on the end.

"What is that?"

"It's a remote switch. It actuates your chronometer's pin function wirelessly."

"Wow. That's awesome." I take the remote from his palm and examine it.

"But let's get back to your other observation," Benji says. "The rock was flying through the air. Why is that relevant?"

"For one, you weren't grounded to anything," I say. "Don't you need to be electrically grounded for the chronometer to work?"

"No. And I'll tell you why. The chronometer needs to be temporally grounded. The electrical ground is a method of conveying the gravitites and activating them with current, but the chronometer only needs a ground in time, to get you back where you need to be in space."

"So my anchor doesn't need to be electrically grounded."

"Nope. The chronometer just needs to be able to connect to something that's not full of gravitites."

"So as long as my anchor is gravitite free, I could be flying through the air and it would still be able to make the jump."

"Exactly."

"What happens if I activate the chronometer when there isn't something grounded in time to connect to?"

"You don't want to do that."

"What happens?"

Benji scratches the whiskers on his chin a moment before speaking. "That's actually a matter of some debate. Some people say you stop existing."

"Whoa. Really?"

"If you think about it, if you have something that can be displaced from the stream of time, and then you displace it without any means of getting it back . . . there's no real reason why you should hope to see it again. You've stopped existing in time."

"Where do you go?"

"I don't know. People talk about it. Some people say you're just gone. Some people claim there is space that exists without time. They call it the Neverwhere. There are some people who say that's what the afterlife is. It sounds like a bunch of swill to me, but I guess it's possible. I'm old enough to know better than to think I have all the answers."

"You ever know anybody who's done it? Gone to the Neverwhere?"

"None that ever came back. I don't recommend trying it. You'd do better to learn how to stick around here on the planet first."

"So what do I do? How do I learn to use this thing better?"

"Let's see what you've got," Benji replies. "Show me a jump."

"Where?"

"Use one of the barrels. Use that one." He points.

I walk to the indicated barrel and look at my chronometer. "How far do you want me to go?"

"A few seconds is plenty," he says.

"Okay."

I find the seconds ring on my chronometer and dial it to three seconds. I look to the side of it and check my directional slider to make sure it is on forward. Satisfied with that, I place my chronometer hand firmly on the lip of the barrel and take a breath. I reach my other hand over to the pin. *Here we go.* I blink.

"How was that?" I say.

"Fine, except I about nodded off while I waited. I think my beard hair got a little longer too."

"Oh."

"I want you to try it at a run."

"What?"

"Running. You know, that thing that you do that's faster than walking."

"Okay. I mean . . . I've never done that before."

Benji points away from the barrel. "Start over there." I walk to the specified spot. "Do five seconds this time, but I want you to set your chronometer while you're running."

"Okay." I look at my chronometer and mentally find the knob for seconds. *Yeah okay. I can do this.*

"Go!" Benji yells.

I start running, but immediately have to slow to a quick trot as I try to dial the seconds ring over two marks. I manage it, but realize I'm barely jogging when I finish. Speeding back up, I concentrate on the barrel. I have to do a couple of stutter steps upon reaching it. I slap my chronometer hand down onto the barrel, and with my right hand over my chronometer, push the pin. I stagger a little as I reappear, and then slow to a stop a couple of yards from the barrel. I turn to look at Benji. He's appraising me with his arms crossed.

"Like that?" I ask.

"Yeah. Though I'm pretty sure Cheeto could have done it faster."

"Who's Cheeto?"

"Cheeto's the tortoise."

"You named your tortoise after a cheese snack?" I ask, slightly out of breath.

"What would you name your tortoise?"

"I don't really—"

"Yeah. Thought so. Get back over there." He points again.

This time he has me regress to a two-second jump and I manage to do it a little quicker. When I'm finished, Benji doesn't comment, but only gestures to the starting point. He holds up four fingers. *Four seconds. Got it.* I run. I get progressively faster over my next half dozen attempts. Just before my seventh attempt, he calls out to me.

"Do five minutes this time."

"Okay." I take a deep breath and start into a run. My legs are moving smoothly and I'm able to find the five-minute mark and set it without breaking stride. I slap the top of the barrel and squeeze the pin in one fluid motion. Smiling, I trot to a stop and turn to face Benji. I'm staring off into the desert. I spin around and see the barrel has moved about seventy yards, and Benji is still back near the start point, leaning against another barrel and sipping his canteen.

"You think you're pretty funny, don't you?" I yell. I walk back, dripping sweat onto the dry, caked ground. When I reach Benji, he hands me my canteen.

"That's better. Now I want you to try jumping it."

"The whole barrel?"

"Yeah. I want you to leapfrog over it and blink while you're jumping," he says.

"Okay. I'll try."

"Don't try it. Do it. I'm sixty-four and I could still jump that, easy."

"Okay Yoda. I'll do it."

Benji smirks at me.

I run various drills till mid-morning. By the time Benji lets up on me, my clothes are soaked with sweat and my canteen is empty. Benji looks at the sun creeping its way up higher in the sky and then nods his head toward the path. "Okay. Let's head back. We'll get some food in us and then keep going."

Cheeto has worked his way around the room and is peering out from under the bed when we walk back into the shack. Benji gestures me to the chair by the table and I slump into it gratefully. He sets a cup and the pickle jar of water in front of me. I pour myself a glass as he rummages through cupboards.

"Looks like I'm out of eggs." He grabs a box of cereal out of the cupboard and after consulting the side of it briefly, sets it down on the table, but keeps a grip on it. "I'll be right back." I barely have time to see his hand go to his chronometer when he disappears. Seconds later he walks back in the front door, holding a paper bag under his arm. He sets it on the counter.

"What . . . where did you go?" I say.

"Grocery store. What does it look like?" He unloads items onto the counter.

I grab the cereal box and look at it. A photo of a grocery store aisle is taped to the side. Cereal boxes line the shelves but one is sticking out at an odd angle. I recognize the labeling that's the same as the one in my hand.

"You're really something else, you know that?" I say. Benji piles handfuls of some sort of grass out of a bag onto a plate. He adds a handful of spinach, then walks over and sets the plate in front of the tortoise. When he comes back to the kitchen, he reaches into the bag and pulls out a carton of eggs. "Where's the grocery store around here?"

"Tacoma."

"Washington?"

"Finding a grocery store that will let you keep a gravitizer on the premises is harder than it sounds."

"Oh. Yeah. I guess that would be an awkward conversation." I watch him rummaging around the bag. "Hey, you mind if I ask you something?"

"Maybe."

"How did you end up here? What's with the desert existence?"

He pulls a bowl out of the cabinet and begins cracking eggs into it. "I like the desert. It's peaceful."

"Yeah. It is, but is this your whole life? What happened that made you want to come live out here?"

He reaches back into the bag and pulls out a few more items. I see bacon and shredded cheese and a jar of salsa. "I needed to be here to train you when you showed up," he says. "I needed somewhere away from the rest of the world where you wouldn't be distracted. But I've been out here a while anyway."

"What kinds of distractions?"

Benji pauses and looks at me. "You have a tendency to booger some things up once in a while if you haven't noticed. Out here . . ." He gestures to the view out the window. "There isn't much to mess up."

"Wow, thanks for the vote of confidence. That makes me feel really great."

He looks me in the eyes. "That's not what I meant. Look, I knew what kind of state you were going to be in coming out of that fiasco in the lab. I knew if there was anytime you were likely to do something rash or emotional, then that would probably be it. I just wanted to avoid that possibility."

"So you knew what I would go through, but you didn't know firsthand what I'd do? So does that mean the lab never happened to you?"

"No. It didn't. Our timestreams split before that point."

"When?"

Benji sighs. "In 1986. But it was 2009 that really made the difference. The other 2009. Not the one you were in. Not after the changes."

"What happened?"

Benji goes back to cracking eggs. "I made some poor choices."

"Oh." I consider him as he pulls strips of bacon out of the package and lays them on a pan. "So then how did you know about the lab? How did you know I would need help?"

He turns on the camp stove and adds the eggs into a pan. "You told me."

"I did?"

"The future you," he says. "You told me what I needed to do to get you back there."

"Really? How did you know it was me?"

"You had the same frequency signature." He turns and points a spatula at me. "But don't go getting it into your head that just because I met a future version of you, that you're somehow invincible and can't die, or any bullshit like that. If you go do something stupid, you won't end up being that version of you at all. You'll end up the version of you who got himself killed doing some stupid shit."

I nod. "Okay. I won't."

I turn my glass around in my hands and watch the last sip of water swirl around bottom. I look back to Benji pushing the eggs around the pan with the spatula. *He's a version of me, but he seems so different. He seems sad somehow.*

"How many versions of us have you met? Are there a lot of us?"

Benji frowns. "Not as many as there should be." He sprinkles some of the cheese over the eggs.

"Oh." I set my glass back down. "You mind if I ask you something else?"

"Shoot."

"Okay, well this has been bothering me since I got here. I'm not completely sure I want to know the answer, but I feel like maybe I should." I

300

feel my chest tighten up. I take a deep breath. "What happened to Malcolm? And Francesca and Blake? This is 1990. Does that mean they died back in '86?"

Benji sets a plate of eggs and bacon in front of me. "No."

I breathe a sigh of relief.

"Actually, it sort of depends . . ." he adds.

"What do you mean?"

He grabs his own plate and drags a stool to the table. "Have you ever heard of Schrodinger's cat?"

"Who's Schrodinger?"

"He's a scientist. He's dead. But he had a theory that might help you understand your situation." He leans forward and puts his elbows on the table and begins to gesture with his hands. "The idea is that you take a cat and you put it in a box. You also put in some sort of device such as a vial containing poison that is set to break at an undetermined time. It doesn't really matter the nature of the device in question, only that it has the potential possibility of killing the cat. Let's say it's fifty-fifty."

"That's terrible," I say.

"Of course it is. But that's not the point. The point is, that due to the imprecise timing or probability of this device going off, until you open the box, you don't know if the cat is alive or dead. Inside the box, it exists in a state that can be considered both alive and dead."

I think about this scenario. "So you're saying that my friends right now could be dead?"

"Or they could be alive. You won't know till you open the box."

"What's the box?"

"In this case, you have to figure out if you are, or aren't, going to go back to 1986 to save them. And if you do, whether you're actually going to succeed."

I ponder my eggs. "So since it's 1990, there could be a grave out there somewhere with Francesca's name on it right now." I point beyond the walls of the shack. "If I don't save her, she died in 1986."

"That's one possibility."

"But it might be one fact. Potentially I could walk out of here and find out the truth one way or the other. I might find that grave."

"You might. But maybe just that knowledge that you failed would be enough to dissuade you from going back to try to save them in the first place, causing the very thing to happen that you were hoping to avoid."

"That's really convoluted."

"Another reason why I brought you out to a desert with no phone and no internet and no other contact. You don't need that kind of distraction right now. It would be too easy to go searching for answers when you need to be finding the answer firsthand."

"So you don't know?" I say. "You don't know if I succeed in saving them when I go back? You met me. Future me. He didn't tell you?"

"No. He told me what I needed to know. And he told me if I wanted to make up for some of the other things I'd done over the years, this might be a good place to start. Helping you."

"But apparently I live," I say.

"One version of you does at least," Benji replies. "That's not to say that you stay him though. Like I said. You can make different choices. Your destiny would change then, along with aspects of your timestream signature. How this plays out is up to you now."

I pick at my food for a little and then set my fork down. "I'll tell you one thing," Benji says. "You go through with this, you'll know one way or the other. You don't, and it will eat at you. If there's one thing I've learned, it's that wondering 'what if' can be the worst of it. You go back there and you might die. That's true. And I won't say that's an easy choice to make, but I'll tell you this, dying ain't the worst thing that can happen to a man."

He takes our plates back to the sink and scrapes the remnants into the trashcan. He gestures me toward the door. "Come on. We got more work to do." He opens the front door and points me to the edge of the porch. "Have a seat, while there's still some shade. I want you to work on setting your chronometer with your eyes closed."

"You don't want me to look at it?"

"You shouldn't have to. You've been wearing that thing on your wrist long enough now. You know where the dials are. Remember where your settings are after each jump and you should be able to set the next one without looking. You have to start using your brain to its full potential before you can get the real potential out of that gizmo." I sit down on the edge of the porch. "And don't cheat, or I'll come out and blindfold you."

He lets the screen door slam behind him. After a few moments I hear the clink and clatter of dishes again. I look down at my wrist. I feel over the face of the indicator and then touch my fingertips to the different dials. *Okay. I can do this.* I shut my eyes and concentrate. *Let's do five minutes.* I let my fingertips find the minute dial. I give it a twist. I reopen my eyes to find it set on eight minutes. *Damn it.* I reset the chronometer and try again. This time I undershoot to the four mark. A hawk keens above me and I see it circling out over the desert, riding waves of thermals. I go back to my chronometer.

It's the better part of an hour before I start getting any kind of consistency. Benji comes out to check on me briefly and gives me my glass of water, but then goes back inside. I keep at it. During one of my longer periods, trying a more difficult combination, I hear a scraping noise behind me. I turn to see Cheeto pushing his way out the screen door. He clumps and scrapes himself along the rough boards behind me, before plopping off the end of the porch into some brittle tufts of grass. I hear more rustling as he burrows himself into the space under the porch.

Once the sun is directly overhead, I lose my shade and slide back against the wall of the shack to get out of the sun. Benji reappears after a little while and gestures me inside. He points me to the bed where he's laid out a pair of khaki cargo shorts, a baseball cap, and a tube of sunscreen. "You're gonna want those. We're going back out."

Once I'm out of my jeans and smelling like a coconut, I rejoin Benji outside. We refill our canteens from a barrel around back labeled, "Drinking." We return to the dry lakebed with the drums. I run drills around the barrels again, alternating between leaps and simple taps. Benji mixes things up by throwing rocks at me, requiring me to time my blinks so as not to get pelted. Luckily, my mess-ups only result in bruises, and I manage to avoid getting anything fused into me. By the time we're done for the afternoon, my clothes are soaked again, and despite the frequent layers of gravitized sunscreen, the skin on my neck and arms is decidedly pink. Once we're back to the shack, Benji gets me out another change of clothes from a trunk near his bed.

"There's a wash basin out back you can use to scrub yourself clean. You'll find water for washing in the rain barrels back there. Should still be some left. There's food in the cupboards too. Nothing cold but it should be enough to tide you over till tomorrow."

"You're not staying?" I say.

"No. Not tonight."

"Where are you going?"

"None of your business," he replies. "Just get some rest. I'll be back tomorrow. We'll carry on from there."

"Okay." I nod and examine the clothes on the bed. When I turn around again, he's gone.

I find the corrugated basin out back like he described and a clean towel hanging from a hook. A big block of soap and a washcloth are sitting on a window ledge of the shack. I strip down and pour some water into the basin out of the barrel labeled "Bathing." It has a slight rust color but I know I'm just going to get it dirtier.

I scrub myself all over and squat down as low as I can, to get my head under the spigot of the water barrel to rinse my hair. By the time I'm done rinsing off, the bottoms of my feet are in a puddle of mud, but I feel better. A lizard watches me from the wall of the shack as I towel off, but the rest of the desert view seems vacant and lonely. I keep the towel and walk around the front of the shack, wiping my feet off and donning my clothes on the porch. Back inside, I idly browse through the books on the bookshelf near the bed for a few minutes before getting myself a glass of water and going back out to the porch. Dusk is highlighting the dunes in reds and oranges.

As I settle onto the porch, I notice the tortoise has partially reemerged from under the shack and is viewing the twilight scenery as well. I close my eyes and try to remember my last chronometer setting. *I think I left it on a thirty-second interval.* I look down. Twenty. *At least I was close.* I close my eyes again and practice for a while longer. As night descends, I admire the stars appearing in the darkening sky. Soon it grows too dim to see my chronometer settings, but I keep practicing anyway until my eyes start to droop. Cheeto has made his way over and is eyeing me from a few feet away.

"It's just you and me tonight, buddy." I watch the stars for a while longer. *The view might not be as good as Montana, but it has to be close.* I stand up and open the screen door. The tortoise watches me.

"You want to come in for the night, dude?" I walk over to him. He watches me but doesn't retract himself back into his shell. "Okay. We'll try this again." I pick him up, and this time he doesn't try to pee on me. I pry the screen door open and set the tortoise on the floor inside.

"There you go, my friend." I refill his plate of grass before lying down on the bed. I try to read some more of Quickly's journal, but in the dim light it gets too difficult to see. I watch the shape of Cheeto munching on his grass instead, and soon drift off.

When I wake in the morning, there's no sign of Benji. The tortoise is waiting near the door, so I let him outside again. I find myself a box of strawberry pop tarts in one of the cupboards and chew on those while I wait. I walk back out to the porch and practice my no-look chronometer settings for a while longer but then find myself at a loss for what else to do. I begin running circles around the outside of the shack, blinking myself forward in twenty and thirty-second intervals as I tap each corner. I gradually move myself up to five-minute intervals. By the time I stop for breath, I look up at the sky and realize that I've fast-forwarded through a couple of hours.

I walk to the top of a large dune and have a look around. Still no sign of anyone. I fill up a canteen and wander out to the lakebed. I run the drills I learned the day before, jumping over barrels and pretending to dodge rocks and obstacles. I practice until I'm soaked with sweat and coated with a layer of dust. When I make it back to the shack a couple of hours later, I find Benji sitting on the front porch.

"Hey," I say.

"Hey."

"Where've you been?"

Benji stands up and gestures toward the inside with his head. "I got you something." When I walk inside, I find a ball of brown waxed paper tied with string, sitting on the kitchen table. "Go ahead," Benji says. "Open it."

I untie the string and unwrap the paper. In the center of the package sits a doorknob. The metal is discolored and darkened around the edges, but it seems to be intact. "You recognize that?" Benji asks.

I pick it up and consider it. I note that it is technically only half of a doorknob, since nothing is on the other side. "It's from the lab?"

"You got it."

I turn the knob over in my hands. I remember Malcolm writhing in the chair with wide eyes as I walked toward him. "I never should have let that door shut," I say.

"Well, now you can reopen it."

"Thank you." I tuck the knob back into its wrappings.

"Look, Ben. I know I've not been the easiest on you out here, but I do think you can do this. I wouldn't have signed on for this job if I didn't think you had it in you. I'm not saying you have it all figured out. Your skills can still use a lot more practice, everyone's can, but you've certainly got enough knowledge and ability to take out a shithead like Stenger."

"What if I don't?" I say. "What if he wins?"

"I would never put 'winning' and 'Elton Stenger' in the same sentence together. That guy lost at life a long time ago. Surviving isn't all there is to winning, Ben. A lot of good men have died in the act of doing something great. That doesn't mean they lost."

I nod.

"Come on. We'll clean up your stuff." Benji helps me gather my clothes from the day before and we scrub them by hand in the washbasin out back. Once they're clean, he hangs them on a line that he strings from the shack to the outhouse. By the time we've finished eating some late lunch and I clean myself up in the basin again, the afternoon sun has dried my clothes enough to wear them. I walk back inside feeling clean, but still hot. I grab the loose wad of hundred dollar bills and my pen that I took out to wash my pants, and stuff them back into my pocket.

"Let me see your chronometer." Benji has a small box of tools out on the kitchen table. I hand him my chronometer and he uses a set of micro screwdrivers to remove the back.

"What're you doing?"

"Seeing if your unit is already wired with a remote receiver. If it is, I can tune a remote switch to it for you."

"Where did you learn how to do that?"

"Abe Manembo. The guy is a genius." He sets the back of the chronometer on a clean white rag and holds the chronometer a few inches from his face. "You should look him up sometime if you get the chance . . . and yes. He put one in here already. That means I just need to see what range it's using . . ." He uses a jeweler's magnifying glass to read inside the chronometer. "All right. I can do that." He pulls one of the tube-like remote switches from his toolbox and pops the end open. He uses pliers to remove a red diode, and replaces it with a blue one. Lastly, he closes up my chronometer and hands it back to me.

"Here. Try that out." He hands me the remote switch. "You just flip over the safety just like on the DGs, and then you can push the button. This is one more thing you don't want going off in your pocket when you aren't paying attention."

"Great, another exciting way to die. I'll add it to the list."

Benji smiles. "Go ahead. Give it a shot."

I dial my chronometer for a two-second jump without looking at the dial, but then double check it as I place my chronometer hand on the counter near the sink. I flip open the safety on the remote with my thumb. "I hope you know what you're doing," I say, and push the button.

When I reappear, Benji is still smiling. "See? Child's play." I look down at my still existing body in relief. "I have something else for you too." Benji moves to the closet and removes a gas mask, a pair of welding gloves, and a large fire extinguisher. "I couldn't get my hands on any real fire gear but this will be better than nothing."

I nod, thinking of the heat I'll be facing on the other side of the doorknob. "Thank you, man. This is all really fantastic."

"You should probably take this too." He pulls a leather jacket out of the closet. "Not like I get to wear it much out here anyway. Are you ready to do this now or do you want to wait for the morning?"

I walk over to the bed and pick up Quickly's journal. "I think I'm ready to go now. The longer I wait, the more time I have to worry about it."

"All right then. You remember what time you're going back to?"

"Yeah. I wrote that one down." I flip open the journal to the page where I scribbled my jump information and dial in my time. My heart begins to beat faster in anticipation. I stuff the journal into my back pocket and don the leather jacket, then pause to take a deep breath. *You're not gonna die, Ben. Get it together.* I slip the gas mask onto the top of my head, but leave it up on my forehead so I can still speak. The welding gloves are next. I pull the left one on first and it covers my chronometer and half of my forearm. The fingers of the glove are thick and awkward for holding anything small, so I realize I can't wear both. I stuff the other glove into one of the jacket pockets, and pick up the remote with my right hand.

"You're gonna do great," Benji says, looking at me approvingly.

I set the remote down on the fire extinguisher and extend my hand. "Thank you. Thank you for being here for this."

"It was my pleasure," Benji shakes it. "Sorry I hit you with so many of those rocks."

I smile and pick up the remote again, readying it with my thumb and forefingers. I then slip my remaining fingers under the handle of the fire extinguisher and pick it up. Benji takes a step back and crosses his arms to watch.

"Hey, Benji?"

"Yeah, Ben."

"Do you think, that when all these different versions of us, however many of us there are . . . when we die, do you think we share a soul?"

"Ha. Now you're asking questions way above my pay grade. But you know, I kind of hope so. Maybe some of your decisions can help make up for some of mine."

I nod. I take a deep breath and pick up the doorknob, careful to keep the keyhole facing the right direction.

"See ya around, kid."

"See ya." I press the remote switch.

Chapter 23

"A time traveler's clock ticks no slower than anyone else's. Guard your minutes and seconds closer than your dollars and cents. You can predict when you'll be out of money, but not when you'll be out of time."
-Excerpt from the journal of Dr. Harold Quickly, 1986

Flames lick out of a crack at the top of the door. The smell of smoke assaults my nose and I take a step back from the hot air in my face. I set the fire extinguisher down on the hallway floor and slip the remote into my pocket. I cough and pull the gas mask down over my face and don the other welding glove. The fire extinguisher seems awkward and heavy as I hoist it back up. I yank the pin out of the handle and mentally prepare myself for what I'm about to do. *Malcolm needs me.*

The moment I turn the knob and push the door open, a wave of fire backdrafts out the top of the door and engulfs the ceiling. The room glows brighter from the sudden influx of oxygen. Dense smoke blackens the hallway. I go in spraying the extinguisher ahead of me. Getting as far as the inner arc of the door, I look around. A dark mass is prostrate on the floor to the right. I block the door open with the extinguisher and rush forward against the oppressive heat.

Scooping my hands under Malcolm's armpits, I drag him backward to the hall as fast as I can manage. His head lolls in my arms but I hear him cough. *Thank God.* I drag him out the door and left down the hall. The flames have begun to consume the doorway.

When we've reached a safe distance, I lay Malcolm on the floor and remove my mask and gloves. "Malcolm!" I roll him onto his side. He coughs violently for a few seconds but then looks up into my face and smiles.

"I knew you'd come back."

"We're not out of this yet, buddy. Can you walk?"

I help Malcolm to his feet and throw one of his arms around my neck. I half drag him past the balcony hallway and into the living room of the apartment. When I reach the doorway to the stairs, I stop and he slumps against the wall.

"Do you think you can make it out from here?" I ask. "I have to go back and find Francesca. That woman with the gun took her."

"Lillith. I heard them talking. If they're taking her with them, they'll be going out the second floor to the office next door. That's how they got in. They busted a hole in the wall of the janitor's closet and came through into one of the classrooms. With the place on fire, they'll probably go back out there too."

"How did they find this place?"

Malcolm lowers his head. "I didn't mean to . . . It started out okay. When I found him with the spectrometer, I thought he was just another displaced citizen like you guys."

"What happened?"

"I didn't realize he was the one you warned me about. He was going by a different name. I told him that Dr. Quickly might be able to help him. He asked me a lot of questions, but when I went to leave, he stopped me. That's when Lillith got involved.

"They were living in her trailer in Pinellas Park. I guess he met her in a bar in St. Pete beach. I think she might be crazier than he is. They tied me up and have been holding me for days . . . I think I talked too much . . ."

"Hey, it's okay." I put a hand on his shoulder. "That guy is a psychopath. You couldn't know what he was capable of. It's not your fault."

"They wanted Dr. Quickly. They kept me alive because they thought he would come for me. When he didn't show up in a couple of days, they decided to come here. They knew where the building was from some of the stuff in my bag. I didn't tell them how to get in, but they figured out a way anyway."

"What do they want with Quickly?"

"I don't know, but it's nothing good." He coughs again.

"Okay. Get yourself out of here. Do you know where the hole in the janitor's closet is? Which classroom is it?"

"On the second level, along the east wall."

"Okay. Let's get down there. I don't know how much time I've got."

I help Malcolm down the first flight of stairs and stop on the landing of the lab's second floor. I lean over the railing and look down the couple of flights to the ground floor. "You going to be able to make it okay?"

"Yeah. Go. I'll get help."

I slap Malcolm on the shoulder and open the door to the second level.

"Thank you," he calls out after me.

"You bet," I say, and plunge into the hallway. I run through the lab, dialing my chronometer for a two-minute backward jump, in case something leaps out at me. The hallways are vacant. I rush past the lockers where I'd found our packs. *I need to find the east wall again. I know I wrote it around here somewhere.* I scan the walls as I turn corners, and finally see my scribbled word and arrow still up by the trim. I sprint down the hall past the stairwell and Quickly's office, then make a left. I push open the doors on two other rooms till I find the one I'm looking for.

A rough hole has been hammered through the drywall. A couple of exposed 2x4s are splintered to a ruin, allowing enough space for someone to crawl through. I hear voices. As I creep closer, I can make out the sound of Francesca's voice. *Thank God she's alive.* I move up to the hole. The door to the janitor's closet on the opposite side is open.

"Get your fucking hands off me, asshole!"

Something crashes to the floor. "Get her, baby!" Lillith's voice rings out. The scuffling subsides. My heart pounds.

"Listen, you little bitch, I'm going to teach you some manners, but first you're going to start talking. Where's the scientist?"

The voices are out of sight, but not far. I crawl gently through the hole, past a mop bucket and a shelf of cleaning products that has been shoved out of the way to access the wall. When I reach the doorway, I'm looking at a cubicle with a typewriter and a calendar of puppies in a basket. To the left, an aisle bisects the office from more cubicles on the other side.

"I told you. I don't know where he is," Francesca says.

Her voice is coming from ahead of me to the left. I keep low and move to the corner of the cubicle across from me. Crouched on one knee, I poke my head around the corner to have a look. Ahead, the aisle opens up into a space with a conference table. Beyond that, nearly against the wall of windows looking out to the east, Stenger has Francesca in a rolling office chair. He looms over her, the gun in his right hand. Lilith, now unarmed but holding a bulging plastic bag, is encouraging him from a few feet away.

"If we have to make this more difficult on you, we will," Stenger says.

Francesca's face is red on the right side where he's struck her, but her eyes are defiant. I see Stenger reach his left hand around his back and up under his shirt to where he keeps his knife. Rising anger overwhelms my nerves. I slip the remote switch out of my pocket and palm it as I step into the aisle.

"Hey, shithead!"

Stenger spins at the sound of my voice and almost instantaneously moves behind Francesca. As he recognizes me, he hooks his arm around

Francesca's neck and pulls her up out of the chair. He kicks the chair aside and holds the gun to her head. He sneers. "Well look who decided to come back."

"Let her go."

"I don't think I will, Benjamin." He smiles. "Oh, I know your name. Does that surprise you? Been doing a little research since I met you at the gas station that night."

"I'm happy for you," I say. "Apparently you didn't learn that it's not nice to beat up women. You might want to keep studying."

Stenger pulls up on Francesca's neck a little harder and I see her grimace. "Oh, you don't like the way I'm treating your girlfriend here? That's just the beginning, Ben. I don't think things are going to end well for any of your friends, now that I think about it. We're having a little foreigner barbeque as we speak."

"It's your ending you should be worried about," I say, stepping closer. I keep my eyes on Stenger and the gun, but I see Lillith is watching me too. Francesca's eyes are on me as well, but her right hand is inching slowly toward her pocket.

"So you're a tough guy now, is that it?" Stenger says. "You found yourself a leather jacket and now I'm supposed to think you're a badass? You gonna walk in here and beat me up? I think you might want to reconsider your plan there, Ace. Unless you want to see your girlfriend's brains all over your fancy new jacket."

"I can give you Quickly," I say. Stenger stops smiling. "That's what you want, isn't it? It's what you're here for." Stenger is eyeing me with suspicion, but I see I have his attention.

"Just shoot his ass, baby," Lillith says. "We don't need the scientist now." She waves a stack of hundred dollar bills from the bag. *They found Quickly's office.*

"Shut up," Stenger says. He narrows his eyes at me. "Where is he?"

"Let her go, and I can take you to him."

"You'll just run off."

"Why do you want him so badly?"

"He's the one who did this!" Stenger yells. "He's the one who cost me everything. I don't let my debts go unsettled."

"You think you're the only time traveler who matters?" Lillith laughs. "My man is twice the man you'll ever be."

"Yeah, you sure know how to pick 'em," I say.

"I told you to shut up," Stenger yells at her.

311

Francesca has finished removing her hand from her pocket. I see the glint of silver. The de-gravitizer. I take another step forward. Stenger retreats against the windows, but he raises his elbow on his gun hand, pressing the muzzle harder into Francesca's temple. "You really want her dead, is that it?" he says.

"It doesn't have to be like this, Stenger," I say. "You could just leave. Go away somewhere. You and Lillith here could take the money. Live happy somewhere with some little pyromaniac children. You really want to tangle with a guy who can master space and time?"

"That old man doesn't scare me," Stenger says. "I'm not going to run away and disappear like a nobody. It's him that should be scared."

"I wasn't talking about Dr. Quickly," I say. "I was talking about me."

I spring forward into a run. Stenger tries to point the gun at me, but before he can aim, Francesca jams the end of the degravitizer against his thigh and depresses the button. I veer sideways toward the nearest cubicle and dial my chronometer as Stenger screams. I jump onto the nearest desk, and as I plant my hand on the top of the cubicle wall, I see Francesca roll out of Stenger's grasp and duck under the conference table. Stenger reels, with one hand on his thigh. With the other, he tries to aim the gun at me as I vault over the cubicle wall. As my feet clear it, I press the remote switch.

The office is suddenly bustling with workers in suits and skirts. The woman occupying the desk I land on, shrieks as I knock the coffee cup out of her hand with my knee. I sprint around the end of the cubicles toward the far end of the conference table. A man's stack of files comes loose all over the floor as I race past him.

"What the— Hey!"

I turn the corner past a fake ficus. The conference table lies ahead of me now, and beyond it the window where I last saw Stenger. Two executives watch my approach with wide eyes from opposite sides of the table. The man standing at the head of the table falls over his chair backward as I sprint straight toward him. *I need to get back to the time I left, plus maybe half a second . . .* I leap onto the conference table.

On my second step, my feet land on some manila folders and I slip and drop to my knees, sliding forward as I dial in my chronometer setting. I regain my balance momentarily just before sliding off the end of the table. My chronometer hand slaps the edge and I press the remote. I land on my feet, directly in front of Stenger. His gun is still aimed past me toward the cubicles where I vanished. Benji's words jump into my mind as I lower my shoulder. "Dying ain't the worse thing that can happen to a man." *I hope he's right.* I lunge forward and plate glass shatters around my ears as I force Stenger through the window.

As Stenger and I sail into the void, three stories above the alley, it's no longer Benji's voice in my mind, but rather Cowboy Bob's. "The sky never hurt anybody. It's hitting the ground that gets you."

But we don't hit the ground.

We hit a truck.

The force of the crash onto the semi-trailer knocks the wind out of me. Pain shoots up my arm as my wrist bends awkwardly. Stenger is under me, but not for long. His elbow shoots up and knocks me in the side of the head. I roll sideways, gasping.

When I look over to him, Stenger is scrambling to his feet. *Why isn't he dead? We were supposed to be dead.* I roll over again and get to my hands and knees. My left wrist buckles under the weight, and my shoulder crashes into the top of the trailer all over again. The side of Quickly's building looms above us. I can see the hole we came out of. Francesca is still up there with Lillith. *I feel bad for Lillith. She's in for a rough time.*

I scan the area around us. Loading dock. Alley. The cab of the truck is behind me. *Is there a way down?* I look back to Stenger. The gun is gone. *That's something at least.* I struggle to get to my feet. Stenger has blood trickling down the back of his neck. *Why won't you die?* I feel something warm dripping down my forehead. I reach up to touch it and see my own blood on my empty right hand. I've lost the remote. I square up to face Stenger.

"You think this changes anything?" he snarls. "I'm still going to gut you." He reaches behind him, pulls out his knife and charges me. I dodge left and block his downward thrust with my left forearm against his, hoping to hit him with a right cross as he passes. The pain in my arm from his blow makes me cringe and miss, and my punch just grazes the back of his skull. I spin away and now we're facing each other from the opposite direction. I glance backward at the loading dock ramp. *I can jump that. There's no way he'd catch me on foot.* I turn to run. I'm not fast enough. Something catches my toe and I go sprawling. I look up at Stenger looming over me. He's smiling.

"Time to die."

He raises the knife and I grab my chronometer and spin it to an arbitrary number.

"No!" Stenger yells. The fingers of his free hand wrap around my ankle, just as I push the pin. The next moment he crashes down on top of me in a rush of wind and noise. The truck vibrates and shakes as it hurdles down an interstate highway. I grab Stenger's arm and attempt to wrench the knife from his grasp. He fights back by elbowing me in the ribs. He clamps down on my bad wrist and twists. I yell out in pain. I catch him in the face with an elbow of my own that forces him upward, and I scramble backward to get away from him. I don't have far to go. A few feet farther, the trailer ends in open air and hot freeway, crowded with speeding traffic.

A pair of senior citizens, enjoying the sunshine in a convertible trailing the truck, gawk and point as I become visible to them. My fingers find the edge of trailer. I make the mistake of looking down. The highway is a blur.

"Nowhere to run now, Ben!" Stenger yells over the din of the truck and the wind.

The truck rattles and sways as it rounds a bend in the freeway but Stenger gets to his feet. The edge of his knife glints in the afternoon sun. Stenger must see the fear in my face because he smiles. He steps toward me and glories in his victory. That same sadistic grin he had in all his mug shots, the face of the famous killer. I realize I'm seeing him happy. But he doesn't know what else I see. While still staring at his eyes, I reset my chronometer for a three second jump. I slam my hands down onto the top of the trailer just as the Twenty-Seventh Avenue pedestrian overpass clears the top of the cab. I close my eyes and blink.

When I reopen my eyes, there's nothing but blue sky ahead of me. I look behind me and see the chaos of a van and a passenger car and another tractor trailer truck that have all tried unsuccessfully to avoid hitting the body that fell from the overpass. Traffic behind the overpass slows to a crawl and eventually a stop, but my tractor trailer takes me away from the scene at eighty miles per hour. I work my way carefully back to the center of the trailer and lie there looking up at the sky for a few moments.

Eventually I crawl to the front of the trailer and hang on to the front edge. I blink myself past a dozen more overpasses until the truck finally comes to a stop at a gas station north of Tampa. The driver never sees me descend. Walking to the edge of the grass near the payphone, I collapse next to an empty bag of Doritos and a couple of cigarette butts. The ground never felt so good.

Chapter 24

"People say, 'Time heals all wounds.' That may be true, but relocating to an alternate reality can sure help too."
-Excerpt from the journal of Dr. Harold Quickly, 1941

As the truck pulls away from the gas pumps, I lift my head. *I probably should have used that to get back to St. Pete.* I lay my head back in the grass and contemplate the sky some more. *I need to find Blake.* The image of the blood splattering the chair comes back to me. *Quickly knew somehow. He saw the blood.*

I get to my feet and walk into the convenience store. I ignore the attendant's sideways glances at my bloody face and buy a bag of sunflower seeds. I ask him to call me a cab, then regress to the outdoors and lean against the edge of a planter. *Quickly saw the blood on the chair days ago. Blake must have gone back in time when he got shot.* I spit a couple of shells out near the curb. *But why not tell us? Why wouldn't he warn us what was going to happen?*

When the cab arrives, I ensconce myself in the back seat with Quickly's journal, shutting down the cabby's attempts at chitchat. I page through the journal for clues. There's nothing about the fractal universe. Not even a mention of jumping timestreams. I'm about to slam it shut when I notice a torn edge of paper sticking from the binding. I examine the little triangle of paper still clinging to the threads. *Somebody ripped some pages out.* I thumb back through and find several more locations where there are missing sections.

I close the book and watch the highway stream by. As we cross the Gandy Bridge, I get a view of St.Petersburg in the distance. *The Sunshine City.* The setting sun is lighting the buildings of downtown in gold. I check my chronometer. It's still January 9th. I look at the clock on the cabby's dash. 5:40. Somewhere on that horizon, Carson and I are scouring the lab for our things. Another me is hiding on the second level with Blake and Francesca. *That feels like forever ago.* In just a matter of twenty minutes, Blake is going to get shot.

I lean forward in my seat. "Do you think you could drive a little faster?" The cabby accelerates, but it doesn't help. By the time we reach North St. Petersburg, we hit a wall of traffic. We crawl along in spurts and stops.

When we get near Thirtieth Avenue, the cabby comments sourly from the front. "Wouldn't you know it? It's not even on our side of the freeway, just a bunch of gawkers. Looks like they've had a mess on the northbound side."

I watch the lights of the emergency vehicles and tow trucks accumulated near the pedestrian overpass. Police are directing traffic around the shoulder. There's no sign of the body. I close my eyes and lean my head back on the seat. After a minute, I feel the cab accelerating again.

I killed someone.

The thought doesn't affect me the way I thought it would. I reopen my eyes and watch the lines of the freeway speed by.

He killed himself.

I direct the cabby through the neighborhood near Ninth Street, careful to steer clear of any areas where I might encounter any of my earlier selves. He drops me a block north of the lab on the opposite side from where Carson and I ran off. I pay the cabby and watch the taillights of the cab disappear around the corner before turning toward the lab.

I approach the lab from the rear. Creeping up the alley till I have a view of the loading dock, I settle myself on a low wall behind a bush and wait. I don't have to wait long. There's movement in the windows above me. The backlit office offers a clear view of the occupants through the glass. Stenger has Francesca backed up almost against the pane. I can hear nothing, but I see his expression of pain as Francesca activates the degravitizer against his thigh. A moment later, the window explodes and Stenger and I plummet out into space.

Our impact into the trailer makes me cringe. *It's a wonder I'm alive after that.* I feel my swollen wrist with my other hand. *I got off easy.* I watch my awkward fight atop the trailer and see Stenger stick his leg out and snag my toe with his foot just as I turn to run. His smile fades quickly as he's forced to drop down and grab my leg. We both disappear.

So long, asshole. Last I'll be seeing of you.

I step out from behind the bushes and walk toward the trailer. Broken glass litters the ground. There is the sound of scuffling still going on above me. Lillith shrieks like a Nazgul beast from a Tolkien film and I hear Francesca shouting as well. *There's a fight I'd pay to see.*

The ruckus subsides, and a few moments later, I see Francesca appear at the hole in the window. Her face is distraught as she searches the alley. I wave to attract her attention. Her face relaxes when she sees me, and she smiles. She looks past me down the alley.

"Where is he?" she calls down.

"We won't have to worry about him anymore."

She nods. "What do I do with this one?" She drags a miserable-looking Lillith into view by her hair.

"I can come up and help you," I say.

"Okay. You better hurry. It smells like smoke pretty bad up here. Actually, wait just a minute..." She disappears from view. When she returns, she pitches a typewriter out the window. It hits the street and breaks apart. "Oops," she says.

"It's okay," I yell back. "I think I can still use it." I examine the front plastic portion of the typewriter that's mostly intact. "How long ago?"

"Maybe thirty seconds?"

"Okay." I spin my chronometer dials to forty seconds, just to be sure, and touch the top of the typewriter. I blink and drop a couple of feet, landing in the back corner of the office. I poke my head over the cubicle wall. Francesca is still talking to me out the window. I duck around the corner of the cubicle and hide behind another desk.

"Actually, wait just a minute." She trails off and I hear her shove Lillith into a chair. "Don't you dare move." I hear her come around the corner of the far end of the row of cubicles. She stops and enters the one I just departed. "This could work." She yanks the cord out of the socket and strides back to the window with the typewriter. I stand up to get another look.

"Oops."

I walk around the corner of the cubicle into view of Liliith. Her eyes widen.

"Maybe thirty seconds?" Francesca calls out the window. She turns to look at Lillith and then follows her gaze to me. She smiles. I move forward and she rushes into my arms. "God, I thought you were dead when you went out that window!"

"So did I," I say.

"What happened to Stenger?"

I glance at Lillith in the chair. She's eyeing the bag of money sitting on the conference table. She notices me watching her and averts her eyes. "I'll tell you a little later." I lean around Francesca. "Hey, don't even think about it, Lillith. We can find you yesterday if we need to."

She scowls.

That wouldn't work, but she doesn't know that. The smoke is starting to get thick. "We should get out of here," I say.

Francesca leads the way to the office stairs with Lillith between us where I can keep an eye on her. By the time we emerge into the alley below, emergency vehicles have begun to fill up Ninth Street. Lillith's eyes widen but she doesn't try to run. Looking through the array of blue and red flashing lights, I see someone waving their arms at me. I recognize Malcolm standing near a pair of uniformed police officers. He points toward Lillith, and the two officers move toward us with hands on their gun holsters.

"She's the one who held me hostage in her trailer," Malcolm says. "I can take you there if you need me to."

The female officer gets on her radio and transmits something I don't catch. The other officer, a man in his mid-forties, looks at Francesca and me. "And what was your part in this?"

"Our friend worked there," I say. "Her boyfriend tried to burn the place down. If you search that alley back there, I'd bet you'll find the gun with both of their prints on it."

"This whole thing was a set up!" Lillith shouts. "They're the ones you ought to be locking up. This one pushed my man out a window. They're time travelers from the future!"

"Okay ma'am, I'm going to ask you to come with us." The female officer says. "We'll need to ask you some questions."

"I'm going to be pressing charges," Malcolm says.

"We'll need to get a statement from you as well," the male officer replies.

As the two of them converse, the female officer leads Lillith toward some other police vehicles. I ease Francesca away from the conversation and step around a squad car. "We need to find Blake."

"What happened to him?" Francesca asks.

"I don't know. Lillith shot him, but he disappeared."

"She shot him?" Francesca exclaims.

"Yeah. But I think he blinked out of there. I don't know what kind of shape he was in but I think I know where he went."

"Where?"

"You remember the day Carson noticed the blood on the chair?"

"Yeah, that was gross . . . Wait, you think that was Blake's blood?"

"He crashed into that chair when he got shot. Lillith was shooting from the balcony. He must have blinked backwards a few days to get away."

"Why wouldn't we have seen him? You think he's okay?"

"I don't know, but we need to find Dr. Quickly. I have a lot of questions that need answering."

Another fire engine speeds toward the blazing front of the lab. We move farther away from the chaos and I put some more vehicles between us and the officers before they decide to question us. I lead us into the residential neighborhood and pause to consider the sign at an intersection.

"Where are we going?" Francesca asks.

"Quickly's apartment upstairs burned down. If he's still in this timestream and here today, he'll need somewhere to sleep tonight."

"The house? I figured that place was just a front for his tunnel."

"Probably is, but I don't know where else to look for him."

Francesca shrugs and we keep walking. "So tell me about Stenger. What happened when you went out the window?"

"Well . . . we landed on a truck. We fought a little bit and then I tried to blink away, but he grabbed hold of my leg and came with me."

"How did you lose him?"

"I hit him with an overpass."

"You what?"

"Yeah, it was crazy. We ended up on top of the truck while it was rolling down I-275. I blinked past the pedestrian overpass but Stenger didn't see it."

"Holy shit. So he's dead?"

"I didn't stop to check obviously, but we had to be doing close to eighty when he got clobbered by the overpass and knocked off the truck. Then he got hit by at least a couple of cars on the freeway, so yeah, I'm gonna go ahead and say he's dead."

"Wow."

"Yeah."

"I'm glad he's gone. He was so awful."

"Are you okay?" I consider Francesca's slightly swollen face.

"Yeah, I'll be all right." She touches her cheek. "I could probably use some ice."

When we arrive at Dr. Quickly's fake house, there are lights on in the window. I'm about to knock on the door when it opens. Mym is holding the door for us. She's older again, the one from earlier in the lab. Her eyes search my face.

"Hey," I manage.

"Hey. Come in." She opens the door wider and Francesca and I enter. Mym shuts the door and leads us into the dining room. As I turn the corner, my breath catches. Blake is at the table with Dr. Quickly. His left arm is in a sling and a bandage protrudes from under the collar of his shirt. He rises from the table and smiles. Dr. Quickly stands up with him.

"Thank God!" I say. "The worry was killing me, man."

As Blake moves around the table, I clasp his good arm with my good hand and gently clap him on the back. "You had me pretty worried too," Blake says. "I've been stuck wondering for days whether you guys were going to make it out of there."

Francesca embraces Blake carefully. I turn to Dr. Quickly. "Hello, Doctor."

"Congratulations, Benjamin. You've had quite a night."

"Yeah, you could say that."

Mym moves around her father and takes a seat. She smiles at me, but it's cautious.

"So what happened to you?" Francesca asks Blake.

"Not much to tell, really," Blake replies. "I got shot, obviously. When I got hit by the bullet, I sort of went into panic mode. I knew she was still up there shooting when I hit the ground. She was shooting at Ben but I was still in clear view, so I grabbed at my chronometer and blinked myself out of there."

"You went back to a few days ago?" I ask.

"Nights, actually. When I showed up in the lab, it was dark and I was bleeding all over the place. Luckily Dr. Quickly heard me blundering around and came downstairs to help me. He patched me up."

"Blake got lucky," Dr. Quickly says. "The bullet passed through the muscles behind his collarbone, but it just grazed the bone itself. It could have been much worse."

"What happened then?" I say. "Why didn't we realize what happened days ago?"

"I wanted to come back and find you guys as soon as the bleeding was stopped," Blake says. "But Dr. Quickly talked me out of it."

"There's a little more to this story than you know," Dr. Quickly says. "We needed to keep Blake here to avoid altering the events that were going to happen. You may want to have a seat."

I look from Quickly to Mym and finally to Blake. He nods and gestures to the chairs. Francesca and I take seats. Mym shifts uncomfortably in hers.

"So what's the scoop?" Francesca says.

"It's a long story, but we'll try to explain," Quickly says.

"We were hoping you would," I say. "It seems like there were a whole lot of things that we probably should have known, that we somehow didn't get told, especially the universe being fractal thing. We could've saved ourselves a whole lot of wasted energy in the wrong 2009 if we'd known that."

"Well, there were reasons," Quickly replies.

"Dad, maybe I should do it," Mym interjects. Dr. Quickly looks to her and nods, then settles back in his chair. "This is mostly my doing," Mym says.

Hers?

"Which part?" I say.

"The leaving-you-in-the-dark part," Mym says. "I know there were things that you needed to know that you didn't, and dangers you would face as a result, but I had to keep it that way."

"Why?" Francesca says. "Why couldn't you guys just help us get home like we asked?"

"Because you wouldn't have come back," Mym says. "And I really needed you to come back."

I watch her face. She looks pained by what she's saying. "I know it was selfish of me, but I had to try. I've tried for so long to do it on my own, and I couldn't anymore."

"Do what?" I say.

"Save my dad."

I sit back in my chair. "Oh." Her eyes are welling up with tears. "But wait, when did we save your dad?"

"Tonight," Quickly says. "Tonight would have been the night I died."

"Wow," Francesca says. "How?"

"Elton Stenger," Quickly replies. "He came back at the same time you did. There were others as well, but Stenger was the one that really changed things. He's a vicious human being. He took Malcolm hostage when he met him, and found out much about what we do. It seems the knowledge only enraged him, however. In his few days here in 1986 alone, he had begun to believe himself unique. He was angry to have been deprived of the spotlight of public fame. He found solace in his new ability to know the future. I think he envisioned himself becoming famous all over again, perhaps for different reasons. I believe he saw other time travelers as a threat to that."

"Carson," I say. "He killed Carson because he recognized another time traveler in the media."

Dr. Quickly nods. "I don't know all the specifics of that encounter, but it would be in line with other aspects of his motivations. He set up the trap with Malcolm in the lab tonight, to get rid of me. And it worked."

"But why did you need us?" I say. "If you knew Stenger was going to kill you, why not just leave?"

"We couldn't," Mym says. "I tried that. Originally Dad had always told me that if he died, I wasn't supposed to try to change it. He said we all have our time and it has to come to an end."

She sniffs and wipes her nose with the back of her hand. "But I couldn't do it. I tried to just let him go. I tried, but I couldn't forget what happened. I went back to try to stop it. I tried so many combinations of ways to keep it from happening but I couldn't find one where everyone would survive. No matter what I did, Malcolm or my dad or someone else kept dying. I saw them die so many times." She looks at me. "I saw you die too." She sniffs again and looks away for a moment. When she looks back, she continues. "But then one day, when I was traveling, trying to research more information, trying to find some way to solve it, I met a man. He told me he knew my situation and that there was a way to work things where everyone survived. He told me the combination of events that needed to happen to reach that timestream. I knew it would be selfish of me to put everyone through that, but I had to try. I didn't want to go on living in a time where I couldn't save them."

"How did the man know what was going to happen?" Francesca says. "Who was he?"

Mym's eyes meet mine again. "He was you."

I stare into her eyes, then look at Quickly. Dr. Quickly is studying Francesca's face. He stands up and disappears into the kitchen. When he returns, he lays a pair of ice packs in front of Francesca.

"So I caused this," I say. "I'm the reason we couldn't know what we were doing."

"If you knew, you never would've succeeded," Mym says.

Francesca holds one of the icepacks to her face and nods to Dr. Quickly. I snag the other one and press it to my wrist.

"So what now?" I ask. "Is it done?"

Dr. Quickly leans onto his elbows. "It's done for now."

"So these other attempts you made," Francesca says, "does that mean there are other versions of this story where we didn't succeed?"

"Yes," Mym replies. "There are other timestreams, but in this version, Stenger didn't win."

"But the Stenger that shot Carson," I say. "That still happened?"

"We're in a new timestream now," Dr. Quickly says. "Stenger is dead, so Carson will live, should he decide to go to L.A. and produce rock music again, but yes, that old timestream still exists. What happened, happened. You can never change the past. Not really. You can just choose to live in a time where things are different."

"So that Stenger, the one who killed Carson and took his chronometer, he's still out there somewhere," I say.

"I'm afraid so," Quickly says. "But he's gone from your original timestream. When you get home, he'll still be gone."

"So we can go home now?" Blake says.

"Yes," Quickly replies. "If you would still like to go back to your old lives, I can see you there safely."

"Getting home perforated is still getting home." Blake smiles. "Mallory will just have to be extra nice to me for a while."

"When would we leave?" Francesca says.

"As soon as you are ready to go."

I stare out the sliding glass doors into the dark backyard. "So the other versions of us, the ones who are still at the hospital waiting on Mr. Cameron, what happens to them now?"

"They keep on with the story," Quickly replies. "They exist in a bit of a paradox at the moment, but if left uninterrupted, they will continue down the same path you have, eventually looping around and becoming you as you sit right now."

"But Stenger is dead now," I say.

"In this timestream, Stenger was dead the day you three left for Boston. You just didn't know it, because you hadn't come back to cause it to happen yet. But had you paid attention to the news that night, it would not just have told you about the lab burning, but it would have mentioned a pileup on the interstate as well."

"That's tonight," I say. "That news program will probably be on again tonight."

"Of course it will. It's the same news program. Would you like to watch it?"

I look at his face. His eyes are smiling again. "The timestreams are splitting, but they've not separated completely yet. Actually, I can give you all a class on the physics of traversing paradoxical timestreams, if you're in the mood."

"That's okay. I trust you."

"So what about Mr. Cameron and Robbie?" Francesca says. "Will Mr. Cameron survive?"

"In this timestream, he will. If I take you home to your original timestream, he has to have always died. You won't find him there. Robbie has a choice to make. If he would like to continue his relationship with his grandfather here, he is welcome to, but he won't be able to go home."

"That really sucks," Francesca says.

"You can't change the past," Quickly says, "you can only—"

"Choose where you want to live," I finish for him.

Quickly nods. I stand up and look at Blake. "Well, I know where you want to live."

He smiles and stands. "Yep. There's only one home for me. She's got brown hair and blue eyes, and she might not be getting a diamond ring, but she'll be getting a whole lot of me."

Francesca sets the ice pack down on the table and gets to her feet. "Can we at least say goodbye? To Mr. Cameron, I mean?"

"If we get you there after the three of you have left for Boston, it will be a new timestream from there on out. You can do what you like after that point, until we take you home," Quickly says.

Francesca smiles. "Good. I like the sound of that."

Chapter 25

"'Time is Money' is an inaccurate statement, unless you are using it in the early twenty-first century connotation of the word, meaning 'outstanding', or 'excellent.' In that case, I'd be pretty 'money.'"
-Excerpt from the journal of Dr. Harold Quickly, 2009

Carson, Robbie and Mr. Cameron are still in the backyard, staring at the space around the bike handle, when we walk around the corner of the garage. Carson bends down to pick up one of the anchors we left behind. Spartacus barks and bounds over to us at full speed. Francesca has to fend off his licks until he gets distracted sniffing Dr. Quickly and Mym.

"That was quick," Robbie says.

"It really is like magic," Mr. Cameron says. "You even multiplied."

"You know, you guys," Carson shakes the piece of chain link fence he's picked up, "there're fines for littering in this state. You really ought to learn to clean up after yourselves."

I'm too happy to see him alive and breathing to come up with a response. I walk over to him, grinning, and give him a hug. "Good to see you too, dude," Carson says. "It's been a long five seconds."

"Oh man, you have no idea," I say.

Dr. Quickly extends a hand to Mr. Cameron. "It's good to see you again. This is my daughter, Mym."

Mr. Cameron shakes her hand and smiles. "How do you do, young lady?"

Mym smiles back. "It's nice to meet you. I've heard a lot of great things about you."

"Clearly from gullible parties." Mr. Cameron winks.

I fist bump Robbie. "So what happened?" he says. "It didn't work?"

"Oh, it worked all right," Francesca says. "Well, most of it."

I scratch Spartacus behind the ears as he leans against me. "It's kind of a long story."

"The important part is we met you in your forties," Francesca says.

"Really?" Robbie says. "What was that like?"

"Pretty bizarre," I say. "You were really happy though."

"Yeah, and you had a hot wife," Francesca adds.

"Really?" Robbie says. "Huh. You sure she was mine?"

"You had the ring to prove it," I say.

He smiles. "Damn. Sounds like a fun trip."

"It had its moments," I say.

"Why are you guys back so soon?" Carson says. "Did you really miss us that fast?"

"We came back to get your punk ass," Francesca says. She stops and hangs her head just a moment, then looks back up. "Sorry. You see what you do to me?" She walks forward and gives Carson a hug. He looks to me in surprise as he pats her on the back.

"Is the world about to end or something? What's with you guys?"

"How about we tell you inside?"

Mr. Cameron invites us indoors, and he and Dr. Quickly and Mym take seats in the library while the rest of us linger in the kitchen.

"All right, tell us what's up," Carson says.

"Yeah," Robbie says, pulling some cups out of the cupboard. "Explain the speedy return trip."

I take one of the cups Robbie offers and open the refrigerator to pull out a pitcher of water. "Okay, so the short version is this. We went home, only it was the wrong version of home. It turns out time is a fractal, and you can go to all kinds of parallel timestreams. We went to the wrong one." I pour water for the others as they hold out their glasses. "The other versions of us were still in the other timestream, because we never left from there. Robbie was old and married." I look at Carson. "You moved to L.A. to become famous, but you died."

"Famous for what?" Carson says.

"You missed the important part of that sentence," Francesca says. "The 'you died' part."

"Well okay," Carson says. "But what was I famous for?"

"Robbie said you produced *Independence Day* but it sucked," I say.

Carson shakes his head. "That doesn't sound like me."

"In any case, we had to come back," I say. "We had to stop Stenger from killing Carson."

"Stenger? That guy is a tool. I could totally take him in a fight," Carson says.

"He obviously pulled some sort of shady shenanigans, because you died," I say. "But we got him. He's dead now. At least the one from here is."

"You got him?" Robbie says.

"Yeah," I say. "But there's a problem."

"What?"

"If we want to go home, we're going to have to go home to the time when your grandpa died when you were a little kid. That's what happened in our timestream. There's no changing it if we want to get home to where we came from, and not another alternate reality."

Robbie sips his water slowly, then looks toward the library. "He can't come with us?"

"I don't think so, unless Quickly can find a way to turn him into a time traveler somehow. I don't know how that works."

"Huh. But you said in the other timestream I got old?"

"Yeah, you stayed and kept living here and never went back."

"And I was okay with that?"

"You seemed pretty happy," Blake says.

"Actually, you gave us a message to tell you," Francesca says. "You said to tell you that everything was going to be okay."

"So what am I supposed to learn from that?" Robbie says. "Am I supposed to go or stay?"

"I don't know," I reply.

"That future sounds kind of lame if you ask me," Carson says. "I can't see me messing up a movie like that, but I guess I'm more of a music guy . . ."

I walk to the door of the library and poke my head in. Quickly and Mr. Cameron are laughing about something. "Excuse me, Doctor?"

"Yes, Benjamin."

"Would it be possible to take Mr. Cameron back to 2009 with us if he wanted to go?"

He looks from me to Mr. Cameron and back. His eyes grow serious. "The process of infusing a human being with gravitites is pretty dangerous, Ben. Robert here has just been through a rather serious medical condition. I'm not sure his body is in a state to handle that kind of additional trauma."

"Oh. Okay."

"It's not completely out of the realm of possibility," he adds. "But I wouldn't try to do it at the moment."

"I see."

Mym catches my eye and smiles briefly. Then she looks back to the others.

327

Still gets me with that.

I return to the kitchen. I tell Robbie what Dr. Quickly said and he nods his head. "Maybe we could try it later on," he says. "You never know what might happen down the road."

"Do you want to come with us then?" Francesca says.

Robbie shifts his feet. "I don't know. I don't think so just yet. We just got him back from the hospital. I'm not sure I should leave him alone. I know it's been a while for you guys, but we just had this conversation last night. We decided I should stay."

"You just want the hot wife, don't you?" Francesca says.

Robbie reddens. "No! I mean, that doesn't sound terrible, but I mostly just want to make sure he's okay. I'm kind of the reason he didn't die. I think I need to stick with my decision."

"It's okay. We understand," I say.

"What are we going to tell your family back home?" Francesca says.

"Oh," Robbie says. "I hadn't thought about that."

Mr. Cameron emerges from the library and asks us if we would like to stick around for some lunch. We agree and he starts getting out barbeque fixings. Over the next hour, we mill about the kitchen, helping prepare the food and running things up and down the stairs to the veranda where we'll be eating. As I carry a pair of drink pitchers through the glass doors, I find Mym setting out silverware on the table. *Finally I get her alone for a moment.*

"So what's next for you now?" I ask. "More meteor showers with Cowboy Bob?"

"Hmm. That was years ago," she replies, as she straightens a place setting.

"Oh. Well it was only a couple of days for me."

She glances up and nods, then goes back to setting knives around the plates. I set my pitchers down and realize I'm out of excuses to be standing there. "Maybe I should grab a broom and sweep this veranda off a bit. There's a lot of leaves."

"Okay." She doesn't look up this time.

When I get back to the veranda with the broom, I'm disappointed to find that she's gone again. *Our conversation under the stars that night was so effortless. What happened?* I sweep the leaves off the veranda with a little more violence than necessary.

Lunch is delicious but I don't get as much enjoyment out of it as I should, since I keep casting glances down to the other end of the table. Mym is chatting happily with Mr. Cameron, but seems to avoid looking my direction. On the couple of occasions our eyes meet, she immediately looks away.

After dinner, Blake and I are doing the best we can to wash some dishes with only two good hands between us, when he suddenly changes the topic of conversation. "Hey, you okay, man? You seem a little off."

"Yeah. I'm fine," I say. "Just feeling clueless again."

Blake sets another plate in the drying rack. "Don't worry. If women made sense, it would take all the fun out of it."

"Hmph."

Dr. Quickly rounds us up after we're done cleaning. "It's decision time." He looks to Robbie first. "Have you decided what you would like to do?"

"Yeah. I did." Robbie walks over to the roll top desk and picks up an envelope. When he comes back he hands it to Francesca. "Will you give this to my mom? I know she'll be upset, but I explained everything as best I could. Maybe you can help her understand."

"Okay," Francesca says. "I will."

"And you never know. This is time travel, right? I might still get back someday."

Dr. Quickly takes the envelope from Francesca's hand, and setting it on the desk, scribbles an address on the front and hands it back to Robbie. "That's going to need gravitizing and I don't have anything with me. Mail it to that address and I'll make sure Francesca picks it up on the way."

Robbie reads the address and nods. "Okay. I can do that."

Dr. Quickly turns to Carson. "And how about you?"

Carson looks at Robbie, then turns back to Dr. Quickly. "If you can promise that you'll help this one out if he ever needs it, then I guess I'll go back with you. Lord knows he's gonna need some serious help though."

"Hey," Robbie says. "Watch it." But he smiles.

Carson grins too. "I'm gonna miss you, man." He moves toward Robbie and gives him a hug.

Francesca's eyes are wet. She steps forward and hugs both of them. A moment later, Blake and I join in and we have a five person group hug. From in the middle, Robbie laughs. "All right you bunch of hippies. Let me out."

We break apart but Robbie is still smiling. Mym and Mr. Cameron come downstairs and join us.

"I guess this is it," I say. "Again."

"We get to say goodbye to you twice in one day," Mr. Cameron says.

"Yeah. Sorry about that."

"It's okay. For all I know, you might be back again for supper."

We shake hands again and then it's time to go. Dr. Quickly pulls one of his glass anchors from his pocket. He also extracts an extra chronometer and hands it to Francesca. "I figure you might want your own again."

"This one won't leave my sight," Francesca says.

"Now if we can get five of us around this thing, it will get us to my office in Belize in '92. I've got a great collection of November Prime anchors there. Should be more than enough to get us all to 2009."

His math doesn't add up. I look to Mym standing by the roll top. She has her hands in her pockets. "Wait, you're not coming with us?"

She shakes her head. "I've got some things I still need to do around here."

"Oh."

Francesca steps over to Mym and gives her a hug. "Thank you so much for everything." Blake and Carson shake her hand as well. She looks at me. The others are gathering back up in a circle around Quickly and his anchor. *I can't leave it like this.*

"Will you guys give me just a second?" I move to Mym and grab her forearm. "Can I talk to you real quick?" She lets me pull her into the library.

Mercutio and Tybalt are squawking at each other on top of their cage. I move us away from the racket they're making and face Mym near the table with the world map on it. "So this is it?" I say.

"Yeah. I guess so," she replies.

"What happened?" I say. "Am I completely misreading things here? Was there never anything else? When I first met you, you made it sound like we were . . . I don't know, something more."

"That was before," she says.

"Before what?" I say.

"Before I put you through all this. Before I made you come back and almost get yourself and your friends killed."

"But it worked out," I say.

"Did it?" she says. "Blake's out there with a gunshot wound in his neck, you got injured and almost died, Francesca got beaten and held hostage. . ." Her eyes are starting to tear up.

"Hey." I put my hand on her shoulder. "It's okay."

She brushes a tear from her eye and looks away. "How can this ever be okay?"

"We're all alive and going home together. It's going to be fine."

She looks back to my face. "You don't hate me for this? For putting you through all this?"

"No. Why would I? I mean yeah, it kind of sucked for parts of it, but I'm not mad about it. I don't think any of us are. We're just glad to be alive, and going home. If anything, we're happy. You really helped us out back in Montana."

"That was when I was younger. I didn't know any better then. I didn't know about any of this."

"It doesn't matter. You still helped. You'd never even met us, and you helped us. That counts for a lot."

Mym wipes away her tears again. She sniffs. "I just didn't know how you would be once you knew what I'd done."

"This is me knowing," I say. "And I'm not mad. I'm frankly relieved."

"Relieved?"

"Yeah, I thought you just stopped liking—"

Francesca pokes her head around the corner. "Hey, sorry to interrupt, but your dad is seeming kind of impatient for us to get going."

Mym nods and wipes at her eyes again.

"Okay," I say. Mym gives me a smile. I reach out my hand and she brushes my fingertips with hers.

Okay. Now we're back in business.

I join the others gathered around Quickly's anchor. Mr. Cameron has provided a stool to set it on, and everyone extends a chronometer hand to touch it.

"March 18th, 1300 Zulu, Ben," Dr. Quickly says.

I dial in my chronometer settings without having to look. Francesca raises her eyebrows at me. I give her a wink.

"So, Doctor," Francesca says. "I know you're taking us home to our own timestream, but is there any chance I can talk you into making a couple quick stops first?"

Dr. Quickly looks up from assessing our chronometers. "Yes. I suppose that could be arranged. Let's just get to my office first. We can sort it all out from there. On the count of three now."

I look up to Mym watching me from next to Mr. Cameron and Robbie. Her eyes are bright and smiling. *Wait, how am I going to find her again?*

Quickly counts off. "One, two, three."

We blink.

The Friday night crowd at the Green Dragon Tavern is lively. I open the door for Francesca and shut it behind me to keep out the winter chill. A quick scan of the patrons shows me the one we're after. I gesture toward the blonde head protruding from a booth near the kitchen. "He's in the back."

331

I watch Francesca cut through the crowd from my position near the doorway. Cole is wiping down the area near the taps at the far end of the bar. Our eyes meet briefly, but he shows no sign of recognizing me. I can't hear what Francesca says as she reaches the booth at the back, but Guy rises out of the booth with a drunken grin on his face. Francesca makes a comment and his smile wavers. He never sees Francesca's knee as it drives upward into his crotch. He crumples to the floor in a heap. A collective "Oooh!" goes up from the crowd around them, and a quartet of girls at a high top near the bar starts clapping.

Francesca next strides across the room and walks straight past a server and behind the bar. I see Cole reach his hands down and cover his groin protectively. Francesca reaches her arms around his neck however, and stretching up on her tip toes, puts a hand to the back of his head, and plants a long kiss on his lips. Cole's hands slowly move around to her back. Francesca eventually releases him and gives him a nod. Without another word, she turns on her heel and walks back through the crowd to me.

"Okay. We're done here."

I open the door and we exit back into the snow.

It's still raining on the softball field. We're standing in the visitor's dugout, looking across home plate at the dugout we left from. The powerline is still popping and snapping around the bench.

"I'm gonna need to do something about that," Quickly says. "I can't have a rash of displaced power company employees bouncing around the universe when they try to fix it." He turns to us and smiles. He points a spectrometer at the bench we just arrived on and then back to us. He shows us the frequency readings.

"They match," Francesca says.

"Just like advertised," he replies.

Home. For real this time.

"I don't know how to thank you," Blake says. He extends his hand.

Quickly shakes it. "I should be thanking you. Without you, I wouldn't have a timestream to go back to."

"What are you going to do now?" Francesca says. "Will we see you again?"

"Oh, there's plenty to keep an old scientist busy in this world," Quickly replies. "And lots of good people to keep in touch with."

"Do we get to be some of your good people?" Carson says.

"The best," Quickly replies.

I remove my chronometer from my wrist and hold it out to him. "I guess we won't be needing these anymore."

Quickly crosses his arms and gives my outstretched hand an appraising stare. "Why don't you hang on to that, Benjamin. The universe is a big place, and time is even bigger. You never know when you might need to get in a little exploring." He winks.

"We also still owe you a lot of money," Francesca says. "We probably disposed of a good hundred thousand dollars of yours."

"Then you still owe me nothing," Quickly replies. "Things that are worth nothing are easy to come by."

I smile and snap the chronometer back on my arm. I extend my good hand toward him. "You really are amazing."

"You flatter me, but I won't hold it against you," Quickly replies. "One does need a good bit of flattery from time to time."

Francesca steps forward and wraps her arms around him. "We'll never forget this."

He pats her shoulder with affection. "Nor shall I." When Francesca steps back, Dr. Quickly walks to one of the support beams and grips it with his chronometer hand. He turns and faces us.

"How will we find you again if we need you?" I ask.

Quickly places his other hand on his chronometer. "In a universe full of variables, you can still find yourself some constants. The rest is trial and error. But if you come looking, I'll bet you'll find what you're looking for." He gives us one last smile and then he's gone.

We file out into the rain. We pause near the home dugout and look at our softball gear still lying around the bench. The power line crackles near the entrance. A puddle of rain has spread throughout the dugout floor.

"Screw it," Carson says. "We can buy more equipment for the team."

"Yeah, I don't want to go on that ride again," Francesca says.

Our cars are still in the parking lot. I pause near Robbie's. "You still have that letter for his mom?"

Francesca nods as she tries to shield her face from the rain. "Yeah, I guess I'll need to go over there after I get dried off. I don't want his car getting towed."

"You need help?" I say.

"No. I think I'll be okay. It might be better if I talked to her alone. I know her pretty well."

"I can go with you," Carson offers. "I know her pretty well too."

Francesca looks at him and then nods. "Okay." I catch the hint of a smile at the corner of her mouth.

"You know where I'll be," Blake says.

I give him a hug. "Tell Mallory I said hi. I'm sorry you don't have a ring this time."

"It doesn't matter," Blake says. "She won't need a ring to know how I feel."

"Good luck," Francesca says, giving him a hug as well. "You going to be able to drive with that sling?"

"It's just a couple of blocks. I think I can make it." He backs up a few steps and gives us a salute.

"See ya, man," I say. He turns and jogs for his Jeep.

Francesca steps over and hugs me next. I wrap my arms around her. "Thank you for coming back for me," she mumbles from the vicinity of my chest.

"No problem, Fresca. That's what friends are for."

"You really are pretty great." She tilts her head up to look at me. "I probably ought to cut back on all the mean things I say about you all the time."

I smile down at her. "You're pretty great yourself. And intimidating. If I ever need to get in a fight with any more murderous thugs, I know who I want in my corner."

She squeezes me and lets me go. She pulls her little fabric coin purse out of her pocket and retrieves her car key. "Maybe next time I come to one of your softball games, you'll actually play a game."

"There's always next week."

Carson slaps my hand and pulls me into a hug. "See you, dude. Thanks for coming back to save me."

"Hey, I owed you one, remember?"

"I still think I could've taken that guy. I'd like to know how he got the best of me."

"Alternate universe, man. And you were probably out of shape from being so rich and famous." I smile. "No way he could beat you in your prime."

"True story," Carson says. He bumps my fist and follows Francesca toward her car. She gives me a wave from the driver's seat.

I find my car keys in my glove box where I left them. When I pull up to the street in front of my apartment, I sit there for a moment and stare at my door. The rain has stopped, but the trees are dripping large droplets into the puddles in the street. I look around my truck but realize I've got nothing to take in. I take the stairs two at a time. When I swing open the door, I find my water bottles and work shoes still on the floor. It feels like I've been gone forever. It's only been a couple of hours.

I close the door behind me and feel suddenly at a loss for what to do. I pick up the empty water bottles and carry them to the kitchen counter. I come back and nudge my work shoes over by the door where I won't forget them. *Work.* I walk back to the refrigerator and read the calendar I have stuck to the freezer. *Damn. I'm supposed to be at work at 7 am tomorrow.*

I open the refrigerator. The usual condiments greet me, but not much else. Closing the door and reaching into my pocket, I extract a zip lock bag that has one last survivor from Connie's batch of chocolate chip cookies. *They were worth the return visit.* I consider saving it as a memento of the trip, but after a couple seconds of deliberation, pull it from the bag and eat it.

I trudge back to the living room and collapse onto the couch. I stare at the blank television. *How am I going to explain to anyone what happened to me? No one will ever believe it.*

With my good hand, I reach around on the couch next to me for the remote. I pick up my junkmail and look under it. It's not there. Surveying the room, I spot it on the edge of the kitchen counter. *Well forget that.*

I begin to wad up the junk mail advertisements as I eye the trashcan in the corner. *Bet I can make it from here.* My junkmail won't compress as easily as I'd hoped. I feel some resistance and give the ads a shake. An envelope flings out and sails into the open area on the floor between the kitchen and me. It lands with the clack of something solid.

I force myself off the couch and check the rest of the ads. There are no more surprises. I drop them onto the coffee table and walk over to the envelope on the floor. There is a slight bulge at one end. Stooping to pick it up, I turn it over in my hands to check for some identification. It's blank. I slip my finger in one end of the envelope and tear. Giving it a shake, a silver, horse-head chess piece tumbles into my palm. As I examine it, my heart starts to race. I reach inside the envelope. The photo is of the stained glass window and the other chess pieces. I immediately flip it over and read the description on the back, written out in Mym's distinctive handwriting. "A great game in the making." The rest of the back of the photo is still blank.

I feel inside the envelope again and extract another slip of paper. This one holds a time description and location information. At the bottom is a personal note of only one line.

"Want to come out and play?"

I feel the grin spread across my face. The calendar hanging on my freezer seems suddenly irrelevant. I toss the chess piece up in the air and catch it again. I set my chronometer.

Work can wait.

Thank You

Thank you for reading! I hope you enjoyed this adventure. The response from readers has been one of the most enjoyable aspects of this process. If you enjoyed the book and would like to share the experience, please consider leaving a review on Amazon or Goodreads.

Read on for a free preview of *The Chrononthon*. Book 2 in this series.

If you would like to stay updated on other novels in this series and check out excerpts from The Chronothon or future releases, visit www.chronothon.com or find me at www.nathanvancoops.com.

THE CHRONOTHON

"Time travel is hard. Let's get that straight first thing. If you think any part of this will be simple, you can stop now and have a safe, happy, life. Of course, if you're reading this, you're likely not content with safe."- Journal of Dr. Harold Quickly, 2037

Chapter 1

I feel very alive considering I haven't been born yet. Across the expanse of grasses and water stretching to the distant shoreline, the rumbling of rocket engines is causing the wild birds to take to the air in droves. As they stream past my perch on top of the abandoned radio tower, their cries are lost in the roar of the machine beyond them. I have a clear view of the amber glow from the Saturn V rocket. Apollo 11 is hoisting humanity's dreams toward the heavens in a historic panorama in front of me, but I can't stop looking at the girl.

This is the third day I've woken up and existed as an affront to the laws of nature. I've bent them before of course, but this is the first time I've journeyed beyond my own lifetime—what should have been my lifetime in any case—and she's the one who got me into this.

Mym's arms are draped on the lower railing while her legs swing gently as they dangle over the edge. Her chin is propped on her arms and her blue eyes are on the rocket streaming its way skyward. After a moment they narrow slightly. "You know, Ben, I may stop taking you awesome places if you aren't even going to pay attention." Her voice is scolding, but when she turns her head, her eyes are playful. She tries to hold her mouth tight in an expression of aggravation, but as I glower back at her, her cheeks start creeping upward until she's grinning uncontrollably.

My legs are crossed below me, a safe distance back from the edge of the platform. A month ago, I wouldn't have dreamed of being this high up. A lot of things have changed about me in a month. For one, I used to stay in my own time. The chronometer on my wrist changed that. Mym's dad let me keep it. I did save his life, but I don't believe that was his reason for letting me have it. I think he wanted to let me into this world of his—the world where time is no longer about straight lines, but about paths , taken, a secret world where consecutive events in your life don't have to be consecutive at all.

Last night, we caught the Beatles in their last concert at Candlestick Park. This morning, I ate my breakfast a table away from Salvador Dali at a café in Spain, and still made it here to Florida in time for the launch. Not a moment was wasted in airport security or waiting for a calendar page to turn.

Mym leans back onto her hands and watches the twisting trail of rocket smoke dissipate in the wind. She looks happy.

"Do you just wake up amazed every day?" I ask.

She tilts her gaze toward me. "Don't you?"

"I do now. This is incredible. It's like every day is your birthday, or Christmas."

"I know a guy who does that." She smiles. "He only does birthdays and holidays. I think every day should be a good day though, if you're doing it right."

"Well, this certainly makes that a lot easier." I twist the dials on my chronometer. "You get to pick out the really good days."

Mym studies me briefly then turns skyward again. "It's easier to have good days now." She closes her eyes, soaking in the sunshine. I nod, though I know she can't see me. In the excitement of our traveling the past couple of days, I sometimes forget that she spent the last few years trying to find a way to keep her father from being murdered. It hasn't been all good days. But she doesn't seem to be thinking about that now. Her face is relaxed, her skin lit by the sun. She looks young. I wonder again how old she is. *Early twenties? Does she even know?* If I hadn't spent the last quarter century with my days encapsulated in sequential boxes, if Thursday could come after Sunday or spring follow fall, would I know my age? Would I feel it somehow? Would I care?

Mym is still an enigma to me. As I watch her chest slowly rising and falling with each breath, I wonder—not for the first time—why she picked me to come with her on this adventure. She's the type of girl who doesn't seem to realize the effect she has on people. I'm the opposite. I feel like I've always known where I stand. I get a few glances from the girls, maybe not all of them, but the ones who don't mind a guy who gets his hands dirty for a living—the ones who don't run off if I occasionally let a long swim at the beach pass for a shower, or pick them up for a date on my old motorcycle. I used to know where I stood anyway until I met her—a petite, blonde time traveler with a taste for adventure. Now it's like starting over.

drift back to the now vacant sky. "So where's the next

her eyes. "Hmm. We're still in the sixties. Anything else you while you're here, or do you want to head to the seventies?"

"You're the pro at this. I'm totally at your mercy."

"Ooh. Totally?"

"Um, maybe I'm going to regret that."

"Nope. You said totally. I know exactly where I'm taking you." She swings her legs up, tucking one underneath her, and faces me.

"Oh God. That smirk on your face is scaring me. Where are we going?"

"You just dial the settings." She rifles through her messenger bag and hands me a long silver tube and a hard rubber wheel. It takes me a moment to identify the wheel without the rest of its parts, but then it dawns on me.

"We're going roller skating?"

"Better. It's roller disco!" She beams. "Degravitize that."

"Oh Lord. Disco?" I roll my eyes, but set to work with the silver degravitizer, scanning it across the roller skate wheel like Mym taught me, removing the gravitite particles inside that enabled it to follow us through time. I consider objecting to the idea, but I have to be honest with myself, I'd probably follow her anywhere.

"So where does one go to roller disco in the seventies?"

"The beginning." Mym rummages around and removes more items.

"And where is the beginning?"

"Brooklyn." She's intent on something in her hands. "I'm taking you to The Empire."

She's studying a photo of a shelf with an iron, a bowl of whisks, and a pair of purple suede roller skates on it.

"Is that at the roller rink?"

"No. We can't make it to The Empire straight from here. It's too far to jump with these chronometers. That's okay, we need to stop and pick up my skates anyway." She stands and adjusts her satchel, then sticks her hand out for the wheel. I toss it to her, and she sets it precariously on the railing. "Okay. Don't shake the tower."

I step cautiously toward her. "What's the date?"

"May 18th, 1973. 1600 Zulu."

I dial the time into my chronometer and reach for the top of the roller skate wheel. "We good on elevation?"

Mym extends a tape measure to the platform at our feet and checks the height of the railing. "Perfect."

My right hand is poised atop my chronometer, the fingertips of my chronometer hand pressed to the wheel, keeping firm contact to our anchor in real time.

"Wait. Hang on." Mym squints at the photo and then rotates the wheel 180 degrees. "We don't want to end up in the floor." She grins up at me. "Ready?"

"Ready as I'm going to be." I eye the long drop from the platform, then quickly bring my attention back to the wheel. Once we're gone, the wheel will likely tumble to the ground, but we'll be years away.

"Three . . . two . . . one . . . push."

I press the pin on the side of my chronometer and blink.

The room smells like dust and potpourri. I take my fingers off the roller skate on the shelf in front of me and eye my surroundings. Old women are picking through clothing racks and bric-a-brac as dim light filters through dingy subterranean windows. In the corner, the cash register drawer dings as it shuts. The chime blends with the muffled sounds of car horns and traffic.

"You keep your skates in a thrift store?"

"It's not easy to find purple suede skates in my size." Mym picks up the skates and holds them to her cheek. "And they have rainbow laces. You have to snatch treasure up when you find it."

"I guess so." I smile and follow her toward the counter. I almost collide with her as she stops at a rack of sunglasses and plucks a pair of men's aviators from among them. She turns and slips them on.

"What do you think?"

"Um, I think they're a little big for your face."

She considers me briefly. "I feel bad for you."

"What? Why?"

"Because you're going to have to keep looking at them. I love them." She grins and spins back toward the counter. A bell rings as the door to the basement shop opens and a gust of wind follows a middle-aged woman inside. It brings the smell of truck exhaust and hot dogs. I step toward the door and grab it before it closes. Outside, the concrete steps lead upward to a sidewalk full of foot traffic, and beyond the road, a six-story apartment building. I glance back briefly at Mym paying for her skates and then climb upward into the urban noise.

Cabs and trucks clog the street as pedestrians stream past me, a fashionable mix of wide collars and ties, plaid bellbottoms, paisley shirts, and a smattering of turtlenecks and sweater vests. I stand on the top step of the thrift store entrance and breathe in 1973 New York. Despite the exhaust and a faint odor of trash, there is a tang of salt breeze in the air and a pleasant mix of ethnic foods. After a few moments, Mym joins me.

"It's great, right?"

"Sure is busy."

"Well, it's the middle of the day in Manhattan."

"Where's this place we're going skating?"

"It's in Brooklyn, but that's not for a couple of years yet. Come on, you want to grab lunch?"

"Yeah, I could eat."

"There's this little Italian place called Angelina's on Mulberry Street that has the most amazing calzones. It's a bit of a walk, but it's worth it."

"I'm in."

It's cool in the shade of the buildings, and I relish the brief moments of sun on my bare arms as we traverse the corner crosswalk. I dodge pedestrians while trying to keep up with Mym's brisk pace as she plunges into the shadow of the next building. She moves with the confidence of someone at home in her surroundings, flitting among the foot traffic with fluid ease, her purple skates hung casually over one shoulder. I narrowly miss being run down by a bicycle and stuff my hands into my jeans pockets to make myself a little thinner. As I skirt past a pair of rabbis, I find Mym waiting for me near a streetlight.

"Come on, pokey. I want to beat the lunch rush."

"Hey, I take up a lot more space than you do. I think these people treat that as a sin."

"People here live fast." She observes me over the rim of her new sunglasses. "Better learn to keep up." She winks before leading the way on. I appreciate her figure as she walks away, watching the curves that my hands have yet to touch. I entertain the thought for just a moment, then jog to catch up.

"You come to New York a lot?" I fall into step beside her.

"I try to. There are some great people here."

"There's certainly enough to choose from."

Mym slows to look at me. "You've never been to New York?"

"I passed through once as a kid with my parents, but I've never explored it as an adult."

"Then today is your lucky day. After lunch I can give you the tour."

"You going to show me the constructing of the Empire State Building?"

"Hmm, that would be a long way back," she muses. "Although I've always wanted to get a picture of me like one of those guys eating lunch up on the girders over the city. We might have to add that to the extended tour."

"Ha. You'll have to have one of the workers snap that shot. No way you're getting me out there on one of those."

"You just wait, Ben. A few weeks of traveling with me, and we'll have those heights issues vanquished."

My heartbeat quickens. I haven't asked how long she plans on traveling around with me. The idea of getting weeks with her makes me feel happy enough that I imagine I might be coaxed onto a few girders after all. I try not to show the eagerness on my face. "I guess we'll see."

An opening shop door halts me in my tracks as a group of women spills out onto the sidewalk from a boutique. A pretty young mother snags a wheel of her stroller on the doorstop, bringing the ladies behind her to a halt. I grab the door handle and open the door farther to help her extricate it.

"Thanks so much." The woman smiles, and another half dozen ladies thank me as I hold the door for their exit. The press of women moves onward along the sidewalk and I stretch to peer over their heads.

Mym is three shops down, shaking her head, but smiling. As I close the door behind the last straggler, another figure lurches up from the next shop entrance. In a tattered corduroy coat and porous straw fedora, he ricochets off a planter near the doorway and staggers toward the women. The group parts like a flock of swallows, reconvening beyond him with titters of consternation and a few hands held to noses.

The vagrant ignores the slight and tips his fedora in delayed cordiality, but stays his stumbling course toward me. I step to the side, but he sways with me, reaching out to my arms, raised to avert our collision. His right hand wraps around my wrist and clamps it with a near painful strength.

"Whoa, buddy. You doing okay?" I plant my other hand against his chest, to keep him at a distance and prop him up. His lean face is lined and dirty, but his stark, gray eyes have a sharp clarity despite his unbalanced state. I recoil from the scent of stale beer and halitosis, but before I can free my wrist from his grasp, he teeters and falls, dragging my arm across my body and down to the ground. Pain shoots up my wrist as my palm strikes the concrete and my vision suddenly goes dark. I've landed partially atop the vagrant, my other hand outstretched to the sidewalk beyond his head. I jerk my left arm out of his grip and jolt back to my feet. The world is changed.

Shaded sunlight has been replaced with an ink black sky. Streetlights illuminate sidewalks only populated by a few restaurant patrons retreating into the night. Mym is gone. I spin around and search the way I've come. I've been displaced. I check my chronometer. It still reads the settings I had from my last jump. *How is that possible? Shouldn't I have ended up on this sidewalk in daylight?*

The vagrant is struggling to get back to his feet. His left hand is crushing his straw hat as he tries to get his legs under him. He stretches a hand out to me for assistance. I sigh and grab his wrist, pulling a little more firmly than necessary. On his feet, the man gives me a scowl. "You didn't have to knock me down!" This is followed by a jerk as he pulls his arm from my grip and staggers toward the wall, a trail of slurred curses in his wake.

I look back to my surroundings and rub my wrist. My pulse throbs against the band of my chronometer. I gingerly remove it and hold it in my hand. This is the second time I've injured my wrist in a week. It was only just beginning to heal from the first fall. On that occasion, I plummeted out a window trying to save my friend. I considered myself lucky to have walked away with just a sprain. Getting knocked down by a random homeless man seems far less worthwhile.

I recheck my chronometer settings. Still set to 1600 Zulu. *So how is it nighttime? Did the jolt from the fall break it?* I study the different concentric rings, seeing if anything is amiss. Nothing is wrong externally. I give it a shake and listen for anything loose inside. Nothing.

Shit. What am I supposed to do now? I look around, hoping that at any moment Mym will suddenly appear to scold me for being careless and take us along our way. There is no one except a cab driver sitting outside a bar at the end of the block, his hazard lights pulsing their warning to the night. At a loss for what to do, I walk back the way I've come. The streets are less inviting in the darkness. The towering buildings no longer look inspiring, but loom overhead on the fringe of night, lifeless hulks obliterating the stars.

I slip my chronometer onto my other wrist and fidget with the dials. I consider trying to jump back to the time I left. *Will it still work? I don't even know how far I've gone. Will I have enough power to get back?* My mind goes back to Dr. Quickly's lessons, and the varied tales he told of ways time travelers could meet their demise. They involved everything from fusing into walls to flinging yourself off the planet into the void of space. *Those were things that could happen with a working chronometer. What about if it's broken? Am I going to blink myself out of existence?* I've heard stories of time travelers not anchoring themselves properly for a jump and vanishing completely. Some say there is a place you go that exists outside of time, but there the line between science and urban legend starts to blur. Every time traveler learns early on to avoid that scenario.

Those lessons feel as though they're a long time ago, though for me it's only been a matter of weeks. History would say it hasn't happened yet. It will be nearly a decade till I'm even born, farther still when I'll first be sent through time. But this is time travel. Middles can come before beginnings, and it's anyone's guess where the end might be.

As I cross to the next block, I glance down the side street and note a cluster of young men loitering on the stoop of an apartment building. A dozen eyes follow my progress. Without my usual method of escape, I feel suddenly vulnerable under their gaze. I check myself to keep from walking faster. I continue with feigned ease for another half block until I'm well out of sight, and then stop.

Get yourself together, Ben. You're fine. You're just in New York . . . in 1973. I glance back at the vacant street behind me and then force myself to think. *What now?* I do a mental inventory of my belongings. Besides a possibly broken chronometer, my possessions are down to a wallet, pen, Swiss Army knife, and Mym's degravitizer that I forgot to put back in her backpack. I also have Dr. Quickly's worn leather journal stuck in my back pants pocket. I pull that out and walk a few steps toward the nearest streetlamp to read it. I flip through the handwritten scribbles and drawings, searching for the section on the workings of the chronometer. The book had been a gift, but a utilitarian one, filled with the carefully depicted details of a lifetime of research.

I stop on a page showing a partially disassembled chronometer. Staring at the drawing of the component parts, I immediately realize I'm out of my depth. *Even if I had the tools, there's no way I would even be able to recognize what was broken.* I slap the journal shut. A murmur alerts me that the men from the stoop have moved to the corner behind me. The tallest of the bunch is eyeing me from under a disheveled mop of hair, one hand conspicuously lingering in the pocket of his sweatshirt. The expressions on the young men's faces range from frigid to glacial. I break my eyes away and continue walking. A subtle shuffling indicates that I won't be alone.

They've just got somewhere to go this direction. Nothing to worry about.

A bus rumbles past but doesn't slow. A single old man is staring into the night from the illuminated interior, lost in a daydream or his own reflection. I'm nearly at the corner and, other than my skulking shadows, all pedestrians seem to have evaporated. *Isn't this supposed to be the city that never sleeps?*

I'm just considering breaking into a run when a smoke-black Cadillac materializes from the side street. It oozes to the curb at the corner ahead of me and, as I approach, hearty chuckles trickle from the darkness of the open rear window. "Benjamin, Benjamin, Benjamin. We've been looking all over for you. You had us worried, my friend."

The door swings open and the dome light illuminates the plush interior and the lounging figure of a substantial, well-dressed man in his forties. His glossy hair matches his Burt Reynolds mustache. I've never seen him before. "You shouldn't just go wandering off around here, Ben. The locals can get territorial in the wee hours."

I stoop to peer into the car. The driver is a hulk in a suit coat. The man in the back pats the seat next to him. "Get in."

"I don't know you."

The man's eyes narrow, but then his face lightens and he gives me a cheek-stretching grin. "I forget how young you still are, Ben. Of course! This is your first time meeting me." He extends a hand. "Gioachino Amadeus. But call me Geo." I let his hand linger in midair. Finally, he pats the seat next to him. "Come on. We'll get you out of here."

I glance back down the sidewalk. My flock of followers has stalled out mid-block and is idling near a barred grocer's shop. A few of them are involved in subtle conversation, but the tall one is still just staring at me.

"How did you know where to find me?"

Geo stretches his arm along the back of the seat with a knowing smile. "We time travelers have to stick together, Benjamin."

"Mym sent you?"

"You don't think she'd just leave you out here on your own do you? You can trust me, Ben. We're destined to be great friends."

"Most of my friends drive themselves."

"Well then, it looks like you're moving up in the world. Now hop in. We've got places to be."

I take one last look at the city skyline, blending vaguely into a motor oil sky, and climb in. The Cadillac ebbs back into the street and, as the dome light fades, we are swallowed by the ocean of night.

Get the rest of the story at www.nathanvancoops.com!

Nathan Van Coops is an aircraft mechanic and flight instructor in St. Petersburg, Florida. When not writing time travel fiction, he likes throwing Cinco de Mayo parties and enjoying the perks of being a founding member of the Saint Petersburg Hammock and Nap Club. *In Times Like These* is his first novel.